MOON BORN

BEN BARRY

Edited by Amy Draemel

ISBN: 979-8-9897820-3-1 - Hardcover
ISBN: 979-8-9897820-4-8 - Paperback
ISBN: 979-8-9897820-5-5 - eBook

To my family, for enjoying my stories
and asking me for more.

1

A New Beginning

A FLURRY OF EMOTIONS was growing into a full-on blizzard as Caroline followed Rebecca out of the cavern. With nothing to keep them in check, too many thoughts crowded her mind for attention. She had just discovered that she had special abilities that are extremely rare, fought in two massive battles, and her parents had packed a bag and sent her away with a complete stranger to go to a school far away from all her friends. Her feet felt like lead weights and with each stair the effort caused her leg muscles to burn hotter so that by the time they reached the top she was breathing heavily and had become somewhat embarrassingly sweaty. Rebecca looked back and saw Caroline's state, gave a warm smile and said, "Roots grow deep for Moon Borns. I know this isn't easy for you, the resistance can be strong. Please know I appreciate your trust."

Caroline didn't know how to react. *Roots grow deep? What does that mean?*, she thought to herself, but she just stayed quiet and tried to reign in all the other questions flying in and out of her mind as another group stampeded through. *What was going to happen next? Where was Rebecca taking her? What will her new school be like? Will we be able to stop for some food? I'm starving…*

As they walked out the back door of the bookshop into the cool night air, Caroline saw a large black car with tinted windows parked across three spaces. The driver noticed them and immediately stepped out, opened the back door, and waited for them to get in. Rebecca placed her hand on the center of Caroline's back and guided her in first, then she slid in next and the driver closed the door behind them without a word. Caroline barely noticed when the car began to move and Rebecca said in a low tone, "It would probably be a good idea to buckle up."

This snapped Caroline back into the moment and she shook her head slightly to clear it before quickly reaching to pull the safety belt across her. Then she turned slightly toward Rebecca and asked, "So… are you going to tell me where we're going?" Hearing her voice in her ears, it sounded so accusatory, like she was being taken against her will. Her face flushed with embarrassment.

"Of course," Rebecca answered, as if she hadn't noticed Caroline's rudeness. "Before I do, it would help if I asked you a few questions so I can explain things in a way that would make the most sense. How much do you know about Moon Borns?"

"Not much. Just that they're pretty rare," Caroline answered uncomfortably.

"Not a problem," Rebecca said, clearly trying to soothe Caroline's nerves. "And when was the first time your abilities were expressed?"

"I don't know… A little over a day ago in the cemetery when I was attacked, I guess?" Caroline replied.

"No, that's probably not the case. Moon Born abilities build slowly, that's why we are so hard to detect early on. When you are able to put up a defense like what I heard you did during that battle, your abilities should have been expressing themselves for quite a while."

The delicate balance Caroline had been able to maintain with her nervousness, fatigue, excitement, and hunger fell apart as frustration entered the mix and she snapped, "I have no idea!"

"Think back," Rebecca coached gently. "Early on, it would have been something subtle. Perhaps something at school that you connected with deeply and didn't understand why? Or sometime when you felt yourself go into a deep meditation or trance that you didn't initiate?"

Trying to reestablish control over her emotions, Caroline leaned her head back and closed her eyes, searching her memories for something she could point to while Rebecca waited patiently. All that came to mind were the times she watched her friends using their abilities while she was unable to do anything herself. Despite her best efforts, the frustration began to grow and she felt Rebecca place her hand on her shoulder.

"Go further back," she said quietly. "Abilities express themselves around your twelfth birthday, but it starts differently for everyone. My first connection to my abilities happened when I was in a movie theater. A scene triggered it and I went into something like a waking dream. When I emerged, the movie was over and my family was looking at me like I had been gone for a long time."

Caroline gasped as a memory emerged from the recesses of her mind and played out. She was in her room drawing while her mom was cooking dinner and listening to music. A song she had never heard came on and the next thing she knew her mom was leaning over shoulder and looking at her drawing. It was completely done, an intricate pattern that filled the page from edge to edge in a variety of shades of green. For the life of her, she couldn't remember drawing any of it. In fact, she saw a ripped out sheet from her book tossed on the floor by her chair that had the start of the drawing she thought she had been doing. Caroline recounted the memory to Rebecca who nodded and grinned.

"Well done!" she said to Caroline. "When was that? About a year ago?"

"Probably a bit longer…" Caroline murmured, thinking back. "It was raining outside, so it had to be winter. Maybe January or February… So at least a year and a half ago."

"Well it's good I came when I did!" Rebecca said with wide eyes.

"Why?"

"Because you are about to enter a stage of your development that can be very difficult to navigate. Having skilled guidance will be necessary if your abilities are as strong as I think they will be."

"What would happen if I didn't have someone guiding me?" Caroline asked with genuine curiosity.

"We'll get to that," Rebecca assured her. "First, you asked where you are going and I'd like to give you a full answer. There are many Moon Borns who live with tribes around the world. As I said to you before, our roots run deep and, when we become attached to people and places, it becomes difficult for us to leave or reestablish ourselves someplace else.

"The highest concentration of Moon Borns is in Terradune, as has been the case for thousands of years. Even before the Calamity. Its location is a secret that has only been shared with a few trusted people throughout time and that has kept us safe even in the darkest times. It is also why we have newly identified Moon Borns begin their training there."

"So, I'm going to Terradune?"

"Yes, I'm taking you to one of the best Wayfarers I know who will be able to get you there. The journey…"

"Wait…" Caroline interrupted, "What's a Wayfarer?"

"Yes, I should probably provide a little more detail. I keep forgetting there is quite a lot you haven't been taught yet." Rebecca replied. "A Wayfarer is someone with the ability to find a path to even the hardest to reach location. Only a very skilled Wayfarer can lead you to Terradune. It's not only a very difficult place to find, but it's also very well protected. Many have sought it out and died along the way."

"Um… You're sending me on a life-threatening journey with a human GPS?" Caroline asked incredulously.

"Well, I wouldn't use those words, but yes," Rebecca said, clearly a little flustered by Caroline's bluntness.

"If it's so dangerous, why don't you take me there yourself?"

"You will be in good hands," Rebecca said, her voice returning to its gentle, soothing tone. "You can trust me, Ranee is the finest Wayfarer I have ever known."

"This is all too much…" Caroline mumbled as she started to tear up. "You're the first Moon Born I have ever met and I have so many questions. Now you're dumping me on someone else. Why can't you just come with me?"

Rebecca reached out and pulled Caroline into as much of a hug as the seat belts would allow. She stroked Caroline's hair as she cried into her sleeve and, when she heard Caroline's breathing slowly returning to normal, she spoke in a voice just barely above a whisper.

"I wish I could come with you, my dear," she began. "We are in a very dangerous moment in history and I need to make sure Moon Borns do not make the same mistakes as we did in the events leading up to and during The Calamity. You see, Moon Borns have always focused on keeping the peace and have studiously tried to not become involved in violence. We view ourselves as a counterbalance to many of the more volatile influences in the world.

"This is why we did not join a side or intervene in any way when war broke out amongst those who believed in Advancement and those who thought it was too dangerous. Our leaders at the time thought they were preserving our values of neutrality and that we would help rebuild once the lunacy of the war ended. They had no idea of the horrors that would come as a result of The Calamity. People being hunted and killed for using their abilities? At that time, it was unfathomable…

"Most Moon Borns fled to Terradune during and after the war. There, in the safety of our hidden city, our leaders debated for many years about whether we should do more to help or intervene. However, fear and tradition held us back from doing what we should have done. As one of our people's most senior leaders, it is my responsibility to travel around the world and speak with as many of our communities as possible to convince them now is the time that we need to end our neutrality. We cannot repeat our mistakes."

They then sat in silence for a while as Caroline absorbed everything that Rebecca had shared with her. She finally turned to Rebecca with a half grin, "Well, I guess that's a good excuse for not taking me yourself."

Rebecca smiled warmly, "I appreciate your understanding."

Then they felt the car slow and come to a stop. Rebecca looked out the tinted window as she opened the door, "My how time flies!" Sun splashed into the car and Caroline turned her head and closed her eyes, unable to adjust to the sudden brightness.

"Come along! We're here!" Rebecca said excitedly.

Caroline opened her eyes to a squint and, just as she found the door handle, the driver opened it for her. She started to get out, but the seat belt pulled her back down.

"Really, Caroline?!" she snapped at herself in embarrassment before unbuckling and sliding out. She could have sworn she saw a smirk on the driver's face as she hurried away from the car to find Rebecca. Before she did, however, she was surprised by the overwhelming scent of the ocean washing over her with a cool breeze and her eyes opened wide even though they still hadn't adjusted to the morning sunlight.

She blinked several times, feeling her eyes tearing, and then began to look around. They were at a small marina with sailboats and small yachts docked in neat rows. Colorful houses were lined up along the waterfront and there weren't many people out and about. Just a random jogger and a few people walking their dogs. Then she noticed Rebecca a short ways away, waving to her.

"Just down this way," Rebecca said, pointing down one of the docks as Caroline arrived.

They walked together quietly down to the dock and the wood deck swayed under them giving Caroline a slightly dizzying sensation. When they came to the very end, there was a small sailboat that looked like it had been through one too many storms. A deeply tanned woman with strong wiry muscles was carefully coiling some ropes on top of the cabin. She looked up as they arrived, gave Rebecca a warm smile, and said, "I was wondering when I was going to see you. Looks like you brought someone along for the ride, it's gonna be a bit crowded."

"Ranee, I'd like to introduce you to Caroline. She will be accompanying you to Terradune. Unfortunately, I am taking a longer path back as there are some things I need to attend to. In fact, I should probably be going right away."

Ranee nodded in acknowledgement, readily accepting the change in plans. Caroline, on the other hand, had lost the calm acceptance she had established during the car ride.

"You're sending me in *that*?! It looks like it could sink at any moment!" Caroline shouted, surprising a seagull that had been resting on a nearby railing and it immediately took flight to find a calmer spot.

Ranee rose to her full height and crossed her arms, clearly offended. "Where'd you find this one, Rebecca? She clearly needs to learn some manners…" she asked in a clipped tone.

"Caroline, that boat has seen me through some pretty sticky situations. You are in good hands. Trust me, this is a journey you will remember for the rest of your life." Rebecca said, looking down into Caroline's eyes and resting her hands on her shoulders. When she felt the tension in Caroline's muscles ease slightly, she knew at least a little bit of acceptance had returned.

"Now, I need to give you one important instruction, so please pay close attention." Rebecca continued. "Ranee can take you to Terradune, but it is up to you to find the entrance and only those who are open themselves are able to unlock the doors. I suggest you spend your time during the journey meditating on that."

"Seriously?!" Caroline shouted again and looked at Ranee with an exasperated expression. She then turned back to argue with Rebecca and saw she was already walking back down the deck talking with the driver who had appeared out of nowhere.

"I suggest you hop aboard now," Ranee called out to Caroline. "We have a few things we need to do before heading out and I don't want to miss the good wind."

"But I have never sailed before…" Caroline said, anxiety making her voice slightly shaky.

"Lucky for you I'm a good teacher. Toss me your bag and be

sure to grab ahold of that rail before you step on. You'll turn into a popsicle if you fall in the water."

∽

It was clear that Ranee had been preparing to leave for a while before they arrived because they were pushing away from the dock less than an hour after Caroline had carefully climbed aboard. She had to admit, Ranee was impressive as she moved around the boat like she knew every inch of it. Occasionally, she would issue calm simple instructions to Caroline, but she was sure Ranee didn't need any help. Clearly, her sailing lessons had already begun.

Ranee slowly guided the boat out into the bay and, despite the steady breeze, Caroline began to heat up from the sun beating down on them from a cloudless sky. The warmth made her feel lethargic and she closed her eyes, letting her mind wander, and the fatigue from the night before caught up with her.

Just as she was about to drift off to sleep, something smacked into her face and she startled awake, pawing at whatever was covering her face. When she finally got a grip on it and pulled it away, she saw it was a hat with a long brim and a large flap on the back.

"Don't be an idiot and put that on," Ranee called from the wheel.

"Huh?!" was all Caroline could respond with as she was still groggy and disoriented.

"HUH?!" Ranee mocked her. "Put that hat on before you get a sunburn. I don't want to hear you complaining this entire trip. The sun is not your friend on the water. I bet you didn't even bring any sunscreen… Why does Rebecca always stick me with the ones who are so clueless?"

Caroline's anger began to bubble up inside her and she thought of an excellent, snarky reply. Before she could say anything, Ranee said, "Alright, we should be able to start raising the sails now. Pull on that green cord to your left and don't stop pulling until I say stop."

Caroline reached out for the cord closest to her and Ranee snapped, "The GREEN cord! Not the blue one. We're just in the bay right now. Once we're out on the ocean it will be much more rough. You need to pay attention and follow my instructions to the letter."

"What makes you…" Caroline started to say.

"You can talk back to me once you've earned it. For now, pull on that *green* cord until I say stop," Ranee said, cutting off Caroline's argument before she could even start it.

Caroline glared at Ranee, sending as much much anger and dislike as she could without words. Ranee just raised an eyebrow and returned the glare with a neutral expression. Caroline began to feel uncomfortable and a cool shiver went up her back, so she turned to her left, found the green cord, undid the knot, and then began pulling on it.

She could barely get it to budge, no matter how hard she pulled, but she wasn't about to show any kind of weakness in front of Ranee. So, she turned her whole body, planted her feet against the side of the cabin, and began to pull with all her strength. Slowly the cord began to move and Caroline reached out and pulled with her other hand, starting to build some momentum.

"Twelve, thirteen, fourteen," Caroline muttered to herself as she crossed her hands over each other and pulled on the cord, establishing a rhythm. Her arms burned and a knot was forming in the center of her back between her shoulder blades, but she tried to ignore the pain and kept pulling.

"That's good," Ranee said just over her shoulder, startling Caroline out of her rhythm so that she almost let go of the cord. "Let me show you how to secure the line and then you'll help me raise the other sail."

Caroline looked up and saw a large white sail had risen over her head all the way up the mast. Then she moved back over to where she had unknotted the cord and watched as Ranee explained how to wrap it around the cleat and knot it again. Then she pulled it apart again and had Caroline redo it several more times. Strangely, Caroline didn't mind the repetition. It seemed to help her calm down and let her anger fade.

"C'mon, help me get the jenny raised so we can get out to the ocean faster," Ranee said, leading her to the bow. They spent the next several minutes learning how to raise the large foresail and then Ranee returned to the wheel, gesturing for Caroline to take a seat on a small bench next to her. They were both silent for a long while as Ranee guided the boat and Caroline just felt the wind build up and push them faster towards the ocean.

As they got closer, Caroline saw the whitecaps of the larger waves and felt a nervous flutter in her stomach. "How long will this trip take?" she asked Ranee, breaking the silence.

"That all depends on you," Ranee answered matter-of-factly.

"I don't understand," Caroline said, searching Ranee's face for more clues.

"You'll see," Ranee replied, clearly communicating there was nothing else to say on this topic.

Soon enough, Ranee began moving around the boat and issuing clear, short instructions to Caroline again. As they got closer to the open ocean, the instructions came faster and more urgent as they pulled down the jenny and raised the smaller jib. Several times, Caroline knew she made mistakes, but Ranee was right there in seconds to correct them. Each time, Caroline expected Ranee to start shouting or issue a terse reprimand, but none came. That didn't stop Caroline from chastising herself, though, and soon a dark mood had descended upon her again.

The boat's rocking grew and finally Ranee handed Caroline a bright yellow raincoat and jet black rain pants. Then she instructed Caroline to sit down and simply hold the wheel while she finished what was left to do. Just as she closed up the cabin, the skies opened up and they were pelted with large drops of rain. Ranee took over guiding the boat and Caroline simply held onto the railing, trying to not slide back and forth as the boat was buffeted with waves.

Time dragged on for Caroline and her body began to ache all over from the effort she had put in. The skies grew darker and she was sure what had just been a steady rain was going to turn into a huge storm. *Is this some kind of test?* she thought to herself, but dismissed the idea. This was just her luck, she was sure of it. *Why can't there be an easier way?* she wondered, but didn't want to say a word to Ranee.

"Ah, there we go!" Ranee suddenly said energetically, turning the large wheel several rotations to the left.

The boat's rocking transitioned into large rises and falls as it went over each wave. Caroline would sometimes catch a little air as the boat descended and then her butt would slam into the bench as the boat started to climb up again. To her surprise, however, she found this hilarious and, after several more occurrences, she began to chuckle. The next time, the chuckle turned into a full on laugh and then a guffaw. A thought crept into her head that Ranee must have thought she was crazy, but she didn't care. She was finally having some fun.

Unfortunately, the fun seemed to peter out almost as quickly as it came. The rain let up and the ocean calmed. Caroline took the opportunity to stretch her weary muscles, letting out soft groans as she moved from one arm to the other, then to her back and finally her legs. When she was done, she felt a prickle on the back of her neck and she looked around to see Ranee staring at her with an amused expression.

"Perhaps there's hope for you yet," Ranee said.

"Uh… OK…" was all Caroline could say and this caused Ranee to let out a huge bark of a laugh.

"Well, it looks like you're not prone to seasickness, so that's a good thing." Ranee said encouragingly. "Most folks I take out the first time would've hurled as soon as we hit the bigger waves."

"Thanks?" Caroline replied, not sure what to say and whether the positivity would last.

"Let's take advantage of the good weather for now and fix a meal. I wouldn't want to see what happens if you get hangry. You might be able to get some shut-eye too if all goes well," Ranee said warmly, securing the wheel and then opening up the cabin.

Caroline could barely keep her eyes open after eating what was a surprisingly good meal that Ranee prepared. She would have put her head down on the small table they ate at and been completely content sleeping that way if Ranee had let her. Instead, they cleaned up and put together a bed below deck, in the far end of the cabin near the space where the sails were stored. Caroline fell asleep before her head even hit the pillow.

2

THE JOURNEY OR THE DESTINATION?

ANEE'S VOICE WAS somewhat muffled, so it was difficult to understand what she was saying. Caroline tried to lay as still as possible because even a slight noise drowned out the words. The more she focused on Ranee's voice, the clearer it became that she was having a conversation with someone. There was no second voice, however, so Caroline struggled at first to understand what they were talking about.

"It's not gonna be easy," Ranee said and was then silent, listening to the other person.

"Don't give me that. You've done this before too and know exactly what I'm facing," Ranee raised her voice and went quiet again. This piqued Caroline's interest because she had not really seen Ranee show any kind of emotion other than bemusement with Caroline's blundering.

"No, YOU don't understand! I have never missed a path before and we came damn close yesterday," Ranee shouted and now Caroline was dying to know what the other side was saying. Ranee was definitely talking about their journey and it sounded like it was not going well.

"You know me better than that. I always finish what I start," Ranee then said so coldly followed by a mechanical click that sent a shiver up Caroline's spine. For the first time, she considered just how dependent she was on Ranee and the amount of danger she might be facing.

She took a deep breath, opened her eyes, and started to sit up, but every muscle in her body complained. She groaned loudly as she rolled her shoulders and turned her head in a large circle to work out the kinks. Then Ranee appeared in the doorway and said, "Well look who's decided to finally wake up. It was starting to seem like you were trying to make me sail this boat by myself."

"What time is it?" Caroline asked.

"Nine," Ranee responded.

"Oh, you are making it sound like I have been out for a long time, but it's only been a few hours."

"In the morning," Ranee said dryly. "You slept for sixteen hours."

"WHAT?!" Caroline shouted inadvertently.

"Consider it a mark of a good future sailor. Not everyone can sleep on a boat, especially after the wild ride we had," Ranee said, shifting to a more encouraging tone.

Caroline slowly slid across the cushions toward the doorway and Ranee took a few steps back to make some room. Caroline then got to her feet and hobbled over to the table that had been set up again.

"You OK with oatmeal?" Ranee asked.

"Sure," Caroline answered simply. Her mind returning to Ranee's conversation.

Moments later, a steaming bowl of oatmeal was sitting in front of her along with a metal cup filled to the brim with water. Taking big bites that scorched the roof of her mouth, she sat there quietly as Ranee started to clean up the tiny kitchen. When she was done, Ranee grabbed a pad and pencil as she slid into the free spot at the table and started to write something.

"That wasn't normal yesterday, was it?" Caroline suddenly asked, surprising herself.

"The ocean is always full of surprises," Ranee answered without looking up, the pencil racing across the lines on the paper.

"Is there going to be more of that?" Caroline asked, deciding to push further.

"More of what?"

"Crazy storms that come out of nowhere and then you suddenly find the one smooth path through it?" Caroline asked tartly and Ranee looked up with cool curiosity.

"Every journey is unique," Ranee said, looking directly into Caroline's eyes.

"Have you ever failed to complete a journey?" Caroline asked and knew immediately she may have overstepped her bounds as Ranee's eyes narrowed and she put the pad and pencil down.

"Never."

"Never? Like not ever?"

"That's what never means, right?"

"What would happen if you did?" Caroline persisted and Ranee's eyes widened in recognition.

"Were you…" Ranee started to say and then stopped herself. She picked up the pad and pencil, pulled open a drawer, shoved them in, and slammed it shut. Then she pulled out some keys and locked the drawer before turning to Caroline and saying, "Finish your breakfast and then go get cleaned up. The shower doesn't work, but there are washcloths in the cabinet over there. Try to be quick, we have work to do if you want to make it to Terradune in less than a month."

"A MONTH?!" Caroline shouted, not able to contain herself.

"Well, that all depends on you," Ranee answered simply and climbed out of the cabin.

The idea of spending a month on a small boat with a surly sailor caused Caroline to lose her appetite. She pushed the bowl away from her and slid out from behind the table and found her bag stowed beneath the bench. She rummaged around for a change of clothes and then proceeded to do her best to clean up. No matter how hard she scrubbed, however, she felt a thin film of salt covering her body.

☙

"Not bad! Do it again and this time try to get the sail raised in less than a minute," Ranee instructed Caroline as she lowered the genoa, careful to make sure it didn't float into the water. They carefully stowed it in the front compartment and Caroline joined Ranee by the wheel.

"Go!" Ranee shouted and Caroline scampered up over the cabin and to the front of the boat. She reached into the compartment and grabbed the corner of the sail, and proceeded through all the steps to raise it. When she was done, the giant blue sail with a big octopus billowed as the wind filled it and Caroline looked back to Ranee to see how she did.

"Alright! I think you've mastered that one! Fifty-six seconds!" Ranee crowed and Caroline let out a whoop of excitement.

It had been three days of these drills and Caroline was steadily getting the hang of the different tasks Ranee was assigning her. When she first climbed aboard, Caroline was certain she would hate sailing, but the daily routine had a comforting quality to it that she had come to embrace. She didn't even mind all the cleaning Ranee made her do, though she made a mental note to make sure her parents didn't find out about that.

Caroline sat down on the bench next to Ranee and took a moment to catch her breath. As her heart rate slowed down, she gazed around at the open ocean and wondered where they were. They hadn't seen so much as a tiny island since they'd left the shore behind.

"We seem to be making pretty good progress, right?" Caroline said idly.

"We're about where we should be," Ranee said without elaborating.

"And where would that be?" Caroline asked, trying to satisfy her curiosity.

"It's best not to worry about that," Ranee counseled. "We will get to Terradune, I will make sure of that."

"I don't get it," Caroline said, starting to feel a bit of frustration break through the calm. "Haven't you done this trip a ton of times? Shouldn't you know exactly how long it takes to get there and where we are right now?"

"Listen," Ranee responded calmly, "I know you've heard me say this before, but it really is true. Every journey is different. Sometimes we are able to move quickly and sometimes it takes a while. What I can guarantee is that focusing on your progress is the fastest way to get frustrated and, once you are frustrated, that can make a journey interminable. It's best to just enjoy the trip and focus on your destination."

Easy for you to say, Caroline thought to herself, feeling a dark mood settle in. She felt that Ranee was acting like one of the Kung Fu masters in the old movies her dad made her watch with him. They always said things in a riddle that the hero had to figure out rather than being direct and explaining what they needed to do. Caroline had been in the dark about things for so long and while she had caught up with the help of her friends, she still often felt like she had missed out on critical information that had already been explained.

As the day wore on, Ranee continued Caroline's training, but her heart wasn't in it anymore. When the sun began to set and dinner was done, they would normally hang out quietly together and listen to music or read books. However, Ranee noticed the wind was dying and had Caroline bring in the foresail.

That night, Caroline had a horrible night's sleep. She kept falling into the same dream where she was stranded on a desert island by herself. The boat was anchored out in the water, but every time she tried to swim out to it, a large wave would come and push her back onto the beach. She tried over and over again despite having the same result each time. So, when she got up in the morning, she was more tired than when she went to bed and her brain was so foggy that she forgot where she was until she was sitting at the table eating yet another helping of oatmeal.

When Caroline made it out of the cabin, she found Ranee sitting on the bench reading a book. She looked up and saw the mainsail was down now too. Caroline turned to Ranee in confusion and said, "Why did you decide to stop?"

Ranee looked up from her book and replied, "I did not decide to stop." Then she waved her hand around, gesturing to the air around them and said, "No wind."

"No wind?! What does that mean? What do we do now?" Caroline asked in semi panic.

"We wait."

"We just sit here and wait?"

"Yup!" Ranee said as she returned to her book.

"You can't just turn on the motor?" Caroline asked, unable to accept Ranee's answer.

"That's just to navigate when we are docking. I don't have enough fuel to just keep running it," Ranee explained.

"But what happens if the wind doesn't pick up?" Caroline asked, her panic starting to spin up to full speed.

"We have plenty of supplies, best to just enjoy the chill-out time," Ranee said and then proceeded to ignore Caroline's sputtering and hyperventilating.

Eventually, Caroline followed Ranee's advice and got out her own book and started to read, but she found that she was reading the same page over and over again since she couldn't focus on anything but the fact they were stuck. She then went and got her sketch pad, but dark thoughts kept clouding her mind as she tried to access the creative energy that always seemed to come easily to her.

What if it's too late for her to start her training?

What if she never learned to master her powers?

What if another storm came and she was lost at sea?

What if they never let her leave Terradune and she never saw her family and friends again?

A downward spiral of anxiety, anger, and depression washed over her so that she spent most of the day just staring out at the slow, shallow waves all around them. She could barely remember all the positive energy that had built up over the prior days. Occasionally, Ranee would assign Caroline a task and she would go through the motions slowly. By the end of the day, Caroline had completely run out of energy and barely took three bites of dinner before she excused herself with a mumble and climbed into bed.

The next day was even worse since Caroline couldn't get out of bed in the morning. Ranee had to pull her into the main cabin and force her to eat a protein bar before Caroline could muster any energy to go outside. They were still stuck in the doldrums and the sun beat down so mercilessly that Caroline spent most of the day back in the cabin drawing flowers like she did when she was in first grade. Her thoughts were consumed with worries that she had made a terrible mistake agreeing to go to Terradune and, by the end of the day, she had filled five pages front and back with the same tiny flower with looping petals, a big sunflower center, and a single leaf on its stem.

That night, during dinner, Ranee stared at Caroline with a penetrating glare, but she didn't care. She just shoved her mashed potatoes around her plate and didn't touch any of the slab of processed meat sitting alongside them.

"How long is this funk going to last?" Ranee asked, but Caroline just rolled her eyes and returned her stare to the volcano of potatoes she had constructed.

"You're just making things take longer, I tried to warn you," Ranee said in the same tone her mother used when she admonished Caroline for trying to take a shortcut through her homework and having to do everything over again.

"Hey! Why don't you make the wind start blowing again and then we can be on our way?!" Caroline snapped.

"It doesn't work that way," Ranee started to explain.

"Duh!" Caroline yelled, cutting Ranee off. Then she picked up her plate, slid out from the table, dropped everything in the sink, and stormed off to her bed.

She didn't fall asleep though. The guilt for how she spoke

to Ranee just started another round of self-critical thoughts and she spent the entire night chastising herself. By the morning, she felt like a zombie and stumbled into the main cabin for breakfast with a mane of tangled hair and dark purple bags under her eyes.

"Whoa…" was all Ranee could say as Caroline walked right past her and climbed out of the cabin.

When she saw the sails were still lowered, Caroline let out a primal scream, collapsed onto the deck, and began to sob. She heard Ranee climb out of the cabin and then felt the shade as she cast a shadow over Caroline standing over her.

"Get up!" Ranee commanded, but Caroline ignored her.

"I said, GET UP!"

For some reason, the second time, Caroline felt compelled to follow the order and she slowly got to her feet.

"I think I know what you need," she said as she placed her hand on the center of Caroline's back and guided her to the stern of the boat. Ranee stepped up on the bench and Caroline followed her lead. Then Ranee gave Caroline a strong shove in the center of her back and she lost her balance, tumbling into the water. The shock of it caused Caroline to thrash around and yell, "Oh my gosh!" over and over.

"Better be careful, you might attract a shark!" Ranee called out.

"WHAT?!" Caroline screamed and then quickly swam back to the boat, pulling herself up the small ladder.

"WHAT THE HECK?!" Caroline shouted at Ranee, an inch from her face as she stood on the edge of the boat.

"Sounds like you need another dip," Ranee said calmly and shoved Caroline hard in the center of her chest.

When she landed in the water this time, however, Caroline knew what to expect and she calmly righted herself underwater and prepared to pull herself back to the surface. Before she could do that, she noticed something very large swimming underneath her and the boat. While her pulse quickened, she didn't move and just stared as it slowly turned and circled back around. Caroline was so transfixed that she was oblivious to the sting of the salt-water in her eyes and it was only when she was in desperate need of air that she finally surfaced.

"There you are, I was beginning to wonder!" Ranee called out brightly.

Just as Caroline was about to shout back a lame retort, however, a whale surfaced alongside the boat. It blew out a large amount of water that proceeded to drench Ranee and then it took a deep breath and dove back down. She stared at Caroline in surprise and disbelief for a couple of moments before she started to laugh loudly. Caroline couldn't help herself and started to laugh too.

"Oh, you think that's funny?!" Ranee quipped and then she dove into the water, surfaced, and splashed Caroline several times.

Caroline returned fire and then stopped suddenly and said in a worried tone, "Wait, won't this attract sharks?"

"Oh, I doubt there are any sharks around here," Ranee said casually.

"You!" Caroline shouted indignantly and started splash-ing Ranee again who just started laughing uncontrollably and shielded her face.

Once Caroline's arms were too tired to splash anymore, they both just floated on their backs relaxing and catching their breath. Eventually, Ranee said, "I guess you made a friend down there."

"Yeah, his name is Fred," Caroline responded without miss-ing a beat, causing Ranee to let out one of her trademark barking laughs.

They made their way back to the ladder and pulled themselves up one by one. Then they sat on the bench letting the sun start to dry them. The warmth began to relax all the tension that had built up in Caroline's body and for the first time in days she felt some contentment.

"Sorry I've been such a pill…" she said quietly.

"Thanks for that," Ranee replied.

Caroline's stomach then growled loudly and Ranee said, "Wow! Has your appetite come back?"

"I could easily eat all the food on this boat right now," Caroline said seriously, feeling a huge hunger pang hit.

"No worries, I saved your dinner from last night. You can heat it back up and then we can see what else you want to eat."

As Caroline devoured several plates of food, she and Ranee settled into an easy conversation characteristic of people realizing they have met someone who could become a good friend. They shared funny stories about their families, talked about their favorite movies, and even told each other some of their guilty pleasures. Soon, the fatigue caught up with Caroline and she was starting to mumble nonsense, so Ranee sent her to bed.

That night, Caroline's dream was one of the most vivid she had ever experienced. She saw a majestic city perched at the top of a towering cliff with a raging sea battering the sheer walls. She was soaring high above it and noticed several birds circling far below her. An urge to join them came over her and she swooped down, enjoying the feeling of the wind whipping around her.

When she reached the birds, one by one, they began to dive down toward the city. Caroline followed them and soon they were darting down narrow alleys and streets with bright colored windows and doors popping along bland beige walls. The game of chase was exhilarating and each of them took turns being "it." When it was her turn, she was determined to fly as fast as she could. She heard the calls from the birds become fainter and knew she was winning as she took a hard turn into a large square at the center of the city.

There was a tall tower in the middle of the square and, feeling triumphant, Caroline began to circle up its outside in a large spiral. When she reached the top, the windows to the room there were shut and there was a light that was so bright emanating from it that Caroline wondered if this was some kind of fancy light house. She was just about to begin searching for a way to get into the tower when she heard a voice call out, "CAROLINE!" Confused and curious who could be there with her, she looked around and saw only the clay tile roofs of the city stretching out all around the tower.

"CAROLINE!" the voice called again, but this time much more loudly, and she found herself taking in a huge gasp of air as she came out of her deep sleep. She looked around and unlike when she usually woke up, she was completely awake and aware. That was Ranee's voice and it sounded like she was excited. Caroline shimmied out of bed, changed quickly, and climbed out to the deck as quickly as possible. She found Ranee at the wheel with a huge smile on her face.

"Look!" she called out, pointing up to the sails, and Caroline spun around to see both had been raised and were catching a strong wind. At the front of the boat, she could also see spray from the water as it cut through the waves. Then she turned to look at Ranee with relief and elation coursing through her. She hadn't smiled this hard since she had left her friends to go on this crazy trip.

"Terradune here we come!" Ranee exclaimed and Caroline let out a whoop in agreement.

"Go grab some food, you're going to need all your strength to harness wind this strong. When you're done, I'm going to show you how fast this puppy can go!" Ranee said, patting the wheel with pride.

Caroline jumped back into the cabin and whipped up a large breakfast of leftovers and wolfed it down as quickly as she could. When she was done, she cleaned up and checked to make sure everything was secure like Ranee had taught her. Then, when she was satisfied that everything was ship shape, she climbed back out and Ranee gestured for her to join her.

Ranee shook her head at Caroline as she was about to take her usual spot on the bench next to her and grabbed her wrist, pulling her behind the large wheel. Then she placed Caroline's hands securely at two points and said with a mischievous glint in her eyes, "Now we're gonna have some fun…"

She left Caroline at the wheel and began to scamper around the boat, pulling out additional equipment and then changing out the sails to one that would help them go even faster. As it filled with air, Caroline felt the boat lean heavily to the left and she held on tight as the wheel tried to turn as the boat adjusted to the new level of force. Ranee then scampered back and climbed up on the high side of the boat, clipped a harness together, planted her feet on the edge, and leaned far out into the air. Caroline noticed the boat begin to balance more and Ranee let out a huge yelp of happiness. Caroline realized she was seeing Ranee completely in her element and marveled at the level of skill and confidence.

They worked together as a team all day, maximizing their speed and, by the time the sun was setting, Caroline was surprised to see even Ranee was exhausted. They ate dinner together quietly, feeling content from the warm burn of their sore muscles.

Then Ranee looked at Caroline with pride and said, "You done good today, kid."

"Thanks…" was all Caroline could respond with, letting Ranee's approval wash over her.

"Whatever you dreamed of last night, do it again. We might reach Terradune tomorrow if we're lucky," Ranee said and then began to clean up their dishes.

Soon after, they had both turned in, but the combination of extreme fatigue and excitement made it impossible for Caroline to fall asleep. After tossing and turning for an hour, she finally gave up and crept into the main part of the cabin as quietly as possible so as to not wake Ranee. She found her duffel and carefully extracted her sketchpad and pencils before returning to her bed and turning on a small dome light. The images of Terradune were bright in her mind and she began to feverishly draw scenes from the night before.

The next morning, Caroline woke with a large snort and wiped the line of drool from the corner of her mouth. She looked around groggily and saw the sketchpad right next to her and an image of the tall tower she had flown up on the page along with a long pencil line stretching from the roof to the side of the page. Clearly, she had fallen asleep mid-drawing. Then she remembered that Ranee had said they could possibly reach Terradune today and she scampered out of the cabin and onto the deck. Ranee was right where she expected her, at the wheel with a big grin on her face.

"Nice job!" Ranee said.

"Thanks?" Caroline responded in confusion, not understanding what she had done.

"We have a straight shot to Terradune and should be pretty close in the next few hours," Ranee continued.

"Really?" Caroline asked excitedly, not allowing herself believe the good news.

"You didn't pick the easiest path though," Ranee said with a note of caution, gesturing with her head towards the stern of the boat.

Caroline looked in that direction and saw huge storm clouds forming several miles behind them and furrowed her brows. How did she have anything to do with picking their path? She had just been following Ranee's instructions.

"Go grab some food and pack up your stuff. I'd say we have about thirty minutes until the sailing will get really fun," Ranee said.

When Caroline returned to the deck fifteen minutes later, Ranee began barking orders and Caroline worked quickly and efficiently to execute them. The last task was to close off the cabin and when she was done, she made her way back to her spot on the bench by Ranee. Suddenly, a huge gust of wind hit the sails and the boat lurched forward. Caroline lost her footing and began to tumble off the back when she felt a vice-like grip close around her wrist.

Ranee pulled her back to her feet and yelled over the wind, "I haven't lost a passenger yet and you're not going to be the first one!" She then clipped Caroline to a storm line, so that she could move around but not fall overboard.

Caroline nodded soberly with gratitude and took her seat, watching Ranee spin the large wheel to navigate the churning ocean waves. Soon after, the storm hit and they were lashed with rain and winds. The sea swells grew huge and multiple times the boat leaned so far over that Caroline was amazed Ranee was able to bring it upright again. All the while she shouted commands over the raging storm and Caroline did her best to follow them, often slipping or needing to hold on tight to a railing to avoid getting thrown overboard.

This went on for several hours and, despite her exhaustion from the effort, Caroline carried on with the help of the adrenaline coursing through her. Sheets of rain drenched them, and Caroline became used to spotting when another dousing would occur. She saw a huge curtain of gray rain in front of them and the boat pitched forward as it descended the back side of a wave. She squinted her eyes in preparation for another salty shower and, as the bow of the boat pierced the sheet of water she was surprised to see sunlight glinting off the railing. A few seconds later, the whole boat was through and they were bathed in the warm sun with a steady breeze and much calmer seas.

"Hoooo! That was fun, right?" Ranee asked rhetorically.

"You have a strange idea of fun," Caroline quipped.

"Hey, I just guide you through the routes, you're the one who picks 'em," Ranee retorted warmly.

"You keep saying that!" Caroline responded in half mock and half serious annoyance.

"Well, it's true!" Ranee said as she squeezed the rain water out of her hair.

"I still have no idea what you're talking about," Caroline said, giving up on ever understanding Ranee's riddle.

"Wait, you're serious," Ranee said, understanding finally dawning on her. "Who has been training you? I'm going to have a word with them about the gaps in your education."

"Nobody has been training me," Caroline responded earnestly. "I only found out I'm a Moon Born a couple days before I met you."

"Oh my... You're serious, aren't you?" Ranee said, dumbfounded and Caroline just nodded.

"Well, now I know why Rebecca wanted to get you to Terradune so quickly…" Ranee continued. "Listen, Wayfarers just navigate the path that the passenger picks. At the start of this journey, it was clear to me that you didn't know where you wanted to go and there was no path for me to find. That's happened a number of times with my passengers, but usually they figure it out a bit more quickly. You're a stubborn one though…

Caroline smiled sheepishly and blushed.

"When you finally decided you wanted to go to Terradune, however, you had one of the clearest, most direct paths I have ever seen. I guess when you finally made up your mind you had to get here as fast as possible."

"Here?" Caroline asked suspiciously, picking up on Ranee's word choice.

"Yeah, look," Ranee responded, pointing off the side of the boat towards some giant cliffs a short distance away.

"No way… It was real?!" Caroline exclaimed.

"What?" Ranee asked, not following her.

"My dream was real!" Caroline yelped.

"Oooooh!" Ranee said, now understanding. "Not exactly… You Moon Borns are drawn to Terradune somehow. When you opened yourself up to finding it, the image must have been very strong. You were able to visualize your destination with such detail that it made my job a piece of cake."

"You call that a piece of cake?" Caroline asked skeptically, gesturing to the storm they just passed through.

"Heck, that's nowhere near the worst I've been through. Still, remind me to tell Rebecca that I'm not taking any more newbies for a while." Ranee said with a cocky smile as she steered the boat toward the cliffs. "Now, go grab your stuff, we should be at a spot where I can let you off in about ten minutes."

Caroline's stomach flipped as anxiety took the place of excitement, but she pushed it down and opened up the cabin so she could get her belongings. As she double checked she had everything, she looked around to take in the small space that she had called home for almost two weeks. When she had boarded the boat, she was sure she would hate being in such tight quarters. Now that she was leaving, strong waves of nostalgia hit her and tears formed in her eyes. She shook her head and tried to focus on how excited she was to explore that city, but the sense of sadness stayed with her.

"You were in there for a while!" Ranee said in a silly, chastising voice. "We're here!"

"What?!" Caroline said, not ready for such a quick ending to her journey and looking around to the front of the boat to see a small beach sandwiched between two large rock outcroppings at the base of the cliffs.

"Yup," Ranee confirmed as she secured the wheel and slid past Caroline to climb onto the cabin. "Help me get these sails down."

When Caroline was done with her part, she looked over to Ranee to see her finish stowing the sail in the front compartment and then she pulled out a large yellow bundle with a rope lashed around it. It looked pretty heavy as she hauled it back to the stern of the boat. She unwound the rope and secured the end to a cleat at the back of the boat. Then she threw the bundle in the water and it immediately started expanding into a modest sized raft.

Ranee took Caroline's bags and tossed them over to the raft where they landed perfectly in the center.

"OK, this is where I leave you. Good luck finding the entrance," she said genuinely to Caroline.

Fear, frustration, and confusion finally broke through and

Caroline stared at Ranee dumbfounded. "You're just going to leave me here in a raft?!"

"I need to go pick up my next passenger and I'm already later than I expected."

"How the heck do I find the entrance then?!"

"Don't ask me, it's a Moon Born thing. Now, hop on out and get on with your task. I've dropped off a ton of new Moon Borns over the years, but you're the first one I am confident will find the entrance."

Caroline didn't know why, but she rushed over to Ranee and wrapped her up in a tight hug.

"Aww… Thanks, hon. I've grown fond of you too. Don't go using any other Wayfarers now. I'm your gal from now on," Ranee said, giving Caroline a tight, bone-crushing squeeze.

With that, Caroline separated from Ranee and pulled the raft in closer. Then she slipped in and Ranee handed her a couple of oars. Then she untied the rope from her boat, tossing the line over to Caroline who caught it like an old hand.

Caroline just sat as Ranee turned her boat back into the storm, losing sight of her much sooner than she expected. Feeling the rock of the waves beneath her, she turned to look at the small beach and realized that it wasn't getting any closer. So, she pulled out the oars and started to row slowly to the first solid land she had seen in what felt like ages.

3

LENDING A HAND

EO WOKE UP slowly to a quiet house and rolled over, squinting his eyes to see the numbers on the clock stationed on his dresser. It was ten in the morning and a smile stretched across his face since he knew his parents were already out for the day, which meant he was able to enjoy a lazy summer day without the judgy looks and encouragement to do something productive. He would have gladly stayed in bed for longer, but his stomach growled loudly and he felt the need to gorge himself on cereal and whatever leftovers he could find in the fridge.

After making his way down to the kitchen and finding a huge mixing bowl, Leo dumped half the contents of a box of O's in and then doused it with the remainder of the milk. A thought occurred to him briefly that he should maybe let his parents know they needed more, but it was quickly gone as he heard a rhythmic buzzing coming from the den. He shoveled a few bites of cereal in his mouth quickly, leaving a small pool of milk that had dripped off his chin on the counter, and went to investigate.

As he started to look around, however, the buzzing stopped. So, he shrugged to himself and started to turn back to the kitchen when it started up again. Commencing his search again, it was clear the buzzing was coming from the couch. He lifted up several pillows quickly, but found nothing. He then placed his hand on a seat cushion and followed the vibration to the crack between it and the next cushion over. He reached down and felt the familiar contours of his phone case. He pulled it out quickly and glanced at the screen to see Aran's goofy face plastered on it with the prompt at the bottom to answer the call. As he was about to do that, however, the screen went black and a dead battery symbol appeared.

"Gah!" Leo yelled as he ran into the kitchen to plug in his phone and Astro ran behind him nipping at his ankles in the hopes that Leo would play with him.

He found a tangled charger where he had left it a couple days before at the end of the counter and plugged in his phone. Then he slid down the huge bowl of cereal and started guiding big spoonfuls into his mouth while he stared at the screen, willing his phone to wake up with the power of his impatience. It wasn't until he was at the bottom of the bowl and getting the soggiest bits of cereal that his phone screen finally lit up. He quickly grabbed it and was about to jab the app to call Aran back when he saw that he had forty unread messages. Ignoring them for the moment, he opened the phone app and saw he had missed twelve calls that morning from his friends.

"What the heck?" Leo mumbled to himself, confused as to why everyone was trying to get ahold of him.

He quickly hit the missed call from Aran and put the phone

up to his ear, feeling his anxiety start to build as the phone rang multiple times.

"THERE YOU ARE!" Aran yelled into his ear as soon as he picked up.

"What's going on?!" Leo asked urgently, bracing himself for bad news.

"Dude, did you forget? Our parents volun-told us to help out with packing boxes to be shipped to the schools today? Ring any bells?" Aran chastised him.

"Oh shoot…" Leo said, acknowledging his memory lapse.

"Uh huh!" Aran agreed. "Don't worry, we've saved the heaviest stuff for you."

"Ha ha…" Leo responded sarcastically.

"Can you just get yourself down to the bookshop already?" Aran said seriously and Leo knew he had actually annoyed his friends.

"Yeah, I'll be down there as quick as I can," Leo responded and tossed his phone down on the counter as he ran upstairs.

He tore off his pajamas and threw on clothes as quickly as he could, not paying attention to whether they were dirty or clean. He then ran back down the stairs, slipping on the bottom step and landing hard on his backside. He stood back up slowly, rubbing the spot that would soon have a huge black and blue mark. Then he shoved his feet in his shoes and ran out the door, not even checking to make sure it was locked. He ran down the street, ignoring the ache from the bruise and the cramp that was forming in his side from exercising so soon after he finished a massive bowl of cereal.

Hurtling himself around the corner, he saw Caroline's house coming up on his left and slowed down to a jog. Since she had left, nothing felt the same. It was like everything was a little less fun. She had always been a central part of their crew and one of its primary instigators. She would come up with fun quests for them to do, tell horrible jokes, make them watch sappy romcoms that they all ended up loving, and bake them amazing treats. Just thinking of her peanut butter chocolate chip cookies made Leo's mouth start watering, but he had to ignore that too as he picked up the pace again and hustled to the bookshop.

He decided to head for the back door first to avoid the risk of getting a disapproving stare from Adam. Instead, he was greeted with obnoxious cheers from his friends when he pulled the door open.

"Look who decided to join us!" Meimei exclaimed.

"Awww… Sleeping beauty is looking ravishing with all that rest he got!" Ania called out.

Even Stella got in a good jab with, "I don't think our dogs sleep as much as you!"

"Let me guide you to your station," Aran said from behind him, placing his hands on Leo's shoulders and steering him to a spot in the far corner.

"You've gotta be kidding me…" Leo said, staring at the shelves filled with heavy textbooks.

"You thought I was joking?" Aran asked with a big grin. "Hey, when you *snooze*, you *lose*."

Leo shook his head slowly back and forth in defeat and proceeded to start taping up a box so he could fill it with volumes of "Math in Your Everyday World!" The rest of the group turned back to their work and picked up on the conversation they were having before Leo's arrival.

"So, they were already down there when you got here?" Stella asked Meimei.

"Yeah, I'm not sure they ever went home," Meimei replied.

"Just because you didn't see them go in, doesn't mean they

were already down there. Maybe they're taking the day off," Aran chimed in.

"First off, there's no way they would take a day off when we have four days until we're supposed to head to our new school," Meimei rebutted.

"Don't remind me…" Ania said.

"Second," Meimei continued, ignoring Ania's comment. "Adam came through not long after I got here with a bunch of breakfast food and I saw him go down to the cavern. They're definitely down there."

"When did you get here?" Leo asked.

"A little before eight," Meimei replied.

"Dude! It's summer!" Aran chastised.

"You try sleeping late when my dad is working on a project in the backyard," Meimei said with an annoyed look.

"So, you're telling us that Maranda and Keiko have been training on The Crucible for hours today already?" Leo asked in astonishment.

"Yup," Meimei confirmed.

"I don't get it, what's the rush?" Ania asked.

"They need Maranda to be one of the schools' Star Born teachers, but she can't do that if she hasn't passed The Crucible yet."

"Wait, she hasn't passed it yet?" Stella asked.

"Not officially," Leo answered.

"Well, we should go check in on her during our lunch break," Stella said sincerely.

"Yeah, I like that idea," Meimei said brightly and the rest of the group nodded their heads enthusiastically.

They all then turned back to their work with renewed energy and time flew by. Before long, it was almost one in the afternoon and they had run out of boxes with just a few things left to pack. Everyone gathered together and settled down in a circle at the center of the room and the rest of the group shared parts of their lunches with Leo since he had forgotten to pack one in his rush to get there. Before long, they had finished all the food and Leo was the first one to hop up and head toward Adam's office. Everyone else quickly followed and, as they walked through the door, Adam swiveled around in his chair and looked at them with a raised eyebrow.

"What's up?" he asked the group.

"We ran out of boxes and there's not much left to pack," Leo responded on behalf of the group.

"Oh, well I guess you can head out then. I'll grab some more boxes later and we can probably finish up tomorrow morning," Adam said as he started to swivel back towards his desk.

Leo turned toward the bookshelf next to him and reached up behind the books on the fifth shelf up, pushing the button to release the lock on the door to the cavern's secret entrance. As soon as he heard the click of the latch, without turning around, Adam said, "Leo, we have already talked about this multiple times."

"We just want to say hi," Leo responded snarkily.

"No," was all Adam said in response.

"C'mon! We haven't seen her in weeks!" Leo said, ratcheting up his frustration quickly.

"Um… What's going on?" Meimei asked.

"We are technically not allowed in the cavern while they're training. They think we will be too much of a distraction," Leo said with attitude.

"You know how hard it is to pass The Crucible, Leo. She doesn't have any time to spare, so just let her focus," Adam said gruffly.

"But…" Leo began to say.

"I'm sure she'll pass today or tomorrow," Meimei interrupted, looking at Leo with her eyebrows raised high to signal him to stop talking. "We will just try and catch her afterward."

"Perhaps," Adam responded tersely and the group shuffled out of his office and back into the storage room.

"Why did you let him win?" Leo asked with a loud, frustrated whisper when the door had closed behind them.

"Just chill out," Meimei admonished him. "Let's just pack up and we can talk more about it on the way to my place."

Leo managed to make it only a few blocks after they left the shop before he couldn't hold his frustration back anymore.

"So, are you going to explain why you rolled over in there?" he asked Meimei pointedly.

"Oh geez," Meimei said in a mocking tone. "Can you use one of your meditation techniques already?"

"Wha… Wha… Wha…" Leo stuttered as his anger increased dramatically.

"Ok, just hush and listen," Stella said calmly and Leo settled into a fuming silence.

"We're going to all sleep over at my place and then sneak in," Meimei said simply.

"That's it?" Ania asked, confirming there was nothing else to the plan.

"You have a better idea?" Meimei responded and Ania just raised her hands in peace and shook her head.

"Sounds good to me," Aran said. "It's been ages since I've had your mom's cooking."

"You had dinner at our house last week," Meimei said in confusion.

"Like I said, ages," Aran answered with a serious face and the rest of the group erupted with laughter. Even Leo couldn't hold onto his anger and joined in.

❧

That evening, after everyone had gathered their things and reconvened at Meimei's house, they devoured several pizzas and goofed off in the backyard enjoying the still long days of summer when the sun wouldn't set for at least another hour. Things got rowdier when they busted out several games and the noise reached a crescendo when Ania and Aran got into an argument about who won a particularly heated card game. Casey strongly suggested they all go for a long walk and Meimei ushered them out the side gate as quickly as she could.

The playful ribbing continued as they walked down the sidewalk with Meimei silently leading them a few paces ahead.

"Hey, where are you leading us?" Aran called up to her.

"The bookshop," Meimei answered.

"What?! Are you thinking of trying to sneak in now?"

"Of course!" Meimei responded as if it was obvious this is what they should be doing.

"But it's still open! There'll be people there, including Adam!" Stella said anxiously.

"Probably just Adam, since he has the rest of them helping with prep for the schools," Meimei said matter-of-factly.

"We don't even have a plan!" Leo chimed in.

"Sometimes you don't need a plan," Meimei retorted.

"Wait, who is this person? It's definitely not Meimei. I think someone must have replaced her with a doppelganger!" Ania said jokingly and the rest of the group started adding more and more absurd theories to explain Meimei's odd behavior. This lasted right up until they found themselves standing outside the back door to the bookshop.

"So what do we do now?" Stella asked Meimei.

"Knock," Meimei answered with a deadpan as she walked up to the door and knocked softly three times.

They all waited nervously, fidgeting and shuffling their feet, but nobody answered the door. Meimei nodded decisively and tried opening the door, but it was locked. So she turned to Leo and said, "You know the code, right?"

"Uh, yeah," Leo said as he stepped forward to the keypad.

He entered the code, but he didn't hear the familiar soft chime that signaled it had unlocked the door. He entered the code again with the same result, silence. He tried a third time and this time the lock emitted a sharp error sound. He was about to enter the code again, but Aran blocked his hand and said, "They obviously changed the code, Leo. Just give it a little juice instead."

Leo thought about it for a moment and then shrugged slightly as he realized that he didn't have a better idea. He placed his hand on the keypad and sent a spike of his energy into it. He felt a sharp sting in his palm as electricity surged into it and he yanked it back, shaking it to try to help dissipate the pain. Some thin tendrils of smoke came out of the keypad and a soft click came from the latch. Stella tried to open the door and it swung open a crack.

"See? You're now perfectly suited for a life of crime," Aran said in a light, congratulatory way. Leo just rolled his eyes in response.

They peered into the storage room and it was dark and empty, so they crept silently across the room to the door that led to Adam's office. Meimei brought up the rear and closed the back door as quietly as she could.

Stella then listened for sounds in Adam's office and hearing none, she took great pains to open the door quietly. Her stomach dropped when she looked through the small crack she had created because Adam was sitting at his desk working on a laptop that looked like it had seen better days. She looked back to the rest of the group and mouthed, "He's sitting right there…" and pointed toward where the desk was situated.

Stella closed the door again and whispered, "What do we do?"

"Wait?" offered Aran.

"We have no idea how long that will take and my parents are going to start wondering where we are at some point," Meimei said, shooting down the idea quickly.

"Hand me your phone," Ania whispered to Leo.

"Why? What are you going to do with it?" he asked suspiciously.

"Just give it to me," she answered impatiently and he pulled it out from his pocket slowly. She grabbed it out of his hand and made her way to the back door.

They all followed her outside as she started searching for something in the browser.

"Got it," she said with satisfaction after a few moments and then she dialed a phone number and held the phone up to her ear.

When someone answered on the other line, she said, "Hi there, I have a dog here. The tag has this phone number on it and says his name is Scout. He was walking around my neighborhood for a while and I figured he might be lost. Anyway, sorry to bother you, I didn't realize this number was for a store. It must be an old number. I guess I'll take him to a shelter or something…"

She paused for a moment and the others couldn't hear what the voice on the other side was saying.

"Oh, he is the owner's dog? That's great! Here's my address, 85 Leroy Street. I'll just have him hanging out in our backyard. He's such a good dog."

They all listened impatiently as Ania finished up the call with a couple of "Uh huhs" and a "Sure thing" before she finally hung up.

"OK, let's see if that did the trick," she said to them and headed back to the door.

They crept in quietly again and Stella looked through the crack in the door to see the office was empty and it was clear Adam had left in a rush. His computer screen hadn't locked and the door leading to the shop was also slightly ajar.

They made their way into the office and closed the door to the shop. Then Leo opened the door to the cavern and the group made its way down the stairs less quietly once the door was closed behind them. When they reached the bottom, they were glad to see the bookcases were slid to the sides of the entryway to the large anteroom that led the way to The Crucible. All the lights were on, so they smiled at each other knowing Maranda was likely there. They walked across the cavern and made their way through the long shelves in the anteroom to the back where they found Keiko standing by herself looking at a stopwatch.

Leo had only met Keiko a few times since she arrived in Kensington and he was absolutely intimidated by her. Based on Maranda's stories from her time studying with Keiko in Japan, he knew she was one of the most knowledgeable Star Borns in the world. She was always perfectly poised and kept her feelings under close guard. But even more than that, she simply radiated power.

"How did you make it past Adam?" she asked without turning around.

"A distraction," Ania said, her voice full of pride.

"Well, you shouldn't be here, but you can stay and say hello briefly when she comes out. It shouldn't be longer than a few minutes."

"How close is she?" Leo asked with excitement.

Keiko turned to him and said, "Very close. She made her first official attempt last night and was only over by about two minutes. She has been practicing all day today and managed to complete it in just under an hour once. However, her times are getting longer and longer since then. I think she needs to rest."

"Who needs to rest?" said Maranda and they all turned with excited smiles to see her standing outside the exit to The Crucible.

"Very nice! Fifty-nine minutes and thirty-eight seconds." Keiko responded.

"Yeah, I would've been here much faster, but I decided to take a short nap after the first few rooms," Maranda replied with false bravado.

"Let's call it a day," Keiko said. "You can spend some time with the kids and we can try again tomorrow."

"No," Maranda said definitively. "I want to make another attempt tonight. I know I have everything I need to succeed this time now that Leo is here."

"Me?" Leo asked incredulously.

"Of course," Maranda said simply. "You can help me with the room that is taking me the most time to get through."

"I doubt that…" Leo responded skeptically.

"Well, let's see," Maranda said with a knowing smile.

"Just help her," Stella encouraged and the others nodded in agreement.

"OK, which room is it?" Leo asked, resigned to the fact they wouldn't let him out of this request.

"The seventh," Maranda answered brightly.

Leo's face twisted up in confusion and he asked, "I never got to that room, how can I help you through it?"

"Well, let me tell you about it," Maranda began. "The room

is different because there isn't just one target you have to address and each one is a different energy pattern. So, you have to figure out the best way to deal with each pattern. I have found out that energy bending is the fastest way to navigate this room, but I am having trouble switching between patterns fast enough. You happen to be good at that, so I was hoping you could give me a few tips."

"Um…" Leo thought for a moment. "I don't really know how I do it so quickly. I mean, I just had to because we were fighting for our lives."

"Don't sell yourself short," Aran said from behind him. "We have all seen you move super fast when we were training together."

"Show me," Maranda said in her usual warm and supportive voice.

Leo settled himself for a moment and then felt all the patterns around him. He visualized them in his mind like when he created the Spider's Web, a sphere of energy, each unique. He pulled the spheres to him, having each one spread around a different part of his body. Maranda's spread across his chest, each of his friends across his arms and legs, and then Keiko's like a helmet around his head.

"Cooooool…" he heard Ania say.

"How are you doing that?" Keiko asked. "I've never seen energy bending like that. You are balancing six patterns across your armor."

"I already told you, I don't know how I can do this, I just do it," Leo said in frustration as his armor sank back into his core.

"That's it! What you did is exactly what I need!" Maranda said in excitement. "Think back to what you were doing to balance all those patterns. Was it a feeling? A technique that you figured out?"

"I…" Leo hesitated. " I suppose I was just picturing everything in my mind."

"A visualization technique!" Maranda encouraged him. "Tell me more!"

Leo explained how he pictured the patterns in his mind and Maranda asked him to pause while she closed her eyes to focus and follow his guidance. Suddenly, Leo saw his pattern flow over her right arm.

"Nice!" Leo said encouragingly. "Now, pick another pattern for your other arm."

They all saw a green pattern begin to wind around her left arm, but suddenly both patterns sank back into her arms and disappeared.

"Hooo! That's hard!" Maranda said as she rolled her shoulders and took a deep breath.

"Like I said, you're tired. Let's get some rest now, you've done well today," Keiko counseled.

"It's OK," Maranda said, looking directly into Keiko's eyes. "I can do this, I just need to find the right way to focus.

"OH!" Leo exclaimed, suddenly remembering one of the key ingredients. "There's a meditation technique that seems to work really well for me!"

Leo started to explain the technique to Maranda, but he stopped when he realized Keiko was looking at him strangely.

"What?" he asked, turning to her.

"How did you learn this technique?" she asked pointedly.

"From the Book of Star Born," he answered, somewhat confused why she was asking. "Don't you know it?

"Yes, I do… But it is a very advanced technique. The Book does not usually present it to someone so early in their training. Some don't even learn it until much later in their lives."

"Yeah yeah…" Maranda interrupted the exchange. "We all know Leo is *special*. Can we just focus on teaching me the technique?"

Keiko nodded and Leo resumed his explanation. They watched as Maranda was able to follow the steps and reach a deeper state of focus. Then slowly, one by one, her arms and legs became encased in different patterns. As a new pattern spread across her chest, Leo noticed it starting to get unstable, and all the patterns began flickering rapidly.

"Connect them together, don't try to keep them separate," Leo coached, and the flickering started to stabilize.

When Maranda was finally encased in a rainbow of armor, she opened her eyes with a big grin.

"Fascinating…" Keiko said with a grin as she too was balancing different patterns on her left and right arms. Leo looked on, filled with pride as he realized he had just taught two powerful Star Borns something new.

Maranda practiced several more times, gradually getting faster. Finally, after many more attempts, she was able to follow the technique without closing her eyes and they all knew she was ready.

"Ok, here goes nothing!" she said and then ran back into The Crucible.

Keiko started her stopwatch and everyone became silent, barely making a sound to breathe. After fifteen minutes or so, they were startled when they heard Emily behind them say, "Yup, we should've known…" They all whirled around quickly and saw Emily and Casey standing with a very angry looking Adam.

"Ok, kids, let's go," Casey said with moderate annoyance in his voice.

"But she is doing her second attempt and we want to stay and see how it goes!" Leo complained.

"No dice," Adam said firmly. "You knew the cavern is off limits for Maranda's training and still you insisted on coming here. And that trick you pulled, I'll admit it was creative, so I'll let it slide this time. Now let Keiko get back to her work with Maranda."

"No," Leo responded firmly.

"Excuse me?" Adam said with an eyebrow raised.

"We'll go after we see how she does," Leo said defiantly.

Adam, Emily and Casey started to corral the group and lead them out when Keiko said softly, "Let them stay."

Adam looked at her in confusion and said, "But Keiko…"

She cut him off and said, "They are helping. It was good they came. Perhaps we should have asked them to join us sooner too. Let them stay to see how Maranda does."

Adam looked to Emily and Casey who simply shrugged to say they didn't mind. So, they all settled in for the wait. The adults talked softly off to the side while the kids wandered around to kill time.

"Looks like the audience has grown," Maranda said when she finally emerged.

Keiko looked down at the stopwatch and said excitedly, "Fifty minutes! Exceptional!"

The kids couldn't hold themselves back as they all rushed over, enveloping her in a tight group hug. Then Maranda pulled back and accepted individual congratulations, chatting excitedly with each of the kids until she reached Leo. Maranda put her hands on his shoulders and said earnestly, "I have to say, you never stop amazing me…"

Leo's face flushed in embarrassment, but, before he could reply, Keiko appeared next to them and said, "I hate to break up the celebration, but we've worked to the very last moment on this and you are needed at your assignment. I suggest you get some food and pack up so you can be off tomorrow."

"Will she be with us?!" Meimei asked excitedly.

Maranda looked at her kindly and said, "Unfortunately, no. I will be at another location. Not all Star Borns have the combat training that we have developed. The teachers at your school are exceptional, though. In fact, your Star Born teacher is someone I regard highly."

While they still had so many questions for Maranda, they followed the grownups' cues and began to make their way out of the cavern recounting how they were able to sneak into the cavern to Casey, Emily, and Adam.

"I guess I need to get a new, Star Born-proof lock," Adam said in mock annoyance.

"Or you can just give us the code since you know we will find a way to break it anyway," Ania said, followed by a chorus of snickers from the rest of the group.

4

FINDING A KEY

CAROLINE LAID IN the center of the raft, soaked to the bone, with sand covering large portions of her clothes. She heaved in huge breaths and threw an arm across her eyes to shield them from the blinding sun. While it didn't seem that far when Ranee left her in the raft, Caroline had spent the better part of two hours rowing toward the beach, battling the buffeting waves as she went. When she finally landed on the beach, she had hopped out and started to pull the raft further onto the sand only to be caught off guard by a huge wave that tossed her around and shoved both her and the raft towards some large rocks. She had to scramble quickly to pull the raft with her up onto the beach before another one came along a few minutes later.

Now that she had finally made it, exhaustion took over and she quickly fell asleep for several hours. When she woke up, the sun was lower in the sky and every muscle in her body felt painful and stiff. Not only that, but she had a massive knot between her shoulder blades that made it painful to move her head in any direction. It took her half an hour of stretching, but she was eventually loose enough to move around again. That's when the huge hunger pangs hit her. She realized that she must have used a ton of energy in her efforts to make it to the beach and now her body was demanding fuel.

"Grrlmph!" came loudly from her stomach.

"Yeah yeah… Give me a second…" she said back to it while she started to rummage around in her backpack. Eventually, she found a crumbled up granola bar at the bottom and fished it out. She debated for a couple moments whether she should ration it, but another "Breeeep!" came from her stomach and she proceeded to dump the contents into her mouth. Then she licked every crumb from the inside of the wrapper and chewed before guzzling some water from her bottle and letting out a satisfied sigh.

"Well, I guess I should look around a bit," Caroline said to herself and she slowly got up. While her clothes had dried during her nap, a loud slurping sound came from her shoes when she stepped out of the raft. So, she took them off and sat them along with her socks in a sunny spot in the hopes the sun could dry them out as well. Then she started to trudge around the beach, looking closely at the jagged rock walls for any clues on how she might be able to find her way up to the top of the cliffs.

It only took her about ten minutes to walk from one end of the beach to the other. It was an oddly calm spot that was bookended by massive waves slamming into the rocky walls and sending sea spray high into the air. She went back and forth three times, trying to find some semblance of a clue, but all she saw was various shades of brown, tan, gray and white. She tried pushing or tugging on every spot that remotely looked like it could be something, but again found nothing.

Feeling a combination of frustration and confusion, she walked back to the raft and scanned the walls that surrounded her. They stretched so high, but she still wondered if it was as simple as having to climb up. It certainly seemed like there were plenty of handholds and footholds. So, she decided to take a test run and walked straight over to the closest section of the wall.

She found a good spot to start her ascent with two very sturdy looking handholds and began to pull herself up. She quickly found the next spots to put her hands and feet and pulled herself a little higher. However, when she tried the next set of holds, one broke off in her hand and she struggled to hold on before she fell the short distance back to the sand. Her heart raced as she rushed to try climbing an alternative path, but now nothing seemed safe to her. Not only that, but the muscles in her forearms started to burn and a cramp began to form in her left foot.

"There's no way…" she said to herself before deciding to climb back down and not entertain any more ludicrous ideas like climbing up a huge rock face without any gear.

After a short break, Caroline started her investigation again, but still struck out and increasingly felt frustration turn to hopelessness. She had no idea what Ranee had seen in her, but she certainly wasn't going to find the entrance to Terradune. Caroline eventually gave up again and returned to the raft, sitting down heavily at one end and leaned against the inflated side while letting her mind wander.

The sun slowly set and she watched the shadows make the rock walls look even more sinister. *What was I thinking?,* she thought to herself as the temperature dropped and she began to shiver. She pulled out some additional layers from her duffle bag and then laid down, staring up at the sky and watching the first stars appear.

Soon, it was nighttime, but it wasn't nearly as dark as she expected because the sky was bright with stars along with the Milky Way stretching across it. She marveled at the view that she could never see from her home because there was too much light pollution and she allowed herself to relax and just enjoy the moment. She tried to find a familiar constellation, but the stars seemed to be arranged differently here.

Then, as she turned her head to look at a different section of sky, something with a faint glow caught her attention at the end of the beach. Curiosity got the better of her and she walked over slowly to get a better look. When she got close, she realized the spot was about ten feet up from the beach. However, unlike earlier, there wasn't enough light to find a safe way to climb up.

A wave of determination hit her and she decided that she didn't want to wait until the morning to check it out. She felt around on the wall and found a spot that seemed like it would allow her to at least get a little closer to her target. Once she was hanging on the wall again, the familiar sense of danger started to nag the back of her mind, but her stubbornness won out and she quickly found the next handholds she could use. Unfortunately, the footholds were a different story and one broke off just as she placed her right foot on it. This time, she fell off the wall and landed flat on her back, knocking the wind out of her.

Caroline gasped for air for what felt like an eternity, but she finally was able to start breathing normally again and proceeded to push herself back up to her feet and step back up to the rock wall to try again. She tried again and again, getting a little closer each time and managing to avoid hurting herself when she fell each time. Eventually, on the eleventh try, Caroline found herself staring at what appeared to be a Moon Born pattern inches from her face. It also seemed to be glowing more brightly now and she had to squint her eyes to examine it at first.

Her eyes slowly adjusted and she was able to look at the pattern closely, but something seemed odd to her. The pattern looked unfinished, but she doubted herself and continued to stare at it so long that her arms and legs began to shake from the exertion. Unable to hang on any longer, Caroline started climbing down and then released her grip on the wall, hopping safely down onto the soft sand.

As she paced around, shaking out her hands, she constructed a mental image of the pattern. Scanning it with her mind's eye, she became more and more convinced the pattern was unfinished, but had no idea what that could mean. Even more, she had no idea what to do. Still, she came up with ideas on what the pattern should look like once it was completed and discarded each one.

She leaned her back on the rock wall and gazed up at the stars again to clear her mind, letting herself relax. She remembered how her mom would always tell her that she over-thought her school assignments and that sometimes things really were as simple as they appeared. As this memory came and went, a new completed pattern formed in her mind and the urge to climb back up took over again.

She excitedly found the path that brought her all the way up the first time and was quickly staring at the glowing lines again. Then, Caroline let go of a handhold and used her left index finger to start tracing the pattern like it was a maze. When she reached the end, however, she just kept going and completed the pattern based on the image that had formed in her head. Her heart raced as a glowing trail was left behind wherever her finger touched and she stopped briefly to marvel at the effect, but the trail began to fade and she began to move more quickly and finished the pattern a few moments later.

Suddenly, the pattern went out, leaving the negative image glowing in her eyes like when she accidentally looked at a car's headlights as it passed by. The wall rumbled briefly and Caroline sensed a section had moved away where the pattern had once been. Without hesitation, she reached her hand inside without worrying about what she might find and soon had her whole arm in as she felt around.

She found a small, smooth section at the back and accidentally pushed on it while trying to shift her weight to more comfortably hold herself up. She heard a loud click as something quickly encircled her wrist and she yelled out in surprise, letting go of her handhold and footholds so that she was dangling painfully by her wrist

"OW OW OW!" Caroline yelled as she scrambled to try and find a way to pull herself back up, quickly managing to get herself stable again.

Calming herself down, she closed her eyes and felt around with her hand as best as she could until it settled on a piece of rock that felt like a roughly cut circle. When she placed her hand on it, it felt like an energy was emanating from it. She lifted her hand up and the feeling faded, then she placed it back down and the feeling returned. With no better ideas, she decided to take a page from Leo's Star Born training and imagined opening herself up to absorb the energy. She was quickly overcome with the sensation of feeling very full, but not like at the end of a big meal. It was more like her whole body was a balloon that had too much air in it. Once the energy stopped pouring into her, the rock came loose in her hand and the trap released her wrist.

Without missing a beat, she pulled her hand out and tried to examine the rock, but she couldn't see anything in the dark and a deep throbbing pain started to grow in her chest. Realizing she couldn't hang on the wall for much longer, she tried to start climbing down and managed to descend a short way before a blast of pain erupted, radiating from her chest out to her arms and legs. She dropped the stone and she heard it ricochet off the wall as she struggled to find another handhold to avoid falling.

"Oh c'mon!" Caroline shouted as she looked down and didn't see the stone in dark shadows below.

She picked her way back down the wall and began to search for the stone, even crawling on her hands and knees for a while. However, it was gone and the combination of her fatigue, the mix of frustration and sadness, as well as the continued painful throbs in her chest eventually helped her decide to take a break and resume the search in the morning.

That night, Caroline was plagued by variations of the same horrible dream. She would be in some kind of innocuous situation, but at some point she would feel a pain in the center of her chest. The pain would steadily grow into something that felt like she was being stabbed by a sword made of molten lava. As she looked down, a blinding white light would appear on her chest and then she would be torn apart. She woke up to the first signs of dawn feeling exhausted, uncomfortable, and famished.

With the faint hope that she had somehow forgotten that she packed some food for herself, Caroline unzipped the duffel bag and started rummaging around. Eventually, she felt the smooth, crinklyness of plastic packaging and yanked out what she found along with a third of her clothes. She stared at the package of turkey jerky and felt utter elation.

"Ranee, you beautiful, weird, thoughtful woman!" she yelled

at the top of her lungs and the sound was quickly swallowed by another large wave crashing into the cliffs. Oddly, Caroline had never tried jerky before sailing with Ranee, but it quickly became a staple part of her diet because it was a quick source of protein that would help keep her going on those long days. Ranee must have thrown a package in her bag when Caroline hadn't been looking.

Caroline exercised a slight bit of self control and ate only a third of the package of jerky and finished the last bit of fresh water in her bottle. She thought to herself, *Well, I better figure something out today or this beach vacation is going to start getting unpleasant.* Then she chuckled to herself briefly before she remembered that she needed to start searching for the stone again.

She twisted around to look at the base of the towering wall, feeling some satisfying cracks in her spine and the muscles stretching out, and noticed it was littered with stones of various sizes. Feeling a heavy sense of resignation, she pushed herself up and absentmindedly rubbed the growing throb in her chest as she began to trudge over to where she had climbed the wall the night before.

"Great… Just great…" she said as she scanned the base of the wall and saw just how many stones scattered about, most of them about the same size as the one she was looking for.

Caroline dropped down on her knees and began picking up stones and tossing them haphazardly behind her as she discarded each one. The process was monotonous almost immediately and her brain switched over to autopilot while she reminisced about the dream where she was a bird flying through Terradune. She was just remembering the sensation of flying around the tower when her hand landed on a stone that had the familiar grooves from the night before. Her mind snapped to attention and she looked down excitedly at the stone she thought she would never see again.

She quickly stood up and began walking back to the raft, turning the rock over and over and trying to feel every nook and cranny on it. There was a bright blue pattern on one side that was smooth to the touch. However, it didn't look like it had been painted on. Somehow, the pattern was part of the rock like veins in marble. It was gorgeous and she was mesmerized by the complex interwoven lines.

As she reached the raft again, even though the air was cool, she began to sweat profusely and the pain in her chest became distracting. She tried to focus and turned the stone over and examined the textured surface that looked like great care had been taken to carve it. However, the pain suddenly intensified to a stabbing sensation and Caroline flashed back to her dreams from the night before. She dropped the stone like it was scaldingly hot and scrambled away from the raft, her feet getting tangled in her clothes and causing her to fall face first into the sand.

Caroline shook off the clump of clothes wrapped around her ankles and ran away from the raft as quickly as she could and felt the sensation in her chest begin to fade. By the time she was halfway down the beach, all she felt was the slight itch in her chest again and she slowed down to a walk and turned around to stare back at the raft.

"What the heck is going on?!" she thought to herself, but no answer miraculously presented itself. She stayed that way for several minutes pondering what she should do, but the only thing she could come up with was that she needed to examine the rock some more and this seemed crazy to her. What if being close to it caused her to be ripped apart by some strange energy like her dreams? Was she really willing to take that risk?

Clearly her subconscious mind did because, while she had been thinking, her legs had started taking her back to the raft. As she got closer, the itch returned to an ache and eventually a low grade burning sensation when she could see the stone again sitting in the middle of the raft. Her conscious mind overrode her subconscious and she stopped abruptly, swaying a bit as she adjusted to the change in her momentum. She stood there, staring at the stone with no idea what to do, and felt the strangest sensation. It was as if her body desperately wanted to be closer to the stone. The hairs on her arms stood on end, pointing at it and she had to focus her attention on not giving into the urge.

"This is too weird…" she mumbled to herself, shaking her head slowly. Then she forced herself to walk back to a safe distance where she could barely feel the itch in her chest. She plopped down onto the sand and sat there without any idea what to do. The dreams the night before had been so intense and the thought of dying on that beach because she couldn't figure out how to get into Terradune started to send her into a self-critical spiral.

"You're being a wuss!" she yelled, chastising herself.

But what if the dreams were a warning?, she thought in response.

This is clearly a test, they wouldn't kill a twelve-year-old girl who had just sailed around the world to get here, she tried to counsel herself.

How can I be sure?, the anxious part of her brain countered.

"Oh no…" she lamented out loud. "I've barely been on this beach for a day by myself and I'm already going insane."

Then she thought, *I have to find that door and that rock clearly has something to do with it.*

Caroline got up and started to march back down the beach to the raft feeling the sensation growing in her chest as she went.

When she got to the raft, she stepped over the side, and snatched up the rock trying to tolerate the intense pain in her chest. She stared at the stone, wondering what she was supposed to do and thought, *if this were a test for Leo, he would just blast it with some energy…*

She was struggling to tolerate the intensifying pain and was considering whether she needed to take a break when a thought popped into her head. *Could it be that simple? Do I just have to give the energy back?*

An intense throb cascaded throughout her body in response.

"But how do I do that?" she wondered aloud.

Another throb wracked her and she let out a grunt in response to it. Then she started to feel lightheaded and dizzy as her legs gave out. She landed hard on her butt and the rough side of the raft scratched up her back, but she held onto the stone. Staring at the pattern, she thought to herself, *I give up…*

She closed her eyes and felt herself losing consciousness, but then felt something welling up from inside her core. It quickly rocketed up to her shoulders, down her arms, and through her fingers. The intense sensation caught her so off guard that her eyes opened wide and she saw a blue light emanating from her fingertips and the stone seemed to absorb it. The pattern began to glow and the brightness intensified as she felt the energy draining out of her.

The last bits of energy trickled out from her fingertips and the excruciating sensation inside her quickly faded. Caroline continued to stare at the glowing pattern despite its brightness, marveling at the intricacy. Then a beam shot out from its side that hit the inflated wall of the raft.

"What the…" she said reflexively.

She lifted the stone up and the beam moved up with it. As it cleared the side of the raft, the beam shot across the beach and it met the far cliff wall near where the waves were breaking in huge sprays of foam. Curiosity replacing the fear she had been overwhelmed by only moments before, she rotated the stone and the beam continued to point at that one spot on the wall.

"Cool…" she said as she marveled at this new development.

Caroline stood up and stepped out of the raft as she started taking slow but unhesitating steps toward the spot the beam was marking on the cliff wall. Her compulsion to solve puzzles took over and she needed to see where this clue was leading her. When she reached the wall she examined the nook where the beam pointed and marveled at how it was completely unremarkable except that it happened to be the exact same shape and size as the stone she was holding.

"Well… the simplest answer is usually the correct one …" she said to herself as she placed the stone, pattern side out, in the nook. Immediately, it blended into the surrounding rock and the pattern began to extend itself into the surrounding rock, forming an intricate maze of lines in the shape of an arched portal. When it had finished its work, Caroline was entranced by the beauty of the pattern and she spent a long time studying its details like she did with the paintings during her visits to the art museums when she went into the city back home.

When her gaze reached the bottom left corner of the pattern, however, she noticed something wasn't quite right. A small section seemed to be missing and, like the night before, she felt the same need to complete it as if it was a jigsaw puzzle and she had to find the last piece. So, she knelt down and reached out her left index finger again, which glowed a bright blue as it touched the end of the pattern. Working quickly, she was done a minute later and took a step back to appreciate the completed artwork.

She started to take a deep sigh of satisfaction, but found herself holding her breath when, to her horror, the beautiful pattern began to fade away leaving just the bare rock again. A feeling of sadness and loss overcame her and her rational mind struggled to make sense of the feelings while she fought back the urge to weep. She almost lost the battle, but was distracted when the wall began to disintegrate as well, leaving an open portal with the walls inside covered in the pattern she had just completed.

"YES!" she yelled in triumph and she immediately stepped inside, enjoying the spectacle of the glowing pattern surrounding her. It only emitted enough light to see a short distance, but she could tell the hallway went further.

Caroline let her hands skim lightly over the patter and she watched it adjust to her touch and then revert back to itself. A grin crept across her face and she took a few steps further in, noticing the pattern moved down the corridor with her. Just as she was about to continue her exploration, a thought popped into her head that she should probably gather her things before she went any further.

She turned back around to the entrance, but it was gone and a seamless wall stared back at her. Feeling a slight bit of panic, she pushed against it and searched for a way to trigger it to open back up. However, she quickly realized her efforts would be fruitless and slowly rotated back to the dark hallway and the pattern coaxing her forward.

5

BIRTH OF A RIVALRY

HE DAY FINALLY came for the kids from the Kensington tribe to travel to their schools and it was all anyone was able to talk about for the days leading up to it. They had managed to figure out that not everyone was going to the same location because kids were being asked to pack in different ways. They had heard that Kellan and Momo had been taken to the local outdoors store to buy tons of cold weather gear. Luckily, it looked like Leo and his friends were being kept together, although they had an extremely long drive ahead of them.

They were all supposed to gather at Meimei's house since her dad, Casey, had volunteered to drive them. When Leo got there, he saw a large delivery van out front and the back doors were wide open with bags and suitcases stacked neatly like puzzle pieces fitting together. Casey came around the side with a wide smile.

"I can take those!" he said cheerily to Ben as he pulled Leo's bags out of their car.

As he added them to the stack in the back of the van, he said over his shoulder, "Everyone's in the backyard if you want to go hang back there."

Leo didn't need to be told twice and he hustled down the driveway and down the side of the house to the gate.

"There he is!" he heard Aran call out as Leo stepped through and he could feel the nervous and excited energy pouring off the group. They were all gorging themselves on a spread of snacks that Emily had put out.

"Did you save anything for me?" Leo asked as he joined them sitting around a big picnic table.

"Nope," Ania deadpanned and smacked his hand when he tried to take a handful of chips. Leo gave her a steely glare and moved out of her range to fill a bowl with some spicy Indian snack mix.

"Did you see the size of that van?" Stella asked him when he sat back down.

"Uh yeah," he responded. "How could anyone miss it? Is that what we are riding in?"

"Totally," Meimei confirmed. "My dad has been working at a garage that Adam hooked him up with all week. They figured a delivery van would be less noticeable and we're technically not allowed to know where we are going, so there are no windows."

"Guess I shouldn't have eaten that bean burrito for lunch," Aran said sheepishly.

"Oh, don't pretend you wouldn't have stunk it up anyway," Ania teased and everyone started laughing, letting out some of their nerves.

"Fair point," he replied through his own laughs.

The levity was short lived though, as more kids they didn't know arrived. Everyone became more quiet, just saying their hellos to be polite. Eventually they just fidgeted or looked at their phones for what felt like an eternity until a familiar face arrived.

"Petra?" Stella said as the new arrival walked through the gate.

"Hey!" Petra responded brightly as she waved enthusiastically.

"We haven't seen you since…" Aran started to say before Meimei elbowed him hard in his side.

"It's so good to see you again!" Meimei said brightly, without missing a beat.

"Yeah, I was so amped when my mom told me we would be at the same school," Petra replied. I'm the only one from my tribe going there and it would've sucked to have not known anyone."

"Yeah, it kinda does…" one of the boys they had just met said. His name was Diego and he had been sitting by himself in the corner of the yard since his parents had dropped him off. They knew he was from Oakland, but that was about it.

"Nice to meet you!" Petra said cheerily in response.

The group started to chatter and debrief with Petra on what they had been doing with the rest of their summers when Emily came through the back door to the house and called out, "Everybody out of the pool!"

"Huh?" a few of the kids said.

"She means it's time to go," Meimei said with a mixture of annoyance and embarrassment.

"Yeah, what she said," Emily said curtly and walked back inside.

The kids all got up and made their way back to the front where many of the parents were still milling about and talking. When they saw the kids emerge from the back yard, many of the parents proceeded to embarrass them with tearful hugs and admonishments to not eat too much junk food and send emails

every day. The kids slowly extracted themselves from their parents' embraces and piled into the van. Casey closed all the doors
and the group was plunged into darkness.

"Well this is going to be a creepy ride," Ania said.

"Oh yeah, sorry!" Meimei responded and she fumbled her
way around, bumping into several others and stepping on some
toes. Finally a light came on at the front and Meimei instructed
Leo to hit another one in the back. A minute later, they felt the
van lurch forward and knew they were on their way.

At first, it was largely quiet in the van, nobody wanting to be
the one to break the silence. Eventually, Petra said to the group,
"Anyone know a good game?"

The group debated several options and eventually settled on
the movie game, which helped them pass the time for a while.
When that wound down, they broke into separate conversations
with whomever they were sitting next to and the time dragged
on. After what felt like an eternity, they felt the van slow down
and come to a stop. Then they heard Casey get out and walk
around to the doors. He let them out and they looked around to
see they were on a deserted road, but the sun was still up.

"Bathroom break! Boys over there, girls down there!" he
called out, pointing out different spots far away from each other
and handing a bag to Meimei.

When Leo came back, Casey offered him a squirt of hand
sanitizer and said, "I've put out some sandwiches on the front
seat if you're hungry."

Leo suddenly felt ravenous and rushed over to see what the
options were. He picked out a turkey sandwich and unwrapped
it quickly, taking extremely large bites. Then he walked slowly
back to Casey and asked, "So, how much longer?"

"Oh, we've only been on the road for a couple hours, I think we will get there around five a.m. or so," Casey replied.

"You're kidding me…" they heard Stella say behind them.

"Nope!" Casey said cheerfully and then, seeing the rest of the group had come back and grabbed sandwiches, "Everyone ready to hop back in?!" There were a few grumbles in response, but they all slowly made their way back to their seats, resigned that this was going to be one of the longest car rides of their lives.

The kids gradually settled into the rhythm of a long car ride and occupied themselves with a mix of conversations, card games, singalongs, and sleeping. Casey would stop every couple of hours for a bathroom break, each time on an increasingly darker and narrower road. The last section of their ride was extremely uncomfortable as it was clear that Casey had pulled onto an unpaved road that was rocky and uneven.

When they finally came to a stop, most of the kids let out audible sighs of relief. Diego, who had been sitting in the back, climbed urgently over the bench seats in front of him. Others let out annoyed comments as his elbows or feet accidentally hit them in his efforts to get out of the van. Just as he reached the doors, Casey flung them open and Diego immediately started unloading the contents of his stomach. In a blur, Casey moved out of the way before he was covered and then he moved around to the back doors, removing some of the bags so the other kids could climb out that way. While Diego finished up, they all took in their surroundings, noticing they were deep in a forest and surrounded by ancient-looking trees.

"Hey, big guy!" Leo heard Ania say as she placed her hand on the trunk of a giant tree. He was caught somewhat off guard by her friendly tone.

"Check it out," Aran said to Leo, directing his attention to the buildings behind him.

It was an odd assortment, including some very old looking cabins that may have been for a camp that had been there a long time ago along with huge lodges that seemed to be recently built. However, none of the new buildings looked like a normal construction crew had built them. Some extremely strong elementals had clearly been there since one of the lodges seemed to be composed of the ground beneath it. Some smaller structures appeared to have been grown from nearby trees and plants.

What was even more bizarre, however, was that it was extremely quiet. They were all whispering to each other, but it still sounded like shouts to their ears due to the lack of even a breeze running through the branches of the trees. Eventually, they heard Casey clear his throat loudly and they took the hint that they should help him unload the van. When they pulled out the last bag, as if on cue, the door to the building closest to them opened up and out walked a slender woman with long, dark hair and holding a clipboard.

She walked directly to Casey and shook his hand, then turned to the rest of the group and said, "Welcome, my name is Sharon and I am the director of this school. You are one of the first groups to arrive. If you come with me, we will get you situated."

Then she turned back to Casey and said, "If you need to rest, we can provide a bed for you."

"That's very much appreciated, but I've never made it to this area before and there's a trail I have been interested in checking out for a long time. It's just a little further down the road, so I am going to head there and camp overnight."

Sharon didn't seem to think this was odd at all and waved

goodbye as she ushered the kids back to the building and Casey gave Meimei a quick hug before hopping back in the van.

Sharon held the door open for the group as they struggled with carrying in their heavy bags. Once they were inside, the kids were struck by how much it looked like a normal school. There was a hall with classrooms and bulletin boards on the walls with different welcome messages. It was eerie how familiar the space felt.

"Why don't you leave your stuff here and follow me," Sharon instructed as she started to walk down the main hall.

"As you can tell, this is our main school building and it is where you will have all of your regular classes," Sharon informed them along the way. "Every day from eight to one, you'll be here. Then you'll have two hours with your respective mentors. After that, you will finish with two hours with your training team."

"Who's idea was it to start so early?" Aran asked earnestly.

Sharon turned to look at him briefly with a raised eyebrow and said flatly, "Mine." Aran's face flushed red from embarrassment and Leo looked over to him with wide eyes and gave him a shrug. Then Sharon turned into a classroom at the end of the hall with tables ringing the perimeter. Each had neatly stacked packets of papers or books and the excitement the kids had been feeling began to mix with a little bit of back to school dread. Sharon stopped at the first table and picked up a stack of papers. As she handed one to each of the kids she said, "This is a map of the grounds. It'll help for the first few days you're here."

She put down the extras and then picked up a tablet. A few of the kids peered over her shoulder and saw she was looking at a long list.

"OK, let's see here…" she said to herself and then looked up, scanning the group. "There you are, Stella!" she said, looking right at her. "You're going to be in bunk eight. You'll find it on the lower right of your map."

Turning to her right, she said, "Petra, you are in bunk two."

"Diego, glad to see you're feeling a bit better. You are in bunk one. There is already one of your bunkmates there unpacking," she continued.

One by one, she informed each of them where they were going to be living for the next year at least.

"How the heck…" Aran said a little too loudly when she was finished.

"I have a list of the whole student body right here," Sharon answered matter-of-factly.

"Yeah, but that doesn't explain how you knew who we were," Mari said. She was from one of the San Francisco tribes and Leo was already thinking how she would be a fun addition to the crew.

"Of course it does," Sharon replied. "I have all of your information right here. Your names, where you are from, your allergies, and of course your abilities. I see here, for example, that you are a Caretaker like Aran over there. There was only one female Caretaker scheduled to arrive this morning and I knew that must be you."

"But… how did you know I'm a Caretaker?" Mari pressed further, unable to accept such a simple explanation.

"Because she's a Star Born," Leo said out loud as it dawned on him.

"Very good!" Sharon said encouragingly to Leo. "Now why don't you all settle in. Breakfast will be ready in about an hour at the cafeteria, which is the large building right behind this one."

Realizing they were being dismissed, each of them slowly shuffled out of the room and made their way back to the front of the school. As they walked, Mari made her way over to Leo and said, "I still don't get it, how does her being a Star Born tell her that I'm a Caretaker?"

"She can sense all of our abilities," Leo explained. "We each have a unique pattern that she can read, but there are similarities in patterns depending on what type of ability you have."

"It's creepy, right?" Aran interjected.

"Actually, I think it's pretty cool," Mari replied. "How do you know so much about Star Borns? I know we have one in our tribe, but I've never met him."

"Well, I *am* a Star Born," Leo answered with a bit of an embarrassed flush blooming on his face.

"Wait, so you're telling us that you can sense our abilities," Terrence chimed in from behind them with a healthy dose of skepticism. Leo didn't let it get to him, he had spent a good part of the ride chatting with Terrence, who had told him some hilarious stories. Leo already knew he liked him.

"Well, I knew right from when I met you that you are an Earth Elemental. It feels like you specialize in manipulating metal," Leo responded confidently.

"Whoa..." was all Terrance could say.

"Like I said, creepy," Aran joked as he gave Terrance a playful shove to shake him out of his thoughts.

When the group reached the front of the school, they consulted their maps and helped each other find out where their bunks were located. Everyone had been assigned different ones and Leo suspected they had been split up deliberately. He felt a nervous twinge in his stomach, but decided not to spiral into worried thoughts. He pulled his heavy backpack onto his shoulders, grasped the handle of his rolling case, and began to drag it outside and down a rough trail.

It took him over fifteen minutes of walking until he reached the edge of what the map showed as the full area of the school site to find his bunkhouse. He had been grumbling the entire time, but stopped short when he finally saw it. It looked like a large igloo and was made of the same glittering rock as the cavern he had trained in for the past year. He walked around it and found an opening on the opposite side with a solid metal door. He let go of his "rolling" case and it fell into a bush right next to the door. Rolling his eyes and letting out a frustrated sigh, Leo pushed down on the handle and the door opened with a loud creak.

He fished his case out of the bush and dragged it inside where he found himself in a large room filled with bunk beds. He quickly counted and determined sixteen kids could sleep there. He also saw a door straight ahead that he assumed led to the bathroom. Along the back wall, there was a long shelf made of the same material as the walls with stools underneath, which also seemed to be meant as a kind of desk area.

"You're lucky you got here early. You can pick your bed. I recommend a top bunk," a voice said from the far end of the room.

Leo walked in that direction and he soon saw a boy laying on a top bunk right against the curving wall. His pattern was nothing like Leo had ever felt.

"Hey there, my name's Leo," he said.

"I'm Miles," the boy replied.

"Been here long?" Leo asked as he selected a bunk across from Miles and started to unpack his stuff into one of the lockers that was set up at either end of each bunk.

"Just got here last night," Miles replied. "Kinda glad there's someone else here now. I have to admit, it was kinda weird being here all by myself."

"Yeah, can't say I would've liked that," Leo agreed.

"So, what can you do?" Miles asked directly, catching Leo off guard and he stopped shoving items into his locker. It wasn't like there was some kind of etiquette he was aware of, it just seemed kind of fast to be asking that question.

"Excuse me?" Leo stammered.

"What's your ability?" Miles asked as if it was a totally normal question to ask and not picking up on Leo's discomfort. "Can you do anything cool? I'm a Librarian, at least that's what we are called nowadays. In the past we have been called other things of course. My favorite is Chronicler."

Leo had no idea what any of this meant, but Miles was staring, waiting for him to answer, so he said, "I'm a Star Born."

"Ah! I was wondering since we are in this kind of bunk house. There are two others they've built here. Clearly they are meant to house a Star Born. Gotta keep all the others safe, right? I mean, nobody inside will be safe if one of you goes off, but I guess it's best to limit the damage and they can't just put all of you in the same bunk house and lose a whole crop of Star Borns."

Leo was taken aback again by the bluntness of Miles' comments, but he decided to ignore it and get an answer to the question that was itching at the back of his mind.

"I've never heard of a Librarian," he said to Miles.

"Oh, we are the rarest of all the types," Miles said, clearly a fact that gave him some pride. "We are the keepers of our people's history and store important memories for future generations. There are only ten of us in the entire world right now since one just passed on about a month ago. I was hoping I would be picked to take on her catalog, but they said I'm still too young for that big a transfer. They said it could harm me given my age. I think that's lame though."

"So, you have other people's memories stuck in your head?" Leo asked, still trying to understand.

"Yup!" Miles answered brightly. "I mean not a ton of them yet, only a few hundred so far. It's actually something we share with Star Borns since you all can share memories as well, but you can only store a small number in your minds before it becomes too difficult for you to manage them. I plan to be the first Librarian to have over one hundred thousand memories in my catalog. A few have gotten close in the past, but nobody has done it yet. I guess it is in our natures to want to grow our catalogs, though. I mean it's kind of a prerequisite to want to acquire knowledge when you're a Librarian."

Leo nodded quietly to himself, thinking back to the memories Maranda had shared with him.

"You alright there?" Miles asked, bringing Leo back to the present.

"Yeah… fine…" Leo replied slowly. "You just reminded me of something."

"I get that a lot," Miles said with a big grin. "Looks like you didn't have that much stuff. Are you done unpacking? We can go wandering around if you like."

This seemed like a great idea and Leo quickly agreed with an enthusiastic nod. Miles hopped down from his bunk and proceeded to walk out and Leo followed close behind. When they emerged, Miles pointed toward a trail that led to the left and said, "Let's go this way, I saw some stuff yesterday that I want to show you."

It seemed like as good an option as any other, so Leo followed Miles' lead.

"So where are you from?" Miles asked Leo as they started down the trail.

"Kensington," Leo replied.

"Never heard of it."

"Bay Area," Leo said simply.

"Oh, gotcha, I'm from DC," Miles responded.

"Whoa, you came all the way across the country!"

"Yup! I had to take two planes and then had a long car ride with a dude named Stan. The guy barely talked and I had to keep up the conversation for the both of us."

Leo laughed at this comment because he wasn't sure if Stan wasn't talkative or if Miles just talked enough for the two of them. Before he could respond though, he stopped in his tracks and stared at the structure that had just appeared in front of them as they came around a bend in the trail. It looked like it had been constructed with the interlocking building blocks he used to play with when he was a little kid.

"Cool, right?" Miles said when he noticed Leo had stopped to stare at the building. "I have no idea what kind of ability you need to create that, but I sure want to find out."

"Totally..." Leo said, still taking it all in.

"C'mon, that's not even the coolest thing I want to show you," Miles said.

"Really?" Leo asked, not believing him, but following anyway.

Miles continued to lead the way, chattering about how he was allergic to poison oak and how he hoped there wasn't any around there, when they both heard beautiful music floating through the air to them. It made them stop and listen for several minutes before Leo turned to Miles and said, "Wanna go check that out?"

"Yeah..." Miles answered in a somewhat dreamlike tone.

They walked slowly, stumbling over an occasional root they had not spotted because their attention was consumed by the music, until they arrived at the source. It was one of the bunkhouses that looked like it had been grown from scratch with multiple tree trunks arching together and then twisting into a helix at the center of the roof. Each trunk had contorted itself to create holes for windows that held a different colored glass.

The two boys barely noticed the crazy engineering that went into creating something like this and walked straight to the door, opened it, and stepped right inside. The music was much louder now and they were held in a sort of rapture, swaying to the notes in unison until it suddenly stopped and they heard someone say, "Hey! What are you doing in here?!"

They slowly came out of their haze and looked around for the source of the voice. There was a tall girl standing a few paces away with her hands on her hips and looking not too happy to see them.

"Lucy?" Leo said as he cocked his head to the side in confusion.

"Leo?!" she responded. "I didn't know we were going to the same school."

"You two know each other?" Miles asked.

"Yeah, she's my cousin. I just didn't know she has abilities."

"How could you not know?" Miles probed, unable to understand.

"Different tribes," Lucy explained. "My mom didn't even tell us Leo was a Star Born until we were on our way here."

"Us?" Leo asked.

"Finn's around here somewhere. You'll probably see him at breakfast,"

"So, you and Finn…" Leo started to say, but Miles interrupted him.

"What was that song we heard?"

"Oh, that explains it," Lucy responded, and nodded her head

in understanding. "Sorry, I guess I drew you here. I didn't think there was anyone nearby so I could just enjoy a little practice."

"You drew us here?" Leo asked, his senses finally feeling sharper.

"You're a Siren!" Miles said excitedly. "I've read a great deal about your kind!"

"You have?" Lucy asked, clearly wondering how this was possible.

"Oh, yes!" Miles continued without hesitation. "You're part of the Conjurer family of abilities with a focus on sonic transmission of thoughts and compelling actions. A very difficult ability to master and only one in ten thousand Conjurers expresses their abilities this way. You're quite a rare breed!"

"Is he always like this?" Lucy asked Leo.

"Honestly, we just met," Leo answered with a grin.

"Well, you're spot on, Trivia Master," she said to Miles. "Since you know so much about me, how about you introduce yourself."

"Oh, sure! I'm Miles and I'm a Librarian."

"A what?"

"I'd never heard of it either," Leo chimed in.

Miles proceeded to explain his abilities and, when Leo realized Miles would keep going for as long as they let them, he decided to intervene.

"I heard there's breakfast?" Leo said.

"Oh yeah!" Lucy responded, giving him a grateful look. "I think it's supposed to be available in about twenty minutes.

"Want to go explore a bit with me and Miles? Maybe make our way over to the cafeteria?" Leo asked.

"Sure!" Lucy agreed and they started to walk out when they heard a voice from the rafters say, "Hey! Wait for me!"

Then a small girl appeared straddling one of the broad tree trunks that made up the roof.

"What the?!" Lucy shouted. "Have you been here the entire time?!"

"Of course! I got here two days ago. I think I was the first to arrive!" the girls said brightly.

"Clearly a Chameleon," Miles chimed in. "Of the Physic family. Can manipulate all forms of light and radiation. Invisibility is an advanced skill."

"Wow… You're good…" the girl said.

"Are you telling me that you have been spying on me since I got here?!" Lucy said, clearly upset.

"Not spying," the girl squeaked. "It was a long trip, so I was sleeping when you got here. When I woke up, you were down there unpacking and I thought I would freak you out if I just appeared suddenly. I figured I would wait for you to leave and then introduce myself later."

"OK, fine, out with it. Name. Where you're from. We already know your ability," Lucy directed.

"Marie. New Jersey."

"OK, cool," Lucy said, accepting the answer and then turning to the door. "Let's get outta here and see who else is around."

They made their way back to the main buildings at the center of the site, collecting Aran, Meimei, and Stella along the way. When they got there, Ania was waiting on a bench right outside the doors to the cafeteria.

"What took you so long? I was wondering if I'm the only one who's starving," she said to the group as they walked up.

"We had to check this place out," Leo responded. "Can you believe what they built?"

"Uh, yeah, I am going to be living in a treehouse," Ania agreed.

"Oh, us too!" Marie jumped in. "I've never seen anything quite like it. Having trees grow together to form a structure must be extremely difficult."

"Yeah, it is," Ania responded in her usually annoyed tone. "But I am actually living in a treehouse. Like up in the branches with a ladder to get climb up and down to get in. At first I had no idea how to get my stuff up there, but then I just had one of the branches pull it up."

"Ooo! A Verdant!" Miles said excitedly. "You must be a powerful one too!"

"Who is this guy?" Ania looked past Miles to the rest of the group.

"Oh, he's fine. Just a font of knowledge," Stella replied.

"Font?" Aran asked her. "Since when do you talk like that?"

"Hey, I saw it in a book and was looking for the right opportunity to use it," she defended herself and Aran just rolled his eyes and shook his head.

Leo introduced Marie and Lucy to Ania and then she stood up and opened the door to the cafeteria. The smell of freshly cooked bacon wafted out and all of their mouths started watering.

"I don't know how you waited out here so long, I would've rushed in and started to gorge myself," Meimei said as they walked in.

"Trust me, I tried," Ania replied. "The head cook is no joke. She chased me out and said nobody was allowed inside until they opened, which was just a couple minutes ago."

Everyone fanned out across the large room, filling plates and bowls with food from various stations. Then they all gathered at a long table and nobody talked while everyone started filling their bellies as quickly as possible. It took several minutes until Lucy noticed that Marie was eating a large bowl of frozen yogurt that was covered in gummy bears.

"Where'd you get that?" Lucy asked, surprised that she had missed it and Marie just gestured with her spoon.

After the group stampeded over to the machine to get large portions, the cook came back out again and taped a sign to it that said, "Small bowls only! One serving per meal!" Then she made her way back to the kitchen staring at the kids and grumbling under her breath.

Over the next hour, the kids sat and ate, telling stories and exchanging information about their tribes. Gradually, more kids arrived and the room filled up with a loud din. Leo looked around with a smile on his face and thought to himself how this may turn out to be really fun, when they heard a commotion a few tables away.

"PROVE IT!" one boy yelled at another kid.

"FINE!" the other shouted back and, as he stood up, all the plates on the table gently rose high into the air over everyone's heads. Then he returned them to the table with barely a sound when they touched down.

"Give me a break," the first boy said, clearly unimpressed. "That's beginner stuff."

Suddenly the plates from their table were up in the air again along with the plates and cups from several tables surrounding them.

"Ugh… Why do boys always start this stuff?" Meimei muttered and Leo chuckled without taking his eyes off the two Physics.

Without any warning, all of their own plates, bowls, cups, and trays flew up into the air, followed by annoyed cries around the room from kids who had their food taken away from them. Some of the plates began to shake and Leo noticed beads of sweat were dripping down the sides of the both kids' faces.

"That all you got?!" the boy taunted.

"I can do this all day!" the other called back.

"Hey Jordan! A little help!" the boy yelled and Leo noticed some movement in the crowd that had surrounded them. A tall boy with a large, dark halo of hair emerged and placed his hands on the back of the Physic who had called him. Immediately, everything he had already levitated became steady and more plates and cups rose into the air as cheers erupted from the crowd.

Leo looked to the other Physic, a tall kid with long hair dyed red at the tips and the left side of their head was shaved. Sweat was now pouring down their forehead and cheeks as they struggled to maintain what they had levitated. He decided the fight needed to be fair and focused himself so he could align with their pattern. Slowly, he started to add some energy until their eyes brightened in recognition of what had happened. A mischievous grin spread across their face and, a moment later, everything hovering over the boy's head began to shake violently. Food and drinks sprayed that half of the table as the boy struggled to stabilize everything.

Another section began to shake violently and he shifted his attention there. This continued quickly until food began raining down on the crowd and everyone began cheering for the clear victor. Leo smiled in satisfaction, knowing he had a part in the win, but not needing to call attention to himself. That is, until a cold shiver ran down his back and he looked around finally settling on Jordan who was staring at him coldly. Leo knew he had been found out, but wasn't worried. He just nodded in acknowledgement and stood up, making his way out of the cafeteria.

As he walked back to his bunkhouse with Miles, Leo felt somehow something may had just started between him and Jordan. He wondered to himself whether it had been the smartest thing to do getting involved in that dumb challenge. He decided not to worry about it for now, there would be plenty of time to learn more about Jordan.

When they got back to the bunkhouse, Leo and Miles pulled out books and began to read. Leo couldn't really focus though since his thoughts kept wandering to Caroline. He wondered how she was doing and something inside him felt that she was also in somewhat of a sticky situation.

6

LOST IN A MAZE

THE BLUE GLOW from the pattern was somewhat eerie and barely cut through the darkness, so Caroline had to walk slowly to avoid the sudden turns the corridor made regularly. She had a feeling all the turns were intended to disorient her, but she could tell that she was gradually descending, which annoyed her since she knew she would probably be climbing all the way up to the top of the cliff if she was successful in this next test.

This went on for what felt like ages to her, but she zoned out to the steady beat of her footsteps and paid just enough attention to not run into the walls. At one point it occurred to her that she was actually way below the ocean's surface, but nothing was different and there was no sign indicating where she was. She just kept on taking a stroll down a magically lit tunnel.

As she pondered this further, the pattern's shape shifted into something unfamiliar, which drew her out of her thoughts. It looked like the intricate lines were now stretching upward and, when she looked at the floor, there were stairs carved into it.

"Of course..." Caroline said to herself sarcastically, putting her hands on her hips. As soon as she put her foot on the first step, however, the pattern stopped waiting for her and proceeded to spiral upward.

"Hey! Wait for me!" Caroline called out, but it didn't stop and she had to hustle to catch up to it.

Constantly turning to the left, it took all her effort to not become completely dizzy. She just focused on each step, willing herself to keep going even as the pattern seemed to speed up and she had to jog to keep up. Then the pattern's speed jumped a few more notches and Caroline found herself dashing up the stairs as fast as she could and running her hand along the wall as she went to try and steady herself. So, when a gap finally opened in the wall, she tumbled out and was just barely able to catch herself as she found herself sprawled out on the floor, breathing heavily, and waiting for her stomach to settle.

Caroline closed her eyes and rolled onto her back, but found this just made her more nauseous since the spinning in her head became more intense. She opened her eyes and what she saw sent a jolt of adrenaline through her body that snapped her back into gear. Just as she had been getting used to the beauty of the intricate pattern, she now looked around to see it had grown to cover all the walls around her. She was in a room about the size of her bedroom and every inch of it, even the floor, had glowing blue lines scrawled across it.

"Holy..." Caroline began to say, trailing off as she stared wide eyed as the pattern started to move and then settle into a new orientation. She just laid there and watched as it shifted every minute or so. Then her stomach gurgled loudly, which snapped her out of her reverie.

"Oh, right. I'm doing a test," Caroline said as she patted her belly and she got up to get a sense of her next task.

She did a slow spin to take in the space and noticed immediately there was no longer an opening into the room. The only way out was to figure out how to move forward, there was no way back. Then, as she did another scan of the room, she noticed a gap in the pattern in the shape of a handprint. She took a few steps towards it to get a closer look and, as she approached the pattern shifted again, but the handprint gap remained.

Even with all the light from the glowing lines, it was still somewhat hard to see details. So, Caroline moved closer until her nose was inches away from the handprint and that was when she noticed it wasn't a flat section of wall. It was actually slightly concave and Caroline thought to herself, "Am I supposed to place my hand in there?"

A wave of anxiety washed over her and she stood back up, taking a few steps away to try and gather her thoughts. Just as she was about to start scanning the room again for other clues, however, her stomach let out another large gurgle and she shouted at it, "Fine! If you're going to be that impatient, I'll just put my hand on the creepy dent in the wall!"

She walked back over to the gap and shoved her hand onto it. At first, nothing happened and she felt how it was much larger than her hand. Then it seemed to shrink to fit closely around her fingers and, similar to the night before, she felt a surge of energy flow into her. The sensation was so strong, it was like she was being filled up with the energy from her feet and quickly running up her legs and torso. Soon, she felt the final bit of energy reach the follicles on her head and it was one of the most bizarre sensations she had ever experienced.

Then a long fissure opened up across the ceiling and the walls began to lean out, making the gap grow wider and wider. When the walls reached a tipping point, spider webs of cracks formed across them and big chunks tumbled into an abyss that appeared around the floor. Caroline listened for the crash of the rocks as they hit the bottom, but no sound echoed up and a nervous shiver went up her spine.

When the last bits of wall and ceiling fell away, she looked around and saw that she was in a huge cavern with long stalactites hanging from the roof. There was an otherworldly glow with no apparent source that allowed her to see everything clearly. Around her all that was left of the room she had been standing in was the small section of the floor that now connected to a narrow bridge of rock leading to the entrance of what was clearly a maze with tall, smooth walls.

Caroline lifted up her right foot and gently placed it on the bridge to see if it was stable. Nothing happened, so she put more weight on her foot until she was slightly leaning forward. Satisfied the bridge wasn't going to crumble underneath her with just her first step, she took a deep breath and then hurried across the bridge as quickly as she could while being careful to not take a wrong step off the narrow path. When she reached the other side, her skin felt clammy and she looked back to see the platform and bridge crumbling and falling into the gaping chasm.

"When I make it through this, I am going to find the person who designed this place and give them a piece of my mind…" Caroline said to herself.

She made her way to the entrance of the maze and peered in carefully, first looking to the right and then to the left. The walls were completely blank, with no trace of the pattern in sight and she could see just far enough to notice that both directions eventually made a turn away from the entrance.

Caroline slowly stepped into the maze and, when she did, her skin began to feel itchy, particularly on the palms of her hands. She turned right and took a few steps and the itchiness gradually decreased. Finding this curious, she turned the opposite direction and, as she walked, her skin became itchier as if she were covered in a rash.

"Huh…" she said and took a few steps backward, feeling the sensation diminish slightly.

She held her hands up in front of her, palms facing away from her like she was trying to push something away, and started to walk forward again. The itchiness returned and stayed at a somewhat constant level all the way until she reached the turn to go further into the maze. Feeling that her idea of using her hands as a detector was a bust, she placed her right hand on the wall to lean and think for a moment. The itchiness sensation jumped up by several orders of magnitude and she immediately jerked her hand back, shaking it like it had touched something scalding.

Her heart was racing and she now knew she was on to something. So, she slowly reached out her hand toward the wall until it was hovering just an inch away from the smooth surface. The intense sensation returned, but she was able to tolerate it this time and she slowly turned the corner to continue further into the maze.

After a few more steps, the itchiness transitioned to heat and she took deep breaths to focus herself on tolerating the pain. As she continued, she started to struggle to hold her hand steady and not jerk it back. The only thing that seemed to help her was staring at her hand and focusing on how it looked completely normal. The skin wasn't scorched or harmed in any way. Still, beads of sweat broke out across her body and she felt her shirt begin to plaster itself to her skin.

Working to master the sensation, she trained her gaze on the wall and saw there was a round section bulging out a little further down the path. As she neared it, the pain in her hand grew more and more unbearable, but she couldn't pull her hand back. It was as if the wall was pulling her hand towards that spot and, when she reached it, she shoved her hand onto it and immediately felt the energy that had poured into her before releasing into the wall. A cool, relaxing sensation spread from her hand throughout her body and she closed her eyes as she let out a sigh of relief. Standing there, savoring the moment, it took her several moments to register the light that was making its way through her eyelids. She slowly opened them, squinting to let them adapt to the brightness.

When she could finally open her eyes fully, she saw the pattern was now green and its gorgeous lines had blossomed from the spot where she was touching the wall. It stretched several feet to the left, and covered the section of wall from the floor to the top where it ended in the open air of the huge cavern. She took a moment to admire the artwork again and followed the gentle curves and geometrically spaced, intricate knots. She removed her hand from the bulge in the wall and started to trace a line, feeling the energy now coursing through it.

Taking another satisfied sigh, Caroline stepped back and looked at the whole pattern and noticed that several lines stopped at an odd spot off to the left, as if they were reaching to go further down the wall but something was stopping them. "Are you going to lead the way again?" she asked, somewhat rhetorically. Then she took a few steps forward and the pattern crawled across the wall with her. However, instead of racing ahead to guide her, this time it seemed to just walk with her and wait for her to make the decisions.

Caroline moved slowly down the corridor and eventually reached an intersection where she could continue to go forward or make a turn to the left or right. She took a moment to gaze in each direction, but they all looked identical. Something about the path to the left felt good to her and she began to walk in that direction. After a few steps, however, the familiar presence of the glowing pattern was missing and she turned around to see that it was still on the wall behind her.

"Come on! Let's go!" she called out like it was a puppy, but it remained stationary.

"What is it? You don't want to go this way?" she asked it, but knew it wouldn't answer.

Letting out an annoyed grunt, Caroline walked back toward the pattern, dragging her fingers idly on the wall along the way when she felt something that caused her to stop and gasp. It was another raised bulge on the wall and she looked back at the pattern with dawning recognition.

"Oh! I get it now…" she said to it and jogged back.

When she arrived at the pattern, just as she expected, it was surrounding a small bulge low on the wall. She chastised herself slightly for not noticing it before and placed her hand on it quickly, hoping to avoid the burning sensation. It wasn't meant to be, though, as she felt her hand erupt in pain and the pattern surged back into her body.

She quickly ran back down the path she had started before and placed her hand on the bulge she found. The pattern erupted out of it and, this time, it immediately started moving down the wall. Caroline felt another leap of excitement and she hurried to keep up as it led her through a rapid series of turns. She eventually gave up keeping track of where she was going because it was simply too hard to keep every turn straight. It also occurred to her there hadn't been any option to go backward up until this point, so there was no reason to expect that would change all of a sudden. Caroline simply needed to trust the pattern would lead her to where she needed to go next.

This went on for quite a while and Caroline began to feel the burn in her muscles from the effort as well as the lack of food in her stomach. A low grade ache began to blossom at the back of her head and she felt the beginning symptoms of hanger building up. Looking ahead, she could see the pattern was leading her up to another intersection, this one a T with branches to the right and left. The pattern screeched to a halt and Caroline nearly ran into the wall as she struggled with the abrupt change in momentum.

She bent over, placing her hands on her knees, and breathed heavily as she tried to bring her heart rate down. She was sweaty again and could tell how bad she smelled after a night camping on the beach and now running around a maze nonstop for hours.

"Ugh… I hope one of my abilities is not repelling people with my stench…" she said to herself and then stood up to figure out what she was supposed to do next.

She noticed immediately this time that the pattern was surrounding another bulge located on the wall several feet before the path to the right. She peered around the corner to try to assess which way she should be going, not relishing another round of hand-searing pain that was about to happen. Before she had a chance to do a careful review, however, a large fireball screamed through the air, just barely over her head, and slammed into the wall behind her. The smell of burned hair overpowered her nostrils as she pulled herself back and plastered her back to the section of wall just next to the pattern. A second later, another fireball erupted against the wall she was now facing, raining down embers on the floor that quickly died out.

When she noticed that whoever or whatever could no longer see her and had stopped attacking, she pulled herself up into a crouch and tried to figure out what to do. She knew the only option was forward and she certainly didn't want to go down the hallway to the right because that would head directly to what was likely a fire Elemental. Going left might buy her some time, but she wasn't sure it would be enough to avoid being roasted alive. She thought herself in circles, realizing she had no idea which way she was supposed to go.

"Hey! I'm just a kid here!" she shouted up to the ceiling of the cavern, her hanger starting to blossom. She expected another fireball in response because that's what she would have done in this moment, but none came.

Emboldened by this, she yelled, "I bet the reason there are so few Moon Borns is because you kill too many of them doing this stupid test!"

Still, there was no retaliation for her words. Finally, she decided to take a chance at examining each direction to see if she could notice anything that would give her a clue on what to do. Staying in a crouch, she quietly crept across the path and, with her back against the opposite wall from before, she gazed down the path to the left. She immediately noticed another bulge located high on the wall about halfway towards another turn. Then, as she was in the process of trying to figure out how she could move quickly enough to absorb the energy again and get to the next bulge to transfer it while also being attacked, another fireball smashed into the floor just a couple feet away from her.

She was sprayed with embers this time and she yelped in pain as she rolled backwards out of the line of fire.

"NOT COOL!" she shouted at her hidden attacker and she laid on her back trying to think.

"Well, I suppose I should see what's behind door number two," Caroline said to herself even though she knew she had barely a couple of seconds to look before she would be attacked again.

She carefully peered around the corner again and was able to get a pretty good look before she saw a stream of fire being sprayed in her direction. She fell backwards just before the fire splashed across the corner right where her face had been. Taking a moment to gather her wits again, she was able to process what she saw. There was definitely another bulge about the same distance in this direction, but it was only chest height.

Pondering which way she should go, neither option looked very appealing to her and she took a while to deliberate when a thought occurred to her, "You're a Moon Born!" She started to laugh at herself as remembered that she could protect herself from these attacks. So, she stood up, squared her shoulders, and walked confidently into danger that didn't seem nearly as scary now. She walked right up to the pattern and placed her hand on the bulge it was surrounding. The pain stretched down her arm this time and was practically unbearable. As the energy poured into her again, she wasn't sure how many more times she would be able to do this.

Then, without knowing why she made this decision, she rounded the corner and started walking down the path to the right. Immediately, another large fireball barrelled down the path at her and she raised her hand, sending rippling waves through the air that disrupted it until it simply faded away. A swell of confidence bloomed inside her and she continued to take confident strides down the hallway as more fiery attacks pummeled an invisible shield she had erected around herself.

She quickly arrived at her destination and placed her hand on the bulge, feeling the welcome cooling sensation again, but not letting her guard down for a second because an increasing number of attacks were hitting her shield with jarring thuds. As the pattern spread back out on the wall, Caroline took a step back, ready to follow it, and the attacks immediately stopped.

Caroline's heartbeat pounded in her ears with the sudden quiet and then, without any indication, the pattern raced down the wall. She broke out into a sprint to follow it, but she kept her guard up as well since she was sure more attacks were coming. She didn't have to wait long either as she saw sections of the wall open up in front of her, sending a potpourri of projectiles at her. The shield in front of her dealt with them easily and she started to take darting strides to avoid stepping on the various sharp implements now cluttering the floor.

She allowed herself a soft chuckle of satisfaction between panting breaths when her right arm erupted in pain. She instinctively grabbed it and stumbled for several steps before forcing herself to keep running and taking a quick look down to see blood seeping between her fingers. Then an ice spike shattered on the inside of her shield and she realized that attacks were now coming from behind her as well. She extended her shield around her fully, like a cocoon, and then ignored the pain in her arm as she struggled to keep the pattern in sight.

Caroline was so focused on that, she barely noticed the corridor was getting narrower in front of her. At first she didn't think anything of it, but when her shield started to graze the walls it occurred to her they were actually closing in on her. A jolt of panic radiated out of her stomach and she felt the pressure of the walls increase on her shield. Marshaling every last bit of her energy, she poured it into her shield and ran as fast as she could, hoping it would be enough to keep her from getting crushed.

Looking ahead and searching for something, anything, that would help her, she saw what she thought was an open area about the distance of her street block down the path. She pumped her arms as hard as she could, panting for air and seeing discolored spots appear on her shield as it struggled to hold back the walls. When she was several paces away from the end of the path, she could see the bright, green pattern illuminating the room she was struggling to reach. She pulled in her shield and threw herself forward with everything she had just as the walls slammed together behind her. She flew through the air briefly and landed hard on her side.

She groaned as she rolled onto her back, stared up at the ceiling and thought about how she would ask many more questions before agreeing to go on a mysterious trip again. When she felt she had it in her, she pushed herself up and leaned on her hands, looked around and saw that she was now in a large, perfectly round room. Separate sections of wall seemed to grow out of the floor and each one was separated by a small gap. The pattern had stopped on a section to her left, surrounding another one of the round bulges. The center of the room was filled with sections of rock, very similar to the walls, but set at different angles. She could see some of the sections had grooves cut into them that could act like a ladder, while others had a step or two carved out. What was even more curious was that she could see more round bulges that seemed to be randomly placed. She walked all the way around the room and saw that less than half of the wall sections had a round bulge. It was also another dead end. She was trapped here until she could find a way out.

Every part of her body ached from the effort it took to get to this point and Caroline felt exhaustion raining down on her. There didn't seem to be any imminent danger to her, so she decided to give into the fatigue and let her hands slowly slide out as she lowered her back onto the floor. Within seconds, she was fast asleep.

⁓

When Caroline woke up, she hadn't forgotten where she was. She still felt sore all over her body and a massive headache had enveloped her brain. She tried to just go back to sleep, but she was now fully awake and needed to just get on with the next challenge. As she slowly stood up, she felt the dizziness of a head rush hit her hard and stumbled backward a few steps, finding a section of wall to steady herself. When the dizziness had passed, she took a deep breath and started to examine the room.

Her first stop was to try to peer through the gaps in the walls to see what might be on the other side. She walked to each gap twice, searching for anything she could fixate on, but all she could see was inky blackness. The same went for the ceiling above her. She could no longer see the stalactites hanging over her, but the echoes of her footsteps told her they were high above her.

Caroline's stomach growled loudly again and she said to it, "Yeah yeah… give me a second to figure this out."

She walked over to the pattern and stared at it. Unlike before, it wasn't straining to move to the next section of wall, it now covered the bulge and the section of wall around it in a large rosetta. Caroline was absorbed by it and was surprised by a sense of joy that cascaded from her core out to her extremities as she took in every inch of the pattern's new form. As she reached the center, she noticed that, unlike the rest of the green pattern, a small section of it emitted a soft white glow.

A light bulb turned on in her mind and she looked around the room, her eyes eventually landing on one of the stone sections arranged in the center. It was basically a wedge of rock that angled up to a tall obelisk next to it and she found a small bulge at the base of it near where it slanted seamlessly into the floor.

"I know there's gotta be a catch…" Caroline said to herself as she fidgeted nervously.

Without a better idea, she shrugged, walked back to the pattern, and placed her hand at the center. She shut her eyes tightly and gritted her teeth as the pain cascaded across all the nerves in her body until the energy was all back inside her and she was able to breathe again.

Before she could even turn around, a lightning bolt smacked down next to her and she scampered away. She turned to look where she had been and another rained down quickly behind her, scorching the side of her shirt as she twisted away. She patted it down to make sure it didn't catch on fire and then ran for the wedge of stone in the center of the room. Meanwhile, more lightning bolts chased behind her, emitting loud cracks as they hit the floor and leaving more scorch marks. Caroline felt the air around her become charged with static electricity.

The lightning bolts caught up fast and, once again, Caroline found herself diving for her target. She landed splayed out on the surface of the rock and desperately reached for the bulge as she felt the lightning bolts hit just inches away from her. When her palm slapped down on the bulge, the familiar feeling of cool greeted her as the energy left her. Thankfully, the lightning bolts stopped raining down as well.

Caroline rolled onto her back and yelled, "I knew there was a catch!"

Then she pushed herself up angrily, impatient to see whether

her theory had been correct. The anger faded quickly when she saw just what she had hoped for. The pattern had reemerged, half on the wedge and half on the floor, with another location lit up in white within the pattern just next to the first section that had been lit up when she had seen it on the wall. She now knew the pattern had become a map and, this time as she examined it, she could tell her next target was on a tall obelisk. She looked up to find it and saw it was at the top of a small section of ladder grooves carved into the side just under the pyramid at the top.

"You've gotta be kidding me…" she muttered.

Then she stood up, examined her options, and decided to do a test run. She took a few steps back, ran up the wedge, leapt off the top lip, and reached for the grooves. She quickly smacked into the rock and tried desperately to hold on to one of the grooves, but she ended up sliding down and landing in a heap at the bottom of the obelisk.

"I didn't realize that Moon Borns are supposed to be experts at parkour too…" she grumbled and set herself up for another try.

It took another four practice runs to finally be able to hold on and by this time, there was a hole in her jeans and her knee was badly scraped up. She let go and landed on her feet for the first time, then decided to try it for real. Taking a few deep breaths, she knelt down like a runner at the start of a race and planted her palm in the center of the pattern. The fire rocketed up her arm and she yelled out in agony as she pushed herself up hard and sprinted up the wedge. Her eyes widened as the maze, ever full of surprises, started to shift all the stone shapes in the center of the room to different positions.

Half in desperation and half in anger, she shouted, "NO!" and let loose a huge blast of disruptive waves around her as she jumped off the lip again. Suddenly the movement stopped and she was so caught off guard that she almost forgot to hold on when she reached out for the bottom groove. She felt a vibration in the rock tickle her fingertips and figured she only had a few seconds before the rock began to move again. Thankfully, the angle of the obelisk had changed and it was now leaning so dramatically that she was able to somewhat scamper up the grooves as the vibrations grew stronger. She planted her hand on the target above her but surprisingly didn't feel the expected relaxing sensation. Instead, her hand was stuck there while all the stones sank into the floor.

"Oh my g…" she screamed as panic erupted inside her.

Her heart pounded in her chest as she tried desperately to release the energy, but to no avail. She then tried to disrupt the movement again, sending weak, shimmering waves into the floor. However, in her state, she could barely focus and was unable to do anything but scream out in fear as she sank towards the floor as the obelisk moved downward.

She closed her eyes and held her breath just as her feet hit the floor, but she didn't sink into it as she had expected. Instead, she was pulled flat onto her belly as the obelisk sank down further and she could feel the cold stone through her clothes. It was only then that the energy drained out of her and into the bulge under her hand. With shuddering breaths of relief, and a few thankful tears, she laid there motionless with her face pressed into the cool rock floor.

When she finally had the courage to open her eyes, Caroline saw the glow of the pattern underneath her. She pushed herself up to get a better look and, out of the corner of her eye she noticed there was now a large opening in the wall. In fact, she saw there were now five openings in the walls around her with a lit path stretching out from each of them into the darkness.

"Oh come on!" she shouted at whomever was watching her go through this ordeal.

She jumped up and yelled up into the darkness, "CAN THIS JUST BE DONE NOW?! I am still alive! That has to count for something!"

Caroline was answered with nothing but silence and she decided she was done being their lab rat running through the maze. She looked down at herself and saw how much of a mess she was. There were streaks of dried blood running down her arm. Her shirt was filthy and covered in scorch marks. Her jeans were ripped in several places and the souls of her shoes were falling off.

She pulled off her left shoe and tore the rest of the sole off and then stomped over to the nearest opening. When she reached it, she realized how absurd she looked and hurled the rubber sole down the path in frustration. When it landed a huge crack formed and the path quickly fell apart leaving nothing but darkness in that direction again.

Caroline let out another huge groan of frustration and yelled, "FINE!" Then she stomped back over to the pattern and stared at it, looking for a clue. It took her a while to calm down enough to see it clearly, but then she noticed a familiar portion of the pattern that looked unfinished like before. Knowing the drill, she knelt down and traced her glowing finger along the bare rock, finishing the pattern again. With a sudden lurch, the floor began to rise and she stayed kneeling as the speed picked up and felt the air rush around her.

Looking up, she saw a small round point of light directly above her and it grew bigger as she approached. She mentally prepared herself for the next challenge as the smell of the ocean wafted around her.

The platform slowed as she rose through an opening in the

ceiling, finally coming to a stop in the open air with the sun shining down on her. It was so bright, she had to close her eyes for a minute to let her eyes adjust. When she could finally open her eyes, she found herself surrounded by a group of what she assumed were Moon Born priests. Each was wearing flowing robes, some with bright colors.

A tall man with a dark complexion and a completely shaved head smiled warmly and began clapping as he walked toward her.

"Very well done!" he said loudly when he was a few paces away.

"Is it over? Did I pass?" Caroline asked with trepidation, unwilling to allow herself any hope there wasn't another test to complete.

"Hardly!" the man said with a chuckle. "But you have found your way into Terradune, so now your true work can commence!"

7

Close Call

L EO RAN DOWN the trail as fast as he could, his backpack bouncing uncontrolled across his back as he struggled to feed his other arm through the second strap to stabilize it. He was so consumed in his anxiety, that he didn't see a large root arcing out of the ground in front of him. His foot lodged firmly in it and he flew forward, splaying himself out on the rough ground and his clothes became covered in dirt and pine needles.

"Shoot! Shoot! SHOOT!" he shouted loudly, knowing nobody would probably hear him. They were all in class after all, which is where he should have been if he hadn't overslept for the third time since school started. Why had none of his bunkmates woken him up? He would totally do that for them after all.

"Selfish jerks..." he grumbled before a memory of Miles emerged in his adrenaline infused brain. He had tried to wake Leo up twice and finally gave up after Leo threw his drool encrusted pillow at him.

Now accepting that this predicament was of his own making, he descended into his anxious thoughts again. Coming late to class was bad, of course, but much worse when you had Ms. Herbert first period. She was supposed to just be their English teacher during fourth period, but she had also been filling in for Mr. Ialongo's first period History class since he had been delayed and wouldn't arrive for another day. What was worse though was that Ms. Herbert was militant about her rules and he remembered the first day of classes a few weeks ago when she listed them off.

"Follow these rules and we'll get along fine," she started with her stern, nasal voice. "No talking in class, get your work done, raise your hand if you don't understand something, and don't come late to class."

Aran, as usual, had the gall to raise his hand and ask, "What happens if you're late?"

"You don't want to find out," was all she said.

Well, they had found out a few days later when Leo had overslept and arrived in class twenty minutes late. She had given him four extra assignments to complete and nobody was allowed to help him. The workload had overwhelmed him, but it also motivated him to get up on time. For a week, that is, until he stayed up too late doing homework and overslept again.

This time, when Leo arrived, a sly grin crept across Ms. Herbert's face and just her penetrating stare caused him to break out in a cold sweat.

"Leo. How good of you to join us," she had said curtly and Leo just waved awkwardly and started walking down the aisle to his seat.

"No need to sit down, Leo. Why don't you come up here to the front." she instructed.

He dropped his backpack in his chair and slowly made his way to stand in front of all the other students in class and saw Jordan, with a deeply satisfied smile on his face, sitting in his seat in the front row.

"Now, how much do you remember about the Boreal Conflict that we discussed yesterday?" she asked him.

He had felt a leap of excitement then because he had paid rapt attention in that lesson. It was a pretty exciting historical era. It was about the early days when Coreolis was still very young and a rather small city. Everything was kind of like the wild west and there had been a warlord named Boreal who had sent his battalions to raid tradelines between Coreolis and other cities in its trade alliance. No matter how many soldiers they sent to protect the caravans, Boreal's forces had decimated them and stolen all the money, goods, equipment, and food.

"Sure," Leo said quietly in response to Ms. Herbert's question, not wanting to let on how confident he felt.

"Excellent!" she said with an enthusiastic voice that sent shivers down his spine. "There is more to this story than may first meet the eye, but let's start with some easy questions as a recap for the class. Who was Boreal?"

"A warlord from the Pandan region," Leo answered briefly. His anxiety had shot up several hundred levels when she had said there was more to the story since he had thought it was a pretty simple action-adventure type of plot.

"Well, I guess that is correct even though it is not a very complete answer," she said in a slightly disappointed voice. "Can anyone else provide some more details about Boreal?"

A couple of students raised their hands, but Leo was staring at one of them. Jordan held his hand high and confidently as he met Leo's stare with glee in his eyes.

"Yes, Jordan," Ms. Herbert acknowledged.

"He was the former head of the Coreolis defense force who had been stripped of his rank and exiled from the city. He was caught taking bribes from several of the wealthiest families who were trying to corner the market on a new metal that only a few Earth Elementals had perfected the technique to create."

"I see someone has been doing the supplemental reading!" Ms. Herbert said enthusiastically and then added, "Five points for you!"

Jordan leaned back in his chair, continuing his staredown with Leo. Meanwhile, Leo felt sweat break out along his hairline and his armpits and he kept thinking to himself, "There was supplemental reading?!"

"Here's another easier one for you Leo," Ms. Herbert said, barely breaking through Leo's panic attack. "How did Boreal go from being an outcast to a warlord?"

Leo hesitated as he gathered as much of the information he could remember from the day before so he could provide a detailed answer. Then he felt a sharp jolt of pain in his right arm that caused him to gasp and lose his focus.

"What's the matter, Leo? Can't remember the facts from yesterday's lesson?" Ms. Herbert said, taunting him.

"No..." Leo started to say before Ms. Herbert jumped in again.

"Perhaps we should have Jordan refresh your memory?" she said, walking over to stand next to Jordan and place her hand on his shoulder.

"That's not necessary!" Leo said forcefully and he felt the flare of anger radiate off Ms. Herbert.

"I appreciate the offer, but I think I remember it well enough," Leo said in a calmer tone, trying to avoid making things worse.

"A large gap had formed between the wealthiest families and the rest of the city's population. They controlled most of the city's economy and prices had been increasing steadily for years. There were protests in some of the poorest neighborhoods where people could barely afford to live and buy food. The protests started out as peaceful, but they had grown to become very disruptive and the defense forces had been called in twice to break them up. A curfew had even been instituted by the time Boreal had been exiled. Some of Boreal's lieutenants had left the city with him and he sent them back to recruit from the younger members of that population. He fed stories to them that the defense forces were set up to maintain the wealthy families' control of the city. This worked and there was a steady stream of recruits for his army."

"Mostly right, I'll give you a little bit of credit," Ms. Herbert said flatly. When she turned to the class, Leo felt his stomach cramp extremely painfully and he doubled over, wrapping his arms around it. It was so intense, he could barely register her words when she asked the class, "What did he leave out?"

Just as quickly as the pain came, it began to dissipate and he put his hands on his knees as he looked up to see who would answer. Nobody was raising their hand this time and he saw Meimei looking at him with concern in her eyes.

She mouthed to him silently, "What's the matter with you?"

He just shook his head slightly and stood back up fully.

"Nobody knows?" Ms. Herbert asked and the rest of the class stayed still, trying not to meet her gaze.

"How about you, Jordan?" she asked softly, turning back to Leo's new nemesis.

"Uh…" he said at first, caught off guard. Then the cocky grin returned to his lips and he looked up to her as he said, "Boreal used conjurers who planted thoughts and emotions in his new followers. This turned them into zealots who thought he was fighting for greater equality when he was really just out to feed his grudge against Coreolis."

"Very good!" she said warmly to Jordan. "A very innovative use of Neural specialties that had not been seen before this point! This was his distinctive advantage during the conflict."

"While I agree that was an innovation, Luella, I think Boreal's unconventional battle strategy had more of a direct impact in his early success," a voice from the back of the room said.

"Mr. Ialongo!" Ms. Herbert said in a nervous, surprised voice.

The entire class turned to see who their teacher was and he walked confidently to the front. He was dressed in all black, had a shaved head, and wore wire framed glasses. He was holding a soft leather briefcase that he set on the desk off to the left side of the whiteboard. Then he took off his coat and laid it carefully over the back of the chair.

"Thank you again for stepping in to cover for me, Luella. I can probably take it from here," he said as he turned back around.

"Oh, I wouldn't mind finishing the lesson if you would like to get settled in," Ms. Herbert responded in a twittery voice that seemed so unlike the controlled person she had been moments before.

"That's quite alright, I have already imposed enough and I am sure you have no shortage of things to do," Mr. Ialongo said to her cooly. Leo felt confused by what he was sensing from his new teacher, unable to tell how he felt about Ms. Herbert.

"Very well then," she said, acknowledging that her presence was no longer necessary. She walked quickly over to the desk and picked up a stack of papers before hurrying out of the classroom.

"You can take a seat if you like," Mr. Ialongo said to Leo with a raised eyebrow.

Leo began to hurry to his desk, but the remnants of the pain in his arm and gut twinged, causing a momentary hitch in his step. He tried to cover it up as best as he could and quickly sat down.

"Hello, everyone, as you all just heard, my name is Ernest Ialongo and I will be your History and Battle Strategy teacher this year. I am not one for formality, so please just call me Ernest. I apologize that I was not here for the start of the term, but I was held up. In any event, I am very glad to be here now and look forward to getting to know each and every one of you."

Aran raised his hand from the back of the classroom and Ernest acknowledged him with an upward nod.

"Um… Mr. Ia… I mean, Ernest. You said you will be teaching us Battle Strategy?"

"Your name please?" Ernest asked in response.

"Uh, Aran."

"Ah yes, you are one of the students from Kensington, I believe?"

"Yeah… How did you…"

"To answer your first question, yes, you will be learning how to construct a strategy when faced with a variety of opponents and environments. This is an essential skill in the event a war breaks out and one of the reasons we have created these schools to train you. Our lessons will sometimes be classroom based and we will analyze historical events to learn from the strategies that were used in those moments. We will also have regular practicum classes where you will try to use the information you have learned in real-life scenarios."

Ernest paused and the weight of his comments sat with the students. Most just stared at him, trying to process what he had said. None of the other teachers up until this point had brought home the purpose of the schools so bluntly. In a few short comments, he had dispelled the illusion and reminded them of why they had been sent away from their homes. A war may be coming and, if it did, they would become soldiers.

"To answer your second question," Ernest started to stay and the students were stirred from their thoughts. "I have a roster with some basic information about each of you."

Ernest walked over to the desk, reached inside his briefcase and pulled out a sheaf of papers. He flipped through several and then pulled out a stapled packet.

"Here we are," he said and turned to the third page in the packet. "Ah paper… It's been a long time since I had to carry this much of it around with me. Alas, it is much more strategically secure in this day and age… Anyway, I digress. It says here, Aran, that you are from Kensington, you're a Caretaker, and that you have received some battle training already. Is that so?"

"I guess so…" Aran replied slowly. "I mean, we had some heavy stuff go down."

"Heavy is putting it mildly," Ernest said. "It was an excellent strategy to train you all and a credit to your teachers there. I am sure that training will come in handy here and I hope you and your classmates are willing to assist me during our first practicum tomorrow."

"Tomorrow?!" Stella blurted out.

"Indeed!" Ernest replied, finally showing a smile. "We've already lost several weeks to my delay, there is no point in postponing."

"But… But… We haven't learned enough!" Stella responded in distress.

"One of the first things you will learn in battle is that you can never be truly prepared. You can plan as much as you want, but, once you're in the fight, your enemy often destroys even the best designed plan. What you will learn in my class is the more you plan in advance of a conflict, the more effectively you will be able to modify your tactics once you're in the heat of battle.

"Anyway, I heard you were discussing the Boreal conflict when I came in. It is a bit early in the term to discuss that one, but I know it is one of Luella's favorites. She does have a bit of a spin on it, though, and I do not exactly agree with it. So, let's dig into it a bit more…"

Just then, the bell to change classes rang and the students started to stir and gather their things.

"I guess we will have to pick that up next time," Ernest said, raising his voice over the din. Then he looked to Leo and said, "Would you mind staying back for a moment?"

After all the other students had exited the room and the door had closed behind them. Ernest walked up to Leo's desk and said, "You appear to be in some pain."

"Oh, it's nothing," Leo responded, trying to brush off the concern. "It's going away."

"Would you mind?" Ernest asked, holding up his hands to communicate he wanted to place them on Leo.

Leo nodded slightly, and Ernest came around and placed his hands on Leo's shoulders. After several moments, he asked, "When did this pain start?"

"In class," Leo answered truthfully.

"When?"

"Not too long after I arrived."

"Could you be more specific?" Ernest probed.

"Well, I overslept and got here late… I'd say maybe half-way through class? Ms. Herbert made me stand at the front of the classroom and answer questions," Leo replied.

"Interesting…" Ernest said softly then Leo felt warmth cascade down his shoulders and the pain in his arm and stomach evaporated. He couldn't help but let out a relaxed sigh.

Ernest stepped away and went back to his desk, rubbing the back of his head in thought.

"You're a healer…" Leo said in recognition.

"Indeed," was all Ernest said in response.

"You seem to know about me and my friends. Does that mean you know Adam too?" Leo asked, his curiosity getting the better of him.

"In fact, I do. We know each other quite well. You could say we have been through a lot together," Ernest replied.

Before Leo could keep asking questions, they heard Meimei from the back of the room say, "Leo, we have to get to Math!"

"You'd best be going," Ernest advised and Leo got up reluctantly.

He had so many questions running through his mind that were struggling to get out. He managed to keep them at bay though and walked out of the classroom to join Meimei.

"What did he want?" she asked Leo once they were walking down the hall.

"He's a healer," was all Leo could say.

"So, there *was* something wrong with you! What was it?" Meimei asked.

"Look at that, here we are at Math class," Leo said, dodging the question.

"You're not getting out of this that easily. We're talking about this at lunch," Meimei responded with determination and Leo knew he would have to explain whether he liked it or not (this might be a good place to put a cliffhanger about what Ms. Herbert had done to him).

The next several periods flew by and Leo even managed to distract himself from the experience during first period here and there, but lunch time arrived eventually and he dragged his feet all the way to the cafeteria. As soon as he walked through the doors, he saw a table filled with his friends off to the side with a seat saved for him. Resigned to the grilling that was about to ensue, he got in line and tried to find something that looked appealing. Usually, he would pile his tray high with almost everything on offer, but today he didn't have much of an appetite and ended up just getting a couple bowls of cereal and some frozen yogurt.

Making his way back towards the tables, he heard someone call out to his left and saw Mari wave to him and then gesture to an empty seat at her table. A combination of relief and elation ballooned inside of him and he walked over, noticing Miles, Marie, Leah, and Finn were sitting at the table.

"That's all you're having?" Finn asked as Leo sat down. "They have a whole taco bar today."

"Yeah, maybe I'll go back for more," Leo responded, feeling his appetite slowly returning now that he knew he didn't have to spend lunchtime explaining something that he didn't understand.

The table quickly settled into idle chit chat and Leo focused on shoveling large spoonfuls of cereal into his mouth. Sometimes, he relished the moments when he could just be quiet and listen to life around him. However, they never lasted that long and this time was no different.

"So, I've barely seen you since we got here. How're you liking it so far?" Finn asked.

"Fine, I guess..." Leo answered.

"That's it? Fine? I mean, I think I've learned more here in the past three weeks than I did in a whole year back home," Finn challenged.

"I don't know… I mean, I had some pretty good teachers back at home," Leo said.

"Well, some of us weren't so lucky," Finn responded coolly.

"Sorry, Ms. Herbert was a total jerk to me today in first period," Leo said, trying to explain his mood.

"Really? She's, like, my favorite teacher here," Finn said enthusiastically.

"Are you kidding me?!" Leo said a bit too loud, his incredulity blasting through the little bit of control he had been maintaining. He felt glances of attention rain on him from the surrounding tables.

"Yeah, she's brilliant!" Finn continued as if he didn't even register Leo's response. "Last Friday, she taught us how to use deflection and redirection techniques and then we practiced by trying to talk our way into different parts of the school we weren't supposed to be in. My friend Arlo had to talk his way into another class and failed miserably. She had me talk my way into the kitchen and I managed to get the cook to show me where she keeps her stash of junk food!"

"What?" was all Leo could say, his brain still unable to compute.

"You probably just have to get to know her a bit better," Finn said simply. "I hear we'll get into advanced espionage later in the year. Can't wait for that."

Leo sat silently and Finn just gave him an annoyed look, joining a conversation that Marie and Leah were having about the best jelly bean flavors when Leo interrupted suddenly.

"Why are you sitting here?" he asked Finn.

"What's that supposed to mean?!" Finn responded angrily.

"S-s-sorry, my bad," Leo stammered realizing how his question had sounded. "I just mean, how do you know everyone here? We're all younger than you and don't share any of your classes."

"That's not entirely accurate," Miles responded. "They don't have a dedicated elective for me because there aren't any other Librarians here. So, they stuck me in the Technic group with Finn. I mean, it makes some sense when you think about it. Librarians have some adjacency to Technics since we have some gifts with computer systems. As a matter of fact, Finn has taught me some very interesting methods for hacking into the school's system!"

"*Miles!* Can you be a bit more *discreet*?!" Finn whispered loudly at him.

"Sorry!" Miles said, an embarrassed flush blooming across his face and his head retreating in between his shoulders like a turtle ducking into its shell.

"Yeah, so that's why I am sitting here today. Miles invited me. I'll be sure to steer clear in the future," Finn said, clearly still angry at Leo.

"C'mon, don't be like that," Leo said in a conciliatory tone. "I'm just a bit off today."

"That reminds me of a good joke!" Marie interjected brightly. "What do Star Borns and Fireworks have in common?"

Everyone looked at her, waiting for the punchline.

"They both go off spectacularly!"

Everyone stared at her for a moment, marveling at just how horrible the joke was. Then Mari started to giggle, followed by Leah, until the whole table was laughing. Leo was wiping tears from his eyes, wondering how that joke had made him laugh so much when the bell to let the students know they had ten minutes until classes started up again.

On cue, everyone made their way to return their trays and a traffic jam formed at the doors. The mass of students started to shove and jostle impatiently, and Leo felt an electric jolt as he was pressed up against someone. He looked to see who it was and found himself staring up at Jordan.

"Watch it," Jordan said angrily.

Leo just rolled his eyes and looked back over to Finn to make a plan to hang out later that week. Before he said a word though, Finn saw Jordan and said warmly, "What up, bruh?"

"Sup!" Jordan responded warmly and reached out to do a quick shake like they were good friends.

"Bruh?" Leo asked Finn.

"Yeah, we're bunkmates. I'm on the top bunk of course," Finn responded. "By the way, your farts were horrible last night, dude. Please tell me you didn't hit the refried beans just now."

"You're not gonna like my answer," Jordan said cheekily as the mass behind them finally pushed them through the doors.

Leo hurried away, saying a quick goodbye to Finn and the others, reeling from the revelation that his cousin and his enemy were friends. He could barely focus on the rest of his classes that afternoon and didn't even notice Meimei when she walked up to him as he made his way to the end of day elective class for Star Borns.

"That wasn't cool of you to avoid our conversation at lunchtime," she said to him sternly.

"I don't know what you want me to say," Leo said in frustration. "I have no idea what was going on in that class."

"I get that, but we're a team and we figure things out together," she pushed on him, managing to break through his negative spiral.

"Yeah... I know... I'm sorry... I just need this day to be over already," he said.

"One more class and then we can all hit dinner together later, alright?" Meimei counseled. "Then we can get into what happened.

"Yeah… Alright…" Leo agreed.

⁂

"I don't get it," Stella said

"What's not to get?" Leo asked, his mouth full from a huge bite of pasta.

"You're both Star Borns and there aren't a ton of you. Why do you need to have a beef with Jordan?" she explained.

"Because he's a jerkface and know-it-all," Leo said in a sing-song voice as he twirled his fork to make another huge bite.

"Great, thank you for such great insights," Stella said sarcastically. "Seriously, though. Can't you just let it go and try to get along? I mean, it'll make things much more pleasant for you and the rest of us."

Aran and Ania nodded in agreement on this point and Meimei looked at Leo intensely waiting for his response.

"Why is it my job to make things better?! You make it seem like he's all innocent!" Leo snapped.

"Well, we're *your* friends and we are asking *you* to try to make things better," Stella pushed harder.

"And what if I don't?" Leo challenged.

"C'mon, don't be like that," Aran interjected. "This place is awesome and we're learning so much! There's just a teensy problem with one other student."

"Easy for you to say…" Leo grumbled as he stirred around the noodles on his plate, no longer hungry.

"No, it's not," Stella snapped. "We've been walking on eggshells around you for weeks now, not wanting to bring this up and the way you're acting is exactly why we haven't said anything before now. I mean… GAH!"

Stella shoved her chair back and stood up, taking her tray with her as she walked out the doors of the cafeteria. Leo, just stared after her, unable to understand what had just happened. He had never felt that kind of anger from Stella before. She was always the careful, studious one in the group who didn't want to take big risks and was always up for what the group wanted to do. The emotions that had smacked into him moments before caused his stubbornness to crumble.

"I… I had no idea…" Leo said softly.

"Yeah, we know…" Meimei responded.

"Has it been that bad?" Leo asked.

"Dude. All you have talked about whenever we see you is how much you hate Jordan," Ania said bluntly.

"Nooo… I'm sure we've talked about something else," Leo said, hoping it wasn't as bad as it sounded. Unfortunately, his friends just shook their heads really slowly.

"Wow… I'm sorry…" was all he could say.

"Don't be sorry. Just make it better," Meimei counseled.

"I will," Leo said with resolve and his friends' faces softened.

"I'll go talk to Stella," Meimei said.

"Should I come?" Leo asked.

"Probably not," Meimei answered. "Plus, I think you need to go take a shower. I have no idea how you got pasta sauce in your hair."

Ania and Aran started laughing and poking fun as Leo used up a stack of napkins wiping down his hair. Eventually it was time to head back to their bunks and Leo trudged down the long path slowly. His bed was calling to him and he knew it would take every ounce of the energy left in his body to get cleaned up before he climbed in and passed out.

As Leo's eyes finally closed that night, the usual swirling patterns appeared in his vision and he felt all the stress from the day begin to melt away from his muscles. Normally it would take him a while to quiet his thoughts before he could relax enough to drift off to sleep. Not that night, however, and he was glad to say goodbye to one of the worst days he had experienced in a long time.

He felt so heavy that he almost worried that his bed wouldn't be able to hold him up, but he didn't have any energy to care and allowed himself to sink further and further. Eventually, something felt like it gave way beneath him and he began falling. He opened his eyes wide, expecting to land hard on the floor next to his bunkmate, but instead all he could see was darkness surrounding him and the dropping sensation just continued.

Leo started yelling and flailing his arms and legs uncontrollably, but that only made it feel like he was falling faster. His heart was pounding in his chest and the little respite he had from the stress of the day was gone. Somehow he managed to gather his wits and realized that something truly bizarre was happening. He forced himself to relax his body and stop yelling and the rate of descent seemed to slow down slightly.

"I wonder…" he said to himself as a thought occurred to him that he should try meditating. He closed his eyes and began to use one of the fastest techniques he had learned and almost immediately he felt like he was sitting on firm ground. He opened his eyes slightly and what he saw made him jump to his feet and lose his calm all over again.

"NO NO NO NO NO!" he yelled as he stared down the long line of doors of the Connector. This was one of the few orders from Adam that he had no issue with following - stay out of the Connector. Since the battle with Gabriel's forces, the Star Born elders around the world had determined the Connector was likely too dangerous for anyone who had not passed the Crucible. Leo had let his guard down a couple of times since then, but had managed to avoid accidentally going there in his mind.

He managed to calm down enough to start getting his bearings and what he saw did not make him feel any better. A number of doors within view seemed to be destroyed or severely damaged. One right next to him was hanging at an odd angle because it had been torn off its two upper hinges. He peered inside the room carefully and saw nothing but darkness. A faint smell of mildew like an old cluttered basement wafted into his nose.

"OK, how am I going to get myself out of this," Leo said to himself, trying to shift into problem-solving mode again. He had never actually left the connector before by choice, something had always woken him up.

He took a step back and turned to his left, deciding that his only option was to explore and see what he could find that might help him. At every closed door that was still intact, he listened carefully and placed his hand flat on the smooth wood trying to see what he could sense. He did this for at least an hour, not that he had any sense of time there, and after walking past countless doors, this approach had been a total bust. He leaned against the wall and slid down slowly until he was sitting on the floor and held his head in his hands.

As he sat there quietly, wishing that he could just wake up already, he heard a faint murmuring. He held his breath and was absolutely still, trying to figure out where the sound was coming from and it seemed to be emanating from one of the doors he had just walked past. He stood up slowly and, using his best ninja skills, tiptoed back to the door and pressed his ear to it to see if he could make anything out.

"…must hurry! … one in the Connector!" the voice of a young man was saying and Leo didn't wait to hear what he said next. He began running down the long corridor of doors as fast as he could as shivers radiated down his back, letting him know a large number of Star Borns were nearby. He held his hands up to either side like he was a little kid pretending to be an airplane, trying to find a door that felt safe.

Suddenly, a door to his right flew open and a hand grabbed his wrist firmly and yanked on his arm trying to pull him through. Leo struggled to get away, trying to put up his armor or send a jolt of energy through his arm, but nothing happened. Then with another strong yank, he lost his footing and found himself tumbling through the doorway and landing in a heap on top of someone. He then heard the door click shut quietly behind him and he pushed up to his knees, cocking his arm to throw a punch as soon as he got a good look at his assailant.

"No, Leo!" a woman's voice whispered loudly in his ear and he felt another set of hands grab onto his arm, holding him back from throwing a punch.

Leo turned his head towards the voice and he saw the person move around so he could get a better look. When he saw her, Leo went from fight or flight to complete relief as he threw his arms around Maranda and hugged her tight.

"What are you doing here?!" she whispered in admonishment.

Leo pulled back out of his hug and said, "I have no idea, I didn't mean to…" He stopped speaking when he saw Maranda hold her finger to her lips and look at him urgently. They heard the thunder of footsteps from a large group outside the doorway and Leo looked to Maranda with panic in his eyes. She shook her head slightly, telling him not to worry and they waited until the sound faded away.

"Um… Can you get off me?" a voice said from the floor. It sounded like the young man's voice he heard before. Leo looked down and saw a man about Maranda's age, maybe a little older, with the faint shadow of a beard.

"Oh! Sorry!" Leo whispered and he stood up, offering the man a hand to get up.

"No, it's alright, I'm good," the man said as he pushed himself up. "I think we're safe for the moment, so we can stop whispering."

"Seriously, Leo! You need to be more careful! You're lucky Gus was nearby," Maranda said, continuing where she left off.

"I know, I know… Trust me, I've been doing a good job avoiding the Connector. I was just so exhausted from the worst day ever and I wasn't careful enough," Leo admitted and Maranda's face softened, unable to stay angry.

"Listen, I don't know how much time we have and we should take advantage of this window to warn you about what's happened," Maranda began to say.

"Mar," Gus interrupted, putting his hand on her shoulder. "I don't think it's a good idea to share this information."

"I know Leo," she assured Gus. "This is important and if there's anyone I would trust, it's him."

Gus put his hands up, accepting Maranda's decision, and took a step back to let her continue.

"One of the schools was raided by Gabriel's forces, Leo," Maranda began. "The teachers were able to fight them off, but they took some of the students."

"What?!" Leo responded.

"Yeah, I know," Maranda acknowledged. "The locations of

the schools were closely guarded secrets. Gabriel must have a spy, but we haven't been able to figure out who it is yet."

Leo felt a sinking sensation as if he already somehow knew this information, but his brain simply hadn't processed it yet..

"All the schools could be at risk," Maranda continued. "The problem is we simply can't move them. It was hard enough to find the current locations let alone figure out a way to transport all the students without getting noticed. So, our best option right now is to find out who we can trust at each school to get up-to-date information. Most of our safest methods of communication are too slow since Gabriel has recruited a large number of Technics who can intercept our electronic communications."

"You're saying that we have to use the Connector to communicate between the schools," Leo said.

"Exactly," Maranda confirmed. "And, as you can see, it's not the safest method either. Just this past week, Gabriel's Star Borns found a group of us meeting. There were too many of them and they overwhelmed our defenses. Keiko fought them back to give us enough time to escape, but…"

Maranda's eyes welled up and Gus came over to rub her back.

"She's gone?" Leo asked quietly, unable to believe it and Gus nodded his head.

Leo's head was swimming with this news. Keiko was one of the strongest Star Born elders in the world. If she could be overwhelmed by Gabriel's forces, what hope did they have? He began to pace and rub his hair back and forth like when he got stuck trying to figure out one of the rooms in the Crucible.

"We need your help, Leo," Maranda said in a shaky voice, breaking through his spiraling thoughts.

"Me? What can I do?" Leo asked in disbelief.

"You and your friends can be our eyes and ears," she answered, her voice growing stronger again. "We will meet here once a week. Never the same day, never the same time, and never the same location. We will agree on the plan for our next meeting each time and I will teach you how to enter the Connector in the right place."

"You gotta be kidding me," Leo started to object. "I don't even know how to get out of here."

"I can teach you that too," Maranda answered.

"He's right, Mar," Gus interjected. "This is too much to ask."

"We don't have any other option!" Maranda said in frustration, walking away from them.

Gus' words of caution rattled around Leo's mind in the conversation lull and they had the exact opposite effect of what Gus intended.

"I'll do it," Leo said quietly.

"You will?" Maranda said excitedly, turning around.

"I don't know how you keep convincing me to do these things…" Leo answered with a smile.

"Rare Star Born ability?" Maranda asked cheekily.

"That'd be my guess," Gus answered.

"Well, I'm not going to waste any time thinking about it now." Maranda said. "Let's teach you how to get in and out of here and make a plan for our next meeting."

8

IF AT FIRST YOU DON'T SUCCEED

CLANG CLANG CLANG! Rang the deafening bell outside of Caroline's window and she bolted upright in bed, disoriented and unable to process what was happening. Her heart thudded in her chest and her head swiveled around rapidly, looking for some sign of emergency. Her eyes settled on her window just long enough to register that it was barely dawn and the first rays of sunlight were reflecting off some scattered clouds in the sky. It would have actually been pretty relaxing to stare at that scene for a while, if it hadn't been for that infernal bell.

The ringing stopped just as Caroline was about to get out of bed and she laid back down, listening to the vibrations of the bell slowly dissipate and allowing her mind to fully boot up for the day. Everything started to come into focus again. When she had made it into Terradune, she had been taken to a large room that reminded her of a church, except it was filled with long tables and benches. She had been given a modest bowl of soup and a piece of bread, which she finished in what seemed like thirty seconds, and then she was walked to one of the nicest bathrooms she had ever seen where she was able to take one of the longest showers of her life. When she was done, a change of clothes had been set out for her. She held up her arm and looked at the light, flowing material. It was like nothing she had ever felt before and its warm golden color seemed to shimmer with the first rays of sunlight coming into her room.

All she could remember after that was being led to this room where she promptly passed out on the bed until being woken up by that bell. With that thought, she wondered why that bell had been ringing in the first place and decided that it would probably be a good idea to find out. She threw off her covers and swiveled her body out of bed, making her way to standing alongside it with shaky legs. She took a tentative step towards the foot of the bed and her left leg nearly gave out. She shot out her arms to both steady herself and have a bit of protection if she happened to fall. Then, when she finally felt steady enough, she took several more baby steps to build up her confidence.

When she reached the end of the bed, she grabbed the corner post to take a short break. She dropped her head, wondering why she was so tired, and noticed her duffel had been carefully placed on the floor there.

"Did they also bring up my raft?" she said to herself as she crouched down and unzipped it. All of her clothes had been washed, neatly folded, and set into tidy stacks organized by each type of garment.

"OK, that's a bit OCD…" she said, marveling at the level of organization she felt she could never attain.

She briefly considered changing into a pair of jeans and one of her tie dyed t-shirts, but there was something about the clothes she had been given that made her feel extremely comfortable. So, she stood back up and walked slowly to the door, feeling the energy steadily returning to her limbs. She opened it a crack and saw the man who had greeted her when she emerged from the maze. What was his name? She wracked her brain for several seconds until it emerged from the cloudiness of her memory - Cecil!

"Rise and shine, am I right?!" he said to her warmly, ignoring her suspicious glare. "I was about to give up on you and send a student to wait until you emerged. I'm glad we are able to have breakfast together, but we should hurry or all the best stuff will be gone."

Cecil started walking down the hall with long strides, his robes billowing around him as he went, and Caroline only hesitated a moment before her stomach encouraged her to follow him with a loud growl. She hurried to catch up with Cecil and when she arrived next to him, jogging to keep up with his pace, he looked down with a grin.

"What you heard a short while ago is the morning bell," he informed her. "It's really loud, right?"

"Uh, yeah… It could wake the dead," Caroline deadpanned.

"Not really! You slept through it yesterday along with the evening bell too," Cecil said.

"Huh?" was all Caroline could say, not following what he had said and Cecil stopped and turned to Caroline, looking down at her with a raised eyebrow.

"You just slept for an entire day," he informed her.

"Nooo…" Caroline said, now understanding why she had such a hard time getting out of bed and walking.

"Indeed!" Cecil responded as he resumed his brisk pace down the hall. "Don't worry, that is pretty normal. Some initiates sleep far longer than that, but you were not in the maze for very long."

This did not make sense to Caroline at all. It had felt like she had spent an eternity in the maze. Before she could ask him more, however, he took a quick left turn and began descending a long staircase that brought them to what was apparently the ground floor. A girl about her age was standing right at the bottom step, apparently waiting for them.

"Norah! Right on time!" Cecil said in what Caroline realized was his normal booming voice not stopping as he continued onward from the staircase toward the cathedral food hall that Caroline remembered.

"I am pleased to introduce you to Caroline," he said to Norah and then glanced down at Caroline. "As you just heard, this is Norah. She will be your guide for the first few weeks here. Norah arrived a couple months ago, so she can still remember what it's like to be a new initiate. These are very exciting times here in Terradune! We haven't had this many new initiates in a long time!"

"How many are there?" Caroline asked, panting a bit from the exertion as she continued to hurry to keep up.

"You make ten," Norah answered quietly.

"Ten?! That's it?!" Caroline exclaimed.

"Indeed!" Cecil continued cheerily. "In recent years, we have only had two or three new initiates come to Terradune. Alas, even with our strong traditions, the pull to stay amongst the tribes can be hard to resist. Until recent events, many Moon Borns would do their initial training with a local elder and then sometimes come here for short periods of advanced training. I can't say that we liked it. While the elders amongst the tribes are very skilled and knowledgeable, there is no way to replace what we can create for a new initiate here… Ah! Hashbrowns! My favorite!"

"Wha?" Caroline said. She had been so focused on what

Cecil had been saying that she hadn't noticed they had walked into the grand hall and gotten in line for food.

"Grab a tray over there," Norah instructed. "You can have as much as you want, it's all really good."

Caroline stared at all the options in front of her and started to feel lightheaded. She gripped the counter in front of her tightly and bowed her head, taking deep breaths.

"Oops!" Cecil said. "Why don't we take you to the table and we will gather a few things for you."

Once she was seated at a small round table, Caroline tried to take her mind off her wooziness by gazing at the variety of stained glass windows. Each was extremely tall and consisted of a myriad of colors that made up intricate patterns. One particular window really captured her and she stared at it open mouthed, taking in the deep greens and blues with random highlights of yellow and white.

"Gorgeous, aren't they?" Cecil said, snapping Caroline out of her reverie.

"Yeah," was all she could say.

"Most of the windows are over eight hundred years old," Cecil informed her. "The one you were looking at is actually a bit newer. It is only five hundred years old. One of our most famous graduates made it to replace one that had been damaged during an incident."

"What happened?" Caroline asked, noticing her dizziness had diminished a bit from the distractions.

"All in good time, all in good time," Cecil responded. "Now might I suggest you start out with some of that toast and jam made by one of the most amazing Chems from blackberries grown by our team of Biologics."

"I thought there were only Moon Borns here," Caroline said

with her mouth full. She had stuffed half a slice in her mouth as soon as Cecil had pointed it out.

"Of course not!" Cecil said, "That would make no sense. There is a whole town outside the walls of Terradune filled with Earth Borns and even a few Star Borns. Of course, we must be very careful about who we invite to live here and only Moon Borns can walk unsupervised within the walls."

Caroline had several questions swimming around her brain as she took several large gulps of orange juice. It was like nothing she had ever tasted at home. It also caused her to miss her opening to ask her questions as Cecil started up again.

"I am going to ask Norah to take you through the curriculum that you will be starting today. I must warn you that it will be quite intensive for at least the first several weeks. We had expected you much sooner."

"Yeah, well…" Caroline started to explain the long sailing trip.

"No need to delve into it," Cecil said, picking up on her embarrassment. "Every Moon Born has their own path to Terradune. Now, Norah, if you wouldn't mind?"

Norah took another quick bite of the scrambled eggs in front of her and then wiped her mouth as she reached down into the satchel by her feet and pulled out a bright red folder. She opened it, slid out a sheet of paper, and handed it to Caroline. As she scanned it, Caroline could tell it was a list of classes and times, but it did not resemble what she expected. There was no sign of Math, English, History, or Science.

"That's a funny face," Norah said warmly, noticing Caroline's furrowed brow and wide eyes. "I know it doesn't make much sense, but I can explain. We will be in all the same classes this year and you can ask me questions whenever you want. Most of the students here were in advanced classes when I arrived, so I didn't get much help figuring things out."

"We're so sorry about that…" Cecil interjected.

"Oh, don't worry about it!" Norah said brightly. "I love a good puzzle. Anyway, when I heard you were coming, I tried to jot down some tips and tricks that will help you get up to speed more quickly. That's our class schedule. I can tell you about each one, but it looks like you already have a question."

"Yeah," Caroline confirmed. "I can see these class names on the left side, but why are there so many times listed next to them?"

"Oh yeah! I forgot about that. We follow the lunar calendar here. I know… It seems like it's a dumb dad joke, but we *are* Moon Borns after all! Those times show when your class is each day of the month. Your schedule is different every day. I had to hang it up in my room and check it every day for the first couple of months. Now I've pretty much gotten the hang of it."

"Every day of the month? You're saying we don't even get weekends off?" Caroline asked, hoping she had heard wrong.

"Nope," Norah answered. "It's not that bad though. The teachers break stuff up and work fun things into the classes."

Caroline looked at her skeptically, but Norah didn't notice because she was already focusing back on the schedule and pointing at the first one on the list.

"Our first class today is Fundamentals. I have to warn you, this one is *a lot* of reading. I think my eyeballs almost fell out of my head the first week. It's pretty interesting stuff though and Sharla is a really good teacher. It's just like it sounds, though. You're gonna learn the basics of Moon Born theory and the three core techniques."

"What are those?" Caroline asked earnestly.

"Oh… They said you hadn't received any training yet, but I had kinda assumed you knew that at least."

Caroline's face turned beet red with embarrassment.

"No no no! It's cool," Norah said, trying to pull her foot out of her mouth. "You'll catch up! The core techniques are reflection, disruption, and absorption. We've only just started diving more deeply into reflection and the other two use up a ton of energy, so they won't start on them until we are a bit further along."

A single, loud "CLANG!" rang out suddenly and Caroline looked to Cecil to explain.

"That means breakfast time is over and you need to head to your first class," he explained.

"But…" Caroline started to protest.

"Don't worry, Norah will be with you all day and I will try to check in on you at dinner time," he assured her.

"C'mon!" Norah encouraged as she shoved the folder back in her bag and hoisted her satchel over her shoulder.

Caroline quickly speared a piece of pineapple with her fork and shoved it in her mouth. She started to pick up her tray, following Norah's lead, but had to stop and lean on the table as she savored the burst of sweet and tart in her mouth.

Norah looked at Caroline and smiled as she said, "I told you the food was good."

Caroline smiled back, grateful to have someone to rely on. It made her feel a bit less alone.

❧

They worked their way out of the hall and then Norah led her on a run through winding passages that Caroline tried to memorize, eventually arriving outside a nondescript wooden door. Norah grabbed the large iron ring and turned it to the right, then she shoved her shoulder into the door and pushed hard. It opened with a large groan and they stepped inside.

Caroline looked around and saw it was a small room with two large, round tables almost filling it. Most of the chairs were filled with kids around Caroline's age or a bit older, so she assumed they were her fellow students. Norah pointed out two chairs open on the opposite side of the room and they shimmied behind some of the students to make their way there. As soon as they sat down, the door groaned loudly again and a woman stepped in briskly, shutting the door with a loud slam behind her and making Caroline jump. She wore flowing blue robes with gold edging that gave her a regal look and she was carrying an ornate book that looked similar to the Book of Star Born.

Sharla scanned the room as if looking for something and then asked, "Has anyone seen Zora this morning?"

All of the students shook their heads or murmured soft no's.

The woman rolled her eyes and let out an exasperated sigh. Then she began to open the book in front of her when the door opened loudly again and a girl hurried in, panting and a little sweaty.

"You're late again, Zora," Sharla said sternly.

"I know! I know! I was practicing Dream Analysis!" she said as she slid behind the chairs to make her way to the last empty chair next to Caroline.

"Got it, you overslept again," Sharla said.

"No! I'm serious! I think I'm getting good at it!" Zora protested.

"Zora, we don't start teaching dream analysis until year three."

"What can I say? I'm an advanced student!" Zora said brightly.

"How about you apply yourself to this class so you don't have to do extra evening study with me?" Sharla counseled and Zora realized it was no good to keep going back and forth.

Sharla's eyes then shifted over to Caroline and they brightened with recognition.

"Ah yes! Our new student is here!" she said warmly. "Why don't you introduce yourself?"

"Well... My name is Caroline and... um..." she said hesitatingly.

"How about where you are from and how you got here?" Sharla coached.

"Well, I'm from a town called Kensington in California," Caroline started to answer.

"Oh! I'm from California, too!" a tall girl at the other table said excitedly.

"Alella, you'll get your chance in a moment," Sharla said.

"So... um... I kinda sailed here?" Caroline continued and the room erupted in murmurs.

"That's great!" Sharla said, signaling the group to quiet down. "Everyone finds their way to Terradune in different ways, but I believe Bea over there also came by sea."

A girl with a long braid hanging down her back gave a huge nod and made a face as if it had been as much of an ordeal as Caroline had experienced.

"Yeah, we kinda got stuck in the doldrums for a while..." Caroline continued.

"Ah, yes! We discussed Resistance quite a bit last week. Can anyone share some of the key points?" Sharla asked the class and a boy a couple seats away from her raised his hand quickly.

"Yes, Niels," she said.

"Resistance is when Moon Borns close themselves off to their abilities," he said in a lightly accented voice that Caroline couldn't place. "It is most common with extreme emotions, particularly anger or depression."

"Very good! Someone did the reading. Can anyone else remember some of the more obscure causes?" Sharla continued.

"Interference?" Norah said tentatively.

"Yes, continue," Sharla said.

"When a Moon Born is misaligned with the natural frequency of their environment, it can sometimes cause a form of interference that blocks their abilities in specific ways. I just can't remember what those are…"

"I can help you out on that part," Sharla said warmly. "Interference is most common when a Moon Born needs to align with an Earth Born. There are only certain types of Earth Borns that we can align with, so it is a very uncommon occurrence. I believe you may have been misaligned with your Wayfarer, correct?"

"Yeah…" Caroline said, marveling at the explanation for what she had experienced.

"What's a Wayfarer?" Zora asked.

"Well that's a whole different lesson and not something we will be covering today," Sharla answered, returning to her book and flipping through pages rapidly.

The next thing Caroline knew, an hour had flown by as they had learned about the reason Reflection takes less energy to perform. The discussion had gotten quite detailed and a lot of it had gone right over Caroline's head, but she was just excited to finally be learning something about her abilities and she couldn't keep a smile off her face. The next thing she knew, Norah was leading her through several narrow passageways and down several flights of stairs with a few of their classmates close behind.

They finally found themselves on a large terrace that overlooked the crashing waves below. There was a small semicircle of chairs facing a man who was intensely focused on a brass plate set on a small table in front of him. He was etching an intricate pattern onto it and Caroline had a strong urge to stand over his shoulder and watch.

"This is my favorite class," Norah said. "Expression is all about how we express our abilities through movement, artwork, writing and music. That's our teacher, Jeremy."

On that note, Jeremy looked up and noticed the group gathered off to the side. He waved his hand, gesturing for them to take their seats. Once everyone was settled, he looked around with piercing blue eyes and asked, "Who wants to share first?"

Nobody moved a muscle.

"Really? Nobody?" he asked.

"I can go," Norah said so quietly that Caroline was sure Jeremy couldn't hear, but he focused quickly on her and nodded.

Norah reached down into her satchel and pulled out one of the most gorgeous books Caroline had ever seen. Just like the book Sharla had pulled out in class, Norah's had an ornate design on it and, even in the daylight, she could detect a faint glow emanating from it. Jeremy stood up and walked over. He held out his hand and Norah placed the book in it tentatively. Then he ran his fingers over every part of the cover, analyzing it as if it were under a microscope.

"This is exceptional work," Jeremy said seriously and Norah's face flushed with embarrassment.

"What do you think?" Jeremy asked as he handed it to Caroline. She took the book and marveled at the fine details of the pattern that rippled across the soft leather on the cover. The glowing of the raised portions entranced her and she followed the urge to open the book. As soon as she did, the blank first page started to write itself and she began to read it.

Confidence is the key.
You can't hesitate for a second or you will not be able to
maintain your focus.
Commit to the idea that feels right. Trusting your instincts
is best when you aren't sure what to do.

"Huh?" Caroline said out loud, though she had meant to just say it in her own head.

"That is a strong connection. You should be able to finish it in the next few classes," Jeremy said to Norah, clearly proud of her.

"But what does this mean?" Caroline asked, confused and feeling frustration tickling the back of her brain.

"The book is a vessel," Jeremy explained. "You will learn how to make your own this year. It will be one of the ways you will learn our ways and find your own path with your abilities."

Jeremy walked back to the table and called on Niels to share, but Caroline's confusion and frustration burst out of her.

"You didn't answer my question," she snapped.

Jeremy's head whipped toward her with surprise in his eyes. "Excuse me?"

"What does this mean?" she said, thrusting the open book toward him.

Jeremy strode over in two long steps and took the book from her and read the short passage that had appeared for Caroline. He took a deep breath and smiled, then closed the book and handed it back to Norah.

"I like your inquisitiveness, but you're going to need to work on mastering that temper," Jeremy said and he saw the fiery anger as it erupted on her face and tensed up her body.

"Wait a moment," he said calmly, "I will explain, but I need to know you are open to listening and that is not possible when you are upset. Please know, I was not intending to be difficult. I like to throw people into class and provide an environment for exploration. However, that isn't always the best approach and I can see from your reaction that you would like a bit more guidance."

"Yes…" Caroline said quietly, feeling the flames inside her die down to a low smolder.

"Alright then," Jeremy continued. " This book contains Norah's learnings since she created it. I am guessing she was thinking about Shijian class when she was working on it last night."

"Yeah… It was a tough class," Norah admitted.

"Does this answer help you understand a bit more?" Jeremy asked.

Caroline gave a slow single nod, accepting his explanation.

"Now, I have a question," Jeremy said, and Caroline cocked her head to the side in anticipation. "How were you able to get the book to reveal itself to you?"

Caroline just shrugged.

"So, you've never interacted with a Moon Born text?"

"No…"

"I see… That's very interesting…" Jeremy responded, clearly absorbed in his own thoughts.

Caroline waited for Jeremy to explain further, but he just stood there, staring at the stone floor. All the other students remained quiet, fidgeting or looking around awkwardly. Just as she was unable to take the waiting any longer, Jeremy looked up and said, "Caroline, would you please return here after Shijian this afternoon? I can explain more then. For the remainder of class, I'd like the rest of the students to share the progress they have made on their books. If we have some time, we may be able to do an exploratory exercise or two."

~§~

At the end of class, Caroline followed Norah and the rest of the students to another narrow alleyway that branched off from the terrace. At first, there was very little of the normal chatter that usually followed kids wherever they went. Then, Niels and Ryan began bantering in the back about how much they were going to eat for lunch and the floodgates were opened. The voices grew louder and the echoes against the high walls around them made the cacophony difficult to decipher for anyone who may have tried to listen in.

"What's Shijian?" Caroline asked Norah as they walked along.

"Ugh… It's our last class of the day, every day. I guess the best way to describe it is the Moon Born martial art."

Caroline's eyes opened wide in excitement, waiting for Norah to explain more.

"Don't get too amped up for it," Norah cautioned. "It is so hard. I mean, I can't figure it out at all. I think Steven is gonna flunk me and I'll be stuck doing the same exercises for the rest of my time here…"

"It's really that bad?" Caroline asked, wondering how something that sounded so cool could be the worst class.

"She's totally right," Bea said from behind her. "We've been stuck doing the same thing for months now and only Ryan has been able to start getting it a little bit right. Steven won't let us move on until we master the first sequence, though."

"Let's talk about something else," Zora chimed in. "Think Marina will make us do a Patience exercise in Symmetry today?"

"If she does, you better figure out a better explanation than 'Dream Analysis' when you start snoring," Bea quipped and the whole group began laughing loudly.

A few minutes later, they arrived at their next class and they walked into the first room that seemed somewhat like a normal classroom. There were desks lined up in the middle and something that looked like a whiteboard at the front of the classroom. However, every inch of the walls were covered with ornate paintings and drawings. There was also a large rug at the front of the class and their teacher was sitting in the center of it with closed eyes.

Zora pretended to stumble and fall asleep and the others struggled to stifle their chuckles. With that sound, Marina's eyes opened quickly and the students hurried to their seats, sat down, and pulled out thick books from their bags along with notebooks and pencils. Marina didn't say a word, she just strode between the desks briskly toward the back of the classroom. Caroline started to turn to see what Marina was doing, but Norah caught her eye and shook her head before facing forward again and staring at the blank board.

Caroline heard the soft padding of Marina's footsteps coming back toward them and then stopped right next to her desk. She looked up and saw Marina was holding a copy of the book along with a notebook and a box of pencils. Caroline reached up and took them and Marina said curtly, "You can get a bag from the supply room at lunchtime."

Marina then walked quickly to the front of the room and said, "Please open your books to page fifty-eight."

Everyone rushed to follow her instructions and Caroline did the same. What she saw on the page, though, made her heart sink. It was filled with complex math that she had never seen before. She looked around and saw the other students opening their notebooks and the pages were filled with their notes and answers to problems. That was when the panic really set in for

Caroline and she felt sick, with beads of sweat forming at her hairline and slowly sliding down the sides of her face.

"So, who did their homework?" Marina asked the group and everyone, but Caroline, raised their hands slowly.

"OK… Who thinks they got the answer to number one?"

Nobody raised their hand.

"Really?!" Marina asked, genuinely not believing them. "C'mon people! This is basic trigonometry."

"Fifty-three?" Ryan said uncertainly from the back of the classroom.

Marina lifted her glasses up and rubbed her eyes while she took a deep sigh.

"People," she said. "This is why you all are having a hard time with Shijian! You need to understand the math of angles to be able to properly perform a redirection defense. All these problems are related to the form you are learning."

Caroline glanced around the classroom and everyone had a nervous or sheepish face. Suddenly, she was not as nervous anymore. All of them were in over their heads together. Then she looked back up and found Marina staring right at her.

"Care to venture a guess?" Marina asked.

"This… is way beyond what I learned in school last year," Caroline responded.

"Perhaps," Marina said skeptically. "I guess a refresher is in order since we have a new student starting today?"

She walked up to the board and made several subtle gestures with her hands and diagrams began to appear showing several different angles. Marina then spent the next hour taking the class through the first two problems on the page they were on in the book. By the end of the class, Caroline's brain felt like mush, but she did think she had learned something. What that was, she wasn't sure yet.

She was in a bit of a haze all the way back to the hall for lunch and it wasn't until she had eaten half of her food that her brain turned back on again.

"Earth to Caroline!" she heard Zora say.

"Huh?" Caroline replied.

"I think she's finally back!" Zora cheered and the others giggled.

"Don't worry, we all had the same reaction during our first Symmetry classes," Bea said.

"It's not always like that," Norah counseled. "We all just seem to have a block on things right now."

"I wouldn't be surprised if Marina's head explodes if we don't get the hang of it soon," Niels said seriously.

"Oh, don't be so dramatic," Bea said in annoyance. "They're just pushing us harder than normal because of the conflict. They need us to be ready as soon as possible."

"How do *you* know so much?" Niels retorted.

"I overheard my mom talking with Cecil yesterday," Bea answered simply.

"Your mom is here?" Caroline asked.

"Yeah, I grew up in the town just outside the gates," Bea explained. "Been here all my life. My dad is an Earth Born, so we couldn't live inside the walls. It's not common that Moon Borns have an Earth Born parent. Guess I'm just lucky!"

Before Caroline could ask any more questions, however, the loud "CLANG!" of the bell rang out and everyone immediately started packing up and bussing their trays before heading to their next class. She followed everyone out the doors, but instead of leading her down another twisting path of alleys, they all just stood around scanning the huge courtyard for something.

"There she is," Norah said brightly. "Cariann! Over here!"

A wide smile spread across a young woman's face who had just entered the courtyard from the opposite side. She waved and then jogged over quickly. When she reached them, the students gathered around her, saying their hellos.

"Ah, Caroline! So great to finally meet you!" Cariann said, finally noticing her new student. Caroline just gave a nervous wave.

"OK, everyone, who's ready to learn more about the origins of the tribes?" Cariann said enthusiastically.

The entire group erupted in excited chatter.

"To the library!" Cariann shouted and they all hustled over to where she had emerged before.

She led them to two large metal doors and placed her hand on the one part of the right door that did not have any ornamentation. The door began to glow around her hand and then it emitted several loud clicks before opening wide. The scent of old books and dust swirled around the group immediately and Caroline felt a pang of nostalgia for Adam's bookshop back home.

Nothing could have prepared Caroline for the scale of the space. It was gargantuan with the walls covered in volumes. Directly in front of them was an elevator that looked incredibly old, made out of sculpted metal to form shapes she didn't know were possible to make by hand. Directly behind the elevator was a large, open shaft that showed floors upon floors of the library that stretched below them, fading into darkness. Above them were several more floors and a beautiful stained glass roof.

Caroline followed the group as they went down a hallway between two bookshelves off to the right. At the end of the hall there was a large room with several tables set up, each holding an ancient-looking book. They spent the next hour and a half looking through the books and hearing about the years follow-ing the Calamity. While Caroline knew the broad outlines of the story, the details she learned that day brought it to life. Instantly, she knew this would be one of her favorite classes.

⁂

As they exited the library at the end of their class, Norah pulled Caroline aside and said, "If you want to change into some of your old clothes for Shijian, we have a little extra time before it starts. Some of the others prefer it."

Caroline shrugged and said, "I have no idea what to expect. Might as well just go there."

Norah nodded in acceptance and they walked over to the staircase where they had met that morning. Instead of going up, however, they went down the steps directly next to it and descended five flights before Norah led them along a cool, dimly lit corridor. At the end of it was another simple wood door that creaked loudly when they pushed it open.

Inside, Caroline was struck by how much it resembled the secret training cavern in which she had spent several months with her friends, helping Leo to master techniques that would help him solve The Crucible. There were targets arrayed around the large room and two men were standing in the center chatting in low tones. They didn't acknowledge Norah and Caroline when they walked in, nor did they stop their conversation until all the students arrived.

One of the men turned to look and see everyone was present and then he looked down at his watch before raising an eyebrow and glaring at the group.

"Never be late to this class," Norah whispered to Caroline and she could understand why. Steven was intimidating. He was tall and wiry, with all the hair on his head closely cropped, even his steel gray beard. It was the intensity that radiated off of him that was his most defining characteristic.

"Today's the day!" Steven called out from across the room. "Today, one of you will redirect an attack with *precision*!"

He gave the other man a slight nod and then took several steps towards the students.

"Bea! You lead warmups today!" he called out and then strolled back to continue his conversation.

Bea immediately started jogging towards the wall and the other students fell in line behind her, with Caroline taking up the rear. She took them around the perimeter of the room five times and then finished up where they had gathered at the start of class. Everyone had arranged themselves in two neat rows of five. Then Bea led the group in calisthenics and dynamic stretches for ten minutes. By the end of it, Caroline felt like she'd had a workout, but it was only the beginning of class.

As soon as Bea was finished, Steven called out, "Ready stance!"

All of the students adopted a fighting stance with one foot in front and the other stretched out behind them. Each of their hands were held up as if ready for an attack, but, instead of making fists, their hands were open with the fingers pressed together. Caroline did her best to copy them as Steven strode around them, looking for something to correct. When he reached Caroline, he adjusted both of her feet, her shoulders, and her hands before he was satisfied with what he saw.

As he walked back out in front of the group, Steven called out, "First form!"

The class began moving through several choreographed motions in unison and she did her best to watch and mimic them. At the end, they all returned to the ready stance and let out a loud "Kiai!" that startled Caroline.

"Again!" Steven called out and the group repeated the pattern. He did this several more times, so that Caroline felt like she had started to get the hang of it by the fifth repetition.

"Shall we, Keith?" Steven said to the other man who nodded in response.

They faced each other and then Keith created a fireball in his left hand.

"Redirection is about awareness," he said as Keith threw a fireball at him. Steven started the beginning of the First Form and moved his body and hands to intercept the fireball and send it smashing into a target on the opposite end of the room.

"Awareness of your surroundings," Steven continued as he moved into the next position of the form and Keith sent another fireball at him that he redirected into the target along the wall to the right.

"Awareness of yourself, both physically and mentally," he said as he moved into the next position and sent Keith's fireball into the target on the left wall.

"And awareness of your opponent," Steven said as Keith sent a large fireball that was reflected into a target directly over him on the ceiling.

"You must not get distracted," Steven said as he finished in ready stance. "With distraction comes imbalance and that can lead to unintended outcomes and possibly catastrophe."

Steven stood up straight and walked over to stand in front of Ryan.

"Would you like to pick up where we left off yesterday?" he asked.

"I guess so," Ryan answered tentatively.

"Such enthusiasm!" Steven said sarcastically.

Ryan followed him into the center of the room while the rest of the group moved behind a set of screens that slid out from a spot in the wall that Caroline hadn't noticed before. Keith created a fireball the size of a softball and waited. Steven muttered a few things in Ryan's ear and then stepped away. After several seconds, Ryan finally nodded at Keith who tossed the fireball underhand.

Caroline watched as Ryan started the first movements of the form, but she noticed he was going a bit too fast. He arrived too early and intercepted the attack when he had finished, sending the fireball above the target on the far wall.

"Slow down," Steven coached and Caroline grinned to herself, relishing that she had been correct.

Ryan was able to correct his pace and managed to strike the outer rings of the remaining targets. When he was done, Steven patted him on the shoulder and said, "You're making progress. Take a break and you can have another go shortly."

Caroline watched Norah go next and could tell immediately why she was struggling in this class. She was so nervous that her movements were not steady and her hands were shaking. The pressure she was putting on herself was leading her to send the fireball careening off in random directions. She was in good company, though. Most of the rest of the class seemed to have the same difficulties.

When everyone else had a turn, Steven finally pointed at Caroline and called out, "Your turn!"

Caroline worked her way around the others standing behind the screens and walked confidently to the center of the room. She immediately got in ready stance and nodded at Keith who looked tentatively at Steven. He stared at Caroline and she felt him sizing her up and deciding how he would react. Then he looked back at Keith and gave him a shrug as if to say, "Let's see what she's got."

Keith lit up a fireball as Steven stepped back several paces. Like the other students before her, he tossed the ball lightly towards her and she started her form, meeting the ball at just the right moment and launching it directly at the target. Excitement rippled through her as she tried to stay focused on the form and move to the next position, but she was too fast and the ball flew off and smashed well away from the target. Then, in frustration, she adjusted too much and went too slow. When she redirected the fireball this time she sent it directly at the screens and the students all screamed as it splashed across the glass.

"Hold up! Hold up!" Steven called out and Keith stopped sending fireballs.

Steven walked over to Caroline and leaned close to her ear and said, "Not horrible. Head on back now."

"I'd like another chance," Caroline said.

"Maybe tomorrow," Steven responded.

"How about now?" Caroline insisted, her voice firm and Steven's eyes flashed in anger.

"How about you listen to your teacher," he whispered back through clenched teeth.

Realizing it wasn't a good idea to go head-to-head with a teacher on her first day, she thought for a moment and realized what she wanted to say.

"I got too excited and fell out of the rhythm," she said. "I think I can get it if you give me another chance.

Steven pulled back, clearly surprised by Caroline's comment, and stroked his beard as he considered what she said. Then he nodded to her and started to whistle *Twinkle Twinkle Little Star* as he walked away. When he was a safe distance, he looked over to Keith and said, "She's going again."

That's when it clicked for Caroline. He had given her a clue! So, after she settled into ready stance and saw Keith send the first fireball, she started to hum the song to herself while moving into her first position. As she finished the first verse, she was in perfect position to send the fireball right at the bullseye of the first target. The same thing happened for the second and third targets. And finally, as she finished the form, she sang out loud, "Like a diamond in the sky," as she sent the last fireball at the target in the ceiling.

A deep sense of satisfaction settled over her and she heard her classmates start to let out cheers of excitement. She turned to Steven and he stood up straight and bowed to her. She returned the bow in respect for her teacher and then strode back to the screens to be mobbed by the others.

When they left the class, Norah was very quiet and Caroline could tell something wasn't right. They emerged from the stairwell into the courtyard and Norah tried to hurry away, but Caroline caught her arm and pulled her back.

"What's going on?" she asked Norah.

Tears immediately started flowing and with a shaky voice, Norah answered, "That was your *first* class and you instantly figured out the form. I feel like a failure!"

Caroline immediately pulled her into a tight hug, feeling such a close bond with her even though they had just met. They just stood there for a minute and, when Caroline could feel the sobs dying down, she pulled back and looked to see if Norah was OK.

"Sorry…" Norah said in embarrassment.

"No, it's fine!" Caroline assured her. "I don't know why it just clicked for me today… But I do know I can help you figure it out."

"Really?" Norah asked, hopefully.

"Definitely."

"Oh, wait! You are supposed to meet with Jeremy now. I can show you the way," Norah said.

"I think I can remember the way," Caroline said. "I'll see you at dinner later."

Norah looked at her as if to say, "Are you sure?" and Caroline gave her a confident nod before turning and heading down the corridor towards the path to the terrace. She did get lost twice, but was able to retrace the path eventually and arrived at the terrace as the late afternoon sun bathed it in a golden glow. Jeremy was sitting there with what looked like one of the older students. His back was to Caroline, but he somehow knew she was there and waved for her to take a seat in the empty chair at the table.

As she sat down, Caroline saw they were looking at pictures of drawings and paintings. When she looked more closely she realized they were looking at *her* artwork and she was mortified.

"How did you… Those are private… I can't believe…" she stammered.

"I'm sorry," Jeremy said, feeling her emotions. "It wasn't our intent to invade your privacy. Your mother provided some pictures of your artwork to Rebecca and she shared them with us so we could determine the best approach to help you catch up."

"These are really marvelous," the older student said, flipping through quickly and finding two of Caroline's favorite pieces.

"You made these more than a year ago?" Jeremy asked and

Caroline nodded, still unable to speak from the shock of her work being shared without her permission.

"It's a shame there wasn't a Moon Born nearby your tribe," he lamented. "We would've been able to start your education much sooner… Anyway, you're here now and we have a plan for you. I'd like to introduce you to Juliet. She will be working with you in the evenings for your first few months here. She is one of our top students and I am very excited to see what you're able to accomplish together."

"I'm very pleased to meet you," Juliet said warmly.

"She will be able to help you catch up in all of your subjects, but I would like the two of you to focus on building your book first. This is a deeply personal activity, so Juliet will just be your guide. Ultimately, you will make all the decisions."

Something didn't sit right with Caroline and she sat there thinking for a minute, trying to take in the new information.

"Do any of the other students have this kind of help?" she asked and Jeremy shook his head.

"Does that mean something is wrong with me?" she asked anxiously.

"Not at all," Jeremy said, clearly surprised this was what she was thinking. "On the contrary, you are a remarkable Moon Born."

"Then why me?" she asked simply.

Jeremy and Juliet exchanged a look and Caroline could tell a whole conversation passed between them without a word being uttered out loud.

"I know this isn't the answer you are looking for and please know we are not trying to hide anything, but we think it is better to not explain anything further at this time," Jeremy said.

"Why?" Caroline pushed further.

"Because our people have learned over thousands of years that sometimes it is better to let things unfold. It's important to provide the right information at the right time," Jeremy explained, but Caroline clearly wasn't satisfied.

"Listen," Juliet interjected. "I promise that I will make sure to share information with you when you're ready for it. We'll be working closely together, so I will be able to know when it is the right time. Do you think you can trust me?"

Caroline looked at Juliet long and hard and felt like she was telling the truth. So she nodded and asked, "So, we'll start tomorrow?"

"Naa…" Juliet said with a wink. "Let's start right now."

9

BETRAYAL

HE BLUE BANNER hung limply on its pole, unable to move since not a bit of wind was able to reach it. Five powerful Earth Borns surrounded it and they had erected a crude set of barriers that made it difficult to see. However, Ania knew it was there as she pulled her hand back from the large tree root she was kneeling next to. She moved quietly back to the rest of her team and smiled.

"They seriously think they can protect it with a small team and that janky barrier?" she asked rhetorically.

"Give us the lowdown," Leo requested.

"There are five of them," Ania began. "All of them are Earth Borns, but I can't tell what kind. Their flag is in the center of that mess of stuff that is blocking our view. There's nobody behind it though, so if we get through them, nothing will stop us from capturing it."

"We should figure out a way to take them out one-by-one quietly, so they don't raise the alarm," Meimei said.

"Are you kidding me?!" Ania responded in frustration. "We are more powerful than them. We are better trained and have more experience. *And* we have a Star Born with us who can make us unbeatable. I say we go for a full frontal assault and just dominate them."

"That's what you always want to do," Stella said in a slightly bored and annoyed voice.

"Yeah and you never listen to me. I go along with your plans every single time, how 'bout we try it my way for once?"

"It's too risky," Meimei responded.

"I, for one, love a little risk," Aran said with a bright grin.

"Yes, we remember last week when you thought you could jump between two trees to get past that flame wall the other team set up," Stella said, rolling her eyes. "You're lucky you just broke your leg and not your head."

"Meh, Ernest fixed me right up," Aran said casually.

"You're not helping here," Ania said to him with gritted teeth.

"Ania is right," Leo said and everyone turned to him in surprise.

"We never try her approach and how are we going to learn if we don't explore all our options?" he added.

Meimei and Stella looked at him thoughtfully, recognizing he was making a decent point.

"So, what's the play then?" Leo asked Ania, assuming everyone was on board now.

"You enhance me to the max," Ania said, an excited grin spreading across her face. "I will incapacitate as many of them as I can while Meimei and Stella pick up anyone I miss."

"And what do I do?" Aran asked, feeling left out.

"I was just getting to that," Ania said, her enthusiasm growing.

"You will sneak one of your critters in while we are fighting and have them steal the flag."

Aran leaned back, satisfied with his role.

"Any objections?" Leo asked the group and everyone shook their heads silently.

"OK, well, I guess we should get this show on the road!" Ania said, looking at Leo as she crawled back to the root she had been using to survey this situation before.

Just as Leo was about to begin enhancing her abilities, Ania turned to look at him and asked very seriously, "What is the real reason you took my side back there?"

"Huh?" Leo said, surprised by the question and not knowing how to respond.

"We've won all of our matches so far and you almost always support the most careful strategy. Why are you backing me up today?" she asked.

Leo thought about it for a moment, trying to decide what he wanted to say, and settled on the truth.

"I want to horribly embarrass Jordan's team," he said matter-of-factly. "He was a fool to leave their flag with such little protection and I want him to feel this loss."

"Dude, really? I thought you were over that," Ania chided.

"Look, I took your side. We're going to bash our way through them and steal their flag. Just give me this," Leo said.

Ania stared at him cooly for several seconds and then said brightly, "Okie doke!"

Then she turned back around and placed both of her hands on the root. Leo began his preparations and synchronized his pattern with hers. When he felt that she was ready, he sent a large amount of energy into her rapidly and heard her say, "That's the stuff!" as she channeled it into the root. Immediately, a large number of tendrils erupted from the ground and wrapped themselves around three of the five flag defenders. Their arms and legs were pinned and they were pushed half a foot into the air, wobbling back and forth slightly.

Out of the corner of his eye, Leo saw Meimei and Stella spring out of the bushes to attack the remaining two defenders. He followed them as they ran past the defenders that Ania had trapped, a mass of paintballs swirling around Meimei and Stella's torso and arms covered in a mass of water. However, one of the defenders began to grow rapidly and the thick root wrapped around her was clearly straining to contain her.

Ania gasped out in pain as the root ripped apart and the now huge defender landed on her feet and began reaching for Meimei.

"Oh shoot!" she yelped as she tried to change direction and duck out of reach.

The defender's giant hand grasped only air as Meimei dropped to the ground and she sent several paintballs hurtling back in response. Two splattered on a giant bicep and the defender let out a roar of anger as she started to run after Meimei reaching with her other hand.

In the meantime, Stella had her hands full as well, battling one of the defenders that Ania hadn't reached. Both were water elementals and it was difficult for Leo to see what was happening as the air was so full of water vapor around them that it created a thick fog.

The battle was not going well and Leo saw that his friends needed help. He began to pull back some energy from Ania so he could jump into the fray, and she gasped loudly.

"No!" she said, panting. "I can't hold them without your help! They're really strong!"

Leo gritted his teeth and stopped pulling back his energy for a moment, but then Jordan strode into view from behind the barriers. Leo realized they had been tricked and he stared angrily into Jordan's eyes. In response, dark black armor erupted all over Jordan's body and a large white sword made of energy extended from his forearm.

A fire ignited within Leo and he withdrew all his power from Ania quickly, ignoring her pleas, and enfolded his body in rippling blue armor. As Leo was about to form his own sword, Jordan charged at him. Leo was briefly surprised just how fast Jordan could run, but he reset quickly and began charging as well. The distance closed in seconds and they slammed into each other, static electricity arcing off their armor and setting dry leaves and pine needles on fire around them.

Jordan raised his sword high and began to swing it down onto Leo's shoulder, but Leo pivoted and created a golden shield matching Maranda's pattern. The sword ricocheted off it and Jordan tipped over as he started to lose his balance. He threw his arms out to steady himself and his sword disappeared. Leo noticed his advantage and formed a huge hammer over his fist, then swung it across his body towards Jordan's chest, who twisted around and grabbed it with both hands. The force of the impact pushed Jordan back, his feet creating deep grooves in the ground, and Leo could barely hear Aran yelling loudly over the crackles of the two competing armors meeting.

Leo turned his head briefly to see why Aran was calling out and saw him holding the blue banner over his head. They had won and Leo smiled, relishing the moment until Jordan slammed him into the ground and raised his arms, intending to slam his fists into Leo's chest.

"That's enough now, Jordan," they heard Ernest say calmly and both looked over to see their teacher standing a few feet away with his usual penetrating glare. They pulled their armor back in and Jordan got off of Leo, who pushed himself up and dusted off his clothes. He saw Ania standing behind Ernest and smiled at her, acknowledging her plan worked. She just stared at him coldly.

"Why are you smiling, Leo?" Ernest asked.

"Well, we won," Leo responded smugly, stealing a quick look at Jordan who was scowling.

"Did you?" Ernest probed.

"We got their flag, right?" Leo answered.

"But at what cost?"

"What do you mean?"

"If this were a real battle, you and your entire team would likely have died. You chose an aggressive strategy and then deviated from it because you were challenged by a rival. You didn't fully assess the situation, got surprised by your opponent, diminished the fighting capacity of your team so you could do what? Get into a fist fight?"

Jordan snorted in satisfaction from the tongue lashing that Leo was receiving.

"You were no better," Ernest said calmly, turning his attention to Jordan. "You had the upper hand. All you had to do was wait, but you had to satisfy your childish impulse to gloat. As a result, you were unable to maintain your defense and they ended up winning."

"Look, it's just capture the flag..." Jordan began to protest.

"Yes! It is just capture the flag!" Ernest snapped and everyone's entire attention was focused on the conversation now. Ernest had always spoken in the same calm, probing tone. Until that moment.

"When are you two going to fully understand that what we do here is meant to prepare you for life and death situations?"

Ernest continued. "At some point, you're going to have to fight alongside each other! How is that going to be possible if you don't find a way to get along?"

Leo hung his head, not knowing what to say, but still adamant that he would never fight alongside Jordan.

"How're we gonna solve this?" Ernest asked exasperatedly, sensing his words were not getting through.

"By mixing up the teams," Stella said from behind Leo. "I'll join Jordan's team."

Leo whirled around, his mouth hanging open, unable to accept one of his closest friends had just volunteered to join his enemy. She just looked back at him with sadness, her face red from holding back her emotions.

"Me too," Ania said from Leo's left and his heartbeat pounded in his ears as he turned to stare at her.

"They're right, this has to end," Ania said, calmly meeting Leo's stare.

"Very well," Ernest said. "You two will join the blue team and Luisa and Vivi will join the gold team. Let's hope for all our sake this works."

With that, Ernest turned and walked away and the group quietly dispersed.

❧

Leo spent the rest of the afternoon and evening in a haze. His mind was stuck in a loop, remembering his friends' betrayal. They were even sitting with Jordan during dinner and the ache in Leo's chest from seeing the sight was so painful that he walked right out of the cafeteria without eating a bite. He just started meandering aimlessly down random paths and eventually found himself near where he started.

It was just past dusk and the moon hadn't risen yet, so the paths were all dark. He didn't want to be around anyone, so he walked over to a tree a little ways off the path and sat at its base. He just wanted the pain to go away and he knew it wouldn't while his mind kept returning to the end of training that day.

That was when he remembered one of the earliest lessons he had studied in the Book of Star Born. Since his sensitivities were both an asset and a liability, he needed to know how to calm his emotions to return to a state of equilibrium. When really emotional, he needed to use meditation to reach that state and he knew the one he should try. It took multiple steps and the first one involved mindfulness. So, he began to take in his surroundings. He smelled the air cooling from a warm day with hints of pine and food cooking in the cafeteria. He heard the rustling of animals going to sleep for the night or just waking up. He looked around and saw the dark shadows cast from the lights outside the different buildings around him.

As he began to relax and feel his breaths become deeper, he saw some movement in the shadows near the building just across from him. Leo tried to continue with his meditation, but there was something about the movement that he couldn't look away from. Then he saw Ms. Herbert emerge from the shadows and into the light by the door to Sharon's office.

"What the..." he said to himself softly and Ms. Herbert's head whirled around, scanning to see if someone was there.

He felt a prickling sensation on his arms and immediately used the technique Maranda taught him to conceal his energy signature. After a long while, Ms. Herbert finished her survey and turned back to the door. She pulled out a small leather case and pulled out several metal tools. She inserted them into the top lock of the door and Leo realized she was picking it.

"Why would she need to break into Sharon's office?" he wondered to himself and then answered his own question immediately. "Because she is a spy..."

Leo watched Ms. Herbert intently as she successfully unlocked the door and then went inside. She closed the door quietly behind her and left the lights off, but Leo could see through the shades that she was using a flashlight. Several minutes later, she emerged from the office clutching a thick folder, which she set down as she used the tools again to lock the door behind her. Leo held his breath and didn't dare to move as she slinked back into the shadows and out of sight. He wanted to follow her, but knew he would not be able to do so without getting caught.

Instead, when he was sure she was far enough away, he ran for his bunkhouse as fast as he could. He yanked the metal door open and it groaned in protest as he rushed inside and looked around to see if anyone was there. Thankfully, everyone still seemed to be at dinner, so he rushed through a shower and got ready for bed to try to arouse as little suspicion from his bunkmates as possible.

When he was finally all settled in his bunk, he closed his eyes and began his preparations to enter the Connector. However, the door groaned loudly again, distracting Leo so that he had to start over again. Just as he was getting relaxed, he heard Miles' bed creak as he climbed up onto his bunk. Leo opened his eyes and looked over to see Miles staring back with concern in his eyes.

"I'm good, don't worry," Leo said.

"Really?" Miles asked skeptically.

"Well... I'm better at least," Leo corrected himself. "I just need a good night's sleep."

Miles nodded in acceptance and jumped down from his bunk to start getting ready for bed. By the time he was done, Leo was already unconscious, making his way to see Maranda.

༄

Leo appeared in front of the exact door he had intended. He had to admit, Maranda was an excellent teacher and she had helped him learn the way in and out of the Connector rather quickly. Unfortunately, this wasn't their scheduled day to meet, so he had to go to one of the doors she and Gus had designated for emergencies. He rapped his hand on the door in a precise sequence that Gus had taught him.

Knock-knock-knock. Pause. Knock-knock. Pause. Knock. Pause. Knock. Pause. Knock-knock-knock.

A moment later, the door opened up wide and a young woman he had never met looked at him urgently.

"Codeword?" she asked, her voice tight with anxiety.

"Shenanigans," Leo answered, trying to remain calm.

The woman nodded and stepped aside, letting him pass. She showed him the safe way to move further into her mind and he found himself in the middle of an empty diner from the 1950s. It even had a big jukebox at the far end that was playing a classic doowop song.

"What do you need?" the woman asked abruptly from the other side of the counter.

"Um… My name is…" Leo began before she cut him off.

"No names," she said quickly. "Why are you here? What's the emergency?"

"Oh… um… I need to speak with someone and they told me to come here if it was an emergency," Leo responded.

"Who do you need to speak to?" the woman asked.

"Uh… You just told me no names," Leo said, slightly confused.

The woman rolled her eyes and exhaled loudly through her nose.

"Fine," she said. "We can use names now. Who do you need to talk to?"

"Maranda," Leo answered and her eyes lit up in recognition.

"You must be Leo," she said and he nodded in response.

"OK, give me a few minutes to go get her," the woman instructed and she evaporated into thin air.

Leo sat down on one of the stools at the counter and listened to the music, but it sounded strange like the jukebox was running out of power and the record was slowing down. The voices became lower and each note longer. Then he noticed the colors seemed to be draining out of the room. The bright reds on the seat cushions had turned gray as had the colorful flowers in a vase sitting next to the cash register. The final straw that made Leo start to freak out was the room's edges began to grow fuzzy and fade away.

He rushed back towards the way he had entered to try to find the door, but it was too late, the door was gone. He stalked across the room looking for a way out and, finding none, began to hyperventilate. Just as he was about to hurl himself at the haze surrounding him, everything returned back to the way it had been and the woman was standing behind the counter again.

"What's the matter?" she asked with concern when she saw the state he was in.

Leo just shook his head and tried to catch his breath. Then they heard the same knock sequence on the door and the woman walked away to let Maranda in. When they both returned, Leo had calmed down enough that he was able to speak again.

"You OK?" the woman asked.

"Yeah… just got a little freaked out…" Leo replied.

"Um… Danielle, he's never been left behind before," Maranda said.

"Oh… OH! I'm so sorry! I should've let you know! Please know you were absolutely safe the entire time," Danielle said.

Maranda walked over to Leo and put her hand on his shoulder, guiding him to sit down at the counter again.

"When a Star Born leaves the Connector, the physical manifestation of their mind space can't be maintained," Maranda informed Leo. "It just turns into a blank space until they return. Once you are inside safely, you can wait there for as long as necessary or leave if you need to."

"Thank goodness…" Leo said, feeling relieved.

"Anyway," Maranda returned to business. "Are you here because you heard?"

"Heard what?" Leo asked.

"You're here and you hadn't heard another school was raided? This doesn't make any sense…" Maranda said.

"Another school was raided?!" Leo exclaimed.

"Yes, it was pretty bad," Maranda responded. "Another group of students was taken and several teachers didn't make it."

"How…"

"Spies, Leo," Maranda said and it jolted him back to why he was there in the first place.

"I think I found one!" Leo said loudly, startling both Maranda and Danielle.

"Really? How?" Maranda asked excitedly.

"It was a horrible day and I was just wandering around," Leo recounted. "When I stopped to sit down, I saw Ms. Herbert sneak into Sharon's office and take a big folder with tons of papers inside. She must've been stealing it because she was a spy."

Maranda gave Danielle a look and Leo recognized that she didn't believe him.

"I'm telling the truth," Leo said defiantly.

"I'm sure you are telling me what you saw, but there's no way Ms. Herbert is a spy. She was probably just getting the file for Sharon," Maranda explained.

"No, she stole it," Leo insisted. "She was so shady, sneaking around. Also, she didn't have a key and had to pick the lock."

"I can't believe it…" Maranda said.

"Why not?" Leo asked, unable to fathom why Maranda would take the side of the meanest teacher at his school.

"Because she is one of the people who was responsible for setting up the schools," Danielle answered.

"It just doesn't make sense. Why would she go through all the trouble to protect the kids and create the schools in the first place?" Maranda added.

Leo had to admit, it didn't make much sense when he factored in those details. He furrowed his brow and ran his hand through his hair back and forth several times. Then, it came to him.

"She wasn't protecting the kids! She was getting them together to make it easier to take them!" he said.

"What?! No…" Maranda said, but Leo could tell that she thought he may be onto something.

"Who are the kids they took?" Leo pushed for more information.

"Mainly Star Borns," Maranda answered as she continued to think. "And a few powerful Earth Borns from well known families. One was even the son of a member of the Council."

"He's amassing power," Leo said bluntly.

"But they're just kids!" Danielle said, still unable to believe.

"Gabriel doesn't care. He'll do anything to get more power," Leo responded.

"But…" Danielle started to protest further and Maranda interrupted her.

"He's probably right," she said. "Gabrielle has broken so many of our core laws. Of course he would abduct kids. They're easier to convert into followers or to steal cores from if they resist."

"Maranda, this is unprecedented," Danielle pushed harder.

"Yes, exactly!!" Maranda snapped. "We don't have the luxury of waiting anymore. I believe Leo and that means we need to take necessary precautions."

"Then we need to tell Sharon right away," Danielle said sternly.

"No," Maranda said definitively, "She lobbied hard to have Ms. Herbert at her school. It will take too much time to convince her she has misjudged someone in her inner circle. We will approach her when we have more evidence that she can't refute."

Danielle furrowed her brows in thought and then nodded in acknowledgement, finally accepting Maranda's direction and disappeared again.

"Listen, Leo," Maranda said as she stood up and turned to face him. "I believe Gabriel and his followers are starting to accelerate their preparations. For what, I don't know. But we need to work quickly if we have any hope of stopping him. We will meet again at our scheduled time in two days and I hope to have more information then. In the meantime, I think you need to tell the rest of the group what is happening. They need to be ready, too."

"Um... That's going to be a little hard because I'm not really speaking to Stella and Ania right now..." Leo said sheepishly.

"What?! Why?" Maranda asked impatiently.

"Well... They kind of joined my arch rival's team..." Leo explained.

"And?" Maranda asked, unable to believe that was the reason for Leo cutting off communication.

"Hey, you don't know Jordan. He's a real jerkface," Leo said defiantly.

"OK, fine. And why would they join a jerkface's team?" Maranda asked and Leo knew his argument was about to sound even flimsier.

"Because… I am obsessed with beating him at all costs?" Leo answered.

"Well, it sounds more like you are the one being the jerkface, Leo," Maranda said coolly.

"You… You're… I mean… No I'm not!" Leo said defiantly.

"You're going to have to get over this. At some point, you and Jordan may rely on each other. This is no time for petty rivalries," Maranda counseled.

"That's what Ernest said too…" Leo grumbled.

"Well, he's right!" Maranda said. "He also happens to be Adam's older brother, so you should trust him completely."

"No…" Leo said in disbelief.

"Yeah…" Maranda said, mocking him.

"Look, I have to go help Danielle act on the information you just gave us," Maranda pivoted. "But I do have one more thing to tell you. You and Jordan are about to start training in The Crucible. I just heard about it today. Act surprised when they tell you, OK?"

Leo couldn't help but show how excited he was at the news and even let out a little squeak.

"I've never seen someone so excited to work on The Crucible. Most Star Borns dread it. You're truly a weird one, Leo," she said poking fun as she began to disappear.

Leo chuckled at that and then looked around, finding himself in a featureless gray expanse. He began the process to leave the Connector and felt himself rising. The next thing he realized, he was waking up in his bunkhouse with the first rays of dawn light streaking through the windows. Too excited to go back to sleep, he just laid there and waited for everyone to begin stirring, daydreaming about what it would be like to start his training again.

☙

Once everyone started to get up, Leo jumped down from his bed and rushed through getting ready for the day. He heard his bunkmates grumble as he pushed past them to head to the cafeteria and then began to jog down the trail.

"Leo! Wait up!" Miles called and Leo slowed down so he could catch up.

"What's gotten into you?" Miles asked him when they began walking briskly together.

"What do you mean?" Leo asked.

"I'm usually your human alarm clock," Miles said in annoyance. "Suddenly, today you are a morning person?"

"I don't know, I guess I just slept really well," Leo said, dodging the question.

"No way," Miles said, recognizing that he was getting the brush off. "Something's up. Tell me."

"Not right now," Leo said, his annoyance coming through.

"It's always not right now with you!" Miles snapped and Leo stopped walking, surprised at Miles' assertiveness.

"It's hard to explain," Leo said, trying to placate Miles.

"Try me," Miles pushed.

"Fine," Leo said. Miles had become one of his closest friends and if Leo couldn't trust him, then he was a bad judge of character.

"Two of the schools have been raided and students have been abducted," Leo shared.

"OK, and?" Miles asked, knowing there was more.

"And it looks like there are spies who are finding out the locations to tell Gabriel's followers," Leo continued.

"Keep going," Miles instructed.

"I think Ms. Herbert is one of the spies," Leo finished with his bullet points.

"See? Was that so hard?" Miles asked.

"How are you not even surprised?" Leo responded.

"I told you the very first day we met," Miles said pedantically. "Librarians are all about gathering information. This is exactly the kind of thing we would gather."

"So you knew everything already?" Leo asked in surprise.

"Well, not that Ms. Herbert is a spy, but I believe it. That lady is evil."

"We need to keep this information quiet," Leo instructed. "I need to tell a few other people, but don't start spreading this around."

Miles pantomimed zipping his mouth shut, locking it, and throwing away the key.

As the path became more crowded with students, they shifted to idle chit chat. Eventually, Mari, Lucy, Finn, and Marie joined them in the cafeteria and soon they were laughing at a series of ridiculous jokes that Marie started telling them. Then Leo caught sight of Stella and Ania and he stopped laughing as guilt washed over him.

He stood up and walked over to the table they were sitting at. It was just the two of them as it was still a bit early and many of the students hadn't come to breakfast yet.

"Hey," Leo said somewhat quietly. They both looked up, but didn't return the greeting.

"So, I messed up yesterday," he continued, but they still didn't respond.

"I'm really sorry and I will try to let the rivalry with Jordan go," he finished.

"Try?" Stella asked rhetorically.

"I mean, I will absolutely let it go," Leo corrected himself.

"We're staying on Jordan's team," Ania said tersely.

"That's totally fine. I get it," Leo assured them, though he did still feel a pang of frustration deep down.

"You were a real jerk, Leo," Stella said, still clearly upset.

"Yup, quite a few people have informed me of that in the past day," Leo acknowledged.

"Good," she responded and allowed the hint of a smile to break through. Leo felt so grateful when he saw it and then he remembered there was more.

"We have some other important things to talk about, but we should wait for the rest of the crew," Leo said.

"What?! Why you gotta be like that?" Ania protested and Leo chuckled in response.

"You just have to wait until lunchtime," Leo said. "We'll grab our food and find a spot outside."

Ania and Stella nodded in acceptance and then Leo returned to his table to finish his food. He was famished from skipping dinner the night before. Though Marie certainly made it hard to keep the food from shooting out of his nose. She seemed to have an endless supply of jokes.

Soon, they were all gathered in class and Ernest strode in and set his briefcase down on the desk. Then he pulled out a sheaf of papers and started looking through them. The class quieted down and waited for him to start, but before he did there was a knock at the door. Sharon stepped in and the whole class turned to look at her.

"Good morning, Sharon," Ernest greeted her.

"Good morning. I was wondering if I could borrow Leo and Jordan for a few minutes before you get started?" Sharon asked.

"Of course," Ernest replied and then nodded to each of them.

Leo made his way between the desks, knowing why she wanted to speak with them and trying to focus on not giving that away. When they were all in the empty hallway, Sharon paused for a moment, wringing her hands nervously.

"I should tell you that I am concerned about what I am about to tell you," she began. "Unfortunately, it is out of my hands."

Leo could see Jordan look at him and then back at Sharon, but he just kept his eyes on Sharon.

"The Star Born elders have determined that you both should begin training on The Crucible immediately," she continued.

"But..." Jordan tried to interject.

"Let me finish please," Sharon requested. "Yes, normally we don't train students as young as you both are, but the elders believe you have the potential to complete it earlier than most and would like you to start the training process. It is incumbent upon me to say that you do have a choice in this and you do not need to start the training simply because the elders believe you should. In fact, I would like to advise you against it due to the significant dangers you will face. Leo, I believe you know what I mean."

Leo nodded, but didn't say anything.

"If you choose to pursue the training, it will be in addition to your other classes and training sessions," Sharon advised. "You would join me at five thirty every morning and I will not allow you to train if you have not completed the work for your other classes."

Leo and Jordan stood there and waited for her to continue, but she stayed silent.

"Is that it?" Jordan asked.

"No, I need to know your answer before I share any more information," Sharon advised.

"OK, I'm in," Jordan said.

"Me too," Leo added.

"Very well," Sharon said in disappointment. "It is my understanding that you both have not been getting along very well since the start of school. That will no longer be tolerated as you will need to train closely together to pass The Crucible. Leo, since you already began your training in it, you will be responsible for instructing Jordan for at least the first three rooms."

Jordan looked at Sharon in disbelief. Leo closed his eyes, trying to remain calm.

"You heard me right and don't make a face," Sharon said tersely. "You will find a way to work together or you will no longer be welcome at this school."

Leo's eyes shot open in surprise.

"That's right," Sharon said forcefully. "If either of you wants to stay at this school, you will need to trust and rely on each other. Jordan, you will need to follow Leo's instruction. And, Leo, there are quite a few things you will need to learn from Jordan in order to complete your training. As I understand, you got stuck on the fifth room and I believe Jordan will be able to teach you the necessary skills."

Leo couldn't believe his ears, but he'd made a commitment and intended to see it through. He looked over at Jordan, who was staring at the floor. Leo wondered if he regretted agreeing to the training.

"Do you both understand the terms?" Sharon asked and both boys nodded.

"OK, that's all then. You can go back to class. I will see you bright and early tomorrow morning."

On that note, Sharon turned and strode down the hallway, leaving Leo and Jordan standing quietly outside their classroom.

10

Difficult Decisions

AROLINE WATCHED AS Juliet coaxed the gold leaf into the fold she had created in the piece of soft leather placed in front of her. It resisted at first, but then slid in smoothly with a subtle flick from the fine tip of the tool she was holding. Now only a thin, delicate line could be seen and Caroline marveled at the craftsmanship.

"Now you try," Juliet instructed and pulled out the thin strip without even the slightest tear appearing.

Caroline took the offered tool from Juliet and slid the piece of leather over. She leaned in close so that she could see the natural lines of the material and the small pocket of the fold Juliet had created. She moved the tool close to the gold leaf and began to make a connection between them as she had practiced several times that evening. As soon as it happened, she felt the satisfying sensation radiate up her arm.

She moved the tool toward the fold, but she felt a strong tug from the connection and the gold leaf didn't move. Caroline took a cleansing breath and refocused, clearing all the thoughts from her mind and letting the world fade away. It was just her and this task, nothing else needed to intrude. She moved the tool closer until it hovered barely a millimeter over the thin metal and then tried the small flick that Juliet had used just before. The gold leaf didn't tug this time and instead slid effortlessly back into the fold. Caroline leaned back in satisfaction and stared at her handiwork.

"Impressive," Juliet said softly and Caroline could hear the pride in her voice. "You're a natural."

"I don't know about that…" Caroline protested and Juliet waved her hand to dismiss the thought.

"Stop with the false modesty," Juliet counseled. "You are good at this. About as good as Norah and she has a head start on you. And you've worked hard at it, so be proud of yourself!"

Caroline smiled in response and looked back down at the practice piece, running her finger along the thin line of gold. A little pulled out of the fold and Caroline let out a little gasp.

"Forget something?" Juliet asked with a raised eyebrow and Caroline rolled her eyes and kicked herself internally. She took the tool and flipped it over so the rounded end hovered just above the fold. She reestablished her connection with the metal and added a connection to the leather. Then in her mind, she pictured them becoming bound together down to the atomic level. After she pulled the tool away, she ran her finger again along the same spot and the gold stayed in place.

"Very good," Juliet said. "I think it is time for you to plan your book. You have mastered all the necessary techniques."

"I kinda already have an idea," Caroline responded.

"Oh?"

"Yeah… I was thinking of doing a knot maze…"

"Really?" Juliet asked in surprise.

"It just feels right," Caroline explained.

"Well, if there is one thing we have been teaching you, it is to trust your instincts," Juliet responded. "Those patterns haven't been practiced in generations, though. I don't know how much I'll be able to help you. Also, you will need to ask for permission. There's a reason they aren't practiced anymore."

"Why?" Caroline asked. She hadn't known this fact and had just found a book explaining them in the library the week before. The patterns were entrancing and she had barely heard the librarian calling to her because it was almost time for the evening bell and she needed to go back to her room.

"First off, they are extremely powerful and can become unstable if they aren't executed perfectly," Juliet explained. "I've also heard the creator and the piece become connected for life. Once the creator dies, the book is locked forever. Nobody can open it, not even the most skilled Moon Born."

"I see..." Caroline responded. She let the explanation sink in, but was undeterred in her decision.

"The tribes have lost so much knowledge because of fear and destruction. The elders have wanted to make sure that all knowledge that Moon Borns gather is accessible," Juliet added. "Anyway, let's go speak with Jeremy and see what he thinks. Then you probably need to get back to your room and complete your homework."

The two of them walked quietly, both lost in their thoughts. So, when they made their way down an alleyway that Juliet had shown her was a shortcut to the terrace, they could hear voices coming out of an open window high on one of the walls.

"Simply out of the question!" a man said so firmly that Juliet and Caroline stopped in their tracks to listen..

"I'm surprised you are so closed minded about this. You were one of the biggest advocates before," a woman said in response. Her voice had a sing-song quality to it that Caroline loved.

"You know that was before Gabriel got the vial. Now it is much too dangerous. War would be a certainty if we break our tradition of neutrality," the man replied, clearly becoming so angry that his voice began to shake.

"He's right," a third voice said. It was someone older, but Caroline couldn't tell if it was a man or a woman. "There may still be a chance to avoid a war, but that is not possible if we get involved."

"War is here whether you like it or not…" they heard the woman begin to reply, but then Juliet grabbed her upper arm and began to pull her down the alleyway.

"Hey!" Caroline whispered in annoyance. "I wanted to hear more!"

"We shouldn't have heard what we did," Juliet responded, her face pale with worry.

"C'mon…" Caroline protested more loudly as they turned a corner and were far enough away. "The window was wide open. If they needed privacy, they should've closed it."

"You don't understand!" Juliet snapped, catching Caroline off guard. "I wasn't supposed to show you this path! It is intended just for Moon Borns who have completed their initiate training. We could get in big trouble if they find out you heard part of their conversation. You *have* to promise me that you won't tell anyone!"

"Why? What could happen?" Caroline asked, though she knew she probably didn't want to know the answer.

"We could be banished!" Juliet said, panic in her voice. Caroline understood why, too. Terradune was a special place and she had quickly become attached to it. The idea that she would never be able to step foot there again was too painful to consider.

"OK, I get it. I won't say a word," Caroline assured Juliet, who became immediately calmer.

When they got to the terrace, all of the chairs and the table were gone and Juliet led Caroline up a small flight of stairs at the far end. There was a metal gate at the top, and Juliet pulled out a set of keys from a hidden pocket in her robes. She selected a small, brass skeleton key and inserted it into the lock on the gate, but didn't turn it and just stood there waiting. All of a sudden, Caroline saw the key begin to glow and it spread onto the lock and across the gate until it was bright enough to make her squint slightly.

Juliet then turned the key and gestured for Caroline to go through. She pulled the gate closed behind them and it immediately stopped glowing. Caroline followed Juliet up another short path that led to a small courtyard and she paused again.

"Jeremy?!" she called out and they heard someone stirring behind a door to their left.

A moment later, Jeremy emerged and he was wearing coveralls that were splattered with almost every shade of color imaginable.

"Shouldn't you be in your rooms by now?," Jeremy asked, confused by their visit.

"Yes, but we needed to run something past you," Juliet explained. "Caroline has mastered all the techniques I can teach her and is ready to start work on her book."

"That's marvelous, but couldn't you have waited to tell me tomorrow?" Jeremy responded.

"Well… I guess so…" Juliet stammered a bit.

"I would like my book cover to be a knot maze," Caroline chimed in.

"Oh really?" Jeremy said, Caroline's words clearly catching his attention. Then he turned to look at Juliet with a raised eyebrow while asking Caroline, "And how do you know about knot mazes?"

"I found a book in the library," Caroline answered and Jeremy's gaze turned quickly back to her.

"Impossible. All books with that information are in the advanced section. You don't have access to that yet," Jeremy said.

"I don't know what to tell you," Caroline said in annoyance. "I was looking through the shelves on the third floor down while trying to find a book to select for our next assignment. There was a book on the far side of the room and I just felt drawn to it. The spine was different from all the other books. It was so intricate and seemed to shine a bit."

"And what was the name of this book?" Jeremy asked in an eerie voice that scared Caroline.

"There wasn't a name on the book," she answered. "But based on what I saw inside it, I think it's called The Book of Connections? Does that sound right?"

"Take me to it right now," Jeremy instructed tersely and rushed down the stairs as Juliet and Caroline chased after him. He waved his hand and the gate swung open, then it shut itself after they all passed through.

Jeremy led the way to the library and one of the librarians protested loudly when he let them in.

"The library is closed to students, Jeremy! You know this!" she said.

"Yes, yes, Greta," Jeremy said, waving away her concerns. "We will only be a few minutes."

Then he looked at Caroline and said, "Please go get the book, we will wait here."

Caroline rushed over to the closest spiral staircase and raced down three flights. She was quite dizzy when she reached the third level's landing, but she didn't pause and rushed back to the spot where she found the book a week before. It was still sitting there and she took it off the shelf, hugging it to her chest as she ran back to the staircase.

When she emerged at the top of the stairs again, she stopped because of the faces Jeremy and Greta were making.

"It's… that's the…" Greta stammered, unable to get any more words out.

"I believe so," Jeremy responded and waved Caroline over to the front desk that Greta had been sitting at.

Caroline placed it on the desk and Jeremy said, "If you wouldn't mind opening it."

She turned to the first page, though she was very confused why Jeremy didn't just open the book himself.

"Can you tell me what you see, please?" he instructed.

"Um… four mazes?" Caroline responded, not knowing what he was looking for.

"A little more detail," Jeremy said tersely.

"Each maze is a different style, but they are all square," she began, frustrated by Jeremy's tone. "The top left has rounded edges to the paths. The top right has hard edges. The bottom left is really ornate with lots of extra decoration. The last one is extremely simple. Even a little kid can solve that one, I bet. There is also a different symbol at the corner of each maze where it meets the corner of the page."

"Very good," Jeremy said. "Can you now close the book for me?"

Caroline rolled her eyes and closed the book.

"Jeremy, we need to tell the elders," Greta said with a tense voice.

"Of course, just give me a moment," Jeremy said in

frustration. "Now, Caroline. If you would be so kind as to open the book to the same page."

"Uh, why aren't you just doing these things?" Caroline said in frustration, folding her arms across her chest.

"I'll explain in a moment, just please do as I've asked," Jeremy instructed again.

"Fine." Caroline snapped and she quickly opened the book back to the same page.

"And what do you see?" Jeremy asked.

"Look for yourself!" Caroline growled.

"Please," Jeremy said quietly.

Caroline looked at the page and caught her breath. The four mazes were gone and now a single, complex maze covered the entire page.

"There's… um… I can only see one now," she said in wonder, her frustration paused as she took in the new image.

Jeremy nodded and took a step back as he stroked his chin deep in thought. Caroline tore herself away from the book that she desperately wanted to understand and waited as long as she could tolerate before finally shouting, "Will someone please tell me what's going on?!"

Jeremy turned his gaze to her and said, "You are correct. This is called The Book of Connections and we thought it had been lost. Actually, stolen would be the more accurate word. Nobody has seen this book in generations."

"OK, great, glad I could find your lost book," Caroline said sarcastically, her temper making her feel hot.

"Let me explain," Jeremy continued. "This book is an important piece of Moon Born heritage. All the people who have learned its teachings are long gone. Nobody has been able to practice these techniques in generations."

"I thought we had chosen to stop teaching the techniques because they lock away information," Juliet said.

"Absolutely not," Jeremy dismissed the thought. "We would never stop teaching these techniques intentionally. While there are some downsides, these patterns are sacred to our people."

"Why are you acting all weird and making me tell you what I see, though?" Caroline redirected the conversation.

"Because the book only chooses one person to read it at a time," Jeremy explained. "When I looked at the pages, they were blank. If I had even touched the book, it would have locked itself and we would have to wait perhaps another generation for the book to select another reader."

"Really?" Caroline asked, unable to believe him and he nodded soberly.

Greta cleared her throat loudly to indicate again that Jeremy needed to inform the elders and he turned to her and nodded. Then he said to Caroline, "Please follow Greta and she will show you where you can keep the book for the time being. Then you can head back to your room and we will discuss this further tomorrow."

"But I want to hear what the elders have to say," Caroline protested.

"And you will, I promise that," Jeremy said and gave her a smile. "But I believe you have a test in Marina's class tomorrow and there is nothing I can do to get you out of it. I think studying would be a good idea now."

Caroline agreed reluctantly and followed Greta to the elevator. They went to the top floor and Greta led her to a dark black door sandwiched between two bookcases. She opened it and Caroline was surprised to see how large the room was. It had bookcases around the walls and was packed with tables. Each had at least one book or scroll that was under glass.

Greta led her to the third row of tables where there was an empty display. She placed her hand on the table and the glass tilted back as if there was a hinge.

"Place the book there," Greta gestured and Caroline followed her instruction.

"Now, place your hand here," Greta said and pointed at the spot where her hand had been resting. Caroline placed her hand in the spot and the glass closed over the book.

"Only you and I can open it now," Greta explained. "This does not mean you have unlimited access to the library though. The same rules apply and you will only be admitted during student hours."

Caroline nodded once to indicate she understood.

"Now, off you go," Greta said, gesturing to the door and Caroline hurried out.

⚶

The next morning, Caroline woke up at her desk with a huge crick in her neck and a page of her open text book pasted to her cheek. She let out a slight groan as she sat up and slowly loosened up her muscles. She tried to remember what she had been dreaming about, but she couldn't piece together any of the details. However, she savored the feeling of genuine contentment that lingered as she continued to wake up fully.

She looked out the window at the gray sky and smiled. She had always loved gray days and there were so few of them at Terradune, so she was filled with the general sense that the day was going to be great. Then she looked down at her desk and was reminded that she had a huge test that she wasn't sure she was prepared for. As if on cue, the morning bell chimed and Caroline simply shrugged as she decided that nothing was going to ruin her day.

She quickly went about her usual routine, rushing around her room to change into her flowing tan clothes and pack up her bag. Then she ran down the stairs to the courtyard and looked across to the hall where she saw several of her classmates entering. Even from this distance, she could see how disheveled they looked and she realized that most of them probably stayed up late studying.

Walking briskly across the courtyard, it felt like Caroline's senses were heightened. The smell of the ocean around them seemed much stronger than normal and a slight breeze tickled the peach fuzz on her cheeks. She couldn't help but grin in enjoyment and continued in her happy state as she stood in line for breakfast.

Once her tray was filled with a tall stack of pancakes, several strips of bacon, and a glass of orange juice, she made her way over to sit with her friends. With her first bite, she let out a contented sigh and closed her eyes as she leaned back in her chair and allowed the sweetness of the maple syrup to fill her mouth.

"Uh… Caroline? They're just pancakes," Bea said.

"Correction. They are *amazing* pancakes," Caroline responded as she opened her eyes and used her fork to cut another huge bite for herself.

"What's going on with her? It's as if she doesn't care there's a test we are all going to fail today," Bea said, looking at Norah across the table.

"It's just a test," Caroline said casually.

"Just a test?! Bea said exasperatedly. "Did you even study?!"

"Sure!" Caroline answered brightly.

"I can tell," Norah said with a grin. "You have a formula from the book on your cheek."

"Really?" Caroline asked as she chuckled and rubbed her cheek with her hand.

"Stop, stop, stop," Norah instructed as she took her napkin and dipped it into her water and then gently scrubbed Caroline's cheek.

"There, got it," she said to Caroline when she was done.

"Thanks, mom!" Caroline responded brightly. Norah couldn't help but laugh as Caroline's happiness infected her.

Soon it was time to head to class and they all walked down the alleys in a tight mass to Marina's classroom. Most were either silent or muttered equations they were trying to memorize. Not Caroline though. She whistled old show tunes that her mom loved to play on Saturday mornings. Norah joined in on a few of them she knew, their out of tune whistles echoing off the walls. Someone closed a window high above them and they started to laugh loudly.

When they arrived at Marina's classroom, she was seated in her usual spot on the carpet with her legs crossed and eyes closed. Everyone made their way to their desks and found a copy of the test waiting for them.

"You may begin when you're ready," Marina said without opening her eyes and all the students rummaged in their bags for a pencil.

Soon the only sound in the room was the faint scratches of the pencil tips on test papers and the occasional furious erasing. Strangely, Caroline still didn't feel the least bit stressed like she normally would be during a test at her old school. She just looked at each question and tried to answer it the best she could, then moved onto the next one.

When she finished the final question. She looked around and saw everyone was still working and Marina hadn't moved from her spot at the front of the room. So, she put her pencil down and began to stare out the window. She remembered the events from the night before and grew excited to hear the outcome of Jeremy's conversation with the elders. She was so absorbed in her thoughts that she didn't notice Marina standing over her.

"All done?" Marina asked and Caroline jumped in her seat from being startled.

"Uh… yes?" Caroline answered.

"It doesn't sound like you're so sure," Marina said flatly.

Caroline looked down to think for a moment and met Marina's gaze with a bright smile and said, "Yes."

Marina furrowed her brow, not used to this kind of response to a test and picked up the papers. She scanned the answers as she flipped through each page quickly and then looked down at Caroline intensely.

"Please stay after class. In the meantime, take out your book and start getting familiar with the next two chapters," she said tersely and then walked to the front of the classroom to sit at her desk and look at Caroline's test again.

It occurred to Caroline that she had never seen Marina sit at her desk before, but then she saw Bea staring at her with a questioning gaze. She simply shrugged in response and leaned down to pull out her book. The rest of the class felt like an eternity and Caroline was relieved when Marina said, "Pencils down!" There were a few protests as she walked around collecting the papers. Ryan and Niels had not listened to Marina's instruction and were still writing feverishly as she pulled the papers out from under them.

The room filled with noise as everyone started exchanging answers to questions as they filed out of the room. Caroline started to follow them, but Marina cleared her throat and called out, "Excuse me? Did you forget?"

Caroline *had* forgotten and she immediately changed course

and walked over to the desk. Marina gestured for Caroline to sit down on the chair right next to it and then stared at Caroline intensely again.

"Cheating is a very serious offense," Marina said and Caroline's eyes opened wide and her jaw dropped, unable to respond to what she was being accused of.

"Who gave you the answers?" Marina continued.

"No… Nobody!" Caroline stammered.

"You expect me to believe that you aced this test?" Marina asked skeptically.

"What?!" Caroline asked, unable to comprehend what Marina was saying. "There's no way… I must've gotten something wrong."

"Don't do that," Marina snapped. "Don't pretend. Just be honest and I will do my best to advocate for you with the elders."

"I *AM* telling the truth," Caroline responded.

"No initiate has scored perfectly on this test since I have been teaching this class," Marina said. "I know you have been studying with Juliet and she's grown quite fond of you. Did she get you the answers?"

"I… didn't… cheat," Caroline said slowly and firmly through clenched teeth.

"Fine," Marina said firmly back. "Then you should be able to answer this problem without any issues."

Marina stood up and walked over to the board. Her hand glowed as her fingers moved quickly and an equation began to scrawl across its surface. She then turned to Caroline and pointed at the problem, clearly expecting her to solve it while Marina watched. Caroline stood up defiantly and walked over to the board to analyze the problem. It took her a minute or so, but she figured out what she needed to do to solve it.

She moved her hand toward the board and it began to glow as she felt her body make a connection to it like she experienced when practicing with Juliet. She slowly moved her fingers in a way that she thought made sense to her and saw her answer begin to appear on the board. Occasionally, she would make a mistake in her instructions and erase a section, but soon it was complete and she stood back and turned to Marina with a stubborn and determined look on her face.

"Who taught you to do that?" Marina asked quietly. Caroline could tell her expression has softened.

"Nobody, it just felt like the thing to do..." Caroline answered, unsure of what was happening then.

"Fascinating..." Marina muttered as she stood up and walked over to the board, standing next to Caroline.

She analyzed Caroline's answer for a moment and then turned to her and said softly, "I'm sorry for not believing you. Congratulations on a job well done." Then she walked to the center of the carpet and sat down.

"That's it?!" Caroline said sharply, her happy mood gone now.

Marina held out a hand next to her, inviting Caroline to sit with her on the carpet. Caroline sat down heavily and stared at Marina, waiting for an explanation.

"You are a remarkable student," Marina said, clearly taking great care in the words she chose. "It has been a long time since I have taught someone with your abilities. I think many of your teachers would say the same."

Caroline just sat silently and stared at Marina, waiting for her to continue.

"We are not used to..." Marina began, but paused as she searched for the right words. "Students progressing at such a rapid pace... As you know, our methods involve slow and steady progress with many years of careful instruction. So, it is… unexpected when we have a student like yourself…"

"You're not telling me something," Caroline said in a low voice.

"Yes, you are right. I need to spend some time with your other teachers before I would feel comfortable sharing more with you," Marina answered.

"Why?" Caroline pushed.

"Because our world depends on balance," Marina said firmly. "And you are anything but balanced."

"What's that supposed to mean?!" Caroline asked defensively.

"I've already said too much…" Marina said, "Besides, you are very late for your next class. Please tell Jeremy I apologize for keeping you so long."

With that, Marina stood up and walked out of the classroom, leaving Caroline sitting by herself.

Caroline muddled her way through the remainder of her classes, unable to recapture the ebullient mood from the morning, but also making every effort to not let her interaction with Marina drag her down. She just kept focusing on making it to the end of the day when she expected to find out from Jeremy if the elders approved her plan to study knot mazes. However, that moment came sooner than she expected because, when she arrived at Shijian class, Steven informed the group that class had been canceled for the day. As everyone chattered about what they wanted to do with the sudden gift of free time, Steven made his way over to Caroline and said, "Would you come with me please?"

Norah looked at Caroline with concern, but she just waved it away casually and followed Steven as he led her out of the classroom and down the dim hallway. They made their way out of the building and then down towards the paths that Juliet had told her were off limits to initiates. He stopped at the door and knocked several times. As they waited to be let in, Caroline noticed the window where she and Juliet had heard the voices arguing. Her heart started to beat rapidly as she realized that she was about to meet the elders.

A moment later, the door opened and, to Caroline's surprise, there stood Rebecca with a smile on her face.

"Come in!" she said warmly.

"You're back?" Caroline asked.

"It would seem so!" Rebecca said playfully. "Come now, let's not keep the others waiting."

Rebecca stepped aside and Caroline saw there was just a closed door to the right and a set of stone steps straight ahead. She stepped over the threshold and went up the stairs with Steven following closely behind and Rebecca bringing up the rear. At the top of the steps, there were just two doorways, one of which was wide open and Caroline saw a large circular table in the center of the room. There were a large number of people standing around the room talking softly, including the rest of her teachers as well as Cecil and several other people she did not recognize. She assumed these were the rest of the elders.

"Shall we get started, everyone?" Rebecca said and they all turned to see Caroline standing just inside the doorway.

Rebecca placed her hand on her shoulder and guided her to a seat at the table as everyone else settled in.

"Would you mind closing the windows, Steven? We don't need anyone listening in on our conversation," Rebecca said and Caroline's face flushed red as she anxiously wondered if Rebecca knew that she had eavesdropped on the conversation just the day before.

"Well, here we are!" Rebecca said brightly. "And what an interesting topic we have for our discussion today!"

"Rebecca, it is highly unusual for us to have an initiate in our chambers," an older man said from across the table. Caroline thought she may have seen him at a meal once or twice before, but she couldn't be sure. His voice, however, she immediately recognized. He was the one who was arguing the day before that Moon Borns should remain neutral.

"Yes, Robert, you have made your feelings abundantly clear," Rebecca said without shifting her tone. "While it is unusual, it is not unheard of and other initiates have been invited to speak with us on occasion."

"But we are here to speak about *this* initiate," a woman sitting next to Robert said and Caroline recognized her voice as well. She was the one who had agreed with him during the argument. Caroline found it interesting that her voice conveyed a great deal of experience and wisdom, but she seemed to be no older than Caroline's mother.

"She has every right to have a voice in her fate," Steven interjected and Rebecca patted the air in front of her to signal him to remain calm. Caroline stared at him in alarm, not understanding what he was saying about her fate, but he just stared straight ahead even though she knew he registered her gaze.

"Yes, Charlotte, it would be preferable to have several conversations before we invite her in for this discussion, but I feel that expediency is warranted in this case," Rebecca replied.

"Can I recommend we hold further comments until Rebecca has a chance to complete her remarks?" Cecil asked and the group quietly accepted his recommendation.

"Thank you very much," Rebecca began. "We find ourselves in a unique moment. We have an initiate who appears to have abilities that we have not seen in a Moon Born for generations. Her teachers are all here and I would like them to provide an assessment of her progress over the months since she has joined us. Sharla, if you wouldn't mind, can we start with you?"

"Absolutely," Sharla began. "Caroline quickly caught up to her classmates in basic reflection techniques. In fact, that only took her a few weeks. I also assessed her in more advanced techniques and she has very strong instincts that have aided in her progress. I asked Steven to incorporate some disruption techniques in his class, which she has also excelled at. The one area of development that I believe needs some attention and, eventually, refinement is absorption. As we all saw when she navigated the entrance maze, she has immense potential. However, she has some mental barriers that cause resistance."

Seeing that Sharla was finished, Rebecca nodded to Steven.

"Not since The Calamity has there been as gifted an initiate in Shijian," he began.

"We can do without the hyperbole," Robert said tersely.

Steven clenched his hands into tight fists and Caroline could tell he was exerting an immense amount of control in order to avoid saying some choice words to Robert.

"As I was about to say before I was interrupted," Steven continued. "I believe there is little benefit to having Caroline remain in the starting class. She would be better suited to training with my advanced class going forward. It will provide her with the proper level of challenge and pace of learning."

"You would have her skip multiple levels and years of training?!" Marina asked, completely shocked.

"It does no one any good if we stunt her development," Steven answered bluntly.

"I can't believe… Are you hearing this?!" Marina sputtered as she looked at Rebecca and the other elders.

"It seems you are ready to provide your assessment, Marina," Rebecca answered.

"Very well… I will acknowledge that Caroline is a very talented initiate. But we all know what has happened when we have rushed training for someone who isn't ready. Caroline can clearly master techniques and absorb information at astounding rates. Her mathematics scores and pattern navigation aligns with what Sharla and Steven have said. However, her patience scores are dismally low. I fear there is a deep imbalance in her that could prove catastrophic if we advance her too quickly."

"Thank you, Marina. Jeremy?" Rebecca said, not lingering on any speaker for very long.

"The Book of Connections revealed itself to her," Jeremy began. "The wisdom of generations must be listened to and she should be allowed to continue her studies under careful observation and guidance. I will volunteer my time and Juliet's to continue to work with her in Expression. This is a path that I believe will bring her greater balance."

Caroline saw that Jeremy was looking at Marina as he made his remarks. She made a slight nod when he finished that Caroline believed might have been a bit of acceptance.

"Since we are speaking of the Book of Connections, it is only appropriate that we finish with our Connections teacher," Rebecca said with her usual warmth. "Cariann, if you would be so kind?"

Caroline looked at her teacher apprehensively. Connections was the one class that she felt was a struggle. She always felt like she understood the point Cariann was making, but then there was some kind of hidden meaning that she had missed. The only reason she was keeping her head above water in the class was because Norah had been tutoring her most days at breakfast.

"Like Marina stated, I see the risk of imbalance in Caroline," Cariann said. "She relies heavily on instincts that often prove to be correct, but will that trust remain when it matters most? I don't have an answer for that…"

Cariann paused for a moment and shook her head before continuing.

"Hoo nelly… This is a difficult one! I know we can all agree on that. What I can tell you is, this girl cares a lot. More than she should sometimes, but never not enough. I know she is struggling in my class, but she hasn't given up and that counts for a lot."

"Thank you, everyone, for your thoughtful comments," Rebecca said. "Now I believe it is time for me and my fellow elders to discuss."

Without any hesitation, Robert leaned forward and said, "Given the potential power in this girl, we cannot take the chance of even the slightest imbalance!"

"She's a child…" Cecil began to respond.

"A child who will be training with adults if we allow it!" Robert interrupted.

"And she is here, in Terradune, where she will be under the guidance and observation of some of the most powerful Moon Borns in the world." Cecil pushed back.

"What about tradition?" Charlotte asked. "Are we ready to throw away years of experience to satisfy our curiosity? So what if she is an amazingly powerful Moon Born? As you noted, Cecil, there are quite a few of those here."

"She's not like us though," a woman with a sing-song voice

said a few seats over to her right. Caroline leaned forward to try to get a better look at her and saw that she was striking. The woman had raven black hair cascading down her back and a warm olive complexion. She had a nose ring and her robes were a deep green.

"She found the Book of Connections within a day after it had been placed in the library and it revealed itself to her," the woman continued.

"I'm sorry, Honore, I don't understand," Jeremy interjected. "The Book has been missing for generations."

"It wasn't missing," Honore answered. "Elders before our time removed it from the library. We have been waiting for a Moon Born who would be able to open it again. When Rebecca met Caroline and sent her on her journey here, she asked me to place the book back in the library to see if her hunch was correct. Lo and behold, Caroline discovered it and, not only did it reveal itself to her, but she was able to read it."

"You did this without consulting us!" Robert shouted indignantly at Rebecca and Honore.

"Oh, calm down, Robert," Rebecca said impatiently like a mother to a child throwing a temper tantrum. "While we operate this Council as a group of equals, you know I have certain privileges in my position and am allowed to take this sort of action."

"You… You can't…" Robert began to say, his face getting red. Charlotte put her hand on top of his and he clamped his mouth shut and leaned back in a huff.

"It would seem our discussion is over," Rebecca said with a raised eyebrow as she glanced over at Robert. "Let's move forward with our vote."

"I recommend that we allow Caroline to accelerate her training," Honore said.

"I agree," Cecil said quickly.

"I cannot believe this… There is no way I can support this," Robert said.

"You've made that clear," Rebecca responded. "Charlotte?"

"I'm very sorry, my dear," Charlotte said, looking directly at Caroline. "I wish this were a different time and we had more time to deliberate. We are responsible for the safety of our people and I feel this is too great a risk."

"So, it appears that it comes down to me," Rebecca said. "I had hoped we would be able to come to a unanimous decision on this and will admit that I am torn. While I deeply respect the wisdom of our ancestors, there is no way they could have anticipated everything that would come in the future. Least of all the situation we are facing in the world today. I simply cannot allow us to make a foolish mistake…"

Caroline's stomach clenched suddenly. She had thought that Rebecca would be on her side, but now it seemed she had been horribly wrong. She looked across the table and saw that Robert was leaning forward again with a grin in anticipation of Rebecca's vote and Caroline felt a deep disdain for him at that moment.

"I'm sorry…" Rebecca said slowly and turned to Caroline with sad eyes. "Caroline must continue her studies with us. I do not see any other way forward… I fear for you, child, and I hope we haven't made a decision today that leads to irreparable harm…"

Robert threw up his hands in disgust and pushed his chair back forcefully. Then he stood up and started pacing angrily.

"There is one more topic on the agenda this afternoon," Rebecca said, ignoring Robert's outburst. "I believe the rest of you discussed this yesterday, but we should make our formal decision today. Given Gabriel's recent attacks on the schools set up by the tribes, is it time for us to enter the conflict?"

"Attacks?!" Caroline said anxiously, unable to stay quiet.

"Rebecca, surely the girl can leave now," Charlotte said.

"This affects her too," Rebecca answered simply, unwilling to entertain any more discussion. Then she turned to Caroline and said, "Two schools have been attacked by Gabriel's forces. I was told that neither of them was the school your friends are attending. We don't know how they found the schools, but they managed to take some of the students before the teachers were able to fend them off."

Caroline was reeling and didn't know what to say. Who would attack a school?

"Charlotte?" Rebecca said, asking her to continue.

"Very well," Charlotte said, reluctantly accepting Rebecca's decision to allow Caroline to stay. "Robert and I believe it is not the time to end our policy of neutrality. Honore believes another Calamity is coming if we don't get involved soon."

"And what do you think, Cecil?" Rebecca asked.

"I do believe that war will surely break out if we enter this conflict," Cecil answered. "But I also believe that war will come eventually, even if we maintain neutrality for the time being. Our ancestors were wrong to stay out of The Calamity and I do not want us to make that same mistake. I just don't know if we are ready..."

"Cecil, you are an elder of the city of Terradune and one of the most trusted members of this Council. You need to make a decision," Rebecca said gently.

"If... If I must make a decision right now... then I believe we should wait," Cecil said haltingly.

"I see..." Rebecca said in disappointment. "Well, as you all know, I believe that we have already waited too long to join the cause and that we should begin supporting our allies throughout the tribes. I have spoken to many of our people over these past months and there is a growing sentiment that we cannot stay neutral."

"Enough, Rebecca, we know where you stand on this matter, but your vote doesn't matter since there are three of us who agree we should wait," Robert interrupted.

"WHAT?! NO!" Caroline shouted and Rebecca took her hand and squeezed it tightly to both offer comfort and ask her for quiet in that moment.

"While you are right that I cannot change the vote of the Council, I still have the right to share my opinion," Rebecca said coolly. "Cecil is right. War is coming regardless. There is no way we can ever be truly ready for a war and I fear that our delay will put everything in jeopardy. For the time being, we must do all we can to prepare ourselves until this Council can agree that we must send our people into danger."

"We are doing all we can," Steven said so softly, that Caroline almost didn't register it.

"Still, we must do more," Rebecca said with steel in her voice as she stared at Robert.

"I will see to it myself," Cecil said, strength and resolve returning to him.

Rebecca simply nodded, stood up, and made her way out of the room quietly. The others followed her and eventually it was just Jeremy and Steven sitting with Caroline.

11

WHEN THE GOING GETS TOUGH

LEO WAS EARLY because he just couldn't wait any longer. He and his friends had been watching Ms. Herbert constantly for weeks. A few days earlier, he had even stayed up all night sitting outside her cabin, but she never left. He was sure they had blown their cover and that she was on to them because she had changed her routine significantly. She was always leaving the cafeteria when it opened, arriving at class just as the bell rang, and generally keeping to herself.

After days of boring stakeouts, he was dying for even the teensiest morsel of information that Maranda could provide. Anything that could tell him what was going on outside of school was welcome. So, he tried to wait patiently for her to arrive as he stood in an idyllic setting. It was a beautiful, sunny day with a clear blue sky. He was standing in a field of flowers with a lone tree for shade a short ways away. The edge of a forest was off to his right and the air was filled with birdsong.

Leo started pacing back and forth, every minute his tenuous hold on patience weakening, until he startled when he heard a voice.

"You're trampling the flowers," an old man said grumpily as he peaked over a small hill and glowered at Leo. He was wearing a wide brimmed hat and gardening clothes.

Leo had quickly forgotten that he was in another Star Born's space after he arrived. Normally when he met Maranda, the space manifested as an interior like her library or a grand house. Come to think of it, he had never been in a space like this. He looked over at the old man who hadn't stopped staring at Leo and could tell that he was not happy to have someone in his space. Clearly, a lot of care went into creating it and Leo looked down at the rut in the lush greenery that he had created with his pacing.

Feeling sheepish, he turned toward the tree in the middle of the field and took long careful steps over to it. The old man muttered under his breath, dissatisfied with Leo's efforts, but he crouched back down and returned to his work. Leo sat down under the tree and settled in for a long wait. Something told him that Maranda was going to be a while.

It turned out, Leo was absolutely right. He continued to wait for what felt like an eternity. The time was only marked by the old man occasionally peering at him from different spots around the small field as he worked his way around it. Each time, he would let out a loud huff to let Leo know he had worn out his welcome and then crouch back down out of sight.

Just as Leo had given up and started to stand up to leave, he saw a figure materialize in the distance. They were too far away for him to make out who they were, but he was certain it wasn't Maranda. As soon as they appeared, it was as if they were a dark cloud pulling all the color from their surroundings that filled Leo with dread. Maranda was so vibrant the mood immediately lifted whenever she was around and this person was the exact opposite. They seemed to notice Leo a moment later and began walking slowly toward him and he looked around anxiously to see if this may be some kind of attack. He caught sight of the old man and their eyes met. Leo gave him a questioning look to see if he knew what was happening, but the old man just shrugged and turned to stare at the approaching stranger.

As they finally got close enough to see clearly, to Leo's horror he realized it actually *was* Maranda. She was in a state that he could never have imagined and out of the corner of his eye he saw the old man stand up and rush toward her. Leo set off to meet them as well and as the old man reached Maranda, she leaned on him heavily as if all her strength had left her.

"Come come..." the old man said. "Let's get you into the shade to rest a moment."

He guided Maranda to the tree Leo had been sitting underneath and then helped her down gently. She just sat there quietly, hunched over and barely moving except for the subtle rising and falling of her shoulders as she breathed. Leo looked at her carefully, trying to see if she was injured in some way, but there was nothing physically wrong with her. She just seemed to be nothing like the Maranda he knew.

After several minutes, Maranda looked up and said, "Thank you, Dean..."

"I'll let the two of you talk now," Dean replied. "If you need anything, just holler."

With that, Dean walked back to where he left off so Leo and Maranda were left alone.

"What happened?!" Leo asked urgently and Maranda gestured for him to join her on the ground.

Leo sat down quickly and stared at her intensely, bracing himself for bad news.

"It's OK, Leo," Maranda began, her voice stronger than he expected. "It's just been a heck of a week and I haven't slept in several days."

"What's happened? Did they raid another school?" Leo asked urgently.

"No… Not yet at least," Maranda replied. "We expect one any day now, but your guess where would be as good as mine. I haven't been at my school since we last spoke. There have been some… developments…"

Leo waited for her to continue, but Maranda seemed to have just disappeared to a far off place in her mind.

"What kind of developments?!" Leo snapped when it was clear she wasn't going to come back on her own any time soon.

"Sorry… It's just so hard to focus…" Maranda said as she returned to their conversation. "It appears that Gabriel may be able to open the vial without the help of a Moon Born, though it would take a very large amount of energy that would be difficult to harness and control. We have discovered another memory from Torrell that references a kind of ceremony that he had uncovered in his travels after The Calamity. Essentially, it creates a kind of power that can overcome almost any barrier, including some of the strongest Moon Born protections. We believe that Gabriel is searching for the pieces to learn how to perform this ceremony."

"How is that even possible?" Leo wondered aloud.

"We aren't sure yet, so we need to find more of Torrell's memories. The one we found was incomplete and there aren't many clues to where we can find the others," Maranda answered.

"Show me the memory you found," Leo said with determination that caught Maranda off guard.

"I… I don't think that's possible to do here…" Maranda stammered in response.

"It is," Dean's deep voice said from behind Leo, causing him to jolt in surprise again. He turned around to stare at Dean angrily.

"Sorry, I was curious and came to listen," Dean said carefully.

"How is it possible?" Maranda asked. "I thought a physical connection is necessary to share memories between Star Borns."

"Usually that's the case," Dean explained. "But the Connector acts as an amplifier. Your connection here is almost as strong as if you were holding hands in the real world."

"Huh… I supposed we should give it a try," Maranda said as she reached out for Leo's hands.

"One moment," Dean said quickly and Maranda pulled her hands back. "Remember what I said, being here in this space, we are all connected. You don't need to hold hands to share the memory here. Everyone present will see it, so I will get out of here and leave you to it."

"That's not necessary, Dean, you are able to see the memory too," Maranda protested.

"You know better than that, Maranda," Dean scolded lightly. "The less I know the better."

With that, Dean faded away in front of them and the scenery around them began to turn gray and disappear. This process never ceased to feel unsettling to Leo, but at least now he knew what to expect.

"What did he mean? Why is it better that he doesn't know?" Leo asked when they were the only two people in the gray void that Dean had left behind.

Maranda sighed and said, "Dean was one of the Star Born members of the Council before Gabriel joined. They became very close during the transition process when Dean stepped down. Several years after he left the Council, Dean heard some rumors that advocates of Advancement were on the Council. He took this information to Gabriel, who assured Dean there was no way this was possible. However, Dean wasn't satisfied with that answer and he kept digging until he found out around the same time as we did that Gabriel had become an advocate for Advancement. It broke his heart, Leo… He thought of Gabriel as his son and he felt responsible… So, he decided to join Gabriel's forces and take on the dangerous role of being a spy for us. Some of the information he has been able to provide so far has proven invaluable."

"Whoa…" was all Leo could say in response.

"Whoa is right!" Maranda said, finally sounding more like herself. "Now hold on, this one is going to be a bit bumpier since the memory is incomplete."

Leo tried to brace himself, but he was still caught completely off guard as he found himself suddenly in a small, dimly lit cave with Torrell and a woman draped in flowing purple robes sitting in front of him..

"…couldn't assemble the necessary pieces. They are too fragmented now," Torrell said.

"You underestimate their determination," the woman said to him disdainfully.

"Siobhan, what you are describing would not go unnoticed. We would know if they found the method to do this," Torrell said in disagreement.

"This is the typical arrogance your kind have demonstrated time and again," the woman responded, clearly quite angry now. "You brought this upon us all and even now you underestimate the danger that still remains. They will find out about the ceremony. They will assemble the necessary participants. And they will break the seal to let Warwick go free again. This is all inevitable."

"What would you have me do then?" Torrell asked earnestly.

"You are the only one with the full set of instructions and they know it. Break them apart and entrust the pieces only to those who you think can carry this responsibility," she instructed. "Have them learn their portion and then destroy any evidence. They will need to pass on their portion to someone trustworthy in the next generation so the knowledge is not lost."

"Why not just destroy it? Wouldn't it be better if no one was able to wield this kind of power? Not even your best Moon Borns would be able to stand against it," Torrell asked incredulously.

"Knowledge is not evil, but people can be," Siobhan answered. "Someday, this ceremony may be the only way to save all of our people."

"What you're suggesting is so dangerous…" Torrell began to respond, but the memory ended abruptly and Leo found himself facing Maranda and wobbling unsteadily.

"As soon as we found this memory, we began our search for the other pieces," Maranda began to explain. "That's what I have been doing for days with very little idea on where to start. It is one of the best kept secrets in history."

"Well, I guess we'll just have to help you find them then," Leo said as if it were the natural conclusion.

"No. Absolutely not. It's too dangerous. You need to stay at your school where it is safe and learn what they are teaching you," Maranda said firmly.

"We have no idea if our school is safe," Leo pushed back. "We have a teacher spying for Gabriel who is staying at least one step ahead of us, so we can't find out what information she's stolen. And, you know what, I'm so over adults acting like they know better. We will find those memories for you just like we fought Gabriel for you last summer."

"Leo, you don't…" Maranda began to protest as she stood up slowly.

"Don't tell me I don't understand," Leo shouted as he jumped to his feet. "I'll come find you when I have something."

With that final comment, Leo disappeared from the Connector, leaving Maranda to wonder how the conversation had taken such a quick turn.

❧

When Leo woke up the next morning, it felt like a fire had been lit inside him. For months, they had been cooped up at school while the threat of Gabriel's forces seemed to continually grow. When other schools began to be raided, there was nothing they could do, but anxiously wait for news or take on menial tasks like watching Ms. Herbert.

Now, he had a *real* mission.

With this new sense of purpose, Leo started his day ready to take on the world. Since he woke up before everyone in his bunkhouse, he got dressed stealthily and then hurried to Crucible practice where Jordan gave him a key idea that helped him pass the fifth room. It turned out the barrier to making it through the room was that he had been going in with the wrong kind of attitude like the darts were an unbeatable threat.

Before he entered the Crucible, Jordan said, "Maybe try to visualize the darts as something completely silly and non-threatening, like flying stuffed animals."

Bizarrely, this actually made a lot of sense to Leo. The idea of one of the darts smacking into him always made him tense up and he sometimes had nightmares about it. It also helped that, in his hyper-focused state and with an influx of confidence, he was able to maintain his clarity as the swarm of "teddy bears" and other squishy animals flew at him. He not only defended himself easily, but he was able to marshall all of his abilities to reach the target at the opposite end of the room. As he reached the glowing target, a deep sense of satisfaction filled him and months of frustration began to melt away.

When he came out of the Crucible, Jordan looked at him expectantly and Leo's first instinct was to give him a huge high-five. Jordan let out a huge whoop in celebration and Leo wondered to himself why they had held a grudge for such a long time.

"I'll see you both tomorrow. You can continue without me," Sharon said with a satisfied smile and made her way to the stairs to leave the underground cavern.

Leo spent another hour coaching Jordan, who was making steady progress as well. By the time he finished his last run, Jordan was covered in sweat and he decided to go get showered before breakfast. Leo, on the other hand, took the opportunity to rush to the cafeteria. He got there so early that he even beat Ms. Herbert there. She scowled at him as she walked up the stairs and Leo felt a burning sensation on his arms suddenly. His instincts took over and he quickly formed a large energy orb and began to toss it from one hand to the other while staring her down. Her eyes opened wide in astonishment and the burning sensation quickly disappeared and Leo felt a deep sense of satisfaction.

During breakfast, he tried to pay attention to the conversation his friends were having, but the bulk of his mental energy was focused on trying to figure out how to approach finding Torrell's memories. He excused himself well before the first bell so he could wander around and have the space to think without distraction. Unfortunately, no moments of brilliance came, and he knew it was dangerous to space out in Ernest's class. He had a knack for knowing when to call on distracted students.

When he arrived at first period, the usual din filled the room, but he just sat down and pulled out his notebook and a pencil.

"Dude. What is *up* with you?" Miles asked from the desk next to him with a confused look.

"Uh… Nothing?" Leo said, not following Miles' question.

"Since you started early morning practice, you usually eat breakfast until the last possible second, but you didn't eat much today and left early. Who are you and what have you done with my friend?" Miles said in a serious tone.

"I dunno. Guess I wasn't that hungry," Leo said, trying to explain away his friend's concern.

"Not. Buying. It." Miles responded with a flat tone, but, before Leo could respond, Ernest strolled into the room and the class immediately became quiet.

Ernest placed his satchel on the desk and pulled out a stack of papers and then began handing smaller stacks of papers to the first person in each row. As they took a copy and handed the stack to the next person behind them, Ernest began to explain.

"We've covered a lot in the past several weeks and I am curious how much you have retained so far," he began to explain. "So, we're having a pop quiz."

The class was immediately filled with annoyed mutters.

"The first person to finish with a perfect score will design the practicum challenge for this Friday," Ernest added and the annoyed mutters were replaced with excited chatter.

"Begin!" he called out and immediately the only sound in the room was of pencils scratching on paper.

Leo glanced down at the copy in front of him and paused for

a moment. Something felt off about this. Ernest was a careful, methodical teacher. He was not prone to doing something like this. In fact, Leo remembered the first week that Ernest had been at the school he had explained how he felt that written tests were "a poor indicator of academic performance." Ernest was teaching them something right now, Leo was sure of it.

A thought crept into his head. Ernest had been drilling into their head for weeks the fundamental steps for building a battle strategy. Step one was "Observe." Leo looked to his left and saw everyone writing feverishly on their pages. Then he looked right and saw Jordan was already on the second page. Leo fought back his anxiety of losing to him, even though much of the iciness between them had thawed since they had started Crucible training together, and forced himself to look away to continue his observations.

Leo looked back down at the first page and noticed the instructions were written at the very top before even the name and date blanks. He read them carefully several times.

Read every question of the quiz before answering a single one. Once you have completed your review, finish your test and place your pencil at the front edge of your desk to signal it is ready to be collected.

"That's it?" Leo thought to himself, unable to figure out what Ernest was trying to teach them. However, he remembered the second step of forming a battle strategy - "Learn." So, he proceeded to follow the instructions anyway and read every single question, flipping through the pages one after the other until he reached the last one. This is where things got even weirder. There were no words to this question. Just a series of numbers separated by commas and periods:

*1,5. 2,12. 3,16. 4,8. 5,22. 6,10. 7,2. 8,8. 9,21. 10,6.
11,7. 12,1.
1,10. 2,4. 3,8. 4,19.*

"What the…" he whispered to himself and looked up at Ernest who happened to be staring right at him. This totally unnerved Leo and it took him a minute to focus again. After taking a look at the series of numbers again, he began step three - "Plan." Leo came up with several different methods that could be used to create a code that they had learned in Ms. Herbert's class. He then moved to step four, "Execute," and tried to decipher the numbers using the methods he remembered, but nothing made any sense.

Leo felt the itchiness of frustration form at the back of his head and stared up at the ceiling trying to figure out what else might work. Nothing seemed right because Ernest was clearly not asking them to apply anything they had learned in another class. Then it occurred to him, the next step was "Adapt." Most plans never work perfectly when you apply them in a battle. You have to be ready to adapt them to the real-life conditions. He ran through several other options until he had an idea that seemed ludicrously simple and decided to test it out. He flipped through the test and looked at each question number that corresponded to the first number and then counted the words of the question based on the second number. He wrote each word he found on the last page underneath the sequence and, when it was done he was surprised that it actually wasn't gobbledygook.

*Explain the process you followed to solving this problem in
five words
Sign your name underneath*

Leo scribbled his answer quickly - Observe, Learn, Plan, Execute, Adapt. Then he signed his name below his answer and looked up at Ernest with a big grin on his face. However, Ernest just stared back at him impassively, not moving a muscle.

"What am I forgetting?" Leo thought to himself and looked back at the instructions. Then he saw his mistake and placed his pencil at the front edge of his desk and Ernest immediately stood up and walked over to collect his quiz. Leo then heard someone slam their pencil on their desk and Ernest strode to the back of the classroom and collected another one. Many of the students started looking around nervously, unable to believe someone had already finished. Ernest just sat at the front of the classroom and quickly looked at the two finished quizzes he collected before placing them in on the desk to wait for the rest of the class to finish.

A few minutes later, Leo heard a loud groan to his left and recognized it was Stella realizing the mistake she had made. Then, with some satisfaction, he saw out of the corner of his eye that Jordan figured it out next with several others following in close succession. A short while later, Ernest collected the last quiz and returned to the front of the classroom.

"So, what have we learned today?" Ernest asked the room.

"That you like messing with kids' brains?" Aran said jokingly from a few rows back.

"I guess that is a reasonable conclusion, but not exactly what I had in mind," Ernest replied.

"Rushing leads to mistakes," Stella said grumpily from the back.

"Yes, that's part of it," Ernest said as he scanned the classroom to see if anyone else had something to add.

"Distractions can be costly," Jordan said soberly and Ernest nodded his head.

"You were all so excited to be the first to finish that you didn't take the time to follow the steps we have been drilling on for weeks," Ernest explained. "This kind of distraction can be very costly in a real battle. Don't fall for tricks! A moment in the middle of a battle to assess your enemy can sometimes be the way you can turn a certain defeat into an unexpected success.

"Only two of you took the time to read the instructions for the test and they happened to finish within seconds of each other. Leo and Meimei, I am going to consider this a tie if you don't mind. You two will work with me tomorrow after dinner to design the Friday practicum."

Leo craned his neck to look back at Meimei with a wide smile and she returned it with an excited nod. Then the bell rang and everyone packed up and shuffled out to their next class. Leo's focus paid off in almost every class for the rest of the day.

So, after a day when it felt like everything was going right, it came as no surprise when, as he was walking back to the bunkhouse with Miles after dinner, he found his first lead for one of Torrell's memories. Leo was recounting his success in the Crucible and Miles interrupted.

"So, you're basically telling me that everything went perfectly today," Miles said snarkily.

"Not *everything*," Leo qualified.

"Name one thing you didn't ace today," Miles challenged Leo.

"Well…" Leo started to say, but hesitated because he wasn't sure he was ready to tell Miles what he learned from Maranda.

"Oh no… You're not holding back on me. I can tell you have something juicy. Out with it!" Miles commanded.

"Fine," Leo relented. "Maranda gave me a tip that could

help us understand what Gabriel is up to. We have to find some memories that Torrell left behind."

"And you're just telling me this now?!" Miles asked incredulously.

"When did we have time to talk about this today?"

"How about breakfast? Lunch? Dinner? Between classes? Before we were half-way back to our bunkhouse?" Miles snapped.

"OK… Fair," Leo admitted.

"Show me," Miles directed.

"How do you know I have one of the memories?" Leo asked.

"My ability may not come in handy in the middle of a battle, but it is very handy in these moments. You reek of information. Now, show me."

Leo led Miles off the path to a spot the lights didn't reach and then placed his hand on Miles' shoulder. After he reached a calm state, he surfaced the memory and Miles took over bringing it into focus. A few moments later, it was done and Miles was staring at Leo intently.

"There's a Librarian in Portland that I heard about a couple years ago," Miles said in a low voice. "He hasn't been seen in many years. Some of our elders believe that he acquired some memories that troubled him so much that they drove him insane and he became a hermit. It's one of the reasons they used to hold me back from acquiring more memories. I bet we could get to Portland in an hour or two, but we'd need some help finding him."

"Wait, why do you think Portland is so close? We have no idea where we are," Leo asked.

"No, we are in Oregon. I've known that since week one. It was actually one of the easiest things for me to find out," Miles said matter-of-factly.

"Now who's holding back information?" Leo said.

"I can't help it if you're the least curious person I know," Miles responded while rolling his eyes.

"Fine… Whatever… Now all we have to do is figure out how to sneak out of school, get to Portland, and then find a Librarian who's been missing for years," Leo said, annoyed at Miles.

"Yup, sounds about right," Miles responded. "I have an idea of who can help us too."

⌘

When Leo and Miles arrived at the cafeteria for lunch the next day, Miles put his hand on Leo's shoulder to hold him back as he scanned the room. A moment later, he found who he was looking for and led Leo to a table where Finn and several of his friends were sitting.

"Hey," Miles greeted him.

"Sup?" Finn responded.

"Uh… We need to talk to you after breakfast…" Miles said awkwardly and Finn's friends looked back and forth between them wondering what was going on.

"You good?" Finn asked, curious why Miles was acting so weirdly.

"Yeah… We just have a question to ask ya," Miles answered, trying to come off as breezy and just sounding even more awkward.

"OK… I guess I'll come find you," Finn said with a look of annoyance.

"Cool," Miles responded and then he started to walk over to get in line for some food.

"Real smooth there," Leo said, poking fun at Miles as they waited for the line to move.

"Whatever," Miles said, unable to come back with a witty retort.

"You could've just told me that Finn can help us," Leo said, shifting into a serious tone. "He *is* my cousin after all."

"Yeah... I suppose that makes sense..." Miles acknowledged.

"So, what do you think he can do?" Leo asked as he heaped potatoes on his plate.

"After breakfast," was all Miles said.

They sat in a weird silence until Mari and Marie joined them a short while later. Leo even became so engrossed in the conversation that he had forgotten about Finn until he appeared at the table, looking expectantly at Miles.

"Oh yeah... Cool! Let's get out of here, Leo," Miles said.

"Uh... I was in the middle of telling a story," Marie said.

"You can pick it up again later," Miles said, clearly unconcerned with her feelings as he grabbed his tray and started to hurry away.

Leo gave Marie an apologetic look and she returned it with an annoyed shrug as she turned to Mari and took another bite.

"What's this all about?" Finn asked Miles as soon as they were out of the cafeteria.

"Not here," Miles answered abruptly and led them to a trail that would take them to a far side of the camp where they had their practicum sessions.

When they were standing in a small gap in the trees, Finn turned to them and stared expectantly.

"We need you to help us steal a van," Miles said.

"What?!" Finn asked.

"You heard me," Miles responded quickly. "Then we need you to hack Oregon's public records system."

Finn didn't even respond this time, he just shifted his gaze back and forth between Miles and Leo, waiting for more of an explanation. When Miles didn't continue, Leo jabbed him hard in the side with his elbow.

"OW!" Miles exclaimed. "Fine, sheesh… We need to get to Portland and find someone as quickly as possible."

"You're gonna have to do better than that," Finn responded.

"We can't tell you more than that," Miles said.

"No dice," Finn said and started to walk back the way they came.

"We have to find him before Gabriel does," Leo said seriously and Finn stopped in his tracks.

"Who is this guy you're looking for?" Finn asked as he turned back around.

"He's another Librarian," Leo explained. "We think he has some memories that we need."

"You two suck at explaining things," Finn said in frustration. "If you want my help, you're gonna have to trust me."

"OK… OK…" Miles responded. "It appears there may be a way to generate enough power to overwhelm any defense. Torrell left behind memories on how to do it, but he made it very hard to find them. Gabriel found out about it and sent people to look for the memories. We need to find them first."

"And how do you two know about these memories?" Finn asked skeptically.

"I was told about them by another Star Born who is looking for them," Leo answered truthfully.

"I assume they're an adult," Finn said. "So why don't you just let them handle this?"

"Because they need all the help they can get and I'm sick of adults underestimating what we can do," Leo said, his face reddening from anger as he thought back to his conversation with Maranda.

"OK, that sounds legit. I'm in," Finn said simply.

"Really?" Miles asked, not sure if he heard right.

"Yeah, my teachers keep trying to hold me back. I'm sick of the training wheels," Finn said, his shared frustration bleeding through.

"Cool, so when do we leave?" Leo asked them.

"After classes are done, we will be noticed if we try to go earlier," Miles answered, his brain spinning up with a plan. "Meet me by the parking area at five."

⌘

Leo, Miles, and Finn converged on the parking lot within minutes of each other. Finn had a large army rucksack that looked extremely heavy. Miles also had a backpack that looked pretty full and Leo wondered why they thought they needed so much stuff for this trip. He had only packed some food since they definitely wouldn't be back by dinner.

"Alright, let's head outta here," Finn said. "No need to be missing too long."

He walked over to a van that was parked in the shade of a large tree. It looked like it had seen better days, with dents and scratches along the side. There was tape holding one of the side mirrors in place. Finn put down his rucksack and opened one of the side pockets, pulling out a small kit. He selected a few tools and then proceeded to unlock the driver side door.

"Why this one?" Miles asked, looking a bit disgusted.

"Because they don't use this one as much. It is less likely they'll notice it's gone," Finn responded as he started to get in and maneuver the seat.

"You know how to drive, right?" Leo asked.

Finn stopped what he was doing and just glared at Leo until

he held up his hands and said, "OK... OK... It never hurts to ask..."

As Leo and Miles walked around to the other side to get in, a voice called out, "What are you guys doing?"

They whirled around quickly and saw Jordan strolling up. Leo's blood ran ice cold and the old anger he thought had run its course flooded back into him. He clinched his right hand into a fist and took slow breaths, trying to maintain the last bit of calm inside him.

"We were bored so we thought we'd go for a joy ride," Finn said casually.

"You are the worst liar," Jordan responded flatly.

"No, it's true!" Miles insisted, his voice cracking from the stress.

"Guys, just cut it out," Leo instructed. "He can feel your emotions and knows you're lying."

"Seriously?" Finn asked with genuine curiosity and Jordan nodded slowly.

"Can you just be cool and let us do what we need to do?" Leo said, trying to give Jordan a shot at being an ally instead of a rival.

"Nuh uh," Jordan said and crossed his arms.

Crackles of static formed around Leo's fist as he tried to hold back his anger. Jordan noticed and took up a defensive posture that Sharon had taught them a few weeks prior. Finn hopped out of the van and rushed to stand between the two Star Borns, holding out his hands as if he could hold them back from a truly destructive fight.

"Guys, let's just talk it out," Finn said.

"There's no talking it out with him," Leo sneered. "And to think I thought maybe you could be a decent person. I should've trusted my original instincts..."

"What are you talking about?!" Jordan growled back. "I never did anything to you! From day one, you were just this cocky brat always thinking you were the best."

Leo opened his hand and formed a large energy orb with red and green swirls. Miles dropped his backpack and rushed to stand with Finn and shouted, "Guys! Listen! We're all on the same side here!"

"I'll never be on the same side as him," Leo said through clenched teeth.

"Jordan, we need to take this van to find someone who can help us beat Gabriel," Miles pleaded.

"What?" Jordan asked, breaking his glare at Leo and looking at Miles.

"Yes! You have to listen! Leo got a tip and I have an idea on where to find a guy who may be able to point us in the right direction," Miles rattled off quickly, trying to take advantage of the moment.

"Don't say any more, Miles. We can't trust him. He'd probably join Gabriel if he could," Leo said with a sneer.

Jordan's eyes opened wide as he formed a long, amber spear with crackling energy. He raised it over his head, preparing to launch it at Leo, and said, "You're gonna pay for that!"

"NO! Both of you just shut up for a second!" Finn commanded and the two Star Borns looked at him like he'd gone crazy.

Finn then turned to Leo and said, "You really don't think before you speak, do you? You also haven't taken much time to get to know Jordan. If you had, you'd know his mom was killed by one of Gabriel's closest advisers right before he came here."

"What?" Leo mumbled as the energy orb sank back into the palm of his hand.

"And you," Finn turned to Jordan. "You accuse Leo of acting like he's the best, but have you looked in the mirror? Do you know how many lunches I've had to sit through while you talked nonstop about how you learned some random ability?"

Jordan took a big sigh as he looked up at the sky and let the spear drop from his hand. It vaporized into a cloud of particles that flowed back into his chest.

"I thought things were getting better since you started working together with Sharon," Miles interjected.

"They were," Leo admitted.

"Then just get over it," Miles said and looked back and forth between Leo and Jordan.

"They're right…" Jordan responded.

"Yeah…" Leo agreed.

"I'm sorry for following you here and… you know… making you think that I'd snitch on you," Jordan said.

"I'm sorry for being such a jerk…" Leo started to say and then a thought occurred to him.

"Wait…" he said as he kept thinking and then made up his mind. "You should come with us!"

"If we're going, we should do it now. I'd bet someone heard us shouting," Finn counseled.

"Really?" Jordan asked Leo.

"Yeah, you should come," he repeated. "It's time we started acting like a team. Everyone has been trying to convince us and it's time we listened. Also, I'm really sorry about your mom. You have every right to help us beat Gabriel."

"Thanks. I appreciate you saying that. Alright, let's go," Jordan agreed and they all rushed to get into the van. Then Finn pulled it out as quietly as he could and made his way slowly down the dirt road.

※

About an hour and a half later, the boys found themselves sitting in a parking lot outside a branch of a ubiquitous cafe chain with Finn typing feverishly on a laptop. They all took turns taking glances at him every minute or so as they fidgeted anxiously.

"Will you all just go in there and get yourself a mocha frappa whatever so I can focus?!" Finn finally snapped and they all took their cue and hopped out of the van quickly.

Leo, Miles, and Jordan sat at a table, slowly sipping on their drinks and barely talking while the cafe buzzed around them. Every so often, a woman with several piercings in her face and arms covered in tattoos would walk by, making it clear that she was watching them. Between that, the time it was taking for Finn, and the caffeine and sugar coursing through them, they became increasingly jittery.

Then they heard the door open and saw Finn walk in, but he didn't stop at their table. He just headed straight for the line and waited to order his drink. The boys all shared annoyed looks, but didn't say a word, even when Finn waited at the counter for ten minutes while the staff created a complicated frozen concoction with a huge amount of whipped cream on top. With his patience exhausted, Leo couldn't hold back when Finn finally sat down.

"So? What'd you find?" he asked Finn in a loud whisper.

"Do you know how many people in Portland are named Lincoln?" Finn answered rather loudly and the others flinched slightly from the thought someone might be listening to them. Finn noticed and rolled his eyes.

"Dude, you didn't give me much to go on," Finn said in a lower tone, turning to Miles. "But, I am awesome and I found your guy."

"You did?!" Miles asked excitedly.

"Totally," Finn answered with a satisfied grin as he leaned back in his chair. "He's a crafty one too. Covered his tracks well, but not enough to fool me."

"So, let's go then!" Jordan said eagerly as he started to stand up.

"C'mon, man! I just got my drink!" Finn protested, but the rest of them were already following Jordan's lead and starting to walk out.

Once they were back in the car, the others chattered excitedly about what they should say to the Librarian when they found him. Finn just drove silently, sipping on his drink, making sure they knew he was annoyed with them. When he finally pulled over on the side of a quiet residential street, slurping the dregs with his straw loudly, the others looked around trying to guess the right house.

"Guys, that's where he used to live," Finn said finally and pointed across Jordan who was sitting in the front passenger seat.

They all looked over and saw the charred remains of a house sitting in the middle of an overgrown lawn. The houses around it were kept perfectly right up to the property line as a sign of anger and defiance since this place was a complete eyesore.

"Uh… You said *used* to live?" Miles probed.

"Yeah, nobody can live in that mess," Finn answered matter-of-factly.

"If he doesn't live there anymore, why did you take us here?" Leo asked in confusion.

"Because I thought you needed to see this," Finn said seriously. "This guy went through the trouble of burning his own house down to not be found. They pronounced him dead even though they never found any remains when they finally put the fire out. It was so hot, it burned down both of the other houses next door. Those are brand new."

"Seriously?" Miles asked.

"Yeah," Finn confirmed. "This guy doesn't want to be found. You sure we should be doing this?"

"It's the only clue we have," Leo responded. "I have no idea what we should do next if we don't give this a shot."

"We're not just talking about getting in trouble with our teachers," Finn pushed back. "This is going to be dangerous. We all might get hurt or even worse. Are you guys sure you wanna do this?"

Each of the others nodded silently and Finn turned back around and gripped the steering wheel tightly.

"Fine," he said, clearly holding back his frustration. "He's not in Portland anymore, it's going to be a bit of a drive."

"Where are we going then?" Jordan asked.

"Some place called Hood River," Finn answered. "I already have it mapped, you can be my navigator."

⋰

An hour later, Finn turned down a small, dead-end street with a few small bungalows spaced far apart and pulled over. He turned off the engine and pointed out the front window towards the house at the very end.

"That's it," he said. "Last chance to turn back, everyone."

Leo opened the door in response and started to walk down the cracked sidewalk that was flanked by tall weeds. Jordan and Miles followed close behind and Finn slid out from the driver's side after they were all half-way down the block.

When they were all gathered in front of the front door, Leo pulled open the rickety screen and gave a few soft raps with the rusty knocker. They heard someone stirring inside and after a brief wait, a man answered the door. He was average height with sandy colored hair and it looked like he hadn't shaved in about a week. He was wearing a flannel bathrobe over a stained t-shirt and sweatpants. His eyes were red around the rims as if he hadn't slept in days as well.

"Can I help you?" he asked.

"Um…" Miles started to say and hesitated.

"Would you by chance be Lincoln?" Leo completed Miles' thought.

The man barely reacted physically, but both Leo and Jordan felt a spike of anxiety erupt from inside him.

"No…" he answered thoughtfully. "My name is Grant. You must have the wrong address."

"We have the right address," Finn said tersely from the back, unable to sense the man was lying and disliking that his research skills were being called into question.

"Maybe a guy named Lincoln used to live here?" the man speculated

"No, you're Lincoln," Finn persisted, unable to let it go and ignoring the looks from the rest of the group. "You bought this house under the alias Grant Thompson for three hundred fifty-two thousand dollars cash eight years ago. Lame alias, by the way. You have lived here by yourself and paid your taxes on time every year since. You also donate to the local library and like to eat at a place called El Pollo Picante a lot."

"I think it's time for you boys to go home now," the man responded angrily as he started to close the door.

"Please, we wouldn't have come to find you if it wasn't impor-tant," Leo blurted out quickly while Jordan shot out a hand to hold the door open.

"Please go!" the man insisted and leaned all his weight on the door, trying to overpower Jordan who squared himself and pushed harder to keep it open.

"We think you have some memories that we need," Miles said, finally finding his voice.

"I'm calling the police," the man said tersely, finally releasing the door and walking back into his house and looking around urgently for his phone.

"As a fellow Librarian, I call on the tradition of Sharaf!" Miles called out to the man. "You are not obligated to share the memories with us, but you must listen to our request and weigh it fairly!"

The man froze, his shoulders tense and his hands flexing into and out of fists. The boys stood quietly at the open door, sensing he was deciding what would happen next.

"Come inside and bolt the door behind you," he said without turning around and then added, "ALL of the bolts."

The boys hurried inside with Finn bringing up the rear. He then shut the door behind him and began to turn each of the five bolts. The man sat down in a well worn recliner and looked up at them. There was no place for them to sit since there was barely any furniture in the house.

"You have five minutes," the man said gruffly.

"So, you're Lincoln," Miles said to confirm.

"According to your know-it-all friend there," he responded. "If you're going to ask dumb questions this entire time, please just do us all a favor and leave now."

"Fine, whatever..." Miles continued testily. "I heard you came across some memories that drove you insane. You don't seem that insane, though. Just more of a hermit who's a jerk."

"Thanks?" Lincoln responded.

"Can you tell us about those memories?" Leo interjected impatiently, feeling the five minutes slipping away quickly.

"I can, but I don't want to," Lincoln answered and then turned back to Miles. "Explain to your friends how this works."

"A librarian is the protector of the memories they carry," Miles said hurriedly. "They are never required to share them or speak of them. Only *they* can determine if the requester has a legitimate claim to the memories."

"We are fighting people who will become an unstoppable force if they get their hands on the memories we are looking for!" Leo pleaded.

"You don't want these memories," Lincoln responded seriously. "They have taken everything from me. My family… My friends… My home… The price is too high!"

"We believe they may be pieces to a puzzle," Miles countered. "The original memories were chopped up to make it hard to assemble them again because they would explain a ceremony that would create a power so strong that it could overcome any defense."

"That kind of power should never be allowed, which is exactly why I can't share these memories with you!" Lincoln responded with a shaky voice.

"So you do have the memories we are looking for!" Miles said excitedly.

"Guys…" Finn chimed in as he looked out the window.

"Yes, it took me years of study to figure out what they were about and I unwittingly raised some alarm bells with the wrong people," Lincoln responded, ignoring Finn. "Then one day, a man showed up at my front door. He was so smooth and dressed impeccably… My kids loved his accent too…

"Guys!" Finn said more urgently, but Lincoln just continued as if he were in a trance.

"We had no idea how dangerous he was… We invited him to dinner! When the meal was done and the kids had gone off to watch a show, that's when he mentioned what he was looking for. At first, I was excited to talk to someone about my research. The more I shared, the more excited he got and his disguise peeled away.

"I got nervous and tried to make an excuse that it was getting late, but he was so fixated on these memories that he wouldn't let us leave the table. When I finally asked him to leave, he got angry and demanded that I share the memories with him. When I refused, we found out that he was a Star Born. He attacked us, but my wife somehow was ready for it and sent all the dishes flying at him. This gave us enough time to run out of the room, but he just kept coming, setting everything in the house on fire as he went.

"We managed to escape… barely… We hid together for a few months after that, but someone found us. We were ready for it that time and ran again, but it was clear that we would be safer apart. It's been years of running… They've found me three times since then, but I've been here for a couple years and I thought maybe we'd finally hidden ourselves successfully. Now, you're here and I know I was wrong. We can never hide from people looking for these memories…"

"GUYS! DUCK!" Finn yelled as he dropped to the ground and something large flew through the front window and slammed into the opposite wall.

Leo dove instinctively to the floor when Finn yelled and looked to see that it was a rusty car wheel surrounded by a deflated tire.

"STAY DOWN! ANOTHER ONE'S COMING!" Finn yelled again and seconds later something large and heavy slammed into the front door, but it held up thanks to it being made of metal and all the locks Lincoln installed.

"How many are there?!" Jordan called out.

"I don't know," Finn answered. "I only saw three. One's a huge Heavy. He's the one chucking stuff at us."

As if to accentuate Finn's report, another object slammed into the door, bending the top third inward slightly. Then several small contraptions flew through the open window and hovered, clearly scanning the room.

"Get those now!" Finn shouted and both Leo and Jordan threw energy orbs at them. They hit two, but the third found a target and swooped down, creating a small explosion as it slammed into Lincoln's chest. He just continued to sit in his chair, eyes open wide, frozen and unable to respond. Miles reached up from the floor and pulled hard on Lincoln's wrist, tugging him to the floor.

"How bad?" Leo asked urgently.

"Very…" Miles answered soberly as he looked at the injury.

"OK, see what you can do for him, we'll try to buy you some time," Leo said as he looked over to Jordan, who nodded in acknowledgement. They pushed themselves up and then jumped through the window with energy orbs glowing in their hands. They immediately saw the huge Heavy standing on the patch of dirt that was once a front lawn. Not only were they intimidating because of their sheer size, but they were also holding a large chunk of sidewalk that had been torn out of the ground.

"MOVE!" shouted Finn from behind them and they both dove in opposite directions as the Heavy sent the concrete crashing through the house's wall just next to the front window.

Leo caught sight of the other two fighters who were standing just behind the Heavy. One was a Technic and fished out another drone from a bag at her feet. The other was a Chimera who had morphed into a giant wasp with human legs and was hovering just off the ground.

"I've got the Heavy!" Finn called out and they saw a large millipede contraption flow out of his backpack.

"Fine! I'll take the Chimera," Leo added.

Jordan didn't say anything, he just started running at the Technic full tilt and the Chimera started rushing to head him off.

Leo jumped up from the ground and, acting on instinct, created a large energy net as he tried to move around Jordan's path to get a good angle. Jordan, in the meantime, had erupted in red, blocky armor that made him look like a demonic robot. The drones began attacking him, but for now his armor was holding up. They both heard a huge crash from behind them, assuming it was another part of the house collapsing and hoping Finn was OK as they focused on doing their parts.

Finally getting a clear shot, Leo cast out the net and it only managed to catch the Chimera's wings. That was enough to keep Jordan safe, though, as the Chimera crashed to the ground making some of the scariest noises Leo had ever heard. Its arms and pincers made sizzling sounds as it struggled to pull off the net and Leo took the opportunity to run as fast as he could to get close to it. He borrowed one of Maranda's tricks and created a giant hook and slammed it into the ground right next to the Chimera. The hook sank deep and wrapped around the Chimera's torso, pinning it to the ground.

Leo looked up to check on Jordan and realized he didn't need to worry. The Technic was lying unconscious on the ground and he was staring with his mouth open wide at the Heavy. Leo looked over and couldn't believe his eyes. The millipede had spawned an army of smaller replicas of itself and they had swarmed all over the Heavy who was struggling to deal with them. Every inch of skin was covered by the bots and they were dragging the Heavy down the ground with black tethers. It struggled, but it was no match for Finn's contraption.

Miles had heard the battle erupt outside and turned back to Lincoln who groaned as Miles pulled away pieces of metal that once made up the device that had attacked the older Librarian.

"Sorry," Miles said as he removed the last of the pieces and pressed a dingy blanket that had been draped over the side of the chair into Lincoln's chest.

"Why do you want these memories so badly?" Lincoln asked through halting breaths.

"To stop *them*," Miles explained, gesturing his head toward the attackers outside. "They want to release Warwick. If they get their hands on these memories, they'll be one step closer."

"A power like this is too dangerous to wield…" Lincoln murmured, closing his eyes. Miles shook his shoulder and Lincoln opened his eyes wide and tried to take a deep breath before it hitched in his chest and he started to cough uncontrollably. When it finally subsided, he saw the concern on Miles' face and gave a slight grin.

"I'll give you what you came for," Lincoln said slowly. "But, this is too much of a burden for someone so young. I am afraid for you…"

Then Lincoln took Miles' hand and closed his eyes. Miles gasped and collapsed to the floor, trembling violently as Lincoln began the transfer. Images, sounds, scents, and feelings pummeled his mind without any rhyme or reason. The onslaught was beginning to overwhelm him, but he drew on his training and began to protect his mind while allowing the information flow to continue uninterrupted. He couldn't track the passage of time, so he had no idea how long it had been when the transfer was completed. It simply stopped and he felt someone shaking him and saying his name over and over. Miles opened his eyes a crack and saw the concerned faces of Leo, Jordan, and Finn looking down on him.

"Are you OK?" Leo asked in a whisper.

"I think so…" Miles mumbled in response. "Are we safe?"

"Yeah, for now." Leo answered. "It was just a small group, but we should get out of here. We're not sure how long we can keep them contained."

"What about Lincoln?" Miles asked.

Leo shook his head solemnly.

"What happened?" Finn asked.

"He gave me his memories…" Miles responded, barely able to hold onto consciousness.

"The ones we were looking for?" Leo asked.

"All of them," Miles said as his eyes closed again.

12

ℰVERYTHING ℊOES ℋAYWIRE

ILES WAS PASSED out on the back bench of the van as they drove as quickly as they could back to school. He shivered violently even though he was drenched in sweat and he alternated between muttering unintelligible sentences and moaning softly. Leo and Jordan looked on with concern, but had no idea what to do to help him. It wasn't as if taking him to a hospital would help him. What would a normal doctor know about what he was going through?

"How's he doing?" Finn asked from the driver's seat and Miles immediately let out a cry of agony in response.

"We gotta get him some help," Jordan said after Miles resumed his muttering. "If he keeps going on like this, I'm not sure we will make it back in time."

Finn pushed hard on the gas pedal and what little they could see out of the windows began to whir past much faster than before.

"We are going to be in so much trouble… I'm sorry I got you guys into this," Leo said.

"Hey, we decided to come and I'm glad we did. You guys were right to look for Lincoln and we got there before his memories fell into the wrong hands. We're in this together," Jordan responded and Leo was so grateful for the sentiment. It felt like a strong bond had now formed between them.

"Yeah…" Finn said and then paused as if he was thinking about what else he had to say.

"Finn?" Leo eventually prodded after the silence had lasted a bit too long.

"Sorry, I thought I had something good to say, but realized I was just going to say what Jordan said," Finn said sheepishly and they all laughed, trying to let some of the nervous energy out.

Suddenly, Miles gasped and sat up straight, looking around in a panic as he tried to understand his surroundings.

"Miles? Are you OK?" Leo asked.

"Pull over!" Miles shouted.

"We can't, we need to get you some help," Jordan responded calmly.

"PULL OVER!" Miles shouted again even louder and Finn began to slow the van down as he neared a small dirt road to pull off.

Miles began to speak so rapidly that they could barely understand him.

"It's all making sense now… I could show them that one… Where was that other one… I'm sure this is the key… Well, maybe not…"

"Miles!" Leo shouted, trying to break him out of what seemed to be an endless loop. "We pulled over. Now, what's so important?

"Well, you see, I need to show you," Miles began to ramp up again. "It's all in there! Every last detail and then some. Lincoln was a master researcher… I still have so much further to go…"

"Miles, you need to focus. We have no idea what you're talking about," Jordan counseled.

"You have no idea?" Miles asked incredulously. "What did we go through all this trouble for? I'm talking about the memories of course!"

"Yes, we get that," Jordan said slowly. "But we don't know what you're trying to tell us about them."

"I think Lincoln found the key," Miles explained.

"The key to making the ceremony work?" Leo asked urgently and Miles nodded enthusiastically in response.

"Can you show us?" Leo asked.

"Why do you think I asked you to pull over?" Miles retorted and gestured for Finn to join the rest of them in the back of the van.

When they were all situated, Miles reached out his hands and they all formed a lopsided circle stretching over the back of the middle bench. Leo's vision began to fade at the edges and he felt the familiar sensations as Miles began to share the memory with them. When everything resolved again, Leo looked around and saw they were in some kind of prison since there were bars and heavy duty doors all around. He also saw Finn and Jordan looking slightly nauseated and realized that he should have warned them about what to expect.

In the corner of the room was a man dressed in torn and soiled clothing. He was huddled in the corner, leaning his shoulder into the walls and rubbing his arms as if the room was frigid and he couldn't get warm. Torrell and a woman were talking to each other a few paces away, but maintaining a wary gaze on the man. They realized this was wise because, a moment later, the man screamed loudly and his hands began to glow brightly as if he was going to attack someone. Then, just as quickly, everything faded and he resumed rubbing his arms as he started to rock back and forth.

"We believe this one absorbed ten cores," the woman said and Torrell couldn't help but turn to look at her in astonishment. She looked quite young, but it was clear she was the expert in the room.

"Ten? Really?" Torrell asked.

"Yes, we are pretty confident in our analysis," the woman said.

"And what's the prognosis for him?" Torrell asked as calmly as he could, but there was clearly hope mixed in.

"He must be an amazingly strong Star Born," she began to respond. "Most would have died immediately after absorbing a fifth or sixth core. However, while he isn't dead, he might as well be. That power has warped his mind so much that he is in constant agony. As I have said to you before, it would be better to put him out of his misery. There is nothing left of the man you once knew."

"There will be no more blood on our hands," Torrell answered tersely. "Besides, Nicole, your research has been instrumental. When you sent for me, you indicated that you have found a way to detect if a Star Born has absorbed a core?"

"Yes," she answered. "If only one or two cores have been absorbed, it requires physical contact to detect since the effects will be subtle. As you can see here, the more they absorb, the more fractured their minds become. What we discovered is that a core doesn't just contain the source of an individual's energy, but it also contains the pieces of what make up their mind and, some would say, their soul. Jacob effectively has ten minds competing for control right now. The people he absorbed appear to be fighting him from inside and there is nowhere for him to run or any way for him to release them."

"Please explain your detection technique," Torrell instructed coolly.

"Well…" Nicole started to respond. "After a core has been absorbed, your pattern is changed. The best way we can describe it is that the pattern becomes less defined. Fuzzier, if you will. The pattern will also now contain traces of the core you just absorbed. Even if someone willingly offered you their core, it would fundamentally alter you in mostly unpredictable ways."

"Mostly?" Torrell asked with deep curiosity.

"Every single Star Born we are observing has begun to devolve into some kind of instability and insanity. There have been no exceptions," Nicole answered soberly.

The memory suddenly went dark and Leo braced himself for a transition, but none came. Then a colorful pattern exploded in his vision and he quickly realized that, since it was Torrell's memory, he had closed his eyes to better sense Jacob's pattern. Just as the woman had described, the pattern was clear in its center, but it had a fuzzy rainbow halo that was expanding and contracting in an unpredictable rhythm. It reminded him of when Gabriel lost his temper during training the year before and Leo felt that cool shiver of fear wash over him again.

Just as quickly, the scene in the prison reappeared and Torrell looked at Nicole with intensity.

"This is excellent work, thank you. I must be going now," Torrell said.

"Wait!" Nicole said urgently, grabbing onto his arm before he could turn away. "There is more. We discovered how Warwick and his followers were able to share memories like a Keeper. It turns out the processes are very different. When a Star Born shares a memory, they are giving a very small piece of themselves away. If you absorb too many memories, it has a similar effect as absorbing a whole core. However, this doesn't happen with a Keeper. They can absorb the content and leave everything else behind, so it won't affect them the way it will for a Star Born. It is even more dangerous to share memories with an Earth Born. So far, it seems that only one to two memories can be shared with them before it triggers a destabilizing cascade in their mind. I strongly urge you to try and find as many Keepers as you can, it will be the only safe way to pass on what we are learning now in the face of the Abatement."

Leo sensed the memory was about to transition and he braced himself right before his vision blurred and he found himself in a room with carefully cut stone block walls and a massive round table in its center. Torrell, Siobhan, and another woman were sitting at the table, but quite far apart from each other.

"You are sure Samareen can be trusted with the most important secret in the entire world?" Siobhan asked Torrell.

"She is the only one I would trust with it," Torrell answered soberly.

"Very well then," Siobhan accepted as she turned to look at Samareen. "How much do you know about Moon Borns?"

"Only as much as you let us know about you," Samareen answered bluntly.

"I supposed that is a fair statement," Siobhan responded with a hint of annoyance. "The most fundamental thing I should explain is that Moon Born energy is almost impossible to harness by anyone other than the Moon Born who possesses it. A Moon Born cannot take another's energy, nor can a Moon Born lend it willingly."

"You just said it's *almost* impossible," Samareen probed.

"Yes, there is one situation when it can be harnessed," Siobhan began to answer and she grew very serious. "Death."

"You can harness a dead Moon Born's energy?" Samareen asked, clearly confused.

"No, you can harness it in the moment just before a Moon Born dies," Siobhan clarified. "This is the only time when a Moon Born loses the connection to their energy and we believe it is the only way to create enough power to overcome the protections on the vial imprisoning Warwick. If someone is able to harness this energy and combine it with that of Star Borns and Earth Borns, it is completely unstoppable. This is the information we are entrusting to you, Keeper."

"I understand," Samareen said softly.

Siobhan turned back to Torrell and leveled a piercing stare at him as she continued, "And this is why our people must maintain a certain level of separation from the rest of you. The Council does not wish to do this, but we must ensure no Moon Born will ever allow this ceremony to be performed. We must be in complete control of our education and training."

"You know how much I disagree with this," Torrell huffed.

"Yes and, thankfully, you're not a member of our Council," Siobhan responded frigidly.

Then the memory faded away and they were all back in the van. Miles let go of Leo and Jordan's hands and then slumped back in the seat, panting shallowly.

"Is that all you got from Lincoln?!" Leo asked anxiously.

"No, he gave me thousands of memories… Way more than what we should have done in a single session," Miles responded haltingly, slurring his words. "They also came over in a complete mess. He was supposed to help keep the memories… organized as they are transitioning over. But Lincoln was dying… I could feel that when we were connected. He basically just did a massive data dump… The ones I just showed you were the first I could find that might be useful… I'm gonna to need some time to sort through the rest. I'm not sure when I will be awake again…"

Miles' eyes grew heavy again and he layed back down. As soon as he was out, he began to shiver and Leo knew that he was back at work, sorting and indexing his mind.

❧

Something wasn't right when they pulled into the parking lot at the school. The air was thick with smoke and the lights that lit the road and paths were all off. After Finn parked the van carefully so it looked like it hadn't moved an inch, they all sat anxiously for a moment until Finn broke the silence.

"Uh… This doesn't look good…" he said.

"Yeah…" Jordan muttered.

Leo didn't say anything, he just tried to stretch his senses as far as they would go and he was instantly blasted with the feelings of fear and anger. The strength of it caught him off guard and he gasped and held his chest before he could regain control.

"What's the matter?!" Jordan asked urgently.

"Something terrible has happened…" Leo said through clenched teeth. "Everyone is awake. I think we weren't the only ones visited by Gabriel's followers tonight…"

A second later, Jordan gasped as well and looked at Leo, confirming he felt the same thing.

"What do we do?" Finn asked Leo.

"We find out what's going on," he responded and opened the side door.

It took all three of them to maneuver Miles out of the van and then Leo and Finn each placed an arm over their shoulders since they were the closest in height. Jordan led the way as they walked slowly with Miles' feet dragging behind them. The smoke in the air caught in their throats and they alternated coughing as they made their way down the wide trail to the main part of the campus.

When they reached what should have been the main area with the school building, cafeteria, and offices, there was nothing. All three buildings were only smoldering pieces on the ground and several elementals were directing heavy streams of water at them. Some of the teachers were barking orders at students who were rushing around in response. There were also several teachers sitting on the ground together near the large oak tree that had been close to the cafeteria. Ernest was kneeling by one of them, his hands healing a particularly ghastly gash on the side of her head. Leo and Finn were so surprised by the sight, they nearly dropped Miles.

Leo began to turn towards Ernest to see if they could help and he tugged Finn with him, but before they could take a step, they heard Sharon calling their names and they froze. A few seconds later, she was standing in front of them looking furious.

"Where have you been?!" she demanded.

"Uh… we were just out on a walk…" Finn said, fumbling for any explanation but the truth.

"Oh really?! And what happened to Miles on the walk?" Sharon asked, clearly seeing through the lie.

"He just got really tired. He hasn't been sleeping well recently," Finn continued, digging himself deeper.

She stared at him in disbelief and then looked at Leo and Jordan for the real explanation. They just returned blank stares, doing their best to mask their emotions. Finally, fed up with the exchange, she turned back to Finn and glared.

"You have some nerve lying to me, but I don't have the time

to deal with you right now," she said. "It was probably dumb luck that you weren't here when we were hit by the attack. There were over forty of them and this is just the start of the destruction they left behind."

"Forty?" Leo said, unable to believe they could get that many people to the school undetected. Then he remembered they had someone on the inside. He began to scan the area, looking for Ms. Herbert. She was nowhere to be found.

"They were looking for you," Sharon continued. "They went straight for your bunk house. It was the first one to be destroyed."

This time, Leo really did drop Miles, whose limp body pulled Finn down with him.

"Is everyone OK?!" Leo asked.

"Yes, only a handful of students were harmed in the attack. All of your bunkmates are safe. However, the same can't be said for your friends from Kensington. All of them were taken during the attack."

"WHAT?!" Leo shouted and many of the students rushing around stopped to look for a moment before carrying on with their assignments.

"You heard me," Sharon said sternly. "Now take Miles over to Ernest to see what he can do to help him. Jordan, you can stay with Ernest and amplify him so he can help the injured more quickly. Leo and Finn, meet me over where the offices used to be in a few minutes and I will give you something to do. We need to be ready to leave when the buses arrive in a couple hours. Once we are settled in at our new location, I will deal with you."

Sharon stormed away and Leo helped Finn carefully pick up Miles.

"How did she know I was lying?" Finn asked in a loud whisper as they made their way over to Ernest.

"Dude, she's a Star Born," Jordan explained. "You were totally giving it away."

"Jeez! Really?! How did I not know that she's a Star Born? Also, I really don't like this particular skill you guys have…" Finn lamented as they reached Ernest.

"What's the matter with him?" Ernest asked, glancing up briefly before returning his attention to one of the wounded teachers.

"Information overload," Leo answered truthfully.

"I see," Ernest said as he multitasked. "How many memories?"

"Thousands," Jordan chimed in.

"And how long has he been out?"

"At least an hour, though he did wake up briefly."

"OK, he probably has a ways to go," Ernest responded simply. "You can go now."

"Um…Sharon assigned me to you," Jordan said nervously.

"OK, please amplify me so I can work on this broken leg," Ernest directed and Jordan got to work.

Leo and Finn left Miles with them and reluctantly made their way over to Sharon who was talking to one of the teachers, Jaime, who oversaw all the advanced elemental classes.

"Ah, there they are," Sharon said and Jaime gave them a nod hello. "Leo, Jaime needs you to amplify the elementals who are dismantling the remaining buildings. Finn, since you're one of our few Technics, I need you to help me undo all of our electrical systems and then secure our computers."

Jaime started to walk away and Leo followed her, giving a small wave to Finn. The next few hours were some of the most exhausting that Leo had ever experienced. By the time they had finished taking apart the entire school campus, it looked like nothing had ever been there. Soon afterward, the buses arrived and they all piled on, filthy and ready to pass out. Everyone was silent as they made their way slowly down the gravel road.

⤳

While Leo was exhausted, adrenaline was still coursing through his body and his mind kept running in circles about how he wasn't there for his friends when they were taken. The sun was rising from behind the mountains before sleep finally came, but he was plagued by nightmares and it wasn't restful. A few hours later he was shaken awake by Ernest for a bathroom break and to have some food, but they were soon on their way again and he could barely keep his eyes open.

The next time he woke up, it was nighttime and highway lights were streaming by. He peered up from his seat and saw that almost everyone was fast asleep except for a few pockets here and there. He saw Marie reading a book in the back. Mari was playing cards with Lucy in the middle. Several teachers were talking in low tones at the front of the bus.

Leo's mind began to spin up and the only thing he could come up with to help his friends was to contact Maranda. He also realized that he had promised to find her when he had found a memory and here he may have found a treasure trove. So, he decided against his better judgment and all the warnings he had received up until that point, that he would go find her in the Connector.

He closed his eyes and prepared himself to enter at one of the several safe spaces Maranda had taught him how to find. Going through the list, one by one, he kept striking out as none of them answered his knocks.

"How is this possible?" Leo asked himself, but he didn't see it as a warning sign and searched for the last one on the list. When he couldn't even locate the last location, he finally became worried and decided to do something drastic. Since she was probably asleep, he rationalized that he could go directly to Maranda and moments later he was standing outside her door to the Connector.

He reached for the knob, but stopped short when he noticed the door was not completely closed. It just looked closed, but it wasn't latched. With alarm bells going off in his head, Leo placed his hand on the knob as quietly as he could and gently opened the door just enough so he could peer in. He saw the usual dim space that was the visualization of her mind, lit only by a few lamps placed around the room, and caught sight of Maranda sitting at her desk. She had her head propped up on her hands as she hunched over a thick book.

Everything seemed safe and he was about to open the door all the way when he noticed a large shadow emerge a few paces away from Maranda. Throwing caution to the wind, he flung the door open and yelled, "LOOK OUT!" as he attempted to leap over the chasm that protected the space.

Maranda immediately exploded out of her chair and reached out for the shadow, gripping it with both hands and hurling it toward Leo. He was still mid-air over the chasm as the shadow flew toward him, so he pulled in his legs and then kicked out hard as the shadow sailed below him. He heard a loud grunt as it was sent deep into the pit.

With the momentum from the kick, Leo found himself flying in a slow arc toward a fight that had erupted around Maranda. Several more shadows had appeared and, when he landed, he dove into the fight. All the hours of training together made them a formidable team and they quickly beat back the intruders, sending them all into the chasm.

"Thanks," Maranda said wearily.

"Who were they and how did they get past your defenses?" Leo asked.

"No time. There are probably more coming as we speak. We need to get out of here," Maranda responded.

"But I need to talk to you!" Leo protested.

"We will talk soon. Trust me!" Maranda said and then disappeared.

As the space began to turn gray at the edges, Leo left the Connector and opened up his eyes in the real world. It was morning again and much of the bus had woken up. There was a soft din of conversations around him. However, he wasn't ready to talk to anyone. Too much had happened and his head was swimming with dark thoughts. So he pretended to still be asleep for a little longer until Jordan sat down next to him and said, "Hey, I know you're awake."

Leo sighed, opened up his eyes, and sat up.

"We don't have to talk about anything. In fact, I think I'd prefer not to," Jordan said.

"Sounds perfect to me," Leo agreed.

"Take a look at this," Jordan said and pulled a hand-held game console out of the backpack sitting on his lap.

"How the heck..." Leo began to ask.

"C'mon," Jordan interrupted. "You know where this came from."

"Finn," Leo said immediately.

"Exactly. He found it during the cleanup when he was searching for all the electronic stuff. Fancy a race?" Jordan asked, handing Leo one of the controllers.

They managed to spend most of the rest of the day playing video games, exchanging stories from home, and eating junk food that had also been smuggled onto the bus by enterprising students. It didn't take the guilt away that he felt from his friends being taken, but it did help him pass the time until it was night again and most of the students went to sleep in their seats. Leo didn't join them, he just stared out the window, and the night dragged on slowly until he was being nudged awake by Sharon the next morning.

"Rest stop?" Leo asked as she moved to the next row.

"No, we're here. Gather in front of the school building," she instructed.

Leo stretched his back and shoulders, trying to work out some of the knots that had developed, and then quickly lowered his arms when he got a whiff of the smell from not bathing in a couple days. He decided that was the first order of business when he had a free moment. Then he joined the line of students getting off the bus.

He hopped down from the last step and looked around to see the teachers being greeted by their colleagues from the new school. One of them looked almost exactly like Maranda and he did a double take before realizing it really was her. He immediately ran to her and wrapped her in a huge hug, which she returned.

"I told you we would talk soon," Maranda said in his ear.

"You could've told me that I was going to see you in person! I mean, I haven't seen you since we left Kensington," Leo admonished her as he pulled back to look at her.

"Too risky," Maranda said and then added, "Besides, where's the fun in that?"

"Listen up, everyone!" Sharon called out from the top of the steps to the school building. "We are going to find a place for everyone to go today, but it will take a little time and we are going to have some cramped quarters. Please stay around this area and listen for your name to be called so we can get you situated."

"I should probably go help with that," Maranda said.

"Yeah, but you owe me a conversation," Leo responded.

"I know, I know," Maranda said as she walked away.

"Today!" Leo called after her and she waved back in acknowledgement.

⁊

Leo waited for almost two hours for his name to be called along with the five other students who were the last to be assigned bunks. He was led to an almost exact replica of his old bunk house, except this one had been retrofitted to cram in as many bunk beds as possible. The only available spot was a bottom bed right next to the creaking door.

"Did they actually engineer that door to be so loud?" he wondered to himself and then inspected the supplies that had been left on his bed. There was a towel, a couple pairs of shirts and pants, a light jacket that was several sizes too big for him, some socks that appeared to be used and stained, a toothbrush, and miniature tube of toothpaste, and a bar of soap. He had felt like he was kind of roughing it before, but this took things to a whole new level.

It didn't help to wallow, so he grabbed the towel and bar of soap so he could wash the multiple days of grime off of him and smell somewhat tolerable. Once he got under the hot water, it felt like paradise and he intentionally took as long as he could to clean up. He would've stayed longer, but one of his new bunk-mates yelled through the curtain that he was using up all the hot water and he reluctantly finished up.

When he walked out with his towel wrapped around his

waist, Maranda was sitting on his bed and talking to a few of the other kids he hadn't met yet. He flushed red with embarrassment, when Maranda noticed him and she grinned in acknowledgement before saying her goodbyes and stepping out so he could get dressed. He hastily threw on some clean clothes and shoved his dingy ones in the locker at the end of his bunk. Then he walked out to find Maranda.

She was sitting under a tree a short way down the path, humming to herself and Leo felt glad that she was looking more like herself. She got up and he approached and gave him another big hug.

"Oh, that's much better than before," she said playfully.

"Hey, you try and smell fresh after days on a bus," Leo said defensively.

"Heck, I probably smelled worse than you when I got here," Maranda acknowledged. "Let me show you around while we talk."

"Uh, I think we should find someplace kinda private?" Leo suggested.

"I know you found a memory," Maranda said flatly. "Don't be so paranoid, we are safe here and there are a ton of powerful Star Borns and Earth Borns here to protect everyone. We even have a Moon Born!"

"You do?" Leo asked, getting distracted.

"Uh huh," Maranda confirmed. "He's been here from the beginning actually. He happens to be married to the head of our school. We've learned a lot from him. I actually have a ton to share with you too."

Maranda then stopped and Leo noticed they were standing next to a bench that faced a small pond. She gestured for him to sit down and then joined him. They stared out at the smooth mirror of water in silence for a minute before Maranda turned to Leo.

"So, let's get on with it," she said and took his hand. "Share the memory with me."

"Wait," Leo hesitated as he wriggled his hand out of her grasp. "How many memories have been shared with you?"

"Six… Why?"

"I think I should tell you about the memories instead."

"What? How come?" Maranda asked in confusion.

"One of the memories Miles was able to find was about what happens to a Star Born if they absorb cores and memories," Leo explained. "While we can share memories, we only have a limited capacity and it can really mess up our minds if we try to push it."

"I don't understand," Maranda said as she furrowed her brow.

Leo took several minutes to describe the memory that Miles had shared with him and by the time he was finished, Maranda seemed to understand his caution.

"OK, fine, we can just share the memories the old fashioned way," Maranda said.

"Thanks," Leo responded with relief and then recounted the second memory that Miles had shared about the ceremony that could harness a Moon Born's energy to break the seal on Warwick's prison.

"Whoa… I didn't see that one coming…" Maranda said when he had finished.

"Neither did I," he admitted.

"And that's everything Miles found?" she asked.

"So far."

"What do you mean?"

"He said that he received thousands of memories in the transfer and they weren't organized," Leo explained.

"Now I understand why they have him in the infirmary," Maranda said as if everything were finally clicking into place.

"Why the infirmary?" Leo asked, seeing that it was his turn to be confused.

"He's a Librarian, right? He might not wake up for days while he is processing all that information. I heard one took a month to process everything recently when a senior Librarian transferred their memories to her," Maranda explained.

"That must've been the one he was talking about when we first met. He wanted to be the one to get those memories," Leo said,

"Well, he should be glad they didn't do that given what he's going through right now. He might never have woken up," Maranda said gravely.

⁓

After several days of acclimation, the break was over and classes started up again. Everyone began to settle into their new routine with the typical friction that comes with having too many people in the same space. Leo, Jordan, and Finn still made a point to eat dinner together every night and then go visit Miles in the infirmary. They would talk to him like he was in a coma, telling stories, cracking jokes, and occasionally trying different methods to wake him up.

This was their rhythm for several weeks until they arrived on a Friday evening and Miles' bed was empty. They rushed to the nurse's office and banged on the door. She took her time opening it and looked at them with disdain.

"What happened to Miles? Is he OK?" Jordan asked, not even letting the nurse get a word out.

"You think it's OK to come here and bang on my door?" the nurse asked, deliberately not answering his question.

"Look, we're sorry. It's just that we're worried about him," Finn said, stepping in front of Jordan to avoid him saying anything else and convincing the nurse not to tell them anything. The tactic worked and her face softened.

"He's fine," she confirmed. "He woke up earlier today and we ran some tests on him. He seems to have completed his indexing and is healthy all things considered. They let him move into his bunkhouse about thirty minutes ago."

Jordan began to open his mouth to speak and she put up her hand to stop him.

"He's in eighteen," she said. "Now go on and let me get my work done so I'm not in here all night long."

The boys had memorized the entire campus within a couple days of their arrival and they knew exactly where bunkhouse eighteen was located. They sprinted down the paths and arrived at the door in less than a couple minutes. It was one of the buildings that had been grown by Biologics and it took them a bit of effort to locate the door handle. When they entered, they saw a group gathered on the far side of the room that included Mari, Lucy, and Marie.

"Hey guys! Did ya miss me?" Miles greeted them when their heads peered over the group sitting around him.

"It was definitely quieter," Leo said earnestly.

"Actually, it looks like you are missing a bunch of yourself," Finn joked, pointing out how thin Miles had become.

"The food was simply inedible in the infirmary," Miles joked back since he couldn't eat normally while he was unconscious for weeks.

"Miles was just telling us that he is now one of the librarians holding the most memories in the world," Marie informed them.

"Really?" Leo asked, not quite believing what he heard.

"Yup! Lincoln transitioned eighty-four thousand memories to me," Miles confirmed.

"What?! You were able to process that in a few weeks?" Jordan asked.

"It's a new record," Miles said with a wide grin.

"You're crazy, man," Jordan responded, shaking his head and the rest of the group chuckled.

"Hey, Leo," Miles said to get his attention. "I heard your friends were taken… I'm really sorry…"

Leo felt the familiar throb of guilt swell in the middle of his chest.

"But, I think I know where they might be," Miles continued.

"Really?!" Leo said hopefully.

"Yeah, I found the rest of the memories we need," Miles said, dripping with nerdy excitement.

"Well, out with it!" Mari said.

It appeared Miles had forgotten there were others there when he was talking with Leo and he hesitated.

"Oh, no you don't," Mari said seriously. "They're our friends too. We want in."

"She's right," Finn said.

Leo and Jordan nodded in agreement too.

"Alright…" Miles began. "Probably the best place to start is that one of the memories explained how there are specific locations around the world that enhance our abilities. One of those places was the temple that held the vial where Warwick was imprisoned. If Gabriel wants to perform a ceremony to break him out, he's definitely going to be found in one of these places."

"OK…" Lucy said. "So, we just have to figure out where the other locations are."

"I have a map!" Miles immediately responded. "It was a part

of another memory and I memorized it. There are about twenty of them."

"So, we have to go search twenty different locations?" Lucy asked.

"No, I think I know where he is," Miles said with a cocky smirk.

"What makes you so sure?" Jordan challenged.

"Because fourteen of them are in remote locations that would make it very hard to gather a large group. Three of them are in cities that would make it hard to not be noticed. One is in Hawaii next to a volcano that happens to be erupting right now. It's unlikely he went back to the temple in Yosemite. So, that leaves just one place," Miles explained.

"And?" Marie asked impatiently.

"It's in Egypt, of course," Miles said, like it should have been obvious to everyone.

"Are you serious?" Leo said exasperatedly to no one in particular.

"What's the problem with that?" Miles asked genuinely.

"Well, we have to start putting together a plan to rescue them and stop Gabriel from performing the ceremony in a country half-way around the world," Leo explained.

"If you have to put it that way…" Miles began to respond before Jordan interrupted.

"We'll figure out a way," he said so confidently the rest of them immediately believed him.

13

IN THE DEEP END

IT WAS so quiet that Caroline could have heard someone whispering on the opposite end of the city. That is, if she had been paying attention to that. Instead, she stared at a piece of silver that had been fighting every effort she made to place it in a particular spot on the cover of her book. She had been at it for hours already and this was the third day in a row that she had stayed up until the wee hours when she should have been getting some rest. It wasn't as if she could afford to lose even half an hour of sleep.

Since she had started attending the advanced classes, it took every ounce of her mind, body, and soul to be able to absorb even a fraction of what was being taught. She would have brief flashes of comprehension and then long periods of complete bewilderment. The only place she had felt like she was in her element in the past month was in the Expression workshop with her tools and her book. Whenever she settled in to work on it, a feeling of calm and deep focus would wash over her and hours would disappear in the blink of an eye.

At least, that's how it had been up until a few days before. She was so close to completing the cover design for her book, but had gotten stuck. Not only that, but she was out of ideas on what to do and was becoming increasingly concerned that she was going to have to start over from scratch.

Caroline tried the complex technique described in the Book of Connections multiple times, but, no matter how carefully she did it, the silver would not slide into place. She gritted her teeth and clenched the delicate tool in her fist as she stood up to hurl it at the wall far across the room. Instead, she drew on the last remaining bit of her rational mind and placed it as carefully as she could with a shaking hand on the table in a small sliver of free space amongst the clutter she had accumulated.

"Impressive," a voice said from behind her and Caroline whirled around in surprise to see Rebecca sitting on a small bench in the corner with a book in her lap.

"I was sure you were going to destroy that alulet," Rebecca said.

"The what?" Caroline asked half panting as she tried to bring her heart rate back to normal.

"Please don't tell me nobody has educated you on the tools you have been using," Rebecca said with disdain as she set her book down and walked over to Caroline.

She picked up the tool Caroline had set down and held it between her thumb and middle finger. "This is an alulet," Rebecca said slowly and clearly with a raised eyebrow and a grin.

"Well, I've been taught how to use it. I just didn't know that's what it's called," Caroline said while massaging a sore spot in her neck.

"Really?" Rebecca asked in a way that made Caroline instantly bristle.

"Look, I don't see how it makes much difference if I know that thing is called an *alulet*," Caroline said petulantly.

"Learning, curiosity, mastery… These are important parts of being a Moon Born," Rebecca said, shifting her tone in response to Caroline's growing anger. "It's not enough to know the basics of using a tool you have been provided. By learning more about it, you can unlock so much more potential."

Caroline scrunched up her face with a mix of confusion, frustration, and fatigue.

"Here, let me help," Rebecca said as she gestured for Caroline to sit back in her chair and pulled another over to sit next to her. Then she took Caroline's hand and placed the alulet in her palm.

"There are only three people alive currently who know how to make this particular tool and it takes approximately three to five years to create each one," Rebecca began. "It's not that they work for years straight on just this one tool, but each one needs time to rest and prepare for the next phase of the process."

"You're talking about it like it's a living being," Caroline mumbled as she stared at the alulet more closely.

"In a sense, it is," Rebecca said warmly. "But only when in the hands of a skilled Moon Born. You loan it a bit of yourself when using it. That's why it is important to pick the right times to use it. If you're tired, angry, sad, distracted… All of this will be pulled in and will be a part of how you use it."

"So, that's why it's stopped working for me?" Caroline asked.

"It hasn't stopped working, it's just using what you are giving it," Rebecca said as she placed a hand gently on Caroline's shoulder. "I have watched you for the past several nights. I think perhaps we have thrown you too far into the deep end without teaching you to swim."

"Wait, no! I'll get the hang of it, just give me a bit more time!" Caroline said urgently, trying to stop Rebecca from taking something away from her that she now loved.

"Don't be silly, child," Rebecca said with a chuckle. "You will have the time you need. I'm just going to teach you to swim a little better."

Caroline visibly relaxed, her shoulders dropping and the flush on her face started to fade.

"Show me what you were trying to do," Rebecca instructed.

Caroline took the alulet and hunched back over the book as she pointed at the small bit of silver and said, "I need to get this piece into this spot."

"I see," Rebecca said and then stood up, walked between the work benches to the far side of the room. She returned a minute later with another tool that looked very similar to what she had been using. Instead of it having a fine tip at the end, it had an impossibly thin piece of metal in the shape of a tiny garden hoe.

"Try this," Rebecca instructed.

Caroline took the tool and felt the weight of it. It seemed no bigger than what she had been using, but it was significantly heavier. She took a moment to practice using it, getting used to the different feel, and then used the complex pattern she had been trying for days. Suddenly, the piece of silver slid effortlessly into place. Caroline quickly fixed it to the spot with a few extra flicks and grinned up at Rebecca.

"That is a gran alulet," Rebecca informed Caroline. "You will notice as you complete a design, especially one as compli-cated and powerful as the one you are working on now, that it becomes increasingly harder. The pattern sometimes fights you and it becomes more and more important to properly prepare before you work on it. That's why you need to rest, eat well, and spend time with friends."

Caroline smiled sheepishly in response since she had done none of those things recently.

"Still, even when you do all that, sometimes you need something with a bit more oomph," Rebecca continued. "That's when you pull out a gran alulet. But use it sparingly because it takes a bigger piece of you to work and that can take a toll."

With that comment, Caroline began to feel completely drained. Her head felt foggy and it took an incredible effort to keep her eyes even half opened.

"Let's get you back to your room now," Rebecca counseled as she helped Caroline up and led her out of the workshop.

⮝

Caroline woke up the next day with the sun shining through her window and directly onto her bed. It was warming her in a way that felt so cozy that she dozed for a while just enjoying the feeling. It occurred to her that she never felt this comfortable when she woke up in the morning. In fact, she was usually freezing cold and huddled in a tight ball under her covers since the stone walls of her room held no warmth by the end of the night. She had thought of trying to find a way to get another blanket or two, but her friends told her it was pointless to ask. The grownups would just say she would get used to it eventually. However, after many months, she was definitely not used to it.

She finally decided to get out of bed and hobbled over to the window since her legs hadn't woken up yet. She stared out at the large courtyard and saw pockets of people talking and individuals walking briskly across the worn stone paths between the beautiful planters. Then the familiar chimes of the bell began. She counted them by habit and was surprised when they stopped at ten.

"What the?!" she yelled to herself, realizing she had overslept. How could she have done that? The bell tower was practically right outside her room, there was no way she could have slept through those chimes. She turned around to start throwing on some clothes and noticed a tray of food was set on her desk with a note next to it. She snatched it up and began to read it quickly.

> *Dear Caroline,*
>
> *It's time you had a day off. In fact, it's time all of the students had a couple days off. So, enjoy some time with your friends. No work allowed!*
>
> *You will also notice that we left you some breakfast for when you wake up. Since you were so exhausted, I took the liberty of asking Steven to help you have a good night's rest. You most likely will not be awake before ten.*
>
> *Don't skip breakfast! It's one of the three most important meals of the day.*
>
> *Rebecca*

"A day off..." she thought to herself. There hadn't been a single day off since she had arrived in Terradune and she wasn't going to look a gift horse in the mouth. She had barely seen most of her friends since she had started advanced classes. In fact, she only really saw Norah consistently and that was because she was promoted to the advanced Connection class too. She had a sneaking suspicion it was because she would likely fail the class without Norah's help.

Caroline devoured everything on the tray and there were barely even crumbs left over when she finished. Then she finished getting changed and ran out of her room in search of her friends. She didn't have to look for very long though, since she found them at the first place she checked. They were all playing Marco Polo in the large pool located a couple levels below the dormitories. It looked out over the cliffs, so it felt like they were staying at a luxury hotel.

"Hey!" Norah called out and waved when she saw Caroline arrive. "Come join us!"

"Um, I have to run and get my bathing suit," Caroline called back.

"No you don't," Norah said, "I grabbed yours earlier because Steven told us at breakfast that you were passed out and I could go into your room without you noticing. What did they do to you anyway?"

"I have no idea, but it felt amazing," Caroline replied.

"I bet!" Norah said. "My bag is over there if you want to get changed."

Soon, Caroline was in the pool with her friends and having a blast. They had been dying to try the pool for months and never had any time, so they tried to soak it up as much as possible. In fact, the only thing that convinced them to get out was the bell telling them it was time for lunch. A short while later, they were all gathered around a large round table and joking around so loudly that many of the adults had taken their trays outside to eat.

"Oh my gosh, can you *believe* the music that Cariann had us listen to yesterday?" Bea gossiped.

"Totally!" Zora agreed. "I think my ears were bleeding by the end of class."

"Was she having you listen to the classical Moon Born chants?" Norah asked.

"Ugh, yes!" Bea confirmed.

"I like those," Norah said quietly.

"Really?!" Bea asked in genuine confusion.

"Yeah, they make me feel zenned out," Norah explained.

"You know, sometimes I really don't get you…" Zora joked and Norah's face flushed red.

Caroline noticed and she felt the prickle of anger run across her shoulders.

"She's allowed to like it if she wants to," Caroline snapped and Bea's eyes opened wide in surprise.

"Of course you're gonna say that, she's the only reason you're able to be in the advanced class," Bea said snarkily.

Caroline felt her anger flare hotter even though she had the same thought. She just couldn't stand anyone making fun of the closest friend she had made since arriving.

"You're just jealous since you are still in the beginner classes. Maybe if you actually tried to like the stuff they're teaching, you would actually make it out of them," Caroline said harshly and immediately regretted it. She watched as Bea just sat there, tears forming in her eyes. Then she stood up quickly and ran out of the hall.

"Really?!" Zora said to Caroline before getting up to go find Bea.

The rest of the table turned to stare at Caroline and she struggled with the guilt that had immediately erased the anger that had been present seconds before.

"It is kinda weird that I like the chanting… I mean, nobody likes it. Not even Cariann," Norah said, trying to break the tension. However, nobody said a word and the awkwardness just began to build.

"Caroline... You oughta..." Alella began to say, but stopped as Caroline stood up.

"Yeah... I know... Me and my big mouth..." she said as she went to go find Bea.

"Na ah bi ahn miiiine!" Niels said as he shoveled another forkfull into his already full mouth. His cheeks were puffed out like a chipmunk as he struggled to chew.

"Can someone make sure he doesn't choke while I'm gone? I want to be here if that happens," Caroline said and the tension was finally broken at the table as they all started laughing.

It took a while for Caroline to find them and Bea was still crying with Zora's arm over her shoulders. They were not happy to see her and it took a good amount of willpower to not just walk away to avoid the discomfort.

"I shouldn't have said that..." Caroline started to say.

"Duh!" Zora answered on behalf of both of them.

"Yeah... Well... The truth is, I don't think I belong in the advanced classes either," Caroline confessed.

Bea looked up at her with red, puffy eyes, but at least she had stopped crying.

"I don't have a clue what they're talking about half the time," Caroline continued, starting to feel tears forming, too. "They aren't doing anything to help me catch up and I spend all my free time trying to figure it out on my own in my room. I haven't gone to bed before two in the morning for over a week."

"Is it that bad?" Bea asked with a shaky voice and all Caroline could do was nod as the tears flowed down her cheeks.

"Well, I guess that means we're going to have to help you," Zora said matter-of-factly.

"Yeah, I've never stayed up until two," Bea joked and they all chuckled.

"I'm so sorry for what I said," Caroline said from the heart.

"I know," Bea said. "But you were right, I am a little jealous and I wasn't really being cool with Norah, or you for that matter."

"Who's bright idea was it to give us a day off anyway? We clearly can't handle it," Zora said and they all chuckled again as they went to go find the rest of the group again.

⌇

That evening, all Caroline wanted was some quiet time with her book, even though Rebecca had said no work was allowed. She rationalized that it didn't feel like work to her, so it technically wasn't breaking any day-off rules. So, Caroline made her way down to the workshop. When she got there, she saw Juliet standing over her table.

"Sorry, I hope you don't mind," Juliet said when she saw it was Caroline who had come in.

"No, it's cool," Caroline replied.

"It really is magnificent... You've come so far in such a short time," Juliet said, marveling at the cover.

"I have you to thank for that," Caroline said genuinely.

"I don't know about that..." Juliet responded, shaking her head and turning to leave.

"You wanna help me with it?" Caroline asked, suddenly not wanting Juliet to leave.

"I guess we could do that," Juliet agreed and pulled over a chair as Caroline sat down in front of her book.

"I only have this section of the center left," Caroline said, pointing at the drawing she had made of the design that was sitting at the top of a messy stack of papers.

"Gotcha," Juliet acknowledged. "That looks pretty complicated… I did something a while back and learned a cool trick that might help."

Juliet got up, went over to her table and rummaged around for a minute, and then returned with some materials and an alulet. She gently moved Caroline's book and placed everything in front of her and began to demonstrate a complicated set of steps that allowed her to do some amazingly intricate patterns.

Soon, the two of them were absorbed in exchanging ideas and testing them before using them on Caroline's cover. By the time the final bells of the night chimed, they were putting the final piece in place. A rush of energy washed over Caroline and she had to hold onto the edge of the table as the room felt like it was starting to spin slightly. She breathed heavily as the sensation continued uninterrupted, though it wasn't exactly unpleasant.

"Whoa… You OK?" Juliet asked.

"Yeah… I think so…" Caroline said as the sensation faded. "Something weird just happened when we put that bit in place."

"Happens every time you complete a piece," Juliet said warmly. "The more powerful the pattern, the stronger the sensation. Looks like this one was a biggie."

"You think so?" Caroline asked excitedly and Juliet nodded with a big smile on her face, but then it quickly faded.

"What's the matter?" Caroline asked.

"Ah… It's fine… I don't wanna ruin the moment…" Juliet responded.

"Hey, I just finished my book and you are now required to share what's on your mind with me," Caroline said half seriously.

"That's not a tradition I've ever heard of," Juliet said.

"It's a new one," Caroline persisted.

Juliet thought for a moment and then decided to stop dodging the question.

"I'm just wondering how many more special moments like this we are going to have as a people… I mean… If we don't join the fight against Gabriel, the whole world is going to become a much darker place… If they become powerful enough, they're going to come for us. I just don't know why the elders can't see that," Juliet confessed.

"I totally agree," Caroline said. "But they can't stop us from fighting if we want to, right?"

"No, they can't stop us," Juliet confirmed. "But if we leave Terradune before graduating, we will never be allowed back in the city. I just… I don't know if I could handle that."

"We'll just have to find a way to convince them," Caroline said simply and they spent hours coming up with ideas until neither of them could keep their eyes open and they had to call it a night.

⋙

"Hey, can I show you something?" Caroline asked Norah after they had finished breakfast and were walking out of the hall.

"Of course!" Norah said brightly and followed Caroline across the courtyard and down one of their favorite paths toward the workshop. Along the way they chatted about what they should do with their second free day. It felt like such a luxury and they didn't want to waste a minute of it. Norah had crammed her bag full of books that she had been dying to read but never had due to schoolwork.

When they arrived at the workshop, Norah looked at Caroline with concern and said, "Dude, the last place we should be today is the workshop. We already spend too much time in there!"

"C'mon!" Caroline cajoled her. "You're only the second person to see this."

Norah stopped in her tracks and stood so rigidly it was like she had been struck by lightning.

"You finished it!" Norah squeaked.

"Just get in here," Caroline said and held the door open for her.

Norah rushed over to Caroline's table and searched around for the book, but it was nowhere to be found.

"Oops! Looks like one of my stacks fell over," Caroline said as she picked up a load of papers, revealing the book. She placed the papers on top of another precarious stack and looked at Norah with anticipation.

"Oh… my… goooooo…" Norah began to say and trailed off as she began to examine Caroline's handiwork. She leaned over it so closely her nose was practically touching it and spent several minutes looking over every detail. Occasionally, she would lightly touch a spot and would quickly yank her hand back as if it was shocking her.

Caroline tried to wait patiently, but the longer Norah took, the harder it was for her to be quiet.

"So… what do you think?" Caroline asked, unable to wait any longer.

Norah stood up and looked at Caroline seriously as she shook her head. Caroline's anxiety spiked and she started to say, "I mean it's my first one…"

"It's amazing," Norah interrupted. "I've never seen anything like it."

"Really?!" Caroline said, needing to hear it again.

"Uh huh," Norah confirmed and then asked, "What did the rush feel like?"

"You mean when I finished it?"

"Yeah, it happens every time one is completed and nobody knows why."

"Juliet told me a little about that last night," Caroline acknowledged. "It felt like the whole world just tipped on its side. I had to hold onto the table so I wouldn't fall over."

"Whoa! That's a good one!" Norah said excitedly and then looked back down at the book as she asked, "Did you open it?"

"Uh… Actually, no!"

Norah immediately stepped aside and said, "It's your book, you *have* to be the first one to open it."

Caroline stepped in front of it and reached out her hand, noticing it was shaking slightly. She wondered why she was suddenly so nervous and shook out her hands and rolled her head around to let out some of the tension. Then she reached out again and carefully opened the front cover revealing the first page. The cover remained open, unlike most new books she bought at Mr. Novickas' shop where they would immediately snap shut if you didn't hold them open. The first page was blank, just the odd creamy paper she had selected from the storage room with Juliet.

"Huh… That's weird," Norah said.

"What's weird?" Caroline asked.

"Well, normally the book has writing in it. Sometimes there are also pictures. It usually captures everything you have learned or found important," Norah explained.

Caroline couldn't help but feel disappointed and embarrassed that her book seemed to be broken. She stared at it for a moment and then gasped when symbols began to appear on the page. They were nothing like anything she had ever seen before, but they seemed to resemble a cross between hieroglyphics and Asian characters. However, that wasn't the weirdest part for her. She found that she could read the symbols too.

"How is it doing that?" Norah said, mesmerized.

"I have no idea," Caroline responded slowly.

"Those look like ancient Moon Born glyphs," Norah said right next to Caroline's ear as she peered directly over her shoulder.

"So that's what they are…" Caroline started to say and then thought to herself, "Of course they are some kind of ancient Moon Born thing."

"I've studied them a bit," Norah said, "Let's see here, the first one there looks like the one for beginnings."

"It's cool, I can read it," Caroline said distractedly as she tried to keep up with the glyphs that were now appearing quickly on the page.

"No way…" Norah said in awe. "What's it say?"

Caroline began to read out loud.

You are a weaver, connecting strands of knowledge.
I am a rich tapestry, created from those strands.
You are a sailor, tying knots as strong as steel.
I am the ocean you must navigate.
You are a student, ever learning and changing.
I am a teacher, giving this gift to others.
You are a caretaker, tasked with keeping it safe.
I am a vessel, empty and ready to be filled.

"Coooooool…" Norah said softly.

"What does it mean?" Caroline asked.

"No idea," Norah answered flatly.

Caroline turned to the next page, but it was blank. She tried staring at it to see if the book repeated what it did on the first page, but it appeared to not want to do that again. She turned to look at Norah who had sat down in the chair that Juliet had dragged over the night before and was rummaging around in her bag.

"So, your book didn't do this?" Caroline asked.

"No. That's what I am looking for," Norah responded. Then she found her own book and pulled it out. She opened it and flipped through the first few pages that were packed with words and images.

"See?" she said to Caroline.

"Yeah… And yours doesn't write itself in these glyphs?" Caroline asked, pointing to the first page of the book.

"Nope, it's in whatever language the creator prefers. Here, look," Nora responded and placed her book on the table next to Caroline's.

The edges of the two books touched and suddenly, they both began to glow brightly. The two girls immediately jumped back to get some distance. They squinted due to the brightness as they watched both of the books' pages flipping rapidly. Then, just as quickly, the glowing faded and the books shut themselves.

Caroline rushed forward and opened her book, flipping to the second page. It was now populated with more glyphs as was the next page and many more after that.

"What does it say now?" Norah asked, picking up her book and examining it to make sure it wasn't damaged.

"Well, the next page has some of the basic principles that Cariann first taught us in Connections class," Caroline said.

"No… way…" Norah said as she opened her book to the first page and showed it to Caroline. It was the exact same information.

"It's a tapestry…" Caroline said, suddenly understanding the first page. "Your book is a strand…"

"My book is a what?" Norah asked, looking at Caroline as if she had gone crazy.

"A strand," Caroline repeated. Then she picked up the book and ran out of the workshop.

14

Re-Discovery

Jeremy's home was just across the terrace from the workshop and Caroline sprinted up the stairs to the ornate metal gate. She tried to open it, but it was locked. So, she rattled it a few times loudly, hoping Jeremy would hear. When he didn't appear, she continued to rattle the gate and started yelling, "JEREMY!" at the top of her lungs. Norah appeared next to her and tried to convince her to stop, but she knew she needed to see Jeremy.

A minute later, he emerged bleary eyed and with an amazing case of bed head. He walked up to the gate, but didn't open it and looked down at Caroline with deep annoyance.

"You know the teachers got a day off too, right?" he said.

"I have to show you my book," Caroline said.

"Sure. Tomorrow," Jeremy said and turned around to probably head back to bed.

"No, *please*, now!" Caroline insisted.

"I'm going back to bed," Jeremy said without turning around, continuing back to his front door.

"I finished it!" Caroline called out.

"Great! Can't wait to look at it tomorrow!" Jeremy called back as he opened his door.

"It sucked up information from Norah's book!" Caroline yelled louder and Jeremy stopped and slowly turned around.

"It what?" he asked.

"Norah's book touched it and they both started to glow. Then all the information that was in her book was copied into mine," Caroline explained loudly.

Jeremy began to walk back to the gate. He stepped on something sharp and yelled out an expletive before hobbling the rest of the way. Then he opened the gate to let the two of them in and closed it behind them. They followed him up to the small patio in front of his home and he held up a finger to tell them to wait. Then he walked back inside his house for a couple minutes.

When he reemerged, he was fully cleaned up and dressed for the day and tucked under his arm was a book. Caroline's heart skipped a beat. She had wondered what Jeremy's book looked like and she was about to get a chance to see it.

He held out a hand without saying a word and she gave him the book. He looked at it briefly and raised an eyebrow. Glancing back and forth from the book to her, Caroline began to feel a little uncomfortable. It didn't last long, though and he turned to place the book on top of a low stone wall that ran along the top of a stairway that seemed to go down to his basement.

"May I?" he asked Caroline as he hesitated before opening the book and she nodded.

"Huh!" he said when he saw the first page. "I didn't know you knew glyphs."

"Neither did I," Caroline responded.

He went quiet again and she watched his eyes move back and forth as he read the first page over and over.

"I am a vessel… Ready to be filled…" he said quietly.

"That's not what it says," Caroline said.

"I think I know my glyphs a bit better than you," Jeremy said with mild annoyance.

"It says, 'Empty and ready to be filled,'" she corrected.

"No, the glyph for 'empty' isn't here," he responded.

Caroline walked over and re-read the page again, discovering he was right. The words had changed.

"But…" she started to say.

"It's not empty anymore," Jeremy said, helping her understand the change. "The books we create are not like the texts you find in a library. They are alive with the knowledge of their creators. But I think you've created something different here. Something we haven't seen in over a thousand years…"

"Shut. Up…" Caroline said.

"Excuse me?" Jeremy asked angrily.

"Sorry! Not you!" Caroline responded, realizing how it had sounded. "I just don't understand. I'm just a student here. How would I be able to make something like what you're describing?"

"The Book of Connections chose you," Jeremy said simply.

"Yeah, but still," Caroline resisted.

"No 'yeah but's'," Jeremy admonished her gently. "The creators of the Book of Connections imparted knowledge to it and the book decides who should learn it. It chose you and gave you a gift. A *wonderful* gift. Something that has been missing for all of the tribes for too long."

Jeremy took the book from under his arm and placed it next to Caroline's. Again, both books glowed brightly and the pages flipped much faster and much longer than the first time with Norah's. When the process was finished, Caroline came over and opened the book to the middle, but the pages were blank. She looked at Jeremy in confusion and he smiled warmly.

"Close it," he instructed. Then he stepped forward and opened the book to around the same spot and the pages were filled.

"You're not ready for that knowledge yet," he explained. "The book is a teacher. It will know when you're ready."

"This is all too much…" Caroline said, her voice quivering, and Norah came up and put her arm across her shoulders to comfort her.

"I know… We often aren't ready when the call comes, but we still have to answer it," Jeremy said cryptically and Caroline didn't bother asking what he meant.

"I need to go inform the Council about this," Jeremy said a few moments later as he closely examined the cover again. He shut the book and handed it back to Caroline.

"Please keep this with you for the time being," he instructed. "I'll come find you when we are ready. And Caroline, excellent work."

With that, he led them out through the gate and then rushed off to gather the Council members together.

❧

"Nooooo…" Zora said as Caroline recounted the story from just an hour earlier. She and Norah had found the rest of their classmates in a small parklet in the east of the city. They all loved going there to study and hang out because they rarely saw any of their teachers. Plus, there was a fountain with lots of mythical creatures spitting water at each other and they all found it hilarious.

"I swear," Caroline said seriously and Norah nodded her head vigorously to emphasize the point.

"Your book soaks up information from other books," Zora said, still processing. "Like, if I put my Symmetry textbook next to it, it would slurp into your book?"

"No, I don't think it works with all books, just the ones we create," Caroline said.

"Darn… That would've made my bag a lot lighter in the morning…" Zora said jokingly.

"C'mon, this is serious. They want me to talk to the Council again," Caroline said while laughing along with the rest of them.

"Yup, there goes another one of your nine lives," Bea said, continuing the joking.

"You guys are no help at all…" Caroline playfully sulked.

"Clearly, this is valuable," Ryan chimed in. "Jeremy said nobody has been able to create a book like this in centuries, right?"

"Over a thousand years," Norah corrected him.

"Right! A millennium! This is definitely valuable," he reasserted.

"He's right, they're gonna want you to do something," Niels added. "You should ask for something in return."

"Boys always want to get something in return for doing the right thing," Alella complained.

"Hey! I resemble that remark!" Niels said indignantly and Alella opened her mouth to argue before all their brains caught up and everyone started laughing loudly. An old lady peered out from her window, glared at them, and then pulled the shutters closed.

"He's right," Bea said in a low tone and everyone turned to look at her.

"About always wanting a prize?" Zora asked, trying to continue the joking, but Bea shook her head seriously.

"Caroline should ask for something in return," Bea clarified.

"Why?" Caroline asked.

"Because you may never get another chance to ask for something important," Bea responded.

"I don't know if that's a good enough reason…" Caroline began to say.

"You should ask them to start training the rest of us in the advanced classes!" Norah interrupted excitedly.

"Hey, some of us are happy in beginner land," Ryan said.

"Think about it," Norah continued, ignoring Ryan. "You've been saying this ever since you got here. We're going to end up in a war and none of us are ready for that. We need to get thrown into the deep end."

"That's what Rebecca said too… I was thrown into the deep end…" Caroline said softly, understanding where Norah was going.

"So, are you gonna do it?" Bea asked.

"Yeah, you're right, it might be my only time to ask for something big," Caroline confirmed and her friends looked at each other excitedly.

"There's another thing I think I'll ask for too," Caroline added.

"What's that? Norah asked, but then everyone was distracted by someone running as fast as they could down the stone steps that led to the parklet.

"There you are!" Juliet said to Caroline when she reached the bottom of the steps. She had clearly been running all over the city looking for her because her shirt had dark patches from where it was drenched with sweat.

"It's time already?" Caroline asked and Juliet just nodded as she tried to catch her breath.

"See you guys later," Caroline said soberly to her friends as she gathered up her things.

❧

Twenty minutes later, Caroline found herself standing in front of the door to the Council's chambers. Her heart was beating so hard it felt like it was trying to jump out of her chest and her hands were trembling. *How do I keep ending up here?* she thought to herself and couldn't come up with any good answers even though her brain felt turbo charged from all the adrenaline in her system.

"Hey, don't worry, I'll be there with you," Juliet said calmly with a smile and it helped Caroline to start breathing a little more normally.

Juliet knocked on the door and it took a couple minutes for someone to answer the door. When it opened, Jeremy was standing there looking more serious than Caroline had ever seen him.

"Ready?" he asked her.

"Not really," Caroline answered honestly.

"Right answer," he said as he cracked a small smirk and winked at her. "C'mon, let's get up there."

When they entered the chambers, Caroline saw that all the same people from her last visit with the Council were there and in the same seats. Her seat next to Rebecca was also there and waiting for her along with another seat right next to it. Jeremy gestured for them to sit and, when they were settled, Rebecca looked over to her and gave her a reassuring smile.

"We have to stop meeting like this," she joked to Caroline and several of the adults in the room chuckled softly. It helped to take some of the tension out of the air.

"What can I say? I really like it here," Caroline joked back and the laughs were a little louder, giving her some confidence.

"That's great!" Rebecca encouraged. "This is a day to celebrate! One of our most treasured traditions has been rediscovered."

"That remains to be seen," Robert said gruffly.

"Oh hush, you old grump," Rebecca said playfully and then returned her gaze to Caroline. "May we see your book please, young creator?

She pulled the book out of her bag and set it in front of her. It suddenly felt like all the levity had left the room and everyone had started to hold their breath.

"Juliet, if you would," Rebecca instructed and Juliet pulled out her own book and placed it on top of Caroline's. Again, both books began to glow brightly and then Juliet's began to slowly levitate. Both books opened and the pages flipped rapidly for half a minute before they closed and Juliet's settled back down on top of Caroline's.

Rebecca handed Juliet's book back to her and then placed her hand on Caroline's book. She closed her eyes and the cover glowed, then Rebecca removed her hands as the book opened itself to a specific page.

"Glorious," Rebecca said, clearly in awe.

"Just because it can absorb another book, does not mean it's a true grimoire," Robert protested.

"Very well," Rebecca responded with a low, annoyed tone. She stood up, walked over to Robert, and handed him the book. "Please choose something that Juliet has not learned yet in her studies, but could be taught to her by one of us in no more than ten minutes. And it should be outside Jeremy's area of expertise since the book absorbed his knowledge as well."

"Fine… Let's see here," he responded, thinking carefully.

"How about the centering meditation before battle? Neither of you know that, correct?"

Juliet and Jeremy shook their heads.

"Check it," Rebecca said flatly and nodded at Caroline's book. Robert rolled his eyes at her and then placed his hand on the book. It began to glow, but faded quickly when it did not find what he was looking for.

"Steven, would you please take Juliet and Jeremy into the other room and quickly train them?" Rebecca requested and the three of them hurried out of the room.

The rest of the attendees chatted with their neighbors, but Caroline sat quietly and counted the seconds. It was an excruciating wait for her and became even worse when ten minutes came and went. She kept counting and finally they reappeared when Caroline's count had reached twelve minutes. They quickly took their seats and Rebecca walked back around to stand next to Robert.

"Go on then," she said to him calmly and he placed his hand on the book. Just like the time before, it glowed brightly, except this time the book opened itself and flipped to a specific page. He looked down at it and his eyes opened wide as they watched his lips move while he read the page. Then he looked up at Caroline with an awed expression.

"It's written in glyphs..." he said and swallowed hard.

Rebecca reached down and gathered up the book. Looking at Caroline as she walked back around the table to her seat, Rebecca said, "You probably don't know this, but Robert is our resident expert on ancient Moon Born glyphs."

"Tell me child, when did you start studying them?" Robert asked, clearly excited.

"I... uh... I'd never seen them before creating the book," Caroline said.

"But… but… but… that's not possible! The book follows the creator's preferences," Robert said, struggling to understand.

"It's not a creator book," Cariann interjected. "It's a grimoire. It is meant to be accessible by all."

"Exactly!" Rebecca agreed.

"This knowledge must be shared so we don't lose the ability to create another grimoire to the ages again," Cecil said.

"I agree," Charlotte said to Caroline's surprise and many of the others around the table nodded their heads.

"I move that we have Caroline begin training others in the lost art immediately," Cecil said energetically.

"One moment please," Rebecca said in a firm, but measured, tone. "As we know, the power to create a grimoire, while intended for the benefit of our people, can also be used for much darker purposes. We cannot train just anyone, there must be a pure intent in learning the art and creating a grimoire. Caroline pursued this because it called to her and she had no agenda other than to answer that call."

The room erupted into several separate conversations, but Caroline could make out that many of them agreed with Rebecca.

"Everyone! Everyone! Please! Can we return to our discussion…" Rebecca called out and pulled the group back together.

When everyone was quiet again, she continued, "I do agree that it would be prudent for Caroline to begin training another so we can resume our role of connecting our society through knowledge. I also believe we have the right person here with us today."

"Clearly you mean Jeremy," Robert responded.

Jeremy began to shake his head slowly and everyone waited patiently for him to speak.

"It is such an honor to even be considered to learn this art," he began, "but I would not be a good choice."

"How can you say that?!" Robert asked incredulously. "You're one of the most talented Expression teachers we've ever had!"

"You flatter me," Jeremy responded. "Unfortunately, I do not believe I can maintain the purity of purpose that Rebecca correctly pointed out is required for these studies."

Robert opened his mouth to disagree further, but Rebecca raised her hand and took back control of the meeting.

"I believe that Juliet would be the best choice to begin training at this time," she said. "They have been working together for many months and have established a strong bond. Juliet also helped Caroline finish the book. I believe this is no coincidence and sometimes we need to follow a sign when it appears."

"I agree and move that we have Caroline train Juliet in the art of grimoire creation," Honore said.

"Seconded," Charlotte followed up.

"All those in favor?" Rebecca asked and all five members of the Council raised their hands.

"Unanimous!" Rebecca confirmed.

"Uh, excuse me," Caroline said.

"Yes?" Rebecca asked.

"I believe that I have a choice in whether I want to take on the responsibility of training someone, right?" Caroline asked as she looked around the table.

"Yes... That is true..." Rebecca said with concern and confusion. "I had assumed you were open to taking on that responsibility due to its importance to our people."

"Oh, I am! I mean... yeah... I am absolutely willing to do it," Caroline said quickly, her nervousness growing rapidly. "But I'd like to ask for something in return..."

"See, Rebecca? Your favorite student is not as pure as you thought!" Robert said, disgusted with Caroline seeking to benefit from the discovery. She turned beet red, but not from his accusation. More from the thought that she was Rebecca's favorite.

Rebecca shot Robert a cold stare that silenced him and then turned back to Caroline.

"What do you want to ask for?" she asked Caroline slowly, enunciating every syllable.

"Well… um… I'd like for the rest of my class to begin training in the advanced classes," Caroline answered.

Rebecca raised an eyebrow and looked over to Steven who shrugged slightly and then nodded. She did the same with Sharla, Marina, Cariann, and Jeremy. Each nodded in response and Rebecca leaned back in her chair and said, "I believe we can meet this request. All teachers seem satisfied that this class of initiates is prepared for the rigors."

"Are you serious?! We discussed the dangers of accelerating training last time she was here!" Robert began to protest again.

"Can we just vote?" Rebecca asked exasperatedly.

"I move that we allow Caroline's classmates to accelerate their training," Cecil said.

"Seconded," Honore followed close behind.

"All in favor?" Rebecca asked and everyone, except for Robert, raised their hands. He looked at Charlotte like she had betrayed him.

"Done," Rebecca confirmed, "Now if there are no other items…"

"One more thing," Caroline interrupted and Rebecca turned to her with a look that said she should be quiet and it almost worked. However, Caroline took a deep breath and said, "I would also like you to reconsider your decision and begin supporting the rest of the tribes that are fighting Gabriel."

Rebecca's expression changed ever so slightly and Caroline

could tell she was struggling to hold back a smile. Nervousness began to melt away and she leaned back in her chair and began to stare at the edge of the table, praying that her plan would work.

"I suggest the Council considers this request privately," Rebecca said before anyone, particularly Robert, had a chance to say anything else. Caroline heard chairs pushing back from the table and she looked around to see everyone who was not on the Council getting up to leave. She began to join them, but Rebecca placed a hand on her arm and said, "Please wait for me in the courtyard after dinner."

✧

Caroline's classmates couldn't believe the idea worked and they were all going to begin advanced training together. It was all they could talk about for the rest of the day and they insisted on waiting with her after dinner. Rebecca finally appeared as the doors to the hall were closed when the last stragglers left.

"Please stay," she said when Caroline's classmates began to say their goodbyes. So, they all settled in and sat on the edge of a planter in a long line.

"That was a bold move," Rebecca said to Caroline. "I honestly didn't see it coming and it isn't often that I am surprised. Did you just come up with it on the spot?"

"Actually, I didn't come up with it. Norah and Ryan did," Caroline acknowledged and Rebecca gave them both a nod of approval.

"Well it was brilliant," she said to the group. "You've given your teachers a great deal of work to do. I expect they will be up most of the night."

Caroline heard her friends muttering to each other about how the teachers would probably get back at them the next day.

"And did they also come up with your other request?" Rebecca asked.

"Other request?" Norah said.

"I guess not!" Rebecca said, chuckling. "Your friend here asked us to join the fight against Gabriel."

"Oh man… I wish I'd been there," Zora said with a huge smile.

"Tell me, why did you choose that moment to ask for something so big?" Rebecca asked Caroline.

"Because it's too important to wait any longer and I had to try," Caroline blurted out.

"And that is what I meant when I said purity of purpose," Rebecca said with pride. "I am not sure yet if it helped our cause, but we are at least talking about it again. We will need some more time though."

"How much?" Caroline asked.

"Are you negotiating with me? I've been surprised twice in the same day!" Rebecca said loudly.

Caroline just grinned awkwardly.

"Fine, how much time do we have, junior Council member?" Rebecca asked sarcastically.

"Uh… I don't know… A week?" Caroline said.

"Do you think you and your friends here can learn enough in a week to enter what might be the biggest war in thousands of years?" Rebecca asked with a sly grin.

Caroline just opened and closed her mouth, not able to make a sound and not knowing how to respond anyway.

"How about we shoot for a month and see how things go?" Rebecca suggested.

Caroline nodded slowly, hoping this would bring an end to the conversation.

"It's been a pleasure doing business with you," Rebecca said, then turned to the rest of the group and said, "Have a lovely evening! I hope you enjoyed your days off, you probably won't get another one for quite a long time!"

On that note, she walked away, leaving the group stunned and silent.

15

READY OR NOT

"THAT'S IT, WE need to find a different place to work!"
Juliet exclaimed after the last visitor left and she
locked the door to the workshop. Ever since the rest
of Terradune had realized that a grimoire had been created, all
the residents wanted to have their book connected to it. For the
first few days, it had been a parade of visitors. So much so that
they had to set the book up in a special spot in the library with
Greta guarding it like a hawk. At least then they hadn't been
interrupted constantly.

The problem was they needed to use the book as a reference
point for their work together, so they had to take it back to the
workshop. As soon as people found out where they were, however, a steady stream of visitors came and disrupted their progress.

"Totally," Caroline agreed. "We've been here for two hours
and haven't made any progress on your grimoire. Now I need to
get back to my room to study."

"Oh my gosh, you're right! We have a test in Symmetry tomorrow!" Juliet remembered.

The following weeks became a complete blur in their classes. Their entire group was in over their heads and couldn't keep up with the material that was thrown at them as if they had been studying for multiple years instead of eleven months. They quickly realized that the only way they were going to survive was to divide and conquer. At least two of them were assigned to each subject and focused their efforts on it. They were also responsible for helping the others understand the daily homework for that subject. This tactic began to bear fruit during their third week of studying together and the bond between them grew immensely tight.

Caroline felt incredibly lucky because she and Alella were picked to focus on Shijian since they were by far the strongest in that subject. In fact, Steven had remarked in their last class that they were stronger than most of the advanced students who had been studying it for years. He attributed their progression to a complete lack of ego or fear of making mistakes. They were willing to try something to see how it worked and learn from their mistakes.

However, he did often chastise them for not being very efficient in their tests since some of their ideas were completely hairbrained. A good example of this was when they decided to launch shields at each other to see what would happen. The resulting percussive wave flattened everyone in the training room and may have caused some hearing loss in a few people.

So it came as no surprise when, at the end of class one day, the two of them decided to let off some steam and spar a bit with Jose, a Physic, and Anjali, an Air Elemental, who had joined their class for the day. This wasn't the first time that Jose and Anjali had helped Steven with a lesson. They were called on somewhat regularly because they had a way of testing the students that led to amazing lessons. In fact, Caroline was always happy when she arrived to find them in the training room waiting for them.

The sparring started off rather slow and lazy with Jose launching a few objects from a bin next to him at Caroline. She easily disrupted them and felt a deep satisfaction as they clattered to the floor. However, his attack was just meant to lure her into a false sense of security. He had been distracting her, so she didn't notice Anjali beginning to spin so fast that a whirlwind formed around her. Then, somehow, she stepped out of it as if it wasn't there and gave it a push, sending it directly at Caroline.

Alella had been watching Caroline deal with Jose's attack, but saw something out of the corner of her eye and immediately erected a shield to block it. Unfortunately, it had no effect on the whirlwind because Anjali wasn't controlling it with her abilities. Alella searched her mental archives as quickly as possible to try to find something that would work, but nothing came to her. So, she just ran for Caroline and shoved her out of the way just before the whirlwind slammed into her.

Jose and Anjali, didn't let up for a second and continued a barrage of attacks on them even though they hadn't been able to get up off the floor yet. The speed of the attacks was astounding and both Caroline and Alella moved quickly to counter every move against them. An intense focus settled in for both of them and their motions became more and more complicated as they combined techniques in innovative ways to not only defend, but also counter attack.

The air seemed to begin to sparkle at first when they simultaneously started a technique they had just learned a few days prior for absorbing energy without requiring a physical connection.

Caroline glanced over at Alella and saw that she noticed it too, so she gave her a sign to follow her lead. She began to modify the technique by changing her hand positions to something more similar to a shield generation technique and suddenly their hands began to have glowing trails follow them. Not only that, but Jose and Anjali seemed to be slowing down.

Caroline wondered if they were getting tired, but then she noticed the objects he had launched at them had also slowed down. Alella had observed the same thing and was looking around as well. The rest of the class who had moved behind the protective screens were also moving in dramatically slow ways.

Alella gave Caroline a mischievous smile and began running directly at Jose and Anjali while continuing the technique that seemed to have slowed down time for them. Arriving next to their opponents, they encased them in containment shells and time thudded back into its normal pace. Breathing hard, they gave each other an enthusiastic high five.

"WHAT THE?!" they heard Zora yell, but the rest of their classmates just stared at them, dumbfounded.

Steven came out from behind the screen and moved his hands in a complex series that led to Jose and Anjali being released. Then he walked over, shook each of their hands, and said, "Thank you for helping with that. Are you both doing alright?"

They each nodded and smiled warmly at Caroline and Alella before walking over to the side and taking long drinks from their water bottles.

"That is what we will be studying over the next several weeks!" Steven called out. "It is a combination of several techniques that allows a short period of time dilation. When used at the right time, it can help turn the tide of a battle, save a comrade from an attack, or allow for a hasty escape. I had a feeling that Caroline and Alella would stumble on it if they were attacked in the right way. Lo and behold, they did!"

"You… staged that?" Alella asked skeptically.

"Indeed," Steven replied.

"How did you know we would want to spar?"

"You were both particularly… what's the best word… *feisty* in class today."

"But… wait… I don't get it," Caroline said in confusion. "How were you so sure we would figure it out?"

"Because Jose and Anjali are very good at what they do," Steven replied as if the answer was obvious. "They have been helping me train initiates for so long and have helped with this specific demonstration at least a half dozen times."

"So, we were just your pawns," Alella said in annoyance.

"I suppose you could say that, but I would prefer to say skilled participants," Steven said. "Anyway, class dismissed!"

Steven went over to talk with Jose and Anjali and the rest of the group gathered around Caroline and Alella.

"That was insane!" Zora said enthusiastically. "You guys were moving so fast!"

"Technically, they slowed us down," Juliet explained. "They used the energy from Jose and Anjali to feed a field that slowed time down in this specific area. This type of technique has a very limited range and everything outside of it stays at normal speed."

"How do you know so much about this?" Bea asked.

"I read the next chapter in our book," Juliet answered simply.

"Wow.. You were able to read ahead? Can't wait to learn that time dilation technique," Zora quipped and everyone started laughing.

᷎

That evening, after dinner, Caroline and Juliet were working in an office located next to Rebecca's since it was one of the few buildings in Terradune that other Moon Borns would not enter unless they had been specifically invited. They had begun to make some significant progress now that the interruptions had been dealt with. Still, they were caught off guard by a knock on the door and a moment later, Rebecca opened it.

"Hello, you two," she said in her usual calm, warm tone. "How is it going?"

"Not too bad," Juliet answered. "We are almost done with the basic grimoire construction and we should be able to start on the cover in the next day or two."

"Yeah, Juliet is a quick study," Caroline said encouragingly.

"That is excellent to hear," Rebecca said encouragingly. Then her expression changed and cleared her throat before saying, "So... I have news on your second request."

As soon as she heard those words, Caroline felt a tightness in her chest and found it harder to breathe. She hadn't even thought about her request to the Council in at least a week if not longer. Between classes and working with Juliet, there was no space left in her brain to think about anything else.

"We took your request very seriously," Rebecca began to explain and Caroline braced herself for disappointment. "And there have been more developments since we last spoke. We are now certain that Gabriel is about to do something significant to escalate the conflict to astronomical proportions."

"Please tell me we are going to help," Caroline interrupted.

"We are," Rebecca said with a smile, but her eyes told Caroline there was more to what she was saying.

"But?" Caroline asked.

"No but's," Rebecca responded. "We have asked Steven to

assemble an initial force of twenty Moon Borns who will travel to join the resistance movement."

"Are you serious?!" Juliet snapped and Caroline was surprised that she was beaten to the punch.

"Listen, this is a big step for some of the members of the Council to make. Just getting agreement on an initial force was extremely difficult," Rebecca explained.

"Listen to yourself!" Juliet shot back. "You just said Gabriel is going to do something huge and we are going to send a tiny group to help?! You're all cowards…"

Rebecca stood there with her hand to her chest as if Juliet had wounded her and Caroline couldn't help but feel sorry for her even though she completely agreed with Juliet. This was a minimal effort to say they complied with her request, but it wasn't a real commitment to join the resistance.

Rebecca collected herself, looked Caroline in the eye, and said, "There was another development that I should share with you."

Caroline did not like the sound of that and she braced herself for troubling news. She even had an idea of what it was.

"Your friends' school was raided and they have been taken."

"And you think twenty people is a good first step…" Caroline seethed with anger.

"We are working with the resistance to find them," Rebecca assured her.

"You won't, though."

"Hey now, that's not fair," Rebecca protested.

"But it's true. You know it will take more than that to rescue them."

"Well, there should be more room on the ship if we are able to find perhaps… five more volunteers."

"If only initiates could volunteer and not get banished," Caroline responded flatly.

"In times of war, exceptions are often made," Rebecca responded.

"Will the rest of the Council support this?" Juliet asked.

"That depends on when they find out about it," Rebecca said with a slight grin. "Sometimes it's best to ask for forgiveness instead of permission."

Neither Caroline nor Juliet responded, the gears turning in their minds already.

"I'll leave you to your work," Rebecca said softly and closed the door behind her. Both Juliet and Caroline knew what kind of work Rebecca was suggesting. They set aside the new grimoire and began to hatch a plan on how they could sneak five people onto a ship. They stayed up late, but Caroline felt so energized that she wasn't able to fall asleep until the wee hours of the morning.

The next day, Juliet arrived outside Caroline's room before the breakfast bell as they had planned so they could go to the hall together and snag some of the other initiates as they arrived. Before the first class bell, they had managed to talk to everyone and all had agreed to meet during the free period between classes and dinner that afternoon.

Unfortunately, that period was shorter than it normally was due to the worst day of classes any of them had ever experienced. Not only were they distracted as they thought about their upcoming meeting, but the teachers had also decided to increase the intensity of all of their classes at the same time. Nobody was prepared for this and most of their teachers held them back in class out of frustration.

They finally all arrived at the parklet in the east of the city as the sun was bathing the sky in shades of gold, pink, and purple. Despite the rough day, the positive energy running through the group was palpable. So, when Caroline and Juliet stood up in front of the group, it took a bit to get everyone to settle down.

"Hey… So… Thanks for being here," Caroline began.

"Yeah, we're so glad you all want to get involved," Juliet added.

"Yeah, yeah, just get on with the plan," Zora called from the back and the group chuckled.

"Fine, we'll get straight to the point," Juliet began. "In a day or so, a ship is going to arrive and the Council is going to send twenty Moon Borns to join the resistance. It's not enough and, honestly, it's not enough even if all of us joined them as well."

"But every little bit helps," Caroline interjected. "We can probably sneak five more people onto the ship without being discovered."

"The rest of us will need to create a distraction and help get them on board," Juliet continued. "And then we'll have to cover for them long enough that they can't call for the ship to come back."

"That's it?" Lyra, one of the older initiates, said sarcastically.

"That's it," Juliet confirmed.

"Seriously? That's your entire plan?" Lyra asked again.

"No, that's all we are going to explain at this time. We need to know who's in or out," Juliet explained.

"If you're in, stick around. If you're not comfortable, you can leave now," Caroline said.

Everyone stayed seated and waited silently for them to continue.

"OK, then, first we have to decide who's going on the ship," Caroline said. "Then we can divide up the rest of the tasks."

"Well, that's obvious, it should be our best fighters," Bea said.

"We have a lot of them though," Caroline responded.

"Now's not the time to be like that," Bea retorted. "We all know who the best ones are."

"She's right," Juliet said. "It'll be Caroline, Alella, Lyra, Gaspare, and Jay."

There were no disagreements from the group and Caroline felt an icy coolness flow through her at the thought that she would have a chance to save her friends. This was what she had hoped for even if she hadn't allowed herself to even consciously think about it. With that decided, for the rest of the evening the group divided up and began working on their pieces of the plan.

The next night, Caroline wasn't surprised to see Ranee walk into the hall for dinner, but she was still so happy that she ran up and gave her a huge hug.

"Look at you!" Ranee said, holding her out and looking at her with pride. "See? I knew you would find your way in."

"You didn't do much to help me, though!" Caroline joked.

"Hey, I'm just the driver. I don't know anything more than that," Ranee protested lightly.

"Suuuure… You know more than you let on," Caroline poked. "Anyway, what brings you back?"

"Oh, just some more Wayfarer stuff. Gotta shuttle some folks around," Ranee said coyly.

"Folks, huh? The two of us barely fit on your boat," Caroline said, playing along.

"I got a bigger boat for this trip. Anyway, I sure hope I have a good sailor or two like you on the trip. I need some help cleaning up the storage room on this behemoth. I can't find a thing in there," Ranee said, giving Caroline a wink. "Anyway, I gotta grab some grub real quick and get back to the boat since we head out tomorrow night. Swing by and say hi if you can, I'm at the docks on the outside of town."

"Docks? There were docks where you could've dropped me off?" Caroline said, only half joking.

"Like I said before, I took you where you needed to be," Ranee explained and then walked off to get in line.

❧

Caroline checked her bag for the third time in ten minutes. Everything was still packed like it had been the other two times she checked and her bed was already made up to look like she was asleep. The clothes she was wearing had a slight stale smell to them from not having been worn in a year. They also didn't fit as well as when she arrived. Her jeans were a bit too short and her shirt felt tight at the shoulders. These were minor inconveniences, however, when compared to the anxiety she was feeling as she waited for Juliet to arrive. She couldn't help but worry they were going to miss the departure time since it was already almost ten.

Two soft knocks came from her door and she walked quietly over and opened the door a crack. Juliet waved for her to come out and she turned around to grab her bag. When she emerged from her room, she tried to close the door behind her as quietly as possible, but it still sounded like every click echoed loudly down the hall. They made their way out of the building and to a deserted street. The stones felt smooth and cold on their bare feet, as they tried to make as little noise as possible.

It took them ten minutes to meander their way down several side streets and alleyways before they saw the gates to the city through the arch at the end of the last street they took. They waited there for several minutes and, one by one, each of the other travelers arrived with their partners. Now that they were all there, it was time for the first distraction and Juliet hugged Caroline goodbye before hurrying out, looking panicked.

"Oh gosh! Where is it!" Juliet said anxiously as she ran around in a haphazard route, clearly looking for something on the ground. There was only one guard stationed there since Terradune was already so well protected and he came out to meet her.

"You shouldn't be here at this time," they heard the guard say to her.

"I know, but I dropped my notebook and I need it for a test tomorrow!" she said a little too loudly and the guard shushed her.

Soon, Juliet had the guard helping her look for the lost notebook on the far side of the large gates and the rest of the group crept silently to the door set in the wall next to the giant gates. They managed to open it quietly enough and slip through undetected. Then they stuck to the shadows in town as they made their way as directly as possible to the docks.

To her relief, Caroline saw the large ship lit up at the docks as they crested a small hill and it made her run ever so slightly faster. It was very different from the small boat that Ranee had taken her in. This one was sleek and expensive-looking. There were three masts, a swimming pool on the main deck, and a motor boat hanging from two small cranes at the back of the boat. Someone very rich must have loaned it to her. Several people were scurrying around on the deck and one of them had Ranee's unmistakable moves. Even on this boat, she looked completely at home.

They got as close as they could in the shadows so they wouldn't be spotted and then the remaining four partners split off and started making their way down the docks to act as decoys. Caroline and the rest of her team began to pull off their clothes, revealing bathing suits underneath. They shoved them back in their bags and then put them inside black plastic garbage bags that Bea had managed to snag from the cafeteria. Slipping into the water between two of the boats that were docked closest to shore, the cold water was a shock to their systems and they all stifled small yelps of discomfort.

They swam as quietly as they could, keeping to the shadows of the other docked boats whenever possible. As they came around one and saw the back of the huge sailing vessel, they heard a commotion and saw several adults climbing down a ladder on the side while three others had surrounded their decoys. One of them was definitely Steven and he looked really angry. Caroline felt a sense of relief and gratitude that she wasn't standing in front of him at that moment.

They reached the stern of the boat and pulled themselves up a small ladder that was right next to the motor boat hanging from the rear. Hearing footsteps from just above them, they crouched out of sight and hoped they hadn't been spotted.

"C'mon outta there," the person whispered above them. "You're gonna catch your death if you don't dry off soon. I'll lead you to where you'll hide."

Caroline recognized Ranee's voice and came out first with the others following her lead. Ranee opened a door to the main compartment and mimed for the last person to shut the door behind them as she moved quickly through the opulently furnished room. Caroline couldn't help but marvel at how fancy this boat was. However, she wasn't going to enjoy any of it, as Ranee led them through the empty kitchen and down a narrow service hallway to a door marked "Storage." She opened it and flicked on a light, then gestured for them to go inside.

"Keep the light off, there are flashlights on the shelf right here and they are fully charged," Ranee started to say and then placed her hand on the door right next to the storage room. "There's a bathroom right here. I'll come a few times a day to let you know when the coast is clear to use it. Otherwise stay in here and out of sight."

With that, she closed the door behind her and plunged them into darkness. A while later, they could feel the rumble of the motor and the boat began to move. They were finally underway.

✍

Caroline was shaken awake, but she had no idea what time it was. She squinted at the brightness of the flashlight that was lighting up Ranee's face just a foot away from her. She felt groggy since she had barely slept in the days leading up to the departure and the rocking of the boat always seemed to relax her.

"Is your brain on yet?" Ranee asked playfully.

"You know, I was having a really good dream just now," Caroline said grumpily.

"Well tough, you need to start thinking about where we're going," Ranee said.

"What do you mean? I have no idea where Gabriel is," Caroline protested in her confusion.

"Calm down, I don't need you to drive us into another storm," Ranee said carefully. "I will find him, that's what I do. I just need you awake and focused on that desire to find him and I can do the rest."

"You weren't lying when you said that you took me where I needed to go," Caroline said, understanding dawning on her.

"I would never lie to you," Ranee said. "But please try to focus as much as possible, I do not want to get stuck in the doldrums again.

"That was me too, huh?" Caroline asked, scratching her head in embarrassment.

Ranee just glared, waiting for her to focus. So, Caroline closed her eyes and began to focus on just her desire to find Gabriel and her friends. Whenever another thought entered, she pushed it aside and refocused on the one place she wanted Ranee to find for her. It was difficult to maintain that kind of focus, especially since she had just woken up, but she committed to herself that she would keep going until Ranee said she could stop.

Caroline felt the boat begin to lean significantly to her right and she wondered if she had not focused hard enough. When she opened her eyes, though, Ranee was gone. Just a few of her friends were sitting in a small circle with a flashlight and speaking in low tones so as to not disturb the sleepers.

Caroline crawled over to them and asked, "Hey, so, when did Ranee leave?"

"Oh, a while ago," Gaspare said.

"Huh..." she said out loud, but in her head she thought, "Well, I hope she got what she needed..."

She crawled back to her bag and layed down on it again. Soon, she was fast asleep and didn't wake up again until Ranee opened the door and brought in a load of food. She kept the coast clear while everyone took a turn using the bathroom. Then they were plunged back into darkness.

This was the rhythm they lived by for days or weeks. Honestly, none of them had any idea how much time had passed since nobody had thought to bring a watch. Squabbles began to break out amongst them and it became harder and harder to smooth things out between them. At one point, each of them had stopped speaking to at least one other person and it became extremely hard to communicate.

Finally, Ranee appeared in the doorway just as a fight was about to break out between Lyra and Jay over the last peanut butter sandwich.

"Whoa… settle down. This is hardly the time for you all to fall apart. You're going to need to act like a team when you get ashore," she said.

"When we get ashore?" Alella probed.

"Yeah, that's why I came down. I need to get y'all off this boat ASAP," she replied. "The adults are pretty angry since they thought I was taking them to the resistance. They went ashore a while ago to check things out, but I am supposed to pick them up in an hour. Grab only the things you absolutely need and follow me."

Ranee's silhouette disappeared from the doorway and everyone scrambled to throw a few things in their backpacks and hurried out of the storage room, retracing their original path to the back of the boat where they found Ranee prepping the motor boat that was now set in the water. She looked up and held out her hands. Caroline knew what she was asking for and tossed her backpack to her before carefully climbing aboard. The others did the same until it was just Gaspare who was left.

He tossed a large backpack that was stuffed full over the Ranee and, before he could move to climb down, she threw it right back.

"Nuh uh!" she said.

"What?" Gaspare replied.

"I said bring only the things you are absolutely going to need. There is no way you need that much stuff," Ranee said firmly.

"But I do!" he protested. "We have no idea what we're going to face. It's best to be prepared!"

"Nope," Ranee said, crossing her arms. "Either dump some stuff in that cabinet over there or you're not coming with us."

Gaspare rolled his eyes in frustration and then set the bag down. He pulled out a smaller bag containing a tent, a solar blanket, and four pairs of socks. Then he zipped it back up and threw it back to Ranee. She opened it up and looked around. Then she pulled out two books and a water bottle, throwing each of them back to Gaspare. When he finally made it into the boat, she gave him a withering stare. Then she disconnected the boat and moved behind the wheel, carefully working the throttle to guide them away.

Once they were clear, she slammed the throttle forward and the lurch was so strong that several of them tumbled over. They had to carefully make their way back to their seats and hold on for dear life as Ranee took them over wave after wave as she rushed to get them ashore as quickly as possible. It felt like no time at all before she guided the boat into a small, calm inlet and slowed down a short distance from a deserted beach.

"This is as close as I can get you," Ranee said. "You're going to need to hop out here and make your way over those sand dunes over there."

They all looked to see where she was pointing.

"One of my friends, Salman, is waiting for you," she continued. "He'll take you into Egypt."

"Egypt?!" Lyra said in surprise.

"Yeah, you are going to an area outside of Alexandria," Ranee explained impatiently, glancing at her watch.

"I'm sorry... I'm still stuck on the fact that you took us to Egypt," Lyra said.

"No, I took you to Libya," Ranee corrected her. "Salman is taking you to Egypt. Now get off my boat, I am running out of time here."

They all hopped out the side of the boat and landed in thigh or waist deep water, depending on their height. Then they waded slowly to the beach, holding their backpacks over their heads. The sound of Ranee turning the boat and heading away came from behind them and Caroline struggled to not look back. They were now past the point of no return.

⚶

It took them the rest of the day to drive from where Ranee had left them to outside of Alexandria. Salman spent the time explaining in detail the history of the city, both the official version and the one only known to the tribes. It seemed he had an encyclopedic knowledge of the area and, as they got closer, he began to explain the cave system that ran underground throughout the area. This was where he thought they would find Gabriel if he was here. Salman didn't seem convinced that was possible, though. He was sure that he would have noticed if tons of people had started making their way into the tunnels.

When he finally stopped driving, they found themselves on a small, dark road and they all eagerly piled out to stretch their legs. Salman walked around the front of the car and made his way over to Caroline.

"This is where I leave you," he said. "You'll find a small cave about a fifteen minute walk down that trail. It's one only locals know about and can lead you into the main cave system."

"Thank you for your help," Caroline said.

"Please don't thank me," he replied. "If what you say is true, then I have led you to the most dangerous place in the world… Be careful."

"We'll do our best," Caroline assured him and then called out to the rest of the group, "Grab your packs, this is it."

"Really? I thought it would look a lot cooler…" Gaspare said as he grabbed his backpack.

Salman walked back around to the driver's side, started the car back up, and drove away slowly as the group started their hike down the trail he had pointed out. It felt so good to be outside and moving again that they started to chat quietly and sooner than they expected the trail dead ended at the cave entrance.

It was a small opening and they had to pull off their backpacks and crouch low to enter. Then they had to stay hunched over until they reached a point where they had to start crawling. Caroline wasn't claustrophobic, but thought she might start feeling that way if it got any tighter for them. Thankfully, after crawling a short way, they emerged into a tunnel so large they could stand up straight and walk three abreast. The walls also emitted a dim glow, but it was bright enough for them to turn off their flashlights so they could save the batteries.

"Which way do we go?" Alella asked and Caroline shrugged as she gazed in each direction.

"We should split up," Lyra said.

"Seriously? That's like the worst idea," Alella responded. "How many movies have you seen where the group splits up and then the monster picks them off?"

"Well, we're not dealing with a monster…" Lyra muttered, but let her idea go anyway.

Caroline decided to go left for no other reason that it felt right. She had learned to trust that feeling when she went through the maze to get into Terradune and figured there was no reason to go against it now. The others followed her, but all the chatter had dried up as a feeling of eeriness seeped into them.

The tunnel felt like it went on endlessly, without any branches or forks, until it finally emptied into a large cavern that was filled with ruins from different civilizations. Obelisks with ancient Egyptian hieroglyphics and Roman pillars mixed with the carved walls that were covered in writing that Caroline assumed was from the tribes. She even spotted several Moon Born glyphs for connection and unity.

There also appeared to be at least five exits and they all spread out as they explored the huge space to see if they could find any clues. Caroline began to walk around the perimeter by herself and examined each exit she came across. When she reached the third one, something looked weird about the opening. Two large sections of rock seemed to be a slightly different shape and color and she stopped to examine them more closely.

Suddenly, the rock changed shape and formed a human hand that clamped over her mouth while the other section of rock changed to reveal a large man who wrapped his arms around her legs. The two Chameleons picked her up as she struggled and tried to get out a scream, but they were too strong for her and were able to pull her into the tunnel without any of her friends hearing. As they made it around a bend in the tunnel, she heard a battle break out in the cavern and she fought harder to escape, biting down on the hand that covered her mouth.

The hand was yanked away with a curse and she fell hard on her back. She tried to kick away the arms that were still holding her legs and yelled for help, but a thick cord of rope was quickly wrapped around them that rendered her efforts useless. Then the large man let go of her legs and pinned her arms to her sides as the other abductor bound them as well. Finally they completed the job with a rough gag and she was picked up and hurried down the tunnel, her stomach bouncing painfully on the large man's shoulder.

They soon stopped outside a rusty iron gate. A familiar-looking small man with thick glasses appeared from behind it and let them through. Then he led them down a narrow hallway lined with more iron gates. He opened one and the large man quickly dropped her inside before the gate was slammed shut. Caroline rolled over and was greeted by Meimei's and Ania's faces looking down at her.

"What are you doing here?" Meimei asked as they removed her gag and started untying her.

"Rescuing you," Caroline answered with a flush of embarrassment.

"Looks like you nailed it," Ania said sarcastically.

"It's a work in progress," Caroline said, annoyed at the welcome. "I have to admit that I didn't expect to be captured so fast."

"It's awesome that you came for us," Meimei assured her. "How many were with you?"

"Five Moon Borns."

"Five?! FIVE?! Against Gabriel's entire army?!" Ania said incredulously.

"Listen, I didn't come to take on his army. I came to get you guys out and that's what I still intend to do," Caroline said with authority. "Now, where is everyone else?"

Meimei walked over to the bars and said, "Stella is across the hall with some kids from the other schools. Aran and Petra are in the next one down. There are a bunch of kids in the other cells too. The walls are made of something that blocks our abilities though."

Caroline tested hers and felt the familiar deep connection as a shield shimmered around her. Then she realized someone was missing.

"Wait, what about Leo?" Caroline asked.

"Not here," Ania replied.

"He wasn't taken with you guys?"

"Nope."

Caroline's mind raced as she thought through her plan and what this could mean.

"Good, that means he's probably working on a plan too," Caroline said confidently.

"What makes you so sure?" Meimei asked.

"C'mon, you know him. He has serious FOMO," she answered with a smile. Then she pulled up her pant leg and removed a velcro pouch from around her calf followed by another one under her shirt wrapped around her torso.

"Now let's see if we can make use of any of this stuff I brought."

16

ALL IN

EO STARED AT the hand-drawn map that Miles had completed from one of the memories Lincoln gave him. It had taken him several days to work on the intricate maze of tunnels and they were all impressed with the details he was able to capture. Unfortunately, it was also probably one of the most complex mazes Leo had ever seen and, no matter how many times he traced his finger in different directions, he couldn't find the way to its center.

"Maybe we can blast our way in?" Jordan asked hypothetically.

"Where?" Mari asked, entertaining the idea.

"Right on top of them?" Jordan offered.

"What if our friends are in there? We'd have no way of knowing," Mari pointed out.

"Yeah… let's toss that idea out…" Jordan acknowledged.

"We're going to have to assume there's a huge number of people there, so the only option is stealth and surprise," Leo said, rubbing his tired eyes.

"This entire conversation is worthless if we don't find a way to get there," Finn added.

"Yeah, does anyone have any ideas on that?" Miles asked and was answered with silence.

"Also, is it gonna just be us?" Marie asked.

"That's a good question too…" Mari agreed. "Would anyone take a risk and do this with six or seven kids?"

"Caroline would…" Leo said absent-mindedly.

"Well, I don't think we're going to solve these problems tonight and I can barely keep my eyes open. I'm heading to bed," Finn said as he stood up and turned to leave. Except, he found himself staring into Ernest's chest as he looked down on the rest of the group.

"What are these problems you are trying to solve?" he asked them, but they were all too stunned to answer.

Ernest knelt down and looked at Miles' map and asked, "What's this?"

"Oh… uh… it's just something I was noodling on," Miles said, trying to stall for time to think of a believable lie.

"It looks like a map," Ernest said, staring directly at Miles.

"No! It's just something I drew…" Miles dodged.

"Your heart rate has increased dramatically and I can see that you are beginning to sweat heavily," Ernest said skeptically with a raised eyebrow. "These are usually indications that someone is lying."

"We want to save our friends," Leo said bluntly. "It's a map of where we think they are."

"Leo!" Lucy admonished him, surprised that he was just telling Ernest everything.

"Guys, he's our strategy teacher. He knows a map when he sees one and I'm pretty sure he knew what we were doing anyway.

I think he's just playing with us," Leo justified as he met Ernest's gaze.

"Well, you just ruined my fun," Ernest lamented. "So, let's go back to my first question. What problems are you trying to solve."

"Well, let's see," Marie started counting off their list of challenges.. "First, we need to figure out how to get out of school with all the extra security. Then we need to find our way to Egypt. If we make it that far, we need to locate an entrance to that maze of tunnels that Miles has drawn for us. Then we need to figure out where our friends are and get them out of there. Oh! And get back here safely, of course."

"Got it," Ernest replied. "So you have no plan."

"Nope," Leo acknowledged.

"OK, I think I can see some potential solutions, but I think Finn was right and you all should get to bed," Ernest advised.

"You're gonna help us?" Miles asked.

"Yes, on two conditions," Ernest replied.

"There are always conditions with adults," Finn lamented.

"Unfortunately, that's true," Ernest said with a smile. "First, I must know the entirety of what you are planning. No holding back. Can we agree on that?"

"Yeah," Leo agreed, but nobody else spoke up. He looked around at them exasperatedly and said, "Guys?!"

A chorus of "Yeah," "OK," and "Fine" followed.

"Good," Ernest continued. "Second, you cannot start acting on the plan without informing me."

This one was harder for Leo to accept and he looked down, thinking hard about what he was agreeing to.

"Will you keep our plans a secret?" Marie asked simply.

"I will," Ernest agreed.

"Then I think we have a deal," she said and the rest of the group nodded in agreement.

❧

The next day, Leo completed the entire Crucible for the first time and, as soon as he emerged, he was tackled by Maranda. It took him over three hours and he almost missed dinner entirely, but he had a determination that he had never felt before. It kept him focused as he figured out his way through the last rooms that Maranda had been coaching him on since they had arrived at their new school. It had also helped that Jordan was able to make it through the fifth room for the first time before he made his attempt, so things were finally clicking into place.

He carried this feeling with him when he arrived in Ernest's classroom that evening, even though he was exhausted. He had high hopes that they would start to solve some of the problems and, within twenty minutes, Ernest had figured out that Miles' map had errors in multiple places where the architecture of the tunnels didn't make sense. Miles closed his eyes and reviewed the memory again to find the corrections. When he had made them on the map, Ernest smiled and said, "That makes more sense."

"Well, you try to draw a map like that with just a memory from over a thousand years ago," Miles complained.

"You are a very impressive Librarian," Ernest said, trying to soothe his ego.

Miles crossed his arms in a huff, but Leo could've sworn he saw him grin a little bit with pride.

Leo and Ernest pored over the map while the others worked on the holes in their plan. A minute later, Leo spotted a potential path.

"See this room here?" Leo pointed out. "It's like an intersection. If we can make our way there, we have at least two options to make our way to the central cavern."

"True," Ernest agreed. "But I would expect it to be heavily defended for that reason."

Then he turned the map to reorient Leo's perspective and pointed out a narrow route that Leo hadn't noticed before.

"This one," he explained, "is a better option because it is harder to defend."

Leo examined it and saw it was an extremely long and round-about route.

"Ugh… That way will take forever," he lamented.

"Yes and that's why they would not expect us to come that way," Ernest continued to explain. "I would expect them to be rather overconfident and only have a small force guarding it so they can focus their defenses on weaker points. There will likely be at least one caretaker who would be used to send for reinforcements quickly. We will have to neutralize them quickly."

Leo had to admit, Ernest knew what he was doing. He couldn't find any flaw in what he was proposing.

"OK, now we have a potential way in," Leo said. "How do we find our friends?"

"I have a feeling they are located here," Ernest answered, pointing at a spot a short way from the central room in the maze. "This looks like a jail to me. See all these little rooms with only a hallway connecting them? It also dead-ends here."

"Perfect!" Leo said excitedly. "And our route takes us close to that spot. Do you think it will be heavily guarded?"

"That I don't know, but it is a much easier location to defend. They could probably hold it with just a few people," Ernest said.

"So, we will just have to find a way to convince them to let us in," Leo thought out loud.

"I like where you're headed," Ernest said with pride before they were interrupted by Finn letting them know their team had an idea for how to sneak out.

It took them the rest of the week to construct their full plan and then Ernest insisted they needed to begin training on it right away. He reminded them about the point he made on their first day of class with him, "You have made an excellent plan, but you know once you're in a maze of tunnels fighting a powerful army the plan will be worthless, right? As we train, we can come up with many of the ways the plan could fail so you can think on the fly and modify it."

They all saw the merits of his argument even though they were anxious to get to their friends. So, they agreed to start training and their schedule became even more grueling. There was no longer any downtime and their daily rhythm consisted of waking up, eating, class, electives, studying, and training. Even with the days being a long slog of work, they were thankful for Ernest because, now that he was on their team, they realized how hard it would have been to accomplish this by themselves.

"Reset!" Ernest called out, reaching down to help Mari up from the ground.

"I almost had it that time!" Mari said excitedly.

"No. You didn't," Ernest replied flatly.

"Great job, Mari! You almost had it that time!" Marie said as she walked by, heading to her starting position.

Mari gave Ernest a look that said, "See?!"

He returned it with a withering glare that said, "Who're you gonna believe?"

"What went wrong that time?" Jordan called out from across

the large cavern that was very similar to the one Leo had trained in with Adam the year before. The big difference was Ernest had enlisted the help of a Geologic, Penny, who had constructed low walls throughout the room to simulate tunnels.

"Let's see here," Ernest began to respond. "Mari was early and out of position. You and Leo did not provide sufficient covering fire. Lucy directed her attack in the wrong direction… Need I say more?"

"Got it, so we were horrible," Jordan confirmed.

"Let's just say there's room for improvement," Marie said optimistically.

"Again!" Ernest called out, ignoring the comments, and the action spun up in the cavern instantly. This time they managed to make it two minutes into the battle for control of the tunnel before Ernest had to stop them again. Finn had been hit by an errant energy orb that had burned his left arm severely and Ernest rushed over to heal him.

"I'm so sorry…" Leo said feeling overwhelming guilt after he saw Finn was alright.

"It's fine. Look, I'm good," Finn said, rubbing his hand over the spot that had no trace of a burn or scar.

"I could've killed you…" Leo said, doubts creeping in. "Maybe we've overestimated ourselves."

"You've just learned a valuable lesson," Ernest said, his voice warm, but firm. "This is what war is like. It's not always heroes rushing into peril and saving their friends without getting a single scratch. You're going to get hurt. It might be from an enemy and it might be because one of you makes a mistake. You still have to keep going, though. People will be depending on you."

Leo stood there quietly, lost in his thoughts and barely moving a muscle. Lucy came over to find out what was happening and noticed his state.

"Oh shoot! Did I accidentally get him?" she said with concern and pulled out the small sonic emulator that Finn had created for her.

"No, that's self inflicted," Finn said with a smile as he slowly got up.

Lucy waved a hand in front of Leo's face, but he didn't respond.

"Yoo-hoo! Earth to Leo!" Finn said loudly in his year, and snapped his fingers in front of Leo's face.

Leo blinked and then looked at Finn with such intensity that he took a couple steps back.

"We're just going to have to be better," Leo said.

"Well, duh," Finn said nervously, never having seen Leo like that.

"Perfection should never be the objective," Ernest cautioned.

"Not perfection, just better," Leo said, shifting his gaze to Ernest. "Make us better than them."

"Again!" Ernest called out with a smile.

The team drilled on the first section of their plan relentlessly for the rest of that evening and then two more evenings after that. By that point, the group had started to become a well-oiled machine and anticipated each others' moves. They began to improvise and think of creative solutions to the random wrenches that Ernest threw into their plan and started to even enjoy themselves as they went through each repetition.

"Nice job, everyone!" Ernest called out after their last attempt and the group gathered together. "I think you're now ready for the hard part."

"That wasn't the hard part?" Mari asked.

"Not even close," Ernest replied. "You just got past the first area where you will potentially face resistance. As long as you're in the tunnels, you will likely be fighting. And the closer you get to the main chamber, the more intense it will get."

"Couldn't you have just let us enjoy the moment?" Marie asked rhetorically.

"Nope!" Ernest said brightly and then turned to Penny. "Can you reconfigure the room for Phase Two?"

Penny nodded and then the walls sank into the floor before sprouting up again in a new configuration around the group.

"Can we start Phase Two tomorrow? I'm beat," Jordan said.

"I'm sure your friends will understand you were tired and that is why they were imprisoned a day longer," Ernest responded.

"Got it… Excellent guilt trip. You are a man of many talents," Jordan said as he walked to take his place.

The others followed suit and, when they were all in position, training for Phase Two began.

⬧

It took another week of practice sessions before the group felt like they were starting to get the hang of their full plan. While they understood the difficulty level of what they were trying to pull off, every practice session emphasized it again. However, they were getting better and their confidence was growing.

The routine was also something they were growing accustomed to and they looked forward to their training sessions with Ernest. So, when he wasn't in the cavern when they arrived on a rainy Sunday night, everyone was thrown off.

"This has got to be a test or something," Marie said. "He's seeing how we'll react without having him around to guide us."

"Maybe?" Leo said skeptically. Something felt off to him.

"Well, should we keep waiting or should we get some practice in?" Jordan asked everyone.

"I guess we should make use of the time," Finn said and the rest of them went along with it, fanning out around the cavern.

Just as they were about to get started, a drenched Miles came running down the stairs yelling over and over, "LEO! JORDAN!"

Everyone converged around Miles as he panted from the exertion.

"What's going on, dude?" Jordan asked.

"Ernest… sent… me…" Miles said between deep breaths. "He needs… you to come… to the office…"

"Did something happen to him?" Leo asked.

"No… He's fine… Just come… He said to hurry," Miles replied and turned to start heading up the steps.

Leo and Jordan looked at each other, shrugged, and then chased after Miles. When they made it outside, they regretted leaving their raincoats and umbrellas in the cavern because it had begun to pour since they had gone inside. As they ran together, it was difficult to see where they were going and they slipped multiple times along the way. So, they were covered in mud by the time they arrived at the school's office.

When they came inside, all conversation in the room ceased and a group of adults turned to see who had interrupted them. When Sharon saw Leo, Jordan, and Miles standing there, filthy and drenched, she was clearly very angry.

"Boys, now's not the time. I'll speak with you tomorrow," she said in a tone that would normally make students scurry.

"Sharon, I sent for them," Ernest said calmly.

"Excuse me?" Sharon asked, surprised and disbelieving.

"We need them here for this conversation…" Ernest began to explain.

"Good to see you again," Rebecca interrupted, smiling at

Leo. "It's been a while! I was just about to share with the group some news that I am sure you would be interested to hear."

"Rebecca, they are students and we are talking about something very sensitive," Sharon said in a low tone, but everyone could still hear her.

The boys just stood there, fidgeting and waiting to see whether they would be allowed to stay. Leo noticed Maranda who smiled and gave an awkward wave.

"I understand your caution," Rebecca acknowledged, "but I think it was wise that Ernest sent for them. I believe they may be critical to helping us determine our course of action."

Sharon leaned back in her chair and rubbed her eyes. Then she turned to Maranda and said, "Can you take them next door to the clinic and get them some of the spare sweats. They're making a mess in here."

Leo began to protest, but Sharon cut him off and said, "Just go. We won't continue without you."

When the boys returned a few minutes later, they were dry and more comfortable even though the clothing they were given was either much too large or slightly too small for them. Leo and Miles were swimming in huge sweatshirts and Jordan's sweatpants barely reached the tops of his ankles.

"You were saying before we were interrupted?" Sharon cued Rebecca.

"Yes, perhaps I should take a few steps back to catch them up on where we were," Rebecca began. "The Moon Born Council decided to begin supporting the resistance and we sent twenty of our most skilled fighters to join you a little over two weeks ago. They should have arrived in no more than a week, but their Wayfarer seems to have made an out of the way stop for reasons not completely clear to us. They are on their way here now and should arrive in about a week."

"Where was this extra stop?" Ernest asked, but it sounded to Leo like he may already know the answer.

"North Africa, near the border of Libya and Egypt," Rebecca replied.

The boys involuntarily exchanged knowing looks and Leo found Rebecca was staring directly at him when he turned back to the group.

"In addition to the official team we sent, a group of five students also managed to stow away on the ship," Rebecca continued. "They are some of our most talented initiates and one of them has become extremely important to us."

She turned to look at Leo again with a very serious expression and said, "That would be Caroline."

It took every trick and technique that Leo had learned to be able to maintain his focus and not dive into the sea of thoughts and anxieties that were flowing through his mind. He looked around and registered that Rebecca had stopped speaking and everyone was staring at him.

"So, Caroline is on her way here?" Leo asked, hoping his hunch was incorrect.

"I'm sorry, no," Rebecca answered.

"She got off the ship at that stop," Leo said, more talking to himself than the group.

"It would seem so," Rebecca confirmed.

"She beat us to it," Leo said, starting to lose his battle and sinking into his thoughts.

"Beat you to what?" Sharon asked pointedly, pulling Leo back.

"She's trying to save our friends," Jordan explained on Leo's behalf.

"This is why I sent for them," Ernest explained to Sharon and the rest of the group. Then he turned to the boys and said, "It's time for you to share what you've found."

Leo knew he needed to follow Ernest's guidance, but he felt like their plan was suddenly falling apart. He took a deep sigh and shook his head slowly before beginning.

"There are about twenty places around the world where our abilities are dramatically enhanced. We believe that Gabriel has found one of those places in Egypt, outside of Alexandria. He will need all the power he can get to open the vial containing Warwick."

"How… How?! You shouldn't know this type of information! You're still only students," Mr. Fredrickson, their History teacher asked, clearly flabbergasted.

"I am now the keeper of a large archive," Miles responded. "As part of that archive, I received a number of memories that explained the existence of these locations among other important details."

"You found the memories!" Maranda exclaimed and Leo nodded vigorously.

"Is this what you were doing when you snuck away while we were being attacked?" Sharon asked sternly.

"Uh… yeah…" Miles confirmed guiltily.

"Of all the crazy things I've seen students do…" Sharon began to lament.

"We're getting off track here," Ernest interrupted. "Please continue, Miles."

"The memories that were assembled in this archive have a ton of information," Miles said, following Ernest's cue. "It was the hardest indexing I could've imagined and I think it almost broke me. But, I was able to find several things that should help us save our friends and maybe mess up Gabriel's plans.

"As Leo said, they helped us figure out where we think Gabriel is amassing his forces and also contained a map of the temple in Alexandria. It is huge and made up of a maze of tunnels. It took us days to figure out the best way to navigate them, but we have figured out a route that will take us to where we think our friends are being held."

"What about the ceremony?" Maranda interjected. "Do you have memories that explain what they are trying to do?"

"Yes…" Miles said hesitantly and Leo turned to look at him in surprise. "Those memories were the hardest to manage… They feel cursed somehow… I don't even like thinking about them…"

"I understand your fear," Rebecca said calmly. "You are safe here with us. Please try to share what you know."

Miles sat silently for a moment, preparing himself. Leo recognized that he was performing a meditation similar to the ones he had learned.

"The memories are not complete…" Miles said, his eyes remaining closed. "It seems the ceremony requires a huge number of people to share their energy and channel it through a single Star Born. It's extremely dangerous because, if the Star Born cannot maintain control, all the participants would have their energy completely drained… I mean… everyone would die…"

Miles stopped speaking as he wrestled with the memories he was accessing. Leo wanted to help him somehow, but Rebecca caught his eye and signaled for him to be patient.

"If the ceremony is performed at the temple, it will increase its effects by a massive amount. But it still won't be enough to break the seal on the vial. They need another source of power…" Miles continued, clearly anxious. "I can't believe I am saying this, but I think they are going to try to kill a Moon Born to harness their energy for the ceremony."

"That's what I thought you might say," Rebecca responded quietly.

Miles opened his eyes and Leo saw they were filling with tears. He shook his head as if to say sorry to Rebecca for sharing this information.

"So, now we know for sure they need a Moon Born," Rebecca said more loudly, looking around at the group. "And I believe they may have one."

"How is this even supposed to work?" Ernest asked. "Anything they throw at a Moon Born would be useless."

"I'm afraid there are limits to our abilities," Rebecca responded.

"What would happen if the Star Born used the ceremony to direct the energy at a Moon Born instead of the vial?" Leo asked, though he was sure he wouldn't like the answer.

"It would quickly overwhelm the Moon Born and, as they die, unleash an immense amount of power like a nuclear bomb. If they could direct that at the vial, it would destroy the protections and Warwick would be free," Rebecca said soberly.

"Well, it looks like our rescue plan just got a whole lot more complicated," Ernest said. It was clear his mind was already at work trying to figure out how to construct a new plan.

"We have to go now!" Leo said forcefully.

"What do you mean, 'we?'" Sharon asked. "You're not going anywhere."

"You don't have a choice," Leo countered. "We have a plan and trained on it for weeks."

"A plan that fails to account for the information you just heard," Ernest pointed out.

"Yes, that's true," Leo acknowledged. "But you have also trained us to improvise."

"We can work on the plan some more along the way," Jordan added.

"We will not send a group of students on a suicide mission!" Sharon pushed back. "We will do the smart thing and gather an experienced team of *adults*!"

"You're both right," Rebecca interjected. "We do need to leave now and we also can't do this with such a small force. Ernest, how many do you think we'll need?"

Ernest stared into space as if in a trance, calculating and adjusting. This went on for what felt like an eternity to the group, but was actually only about a minute. When he emerged, he looked directly at Rebecca and said, "We will need at least fifty to have even a remote chance of success to stop the ceremony and save the captured students. There would be three teams. One will be at least thirty fighters and will act as a decoy to draw attention away from the other two. We will need the small team that has been training to focus on the rescue as originally planned. The third team would be focused on disrupting the ceremony."

"I will have our Moon Borns turn around and meet us there," Rebecca said as she stood up. "Ernest and Sharon, can you please work to identify who we will need for the other teams?"

Then she turned to Leo and Jordan and said, "Would you please gather your team and anything you will need? I will arrange for transportation to arrive in about an hour."

It was so surreal for Leo as he bounced in his seat from the deep ruts and bumps the van was navigating along the unlit gravel and dirt road leaving the school. Everything had happened so fast after the meeting in the school office broke up. Everyone had stuck around in the cavern, so they were easy to find. Even then, it was a rush to pull together everything they needed. In the end, it had taken them over an hour and a half to be ready to go.

It was only once he and his friends were crammed into the back two rows of the school's biggest van along with their gear that he had a moment to think about what they were embarking on. He tried to stay in the moment and listened as Mari, Finn, and Miles were chatting in the back row about video games. Leo could feel them trying to distract themselves from their nerves. Marie was in her own world humming a song to herself and making her hand blend into the blue plastic seat. Rebecca and Ernest were sitting on the first bench, talking in low tones so he couldn't make out what they were saying.

"Do you think Finn will really use all the stuff he brought?" Jordan, who was sitting right next to him, asked.

"I can't see how," Leo said with a smirk. "I mean, most of us just brought a backpack. All this other stuff is his!"

"I just hope he has some cool gadgets like the one he used to take down that Heavy in Portland. That was dope!" Jordan joked.

"Yeah, remind me to never get on his bad side," Leo agreed.

With a big lurch, the van climbed onto a paved road and everything smoothed out. Soon, the adrenaline wore off and most of the group fell asleep. When they woke up, the van had stopped and the first rays of dawn were peeking out over a nearby hill. Leo rubbed his eyes and looked out the window to see a chain link fence with a line of small airplanes on the other side. He turned to ask Rebecca and Ernest where they were, but they weren't in the van.

Leo unbuckled his safety belt and crawled on top of the bags that were crammed into the bench in front of him.

"Try not to break my stuff," Finn grumbled from behind him as Leo awkwardly shimmied over to the side door and nearly tumbled out when he opened it.

All of his joints protested as he stretched the stiffness of a long drive out of his body. The rest of the group pried themselves out of their seats and joined him in stretching. While he waited for them to be finished, Leo noticed there was an unmarked door to the building that the van had parked in front of a few steps away. Just as he was about to check it out, Ernest and Rebecca came out, followed by a man dressed in a grimy flight suit.

"Excellent, you're all awake," Ernest said.

"Where are we?" Leo asked.

"At an airfield. I thought that was pretty obvious," Ernest answered and Leo rolled his eyes.

"I'd like to introduce you to Reginald," Rebecca said, gesturing to the man in the flight suit.

"Y'all can call me Reggie," he said as he walked around the group and shook each of their hands.

"Reggie is going to take us most of the way to our destination," Rebecca explained.

"Yup! And we better hurry, wheels up in thirty minutes," Reggie added. "Everybody grab a bag and follow me."

Following Reggie through the building, he led them out the other side and then along the line of small airplanes until they reached a hangar. He pulled out a large set of keys and flipped through them until he found the one he was looking for. He fed it into a lock and a motor groaned to life as the huge hangar doors accordioned open to reveal a plane that looked like it had seen better days. It had a large propeller on each wing and a fat, square body that seemed to have been patched in a variety of places.

"We're gonna fly in that?" Miles asked, unable to turn off the connection between his brain and mouth.

"Old Bessie here doesn't look like much, but she's got some

tricks up her sleeves," Reggie said as he patted the side of the plane and then climbed through the open door.

"That thing has some mods," Finn said quietly from behind Leo and Jordan. "A really good Technic has worked on it. I can sense it."

"Yeah, but can we make it all the way to Egypt in it?" Leo asked, turning around to face Finn. "I mean that's thousands of miles."

"We'll have to make one stop at least. Maybe two," Reggie said as he walked past them toward a small office on the side of the hangar. Leo huffed in surprise and wondered how people kept sneaking up on him.

"Depends on how fast we wanna fly and weather conditions," Reggie called over his shoulder as he walked into the office. He walked out again a moment later with his own bag and, without missing a beat, picked up where he left off, "Like I said, she's got a few tricks and I'll find us a good route. Now, follow me with those bags, we can stow them in the back of the compartment."

Once they were inside the plane, some of their worries melted away. The cabin was kept immaculately and there were three rows of comfortable looking seats separated by an aisle. Behind that was a large open area with a small table and a bench, along with a wall of cabinets.

"I assume you're gonna need to tinker a bit along the way, so let's secure these by the table back there," Reggie said to Finn.

"How did you…" Finn started to ask.

"Spend enough time with Technics, you know how to spot 'em," Reggie replied before Finn could finish.

Sooner than anyone expected, they were airborne and Reggie gave them the go-ahead to move around. Finn immediately retreated to the back and started pulling things out of different bags. Rebecca joined Reggie in the cockpit, so the seat next to Ernest was open. Leo moved over to the open seat and looked at what Ernest was working on. As he was about to start asking questions, Ernest held up a finger and said, "I'll be with you in a moment." He wrote a few more things down and then turned to look at Leo.

"It took some time, but I now have a modified plan that I believe has some potential for success," Ernest said.

"You didn't think we could succeed when you agreed we should do this?" Leo asked in surprise.

"As you said, we had to leave right away," Ernest replied. "Let's go to the back so I can take everyone through it."

The plan was extremely complex and Ernest had to explain it multiple times before the group completely understood it. Then they spent hours finding flaws before they modified it enough so that everyone was satisfied with it. By the time they landed on a small island in the middle of the Atlantic to refuel, everyone had studied the plan enough that they had memorized parts of it.

When they were all back on the plane again, Ernest informed the group that he was able to confirm everyone should be arriving in Egypt within hours of each other. Still, it didn't feel real to anyone until they were about an hour away from landing at their destination and Reggie suddenly took the plane into a steep dive.

"I'm sensing some unexpected air defenses ahead!" his voice rang out through the intercom. "I sure hope everyone's buckled up!"

They all gripped their armrests tightly as Reggie took a series of tight turns while still in a steep dive. They could feel the strong vibrations running through the plane and Leo was certain it was about to break apart. However, a few moments later, he felt his weight sink deeply into his seat as the plane leveled off and he looked out of the window to see they were flying low over a sea of sand dunes.

"I don't think they spotted us," Reggie called over the intercom again.

As the group tried to relax and release their white knuckled grips, they felt a sudden thud and the left engine began to sound like it was struggling.

"Never mind, they definitely spotted us!" Reggie informed them as birds started slamming into the exterior of the plane. He took the plane through a dizzying array of motions that started to make Leo feel queasy and he prayed silently that they wouldn't crash. When he opened his eyes again, he glanced over and saw Marie had made a section of the plane completely invisible and she was sweating profusely with the effort.

His instincts took over and he quickly matched his pattern to hers. With all the practice he had over the past year, it had become completely natural to him and he was able to feed her a large amount of energy in seconds. The plane and everything inside it began to fade away until they were disoriented by the sensation of flying at hundreds of miles per hour with nothing between them and the ground. Even more disconcerting was that their bodies had disappeared as well. It was as if they didn't exist anymore and the bombardment ceased immediately.

"Don't stop what you're doing until I give the all clear!" Reggie called out.

He clearly knew every inch of his plane because they continued to swoop and turn to avoid different obstacles until they came over the last of the dunes and saw a small airfield appear in the distance. As if on cue, the left engine gave up with a loud screech and the plane lurched violently.

"It'd help if I could see the plane again!" Reggie requested urgently as he regained control, though the plane continued to buck and shudder and the right engine was clearly struggling to carry the weight.

The walls suddenly appeared around them just as the right engine quit and the eerie sound of the wind outside the cabin was all anyone could hear.

17

ʙOOMSHAKALAKA

THE POLICE BATON banged loudly against the bars, startling everyone awake, and then several thuds followed it as the prison guard tossed several boxes of food in the center of the small cell. Everyone rushed to get a box as quickly as possible, but it was only to ensure the rats didn't get them. The food inside was horrible and sometimes gave them stomach aches. Still, they made sure to eat it all to avoid any visits from the furry scavengers.

It had been two days since Caroline had been captured, at least that was her estimate based on their sleeping schedule, and her plan had not been going as well as she had hoped. She had intended to get captured as a way to find her friends more quickly, but she did not anticipate their abilities would be completely nullified. She had also assumed the tools she had brought would help them, but none of them had the dexterity to pick the lock of their cell.

Being stuck and settling into her friends' endless routine of sleeping, eating, and bored conversations was starting to take a toll on her. She could feel her frustration building as each day wore on along with the creeping sense of defeat. At least they were largely left alone since the guards only came during meal times. This morning was much like the one before, with Ania and Meimei talking about all the things they would eat if they made it out of the prison.

Caroline wasn't in the mood to participate in the conversation, so she sat with her back against the cold stone wall and created a reflective bubble around herself. She manipulated the bubble to change its shape so it looked like she was encased in an egg. Then she expanded it to press tightly against the walls of their cell. Stretching out her powers felt good, like she was an elite athlete and getting to the satisfying part of a training session.

"Holy... How is this possible!" Memei said excitedly and Caroline looked over to see that she was levitating one of their meal boxes.

Caroline's heart leapt and she pulled the bubble back into herself as she scrambled to her feet.

"GAH!" Meimei exclaimed in disappointment as the box suddenly dropped to the floor again.

"How were you doing that?!" Caroline asked.

"Dunno..." Meimei answered, furrowing her brow as she tried to make sense of things. "We were just talking about the disgusting food and I was daydreaming about chucking one of those boxes... Then I felt a connection to that one and it was the first time since we got thrown in here... Whatever... It's gone now, I can't feel anything again..."

Caroline was not going to give up so easily. Something had changed briefly and she was going to figure out what it was. She began to examine every inch of the room, but found nothing new since the last time she had done that the night before. Pacing back and forth, she tried to wrack her brain for an idea of what she could do next.

"Can you just sit down? You're stressing me out," Ania complained.

Caroline returned to her spot against the wall and felt the heat of anger and frustration begin to crawl across her skin. Unwilling to let that take over, she returned to her exercises from before and focused her attention on creating the reflective bubble again. It encased her and grew bigger and smaller as she took deep cleansing breaths to get rid of the negative emotions. Then she took a deep breath and held it, allowing the bubble to expand to the walls again to feel the satisfying sensation as it pressed against the rocks.

"It's back!" Meimei shouted.

"QUIET!" the guard down the hall shouted, startling Caroline.

As the bubble winked out of existence, the box fell out of the air again.

"Aw… C'mon…" Meimei lamented, but Caroline was filled with excitement.

She crawled over to sit between Meimei and Ania and then surrounded them with a bubble that stretched just far enough to reach the first box in the middle of the floor.

"Try now," she instructed Meimei.

The box levitated slowly in the air and rotated lazily.

"What are you doing?" Meimei asked in awe.

"Now you try," Caroline said to Ania, pointing to a web of spindly roots that was squeezing out between several rocks above them.

The roots began to rapidly stretch across the ceiling until they reached the edge of her bubble.

"They're back!" Ania whispered loudly, her eyes wide and a huge smile stretching across her face.

Meimei then sent the box flying at the small segment of wall next to the gate, but it tumbled to the ground as soon as it left Caroline's field.

"Seriously?!" Meimei complained. "We can't do much with that…"

Caroline expanded the bubble all the way to the walls again and grinned knowingly at Meimei who felt the connection again. All the boxes lifted off the floor this time and began weaving through the air in an intricate pattern.

"How is this possible?" Ania asked.

"I'm reflecting whatever is coming from the walls," Caroline explained.

"How far can you stretch it?" Meimei asked and Caroline could tell she may have an idea.

"Let's find out," she answered and started to expand the field into the walls where it met resistance. However, the door to their cell offered no resistance and a section of the field bulged out into the corridor and stretched across the hall to the opposite cell.

"Is that shimmery stuff in the air where your reflection stops?" Meimei asked.

"Yeah, why?"

"How long can you hold it?"

"Pretty long, it doesn't take much effort. You gonna let us know what you're thinking?"

Several of the tools Caroline brought lifted off the ground and flew through the air to the door, inserting themselves into the lock.

"I'm getting us out of here," Meimei answered as she began to work.

⟡

Leo had to hand it to Reggie, he got them on the ground in one piece. Still, he was pretty sure a nasty bruise was forming across his legs where the belt had held him to his seat while the plane jostled them around as they landed. They'd all had to get out and push the plane off the runway when they arrived since it looked like this airfield was barely in use. There were just a few single-engine planes covered in dust and sand parked in the distance and a building with a glass office on top of it that probably functioned as its tower.

They saw someone come out of the building and hop in the jeep that was right next to the door. Then he drove directly over to their plane and pulled up just shy of the end of the wing. Reggie walked over to meet the man and they proceeded to talk for a couple minutes in what Leo assumed was Arabic. When they were done, Reggie pulled out some money from his pocket and handed it to the man who just put it in his own pocket without even counting it. Then he hopped back in the jeep and drove back over to the building.

"Everything out?" Reggie asked when he returned to the group.

"You speak Arabic?" Leo asked.

"Yeah, I speak most languages. One of the perks of being a Wayfarer," Reggie answered. "Mustafa is a good guy. I stopped here about fifteen years ago and he remembers me. There shouldn't be anyone landing for a few days, this is a light season. He is going to call his cousin who will lend us a truck so I can get you the rest of the way there."

"Wow… being a Wayfarer must be awesome," Miles said, nerding out.

"And you're clearly a Librarian. Don't know how I missed that before," Reggie said, giving Miles a wink. Then he looked over at Finn and asked, "Mind having a look at these engines with me while we wait?"

The rest of them sat in the shade underneath the wing while Reggie and Finn worked on the engines. Several hours later, as the sun was starting to get lower in the sky, Mustafa's cousin showed up in a beat up pickup truck. The kids loaded all their gear into the back and then wedged themselves into a small open space in the center. Rebecca and Ernest slid into the cab. Finn hopped down from the plane and found the last tiny bit of space in the truck bed. Then they followed Reggie as he powered up the plane and taxied it over behind the building. He said a few words to Mustafa and his cousin before hopping in the driver's seat and setting off for a small dirt road that dead-ended into the runway.

If they thought their landing was uncomfortable, it couldn't hold a candle to the drive as their butts slammed over and over into the metal floor of the truck bed whenever they went over even the smallest bump. Unfortunately, there were many. By the time Reggie pulled over, it had grown dark and they all eagerly got out and gathered at the back of the truck. Most of them grabbed their backpacks, but Finn started opening up all of his bags and picking things out, placing them one-by-one on different parts of his body until he was covered head to toe in matte black armor.

"What the heck?!" Marie said in amazement.

"I've been working on this all year," a slightly robotic version of Finn's voice said. He glanced down at a display on his arm and touched a few buttons. Then several devices emerged from the bags and gathered at his feet and on his shoulder.

"Ready?" Reggie asked and the group all nodded. "OK, good. The entrance you are looking for is right over that hill. Please be careful, I like you guys."

"Awww…" Lucy said, feeling touched.

"Good luck," Ernest said. "And take care of Miles. He should be able to lead you back to the airfield."

"Wait, where are you going?" Marie asked.

"You weren't paying attention when we went over this?" Ernest asked.

"I have a lot on my mind," Marie answered, guiltily.

"I swear…" Ernest grumbled. "I'm leading the decoy group and Rebecca is leading the group that will disrupt the ceremony."

"Remember, being a decoy doesn't mean you're expendable," Leo said seriously.

"I'll be careful," Ernest said and clapped Leo on his shoulder. "Now get moving. We have to meet our teams and we are already late."

"You can do this!" Rebecca said as she slid back into the truck. Ernest and Reggie joined her and then they were off with a big cloud of dust trailing behind them.

"So… this is Egypt…" Marie said, feeling the weight of the moment and not able to think of something cool to say.

"Yup, but no time for sightseeing," Jordan replied with a grin as he started to walk over the hill that Reggie pointed out. "This trip is all business."

The entrance to the cave was obscured by some thorn covered bushes, but it was still easy to pick out. They walked straight in and felt the cool dampness of being underground within a couple of minutes, despite the dry desert climate outside. The clanking of Finn's armor echoed off the walls and Leo couldn't help but make a crack.

"Does that suit have a stealth mode? They're going to hear us coming from a mile away," Leo whispered loudly.

"Shut it, Leo," Finn said testily. "You're gonna be happy I came prepared."

Leo chuckled to himself and he noticed that Jordan had joined him. However, the moment of levity was brief as they went deeper into the tunnel and carefully scanned for enemies and traps. As expected, this section of the tunnel was left unguarded, but that just made the group even more nervous. At some point, their plan was going to get tested and, to an extent, they just wanted to get on with it.

Before long, Mari asked them to stop and be silent as she reached out her senses and connected with a collective of bats not much further down the tunnel. They waited patiently until she returned to the group and reported out.

"There are three guards stationed in the wider section that's coming up," she shared.

"That's fewer than we expected to be there," Jordan commented.

"Yeah, and they don't seem to be very active from what I learned, so we should be able to sneak up on them. I can't tell what their abilities are, but I'm pretty sure one of them is the Caretaker we are looking for. I can feel their fingerprints in the bats."

"What does a fingerprint feel like?" Miles asked.

"Not now," Jordan said, cutting him off.

"Fine…" Miles said in disappointment.

"I guess this means I'm up," Lucy said as she slid her way along the wall where everyone had crowded and started to creep quietly ahead. Then she stopped and turned to the group.

"I just had an idea. You better put on your earmuffs and hang back," she added.

"Lucy, now's not the time to make changes, we just got started!" Leo cautioned in a loud whisper, but she had already disappeared around the bend. Shaking his head, he pulled off his backpack and fished out a set of heavy-duty sound dampening earmuffs.

They all waited for Lucy to get well ahead before they followed and took their time reaching the guarded section of the tunnel. When they peered in, they saw Lucy standing in the center pressing the keys on her sound emulator, but couldn't hear what she had created. She caught sight of them and gave a nod that it was safe, so they all walked confidently down the center of the path. Two guards were passed out on the floor and they found the third after walking to the other end of the section where the tunnel narrowed again. This was clearly the Caretaker since there was a moderate sized cat passed out next to her.

They continued until they were well away and then paused. Lucy held up her hands to say it was safe to take off the earmuffs and they all pulled them down so they were hanging around their necks.

"What was *that?*" Marie asked, clearly impressed.

"It's something I've been working on for a while now," Lucy explained. "It was originally supposed to help some of my bunkmates sleep when they were stressed out before tests. The problem is, a little goes a long way. They would pass out instantly and then not be able to wake up for hours. Every minute I played led to at least another two hours of sleep and the worst part was they all woke up with splitting headaches."

"Why'd we have to wear these?" Leo asked, gesturing at his ear protection.

"I haven't been able to figure out how to direct it. If you are within hearing distance, you pass out," Lucy said gravely.

"Got it. Let's hope we don't need that one again," Leo said.

"We're almost at the intersection with the tunnel that leads toward the prison," Miles advised in his role as navigator.

"Mari, are you able to sense if it's guarded?" Jordan asked and she closed her eyes to reach out for the nearest creature to connect with.

"No…" she said. "The closest animal I can sense is an ornery rat that is well past the intersection."

"I've got this," Finn said confidently, and a piece of armor on his left calf popped off and landed on the ground. Then it righted itself and scurried ahead extremely quickly, but barely made a sound.

"What the heck is that?" Miles asked.

"A scout," Finn answered as if it was obvious. "Now let me focus, it's coming up on the intersection."

They didn't have to wait long to hear the bad news.

"It's crawling with people," Finn said. "Not guards, just people moving between different tunnels. There's no way we can get through there without being noticed."

"Well, I guess it's time to get a little dirty," Jordan said confidently, slamming his a fist into the palm of his other hand.

"That's not the plan," Marie chastised. "We're supposed to wait for the decoys to make a distraction."

"That could take forever! We don't even know if they're going to be *able* to make a distraction," Jordan countered impatiently.

The cave suddenly shook with a loud rumble and dust rained down on them from the ceiling.

"See? Distraction!" Marie said and everyone turned to Finn to find out what he could see.

"It seems to be working," he said with his dispassionate electronic voice. "There was a bit of a rush at first, but now there are far fewer people coming through. Definitely more manageable for us to handle them."

"Alright, let's go!" Jordan said excitedly as he hopped up and began to run ahead.

The others shook their heads in frustration, but followed him none-the-less, and arrived at the intersection a minute later. They were immediately noticed and a variety of projectiles flew at them. Jordan had created a large, dark shield that was taking the brunt of the attacks while the others fended off what made it past him. Then he ran at full tilt, slamming the shield into two fighters and pinning them against a section of wall.

"GO!" he yelled to the rest of them, yanking his head toward the direction they needed to run.

Mari and Marie followed his directions while Leo tossed two blue and white balls down the other corridors and a huge explosion erupted in each, sealing them partially. Miles crouched down and grabbed one of the fighters' ankles and closed his eyes.

"What are you doing?!" Jordan shouted.

"Intel!" Miles yelled back and then let go and ran after Mari and Marie.

Lucy came up behind Jordan and said, "OK, release them, I can handle it from here."

Jordan dropped his shield and immediately ran after the others. Lucy's fingers flew over her modulator and a sonic attack slammed into the fighters. They winced and plugged their ears, trying to withstand it. However, it was futile and they quickly dropped to their knees, their hands falling to their sides and swaying to a song in their minds.

"We've gotta go, that's not going to last very long," Lucy said to Leo and they both took off down the tunnel.

Two narrow tools were inserted in the lock of the cell across from theirs and Meimei manipulated them up and down extremely gently, trying to find the right angle so the lock would turn. This was her third attempt with different tools and what had once seemed so promising was starting to feel like an exercise in futility.

"Take a break. We need to figure something else out," Ania advised.

"I think I've almost got it…" Meimei said, trying to focus.

"If I hear that one more time," Ania complained.

"Just give her a sec," Caroline said calmly.

A soft click emanated from the lock and Meimei pulled the tools out.

"Did I get it?" she asked.

Stella gently pulled on the bars and the door emitted a soft whine as it swung inward an inch.

"BOOMSHAKALAKA!" Caroline yelped, unable to contain her enthusiasm.

"Shut up!" a guard yelled from down the hall and she clamped her hands over her mouth.

"Boomshakalaka?" Ania asked in a whisper and began to chuckle.

"Yeah, it's a common word used to express joy," Caroline said awkwardly.

"Common? Really?" Ania challenged.

"Fine, I just like it and have been dying to use it. It's a great word," Caroline admitted.

"Great? I am sure we can come up with something better," Ania said skeptically, still giving Caroline a hard time.

"Guys, I need Caroline to focus. We need the field to stretch down to the other cells," Meimei said impatiently.

"Good luck trying to find a better word…" Caroline muttered under her breath as she joined Meimei and reached through the bars of the door to spread her reflective field all the way down the corridor.

Within minutes, all the doors were unlocked except for their own. Meimei brought the tools back to start working on it when something that sounded like a huge explosion shook the cells roughly. All the unlocked doors swung open slightly and the occupants rushed to close them as quietly as possible while they heard shouts coming from the guards stationed at the entrance to the prison. One came running down to check on them and found all of the captives huddled and looking scared in their cells. Satisfied, he ran back to his station.

"What was that?" Stella whispered from across the hall.

"I don't know, but it was close,"Ania replied.

"Maybe it's a rescue attempt?" Petra asked hopefully.

"Maybe… But let's not get our hopes up. We are so close to getting out of here," Caroline cautioned.

There was another commotion with the guards, but this time it was different. It didn't sound like they were scared. In fact, they sounded excited and a moment later the clicks of fancy shoes on the stone floor echoed down the hallway. They stopped just outside the door of Caroline, Meimei, and Ania's cell and there stood Gabriel. As usual, he was dressed impeccably in a custom suit with every hair on his head perfectly in place. Much of the injuries he had sustained in their battle the year prior had healed, but there were scars that rippled across the left side of his head and his ear was still missing.

"Ah… It's so good to see some of my old pupils," he said

with a sneer. "I have been meaning to visit sooner, but I've been consumed with the preparations for something special. Don't worry, you're all invited, especially *you*, Caroline."

An involuntary shiver ran down Caroline's spine and Gabriel's sneer grew into a large, creepy smile. She saw Stella's hands on the bars to her door and she shook her head slightly to say they shouldn't reveal their secret. Gabriel didn't seem to notice and just continued his classic villain monologue.

"A whole team of Moon Borns arrived on our doorstep, just when we needed one, thanks to you. It was our missing ingredient if you will. Alas, I'm sure you surmised by now that we were only able to capture you. Which seemed odd to me at first, but then it made complete sense. You actually wanted us to take you to your friends! Such a noble intention and completely predictable... Whatever your reasons, I don't really care. Your foolishness will now be your downfall and you're trapped here."

Caroline ground her teeth together in anger, but didn't say a word. She was just looking for the right moment. Gabriel nodded to someone Caroline couldn't see and the small man with thick glasses appeared, holding a key. He unlocked their door and pushed it slightly so that it creaked loudly as it slowly opened and clanged against the wall.

"Rushing into an unfamiliar place is a rookie move," Gabriel commented with a mock concerned expression. "You had no idea that we would place you in a cell that blocks your powers."

He formed an energy orb in his palm and reached inside their cell. It dissipated as soon as it crossed the threshold. Pulling his hand back into the hall, he formed another orb and tossed it lightly up and down with a smug grin on his face. Caroline knew this was it and she copied his expression.

"Hey guys?" she said as she stared him down. "You up for a little fun?"

"Definitely," Ania said from behind her. "I've been so bored since we got here."

Caroline created another reflective field and it quickly filled their cell. She saw in her peripheral vision the roots on the ceiling beginning to thicken and stretch further toward their door while Meimei stood up and pulled out some of the sharper tools that Caroline had brought with her. As the field ballooned out into the hallway, Gabriel's energy orb was pushed off its path and tumbled to the floor. His eyes widened with shock.

"Grab her! NOW!" he shouted and a muscular man and woman rushed into the room, grabbed her arms, and began dragging her out of the cell. She put up a huge fight and they struggled to maintain their grips on her, but still managed to steadily pull her into the hall.

All the cell doors flew open and their occupants flowed into the hallway to fight their captors. Ania sent the roots shooting through the wall and Gabriel was almost showered in rubble, but the small man that had opened their cell grew dramatically to fill the entire space in a fraction of a second and took the brunt of her attack.

"GO!" Gabriel shouted at the two guards holding Caroline and they began to shove her down the hallway like football linebackers instead of trying to restrain her. This technique was much more effective and Caroline stumbled repeatedly, unable to resist them. Gabriel hurried ahead of them to lead the way and a group of soldiers met them at the entrance to the prison.

"Restrain her!" he yelled at the woman who appeared to be their commander and she quickly moved to bind Caroline's hands and feet with zip ties.

"Go assist Nelson!" he yelled at a group of four soldiers that were wearing some kind of odd, black armor. Caroline saw one begin to morph and she reached out her hands, sending a jolt of disruptive energy at them. The fighter cried out in agony and collapsed on the floor, but their comrades ignored him. They just continued to follow Gabriel's orders and made their way into the prison.

"Get control of her," Gabriel growled at the commander who, with the help of another soldier, threw her over the shoulder of the large man who had originally captured her. They all began to run down the tunnel quickly and Caroline could feel her vision begin to become fuzzy from lack of air as she struggled to take breaths between each stride.

A crash and more shouts erupted in front of them as Leo and Mari raced down the tunnel at the head of their group. There was no other way for them to go but forward, so they prepared themselves for battle. Leo had blue, undulating waves of armor covering his arms while the large black mamba in Mari's backpack slid out and coiled itself around her right arm. They knew Finn was not far behind because they heard the loud clanks of his armor on the stone floors. Leo could also feel Jordan's energy surging as he prepared for the coming fight.

They arrived at a small open area where several tunnels intersected and a large, rusty iron gate stood wide open exactly where they expected the prison to be. The shouts they had heard were coming from inside and it sounded like it was getting more intense by the second. There was also a man passed out on the floor, who they guessed was a Chimera based on his limbs that looked painfully distorted as if they had been frozen mid-transformation.

"Get back in your cages, you little brats!" they heard a voice boom from deep inside.

"Well, at least they left the door open for us," Leo said as he glanced around at the group. Then he noticed something missing, "Hey… wait a sec… where are Lucy and Marie?"

"Over here," they heard Marie say from the direction of the gate, but they couldn't see anything and looked around aimlessly.

"Oh… sorry, I forgot," she said and then appeared, holding Lucy's hand right next to the gate. "We decided to scout ahead and it's a good thing we did. Gabriel just took Caroline down that tunnel."

Marie paused for a second to point at the left-most opening in the wall and Lucy picked up where she left off.

"Our friends are in there fighting five guys. One of them is huuuuge! I mean, bigger than any human I've ever seen. I don't know how long they can last…" she said.

Leo's impulses warred inside him. He knew he needed to help his friends as soon as possible, but he also knew he needed to save Caroline so Gabriel could be stopped.

"Fine… Let's take care of this as quickly as we can," he said determinedly and ran into the prison. He heard the others follow close behind and several seconds later they were standing at the end of a long hallway where pandemonium was in full swing.

Lucy's description of 'huuuuge' did not do the man justice. He was simply the biggest Heavy that Leo had ever seen and every movement he made sent showers of rocks and debris flying around him. There were six students, including Aran, trying to contain him and he was advancing on them as if their efforts were barely a slight irritation.

There were also the four other soldiers who were battling in close quarters with Meimei, Stella, Ania, and Petra. They all looked a little worse for wear, but seemed to be keeping things relatively under control. So, the first order of business was clearly to deal with the Heavy.

"Jordan, I think we're gonna need to tackle the big guy together," Leo said in such a calm voice that it even surprised him. He brought his hands together and then slowly pulled them apart to create a thick band of energy. Jordan followed what Leo wanted to try and formed a large, dense energy orb. He placed it in the center of the band Leo had created and then pulled back, stretching it like a slingshot. They aimed carefully, straining against the tension, and then Jordan let the orb fly. It slammed into the back of the Heavy who grunted and knelt down on one knee as he took deep breaths to tolerate the pain. A huge burn blister began to form in that spot and Leo and Jordan grinned with satisfaction at each other.

Aran took advantage of the moment and sent a pack of rats swarming over the Heavy who roared with frustration and rose up, trying to smack the small animals off his body. They were too fast and he rammed his side into the wall, creating a huge hole and a swath of the rats fell off his body. He then turned around to face the newcomers and that's when Leo realized who they were fighting. It was the same Heavy from their battle in Yosemite the prior year, but he was significantly bigger and stronger this time. He also recognized Leo and gave him an angry sneer right before he began to run full tilt at him like a juggernaut.

Petra was quick to notice what was happening and sent blasts of wind at Meimei, Stella, and Ania to move them out of the way. Unfortunately for the soldiers, the Heavy didn't try to avoid them and he trampled two on the way towards his target.

"Oh, cra…" Leo started to say as he backpedaled, but he immediately ran into a wall and realized he didn't have anywhere to go.

The Heavy snatched him and Jordan up in each of his giant hands and began to squeeze. Thinking quickly, Leo sent a large jolt of energy through his entire body and into the hand so that the Heavy dropped him in surprise. Still, Leo was cornered and had nowhere to go, so the Heavy took his time pulling back his arm in preparation to swing his fist so that Leo would be crushed against the wall behind him.

Out of nowhere, a boy appeared at Leo's side and sent a shimmering wave of disruptive energy at the Heavy's arm. It suddenly shrank to its normal, shriveled size and the Heavy yelled in agony. He dropped Jordan hard on the floor and reached over to hold his other shoulder as if he was protecting it from harm. However, this was completely ineffective as the boy sent more blasts at the Heavy and he shrank to his normal size in a disjointed and painful process. By the end, he laid on the ground unconscious, breathing shallowly, and covered in gashes.

"You're a Moon Born," Leo said, stating the obvious as he looked at the boy who'd just saved him.

"Yeah, name's Gaspare," he replied. "We're here to help save you guys and find our friend Caroline."

A girl ran past them and reached one of the soldiers who was still fighting Ania. She approached him from behind and placed her hands on the sides of his head. He screamed and fell to the floor, lifeless, while she pivoted and ran to the remaining soldier and released a blast of energy that vaulted him across the room and slammed him into a wall. He slid down to the ground unconscious and the fight was suddenly over.

"That's Alella," Gaspare said, clearly proud she was on his team. Then he asked, "So, where's Caroline?"

"Gabriel took her," Jordan said from the ground, rubbing his bruised ribs.

"Say what now?" Gaspare asked and a couple more Moon Borns filed into the already crowded hallway.

"He and a bunch of his goons took her a few minutes ago. They were in a hurry and she was tied up," Marie explained, appearing next to Gaspare suddenly.

"Are you guys good?" Leo called out to his friends and the other former prisoners. "We should get moving."

Then he reached down to help Jordan and walked out of the prison, straight to the tunnel that Marie had said Gabriel's group took. Everyone else filed out of the prison and the small space of the intersection outside became crowded.

"NO!" Miles called out from Leo's right as he was about to cross through the entryway. Leo could see him shoving and jostling his way through the crowd to get to him.

"Not that way," Mile said to finish his thought as he emerged next to Leo and pointed at the next tunnel over. "You wanna go that way."

"But…" Leo started to protest.

"Trust me," Miles urged and pointed to his head.

That was all Leo needed to hear and he pivoted to the next tunnel over. Finn was already walking through it with Gaspare and Alella. Several more explosions shook the walls around them and they began to run as quickly as possible, a stampede of footsteps thundered close behind. Finn was surprisingly fast and led the way even though he was weighed down by his heavy armor. He consulted his copy of the map constantly and they made several turns before he held up his hand for them to stop. A wave of whispers and murmurs crashed over them as everyone pulled up behind them.

Leo looked around the shallow bend of the tunnel and didn't see anyone. The entire tunnel had been deserted so far. It occurred to Leo that it was odd they hadn't run into a single soul or faced any kind of organized resistance.

"Why'd we stop here?" he asked Finn.

"I sent a scout ahead to keep tabs on things while we dealt with things at the prison," Finn explained. "We need a different plan. There is an entrance just a bit further on, but the temple is much bigger than we thought."

"How much bigger?" Leo asked.

"I can't even explain it…" Finn said. He pulled off his face shield and handed it to Leo who placed it over his face. A video feed covered the entire screen that was inches from his face and it portrayed a startling sight. They had expected a large space around the size of a modest sports arena based on the map they had been using. However, the map was only two dimensional and it didn't account for how deep the space for the temple went. There were stories and stories running deep underground with tiers of steps and balconies that circled around a small altar at the very bottom. Even worse, it was filled to the brim with Gabriel's army.

"Yup…" Leo agreed as he pulled off the face shield. "We didn't plan on that…"

⟋

"Put her down there," Gabriel commanded and Caroline was dumped face-first on the floor. She rolled over slowly, trying to catch her breath since it had been knocked out of her over and over again during the run from the prison as she banged against the shoulder of the soldier carrying her. She thought she had heard more explosions, but they were so muffled that she couldn't be sure.

Looking around to check out her surroundings, she couldn't

believe her eyes. A sea of fanatical faces stared at her and it stretched back to high walls where more and more people were quickly filling the tiers. A bright light source at the very top of the space washed out her vision, so she couldn't see how high the space went.

"Are we ready?" Gabriel asked one of the acolytes bowing before him.

"Almost, sir. Just a few more minutes" he replied.

"Good," Gabriel said with a satisfied smile.

He turned to Caroline and chuckled, then he winced and groaned slightly as he placed his hands on the side of his head as if to try to keep it from splitting open. He muttered softly, talking to himself, but Caroline couldn't make out what he was saying. Whatever was happening to him passed quickly though and he looked down at her once again.

"I must hand it to your friends, they have accomplished much more than I expected," he said. "But don't worry, nothing should ruin our fun today. Our timeline has just been moved up a bit. Please remind me to thank them for that. Oh wait... Nevermind... I don't think you'll be in any shape to speak with them after our little ceremony here."

He turned to the acolyte he had spoken to before and said, "Nestor, please remind me to thank our visitors for helping us get to this point sooner."

"As you wish, Gabriel," Nestor replied, with adulation in his voice.

A cluster of three people guarded by four heavily armed soldiers emerged from a dark shadow that Caroline surmised was another tunnel entrance. She could tell they were Star Borns since energy was flowing out of their hands and into a bright white orb they were surrounding. When they were a few paces from her, they leaned over in unison and placed the orb on the ground. They retracted their energy and stepped away to reveal a small Moon Born vial.

Caroline couldn't believe her eyes and, without thinking, she lunged to grab it. Out of the corner of her eye, though, she saw Gabriel move quickly and she instinctively rolled onto her back to put up a reflective shield before his attack splattered against it. He sent several more at her, which the shield dealt with easily, but it was clear that he wasn't really trying to hurt her.

"Uh uh uuuuh…" Gabriel said tauntingly to her. "You wouldn't want to ruin the surprise!"

He raised both of his hands high over his head and formed two fists. His sea of followers quieted immediately and the speed with which the silence arrived sent a spike of anxiety through Caroline's body. Gabriel brought both of his fists down slowly and the crowd began chanting rhythmically, but she couldn't make out what they were saying. She didn't have time to focus on that, however, because thin streams of energy began emerging from each individual chanter. It was an amazing sight to behold as a rainbow of streams twisted together to form a rope that thickened into a bright white column. It descended slowly from the upper reaches of the temple, eventually connecting with Gabriel's back.

Caroline watched as he struggled to adjust to the massive amount of energy flowing into him. He closed his eyes and took rhythmic, deep breaths in an effort to maintain control. Caroline had no idea if it was working until two beams of concentrated light shot out of his eyes and hit her like a spotlight. She flinched in anticipation of pain, but nothing happened and she met his gaze as bravely as she could.

"While you and your friends thought you were keeping the

secrets of this power away from me, in actuality you were helping me find them," Gabriel gloated with a distorted voice that was strained and twisted by the energy coursing through him.

He raised his hands and they glowed so brightly that Caroline had to squint. Realizing he was about to direct the energy at her, she threw all of her energy into a disruption shield in front of her. A moment later, his attack slammed into her shield like a freight train and she was astounded by the force. It was like nothing she could have imagined and, for the first time since she arrived, she wondered if she was strong enough to stand up to it.

Gabriel ceased his attack suddenly, but Caroline kept her shield up. She knew better than to let her guard down and repositioned herself so that she was kneeling in between him and the vial in the hopes that her shield would keep him from opening it.

"You realize what your role is here," Gabriel said conversationally. "That was only a fraction of the power channeling through me. There is no way you can stand up to it if I direct its full force at you."

Caroline shuddered involuntarily and Gabriel laughed maniacally before sending another blast at her. This one was even more intense and Caroline had to exert more effort to maintain the composition of her shield. Based on what he had said, she was pretty sure this was still only a fractional increase in power. Then, again, Gabriel cut off the bombardment to toy with her some more.

"See? There is no point in resisting. Why not join me? There's no need for you to die. Just open the vial and help put our people back on the path that was interrupted by unnecessary fears so long ago," Gabriel said in a conciliatory voice.

Caroline surprised herself when she started to laugh in response to his invitation. It was like when she and her friends were in the zone and making each other laugh so hard that their sides hurt. Gabriel just stared at her with his glowing eyes and waited for her to regain control. As she took a few deep breaths at the end of her laughing fit, she wiped some tears from her cheeks and looked back up at him.

"You actually believe that," Caroline said with a smile and stifled another laugh that was brewing. "I bet that's what you have been telling yourself for years. Something like, people will understand someday and that you are going to save the world. Maybe not exactly that, but something along those lines…"

Caroline trailed off and her face grew cold and serious before she continued. "It's how you've justified hurting or killing people as you sought more power," she said, glaring at him. "That power has twisted you and I will never willingly help you. So, bring it on. Show me what you've got."

Gabriel's face twisted with rage and a massive blast erupted from his entire body. Caroline gasped as it hit her shield, which flickered momentarily while she summoned more energy to reinforce it. Using every technique that Steven had taught her in Shijian class, she closed her eyes and focused her mind on resisting as long as she could.

As the minutes dragged on at a snail's pace, streams of sweat began to course down Caroline's face and back. She gritted her teeth as the effort took its toll, but she didn't let a doubt enter her mind. Her sole focus was her shield and nothing else until she felt the stream of energy vibrating off her shield become choppy. She opened her eyes a crack and saw the bright column of energy vibrating oddly and becoming unstable. Scanning the crowds of followers, she could see swaths of the rainbow streams that fed the column were winking out. Looking more closely, she could see fights erupting everywhere as small groups of resistance fighters disrupted the ceremony.

A glimmer of hope was kindled inside her and it was exactly what she needed to keep up her fight.

⸙

The hair on Leo's arms stood on end from the amount of energy crackling around the temple. His senses were heightened and threatened to be overwhelmed as he focused his efforts on disrupting as much of the ceremony as they could. That was the plan they came up with after less than a minute's debate. They realized there was no chance they could come up with anything that could account for fighting over a thousand of Gabriel's fervent followers. So, they had divided the group up into multiple smaller teams and entered the temple from different tunnels so they would be harder to deal with.

Leo was paired with Gaspare, Meimei, and Aran. He began peeling away streams of energy that fed the column and directing them into groups of mindless, chanting drones. He had incapacitated twenty people this way, but none of their neighbors seemed to even notice. Gaspare had created a huge reflective umbrella that sent the energy streams back down, knocking out even greater numbers. Leo would've been competitive with Gaspare in a different situation, but in that moment he was just glad they were working together.

"I don't know how, but Caroline is fighting Gabriel!" Aran yelled excitedly as he returned from looking through a salamander's eyes that was stuck to a wall next to the altar.

"Meimei, can you get us down there?!" Leo asked urgently and, without responding, she lifted him and Gaspare up and sent them gliding quickly down to the lower levels of the temple. She let them down gently near the back of the crowds that surrounded the altar on the lowest level and they began to run to help Caroline, disrupting as many streams of energy as they could along the way.

Three Star Borns stationed around Gabriel noticed them and began sending a flurry of attacks their way. Leo's instincts and training took over as he batted everything away to allow Gaspare time to leap over the last row of chanting followers and sprint to join Caroline. He immediately added his energy to her shield and, with their combined efforts, it pushed back against Gabriel's blast that seemed to be faltering through their efforts.

"You came back," Caroline said, half excited and half relieved.

"Never left," Gaspare responded. "Couldn't let you have all the fun."

"Be my guest! Take as much fun as you want," Caroline said, her grimace shifting into a smile and then she noticed Leo battling the three Star Born guards, and nearly losing her concentration.

"Caroline… what's… going… on?" Gaspare asked as he struggled to handle the bulk of effort needed to maintain the shield.

"Sorry!" Caroline grunted and dug deep for more energy. "I don't know how much longer I can keep this up…"

Leo dispatched one of the guards by creating a large bat of energy and swinging it at an orb they had thrown. It smashed directly into the guard's chest and knocked him into one of his comrades, trapping him underneath. This gave Leo enough time to sprint across the distance between them. He placed his hand on the guard's face who was now struggling to push his friend off him and drew out a large amount of energy. The man cried out briefly before passing out and Leo directed the new reservoir of energy, along with some of his own, into crackling bolts of energy that came out of his fingertips and into the last of the guards who twitched violently like he was being electrocuted.

He looked over to Caroline and Gaspare, saw how much

they were struggling, and tried to think of how he could help. It wasn't as if he could amplify them, that wouldn't work on a Moon Born. Then he came up with a truly ludicrous idea to connect with Gabriel and try to redirect at least some of the energy away from them.

"I think I can guess what you're about to try and I wouldn't recommend it," Ernest's voice said from behind him.

"You made it!" Leo said excitedly when he turned around to confirm his favorite teacher was actually there.

"Most of us did," Ernest confirmed and gestured around the temple to show different teams working to disrupt the ceremony.

Rebecca appeared from behind Ernest, breathing hard, and paused to take in the scene before looking at Ernest with determination.

"Ready?" she asked him and he nodded once. Then she gave Leo a familiar warm smile and said to him, "I need you to promise me that you will follow Ernest's instructions no matter what you see happening."

Leo hesitated, unsure whether he could make that commitment.

"You need to trust us," she insisted.

"Fine…" Leo said, looking over her shoulder to see Caroline and Gaspare flagging in the face of Gabriel's onslaught despite the disruptions that were clearly destabilizing the column of energy feeding into him.

"I need to hear you say it," Rebecca said gently.

Leo took a deep breath and let it out slowly before saying, "I promise to follow Ernest's instructions no matter what I see happening…"

"Thank you," she said, placing a hand on his cheek. "Now, get ready. Things are going to get a little hairy."

Then, with surprising speed, Rebecca ran to join Caroline and Gaspare.

∽

"This sure looked… a lot easier… when you were the only one doing it…" Gaspare struggled to say to Caroline.

"Remind me to… never come back here… the service… is horrible…" Caroline joked back, feeling that she had been reduced to the final few ounces of energy in her body. She knew as soon as she gave out, they would be overwhelmed by Gabriel's attack. Strangely, she wasn't scared at all, just exhausted.

It came as a surprise, though, when their shield suddenly strengthened and pushed away from them, creating some space again.

"How about I take it from here, you two?" Rebecca said from behind them.

Caroline felt an immediate sense of gratitude and let go of her connection to the shield. Her shoulders slumped and her body felt bone tired like she had just run five marathons. Still, she could register what was going on around them as she began to shut down bit by bit.

"Get her to safety," she heard Rebecca instruct Gaspare and then she felt two hands grab her from her armpits and begin to drag her away. She was let down gently on the ground and then her bindings were cut away.

"Is she OK?" Leo asked Gaspare.

Caroline opened her eyes and gave him a smile. Then she said, "I knew you couldn't resist a good party."

"You know me so well," Leo replied, trying to keep his voice calm so that she wouldn't worry.

Gabriel's energy feed began to destabilize further and the

beam he was sending against the shield Rebecca was maintaining began to narrow.

"Gabriel, you were once one of the most trusted leaders among the tribes. You know this is not the way," Rebecca called out.

"You are too weak to see that our world is poisoned," Gabriel yelled back. "I will make sure it is purged and we return to the strength that we lost too long ago."

Leo, Caroline, and Ernest heard many of the chanting followers begin to falter and then they began to cry out in agony as Gabriel pulled all of their energy from them. The temple was soon filled with screams as the column of energy solidified and Gabriel channeled its full force at Rebecca. She dropped to one knee from the exertion, but the shield remained strong.

"You're hurting them!" Rebecca called to Gabriel, still trying to make him see reason.

"They will make the ultimate sacrifice for the greater good! They came prepared for this," Gabriel shot back and somehow dialed up the intensity of his attack further.

Nobody, not even Rebecca, could stand up to power like that and she dropped down to her knees, bracing one hand against the floor. Still she kept reinforcing the shield as best as she could as it shrank around her.

"NO!" Caroline called out in despair feeling Rebecca losing the battle, but there was nothing she could do to help her mentor.

Leo began to rise to help Rebecca, but Ernest put a hand on his shoulder and said, "We need to go. She knows what she's doing and you made a promise."

His shoulders sagged as he recognized Ernest was right and he knelt down next to Caroline, preparing to help Gaspare lift her up. Before they could do that, however, there was a bright flash from where Rebecca had been and a concussive blast immediately flattened them and everyone around them to the floor.

Seconds later, with his ears ringing, Leo propped himself up on his elbow and saw the column of energy had disappeared and Rebecca laid motionless on the floor. Then his stomach dropped when he saw a bright light emitting from a crack in the side of the vial containing Warwick. The crack widened rapidly and then the vial shattered as Warwick appeared in the same spot looking not a day older than the memory Maranda had shared with Leo.

The temple was eerily quiet as everyone stared at Warwick, who returned their gazes with a cold and calculating glare before his face softened into a smile.

"My friends," he said warmly. "Thank you for releasing me."

"It is such a pleasure to meet you," Gabriel said, taking a few steps forward.

"It appears many years have passed," Warwick said as he looked Gabriel up and down, taking in his clothing that looked nothing like what people wore in Coreolis.

"It's been thousands of years, I'm afraid to say," Gabriel confirmed as he took another step forward.

"Thousands?" Warwick asked, looking down for a moment trying to process the information.

Gabriel took several more steps to close the distance between them and stood next to Warwick. His followers began to chant softly again and Warwick looked up quickly, seeming to recognize the words.

"How did you break the seal on my prison?" he asked Gabriel and Leo could suddenly sense Warwick's unguarded emotions. There was a healthy dose of fear, but the dominating feeling he got was pure aggression.

"We performed a ceremony," Gabriel answered simply. "I believe you recognize which one."

"While I am grateful to be free again, no one should use that ceremony. It is too powerful," Warwick said, carefully concealing his emotions again.

"You see, that's why you failed and were imprisoned. You weren't willing to do what was necessary. You feared power when you should have embraced it. I won't make that same mistake," Gabriel replied and placed his hands on the sides of Warwick's head.

The column of energy reignited and connected to Gabriel while Warwick struggled to pull his hands away. Leo watched in horror as he realized that Gabriel was reaching inside Warwick to take his core. Coming to his senses, he scampered to his knees and pulled one of Caroline's arms over his shoulders.

"Help me! We have to get out of here now!" he said to Gaspare who quickly followed Leo's lead.

Then they stood up and began running for the tunnel that Ernest and Rebecca had come from. Caroline was jostled uncomfortably, but she couldn't muster the energy to care and she soon passed out from the trauma of the experience. As they went, several more teams joined them from tunnels that connected to theirs and soon they were in the large cavern where Caroline had been captured.

"That way!" he heard Miles call out and then saw him pointing to a tunnel at the far side of the cavern.

More teams joined them and they all snaked their way through the various ruins. Suddenly, they heard a huge cheer echo through the tunnels from the temple and Leo's heart sank as he was one of the few people there who truly understood how powerful Gabriel had just become. The only thing that mattered now was to get out of there as fast as possible.

Finn and Jordan appeared next to them and offered to take over for Leo and Gaspare, who gratefully passed Caroline off to them. Then Leo noticed that Finn's armor had been reduced to just a patchwork around his body. There was only a gauntlet over his left forearm and two pieces that wrapped around his torso. He made a note to ask him what happened. For now, he just focused on following Miles as he led them towards the daylight they could now see at the end of the tunnel.

18

ᴛOMORROW IS ᴀNOTHER ᴅAY

ʙʀɪɢʜᴛ sᴜɴʟɪɢʜᴛ ʙʟɪɴᴅᴇᴅ them as they emerged from the tunnel and everyone screeched to a halt as they blinked and looked around to get a sense of their location. A thunderous noise of countless footsteps echoed from the tunnel behind them and they knew there was only a short window of time for them to figure out where to go before they would be overwhelmed by Gabriel's army.

"How fast can you get to us?" said a clipped voice of someone who was used to being in command. Leo looked over and saw a lean, athletic man with all the hair on his head buzzed short in military style, talking on a clunky looking mobile phone with a large antenna. He didn't recognize him, but could tell he was a Moon Born since Leo couldn't detect anything about him.

"At least fifty. Probably sixty to be safe," the man answered the person on the other end of the line, looking around to do a quick mental count.

"No, that'll take too long," he responded again as the group grew more anxious about the growing noise coming from the tunnel. He listened intently for a few moments longer, nodding to himself as he was clearly taking in instructions.

"Got it, wish us luck," he said and ended the call.

"I need to speak with someone named Miles!" he called out while he stowed the phone in a small pack.

Miles came running up quickly, looking confused, and gave an awkward salute to the man.

"I understand you have a map?" the man asked, not bothering with any pleasantries.

"Uh… yes, sir…" Miles responded.

"Good, we need to split up into three groups and I need you to point each one in the right direction so that Wayfarers can find us along the way," the man explained.

"Excuse me, but they probably already know where we're going. A phone signal is pretty easy to hack," Finn chimed in.

"I'm aware of this and don't have time to explain what is happening right now," the man said, clearly annoyed, and turned back to Miles. "One group will need to head back towards where you left Reggie."

"OK… Yeah… Take the road right there and head west. There will be an intersection in a couple miles and you should turn left," Miles explained.

"Lyra! Take fifteen people with you and go!" the man instructed. A girl a few years older than Leo and his friends began moving around the group and pointed at people who immediately followed her at a fast jog as they set out.

"Gaspare, do you remember where you were let off by Ranee?" the man asked.

"Uh, yeah… But it was pretty far from here, Steven," he replied.

"Don't worry, you won't have to go very far," Steven assured him. "Explain the location to Miles and then take around thirty-five people with you. Make sure that includes Caroline. Now go!"

"But what about the rest of you?" Miles asked.

"We'll figure something out," Steven said sternly. "I just need you to go *now*."

"I have a map, too," Finn chimed in again. "I can figure out where we should go."

"Good, come with us. I think we have a few minutes head start on them at most," Steven agreed.

Finn and Jordan then passed Caroline's arms back to Gaspare and Leo. They broke into a sprint to catch up to Steven and the remaining people in their group. Leo and Gaspare followed suit as the rest of their group had already almost disappeared over a hill. They put everything they had into trying to run with Caroline, but she was dead weight and very difficult to support given everything that had already drained them.

When they reached the top of the hill, as expected, everyone was far ahead of them and the gulf between them was rapidly growing. That is, everyone except for Meimei who was running to them at full tilt.

"What are you guys doing?!" she admonished.

"You try running with a fully unconscious Caroline and tell me how easy it is for you!" Leo said defensively.

"We don't have time for this…" Meimei muttered as she turned around and began to run to catch up to the rest of their group. Leo rolled his eyes in frustration, but then he noticed that Caroline barely weighed anything at all.

"C'mon!" Meimei yelled without turning around.

Leo and Gaspare proceeded to run as fast as they could while still keeping control of a now floating Caroline. They reached Meimei in short order, but it took the three of them at least fifteen minutes of hard running before they caught up to the rest of the group. At that point, they were all hot and out of breath. The redness of their skin suggested they were not a little bit sunburned as well.

The events started to catch up to them as the adrenaline faded from their systems and their pace slowed considerably. They ran along a deserted road with nothing but weeds and rocks around for as far as they could see and were wondering how much longer they could continue when they heard the roar of a large, diesel engine from behind them. They turned around and saw a huge cloud of dust barreling toward them and everyone scattered to hide behind whatever they could find.

Whatever was creating the cloud stopped abruptly right by them and when the dust cleared there was a battered, decrepit school bus standing there. Ranee was behind the wheel and she looked around quickly like she had drunk too many cups of coffee.

"Get in!" She yelled. "NOW!"

Everyone hustled to get onto the bus and Ranee began driving before everyone was even able to get seated. Leo held on tight to a bar at the front of the bus staring out the front window as Ranee kept the pedal to the metal and swung the bus hard into each bend she encountered.

"Who the heck are you?!" Leo shouted over the straining engine, but Ranee didn't reply. She was completely focused on the road.

Leo looked down to Gaspare who was holding onto Caroline and making sure she didn't get injured as the bus threw them around violently.

"That's Ranee," Gaspare said, answering Leo's look. "She's our Wayfarer."

"Shoot…" Ranee said to herself, glancing in her side mirror.

"What?" Leo asked anxiously.

"We have company…" she said gravely.

Leo looked through the side and back windows of the bus, but he couldn't make anything out due to all the dust billowing around them.

"How can you tell?" he asked.

"Trust me, I know," she assured him.

"We can deal with them if you tell us where to aim," he told her.

"Fine, but no explosions. This thing is barely holding together as it is," Ranee informed him.

"Got it!" he responded and then he made his way to the back of the bus where Ania, Meimei, Stella, and Petra were helping with some of the wounded.

"Don't get too comfortable," Leo informed them. "We're gonna have to deal with some visitors soon."

"I had a feeling," Stella said.

"Well, I *was* getting a little bored back here," Ania said with a smirk.

Meimei just looked at Leo with her full attention, waiting to hear what they needed to do, and Petra had her usual up-beat smile, ready to take on any challenge with enthusiasm.

"Ranee is going to call the shots," Leo said, gesturing to their Wayfarer driving the bus. "We just have to be ready to respond. And no explosions."

Right on cue, Ranee called from the front, "We have something fast approaching from directly behind us!"

"I got this," Ania said confidently and she closed her eyes.

At first, it didn't seem like she was doing anything, but then they started noticing some movement in the dust. Something was darting around and only emerging from the dust briefly before fading away. It wasn't exactly clear what it was until it emerged suddenly on the other side of the emergency exit door at the back of the bus. It was another Chimera that had morphed into some kind of combination of cheetah and man. He smiled at them with an array of sharp teeth, preparing to jump onto the bus, but suddenly he tripped and fell face first into the road.

"There," Ania said.

"What did you do?" Meimei asked.

"Just tripped him up and then wrapped him with some prickly branches from the bushes that seem to grow everywhere around here," she explained casually.

"Nice job back there!" Ranee called to them. "But we have more coming! I can't tell how many, but it's a lot!"

"*That* doesn't sound good…" Leo said to no one in particular.

"I think I have an idea," Petra said excitedly.

"Let's hear it." Meimei said gravely.

"Well, I've never done it before, but my teacher has told me about a way to create a huge dust storm," she explained. "It's kinda dangerous though and it takes a lot of energy. I don't even know if I could do it at this point."

Suddenly something slammed into the left side of the bus and it tipped onto its right wheels. Ranee was just able to get it to slam back down safely, but she was right that the bus couldn't take any kind of punishment. That one hit had done something bad and they were traveling at a noticeably slower speed than before.

"Can you keep us safe from the storm?!" Stella asked urgently.

"Of course," Petra said brightly, as if it wasn't a life or death moment.

"Then DO IT!" Stella shouted.

Petra gave an enthusiastic nod and closed her eyes. The dust cloud around them ballooned and the winds whipping through it became more violent. The visibility improved briefly as the weather conditions changed rapidly and they saw just how dire their circumstances had become. A massive force was on their heels and two narrow fingers of soldiers, primarily Kinetics that could easily outrun them, were on either side of the bus. They were about to be surrounded.

More dust and debris from their surroundings flew into the maelstrom that Petra was creating and they heard a cry from one of the soldiers to the right that was probably hit by something hard. However, it seemed that Petra had reached the limit of her abilities and it simply wasn't enough for what they needed.

"Boost her!" Ania shouted at Leo.

"I'm almost tapped out!" Leo responded.

"Then borrow ours," Stella said.

"Borrow as much as you need from the rest of us too," said one of the adults he didn't recognize who was sitting a row away.

Without hesitation, Leo proceeded to align his friends' as well as a number of unfamiliar patterns and channel them into Petra. It had been a long time since he had last performed a Spider's Web, but it felt like it had been just the day before given how quickly he did it. Immediately, the storm created pure chaos around them. The swirling winds picked up anything that wasn't already partially buried and they heard more cries from the soldiers who had tried to start surrounding them.

"It's working!" Ranee called from the front.

Petra had a satisfied look on her face as she let go of the seat back she had been bracing herself against and then extended them ahead of her like she was pushing something heavy. The air around the bus immediately cleared, but the storm became a giant wall from the ground to high up in the sky behind them that nobody could penetrate. Petra remained focused, but the rest of them anxiously stared out the back looking for any sign of danger. The storm was so large, they could still see it an hour later when Petra finally signaled she needed to stop.

Time began to stretch out slowly and the bus began shimmying more and more until it was clear they weren't going to get many more miles out of it. Thankfully, the azure sea had emerged in front of them, so they were growing more optimistic that they might make it out of this mess alive and uncaptured. Unfortunately, just as they reached a narrow road that ran along the coast, the bus finally gave up and Ranee guided it onto a narrow shoulder. It was now late afternoon and exhaustion was hitting many of them hard. Leo himself was struggling to keep his eyes open.

Ranee walked down the center aisle to the back of the bus and stopped next to Meimei's seat.

"You're a Physic, right?" Ranee asked.

"Yeah…" Meimei answered, wondering what Ranee was thinking.

"How good are you at tearing stuff apart?"

"I did a whole unit on it last semester," Meimei answered.

"So, does that mean you're good at it?" Ranee confirmed.

"Yeah, pretty good," Meimei said, but everyone knew she was being modest.

"OK, Ramon over there is a Geologic," Ranee explained. "I need you to tear this bus apart into as many pieces as possible so he can bury them. Try and spread it out as much as possible in that open area across the road. Oh… and make sure it doesn't look obvious."

Meimei thought for a moment and then nodded.

"OK! End of the line! Everybody off!" Ranee called out and the bus slowly emptied.

Once everyone was off, Meimei lifted the bus a few feet off the ground and guided it into the middle of a dry field of scrub brush and a few thorny acacia trees. Ramon began making a random series of holes and Meimei began tearing chunks off the bus and sending them into the freshly made holes.

"I think this might be the first time I am jealous of somebody else's abilities…" Ania marveled.

"Quit your gaping and follow me," Ranee snapped. "We need to get out of sight as quickly as possible."

They all followed her down a steep hill that led to a small, rocky beach. There was a shallow cave along the rock wall below the road that was clearly sometimes used by locals as a private place to not be disturbed. There were remnants of a small fire and some random trash strewn about.

"I'll be back as soon as I can, but it may be an hour or two," Ranee explained to the group when Meimei and Ramon joined them. "Don't go back to the road, it's too dangerous. Just stay here and try not to do anything that will draw attention."

"What happens if you don't come back?" Stella asked.

"Stop worrying and get some rest. We still have a long trip ahead of us," Ranee counseled and then set off the way she came.

Leo, Ania, Meimei, Stella, and Petra all gathered with Gaspare and took turns dozing and helping to care for Caroline. The sun made its way lower in the sky and the hot desert air steadily cooled. At first it was a welcome relief, but the temperature eventually began to drop to uncomfortable levels. Combine that with the growing anxiety from Ranee being gone longer than the two hours she estimated and the group was very relieved when a motorboat slowly made its way into the small pocket of calm water just off the beach.

"This is going to take a couple trips!" Ranee called out to the group. "I'll take half of you now and then come back for the rest."

Leo and his friends lifted Caroline up and carried her to the boat. They placed her gently on the floor and then gathered around her to hold her steady for the ride. Stress and fatigue made it feel like time was moving at a snail's pace, but they eventually arrived at the fanciest sailboat they had ever seen. Ranee helped them board and then set off to pick up the rest of the group.

When everyone was on board, Ranee had them gather in the large common room that still struggled to fit the group. Many people were standing or kneeling wherever there was free space.

"So, we've made it pretty far, but we're not out of the woods yet," Ranee informed the group. "And before you ask, I have no idea if the other groups are safe. We will find out when we arrive at Terradune."

The news they were going to Terradune led to excited whispers from many of the group who had only heard of the place and assumed they would never see it.

"Quiet down now," Ranee directed. "This trip is going to take longer than normal because I need to be sure we are not followed. So, that means I'll need a Moon Born with me at all times. Y'all will need to take shifts and I'll trust you to figure it out yourselves. The rest of you will need to help run the boat. I don't wanna babysit ya, but I'll assign jobs if you can't figure it out yourselves. Also, a couple house rules. We only have five bedrooms, so you'll need to take turns. I had a chance to stock up on food and water because I had a feeling things would go south, but that doesn't mean we'll have enough for the entire trip. For now, nobody can take a shower. I know that sounds gross, but we'll just have to get by with bucket baths for now."

On that note, Ranee pointed at one of the more senior looking Moon Borns who followed her out of the room and then some of the other adults began to organize jobs. Before long, Leo and his friends were in one of the bedrooms looking after Caroline and Leo finally let his exhaustion send him into a deep sleep.

⤫

The next day, Caroline woke up just long enough to eat something before she fell asleep for another day. Each day after that, she was able to stay awake longer and, by the end of their first week at sea, she was almost on a normal schedule with her friends. She was quieter than normal though and didn't have her goofy energy that everyone enjoyed. However, her friends didn't expect it given what she had been through and let her have the space she needed to heal.

For the most part, she spent a great deal of time with Ranee running the ship. This was what surprised her friends the most, because she clearly knew how to sail somehow. She understood every direction that Ranee provided, though it often sounded like a completely different language to the rest of them. They could tell that she and Ranee had a deep bond and they were endlessly curious about it.

It took them another two weeks to arrive in Terradune and they were in awe from the moment they laid eyes on it. By the time they docked in the marina, Caroline's friends were champing at the bit to see where she had been living for the past year. Everyone was in high spirits because it turned out they were the last group to arrive and the other two groups had been back for at least a week. Aran, Finn, and Jordan were there to greet them, but immediately took several steps back and insisted they all needed to get cleaned up before they could spend any time together.

An hour later, they all gathered again in a beautiful courtyard and Caroline introduced them to her Moon Born friends. The group seemed to gel naturally and they set out on a tour of the city so Caroline could show off all her favorite places. It felt good to let go of their worries for a while and just be kids again, but Leo could tell that something was weighing on Caroline underneath the cheerful facade she had put on.

They eventually made their way to the small park Caroline and her friends liked to frequent and spent the afternoon joking and playing games until Aran stood up abruptly as if there was something urgent he needed to say.

"Guys, I'm loving this, but I gotta go. I heard they're serving lasagna tonight and I will be so bummed if I miss out on it," he informed the group.

Everyone burst out laughing and agreed it was a good idea to get some food, so they made their way to the hall and occupied a cluster of tables in the far corner of the large room. They stayed there and talked even after they had all eaten so much that they were uncomfortably full. By this time, most of the room had emptied and a few of the staff members were cleaning up.

Two adults entered the hall and began to make their way over to their tables. All the Moon Born students immediately noticed and stopped talking. One of them was a tall, powerfully built man with a dark complexion who wore flowing robes in earthy colors. The other was a striking woman with dark hair, olive skin, and deep blue robes.

"It's so good to hear joyful voices," the woman said, looking around at the group. "My name is Honore and this is Cecil."

"We are very happy to have you all here with us, even given the circumstances," Cecil added.

Leo looked over at Caroline and saw she was gripping the

table so tightly that her fingers were turning white. He could also see that tears were forming in her eyes. He looked over at Gaspare who gave him a slight shake of his head, clearly sharing Caroline's anxiety.

Honore looked over to Caroline and her smile shifted briefly to a look of concern, but then returned as she continued to speak.

"I'm sorry that we are coming to speak with you so soon after your arrival. We would've preferred to give you more time to acclimate, however, we find ourselves at the beginning of a terrible conflict. So, time is no longer in abundance," she said and Cecil nodded in agreement.

Before she could continue, they heard the loud slaps of someone in sandals running and a moment later a young woman came barreling into the hall and rushed over to their tables. When she found Caroline in the group, she rushed around the table and Caroline bolted up from her seat. They shared a tight hug and Caroline began crying.

"I'm so sorry I wasn't there to meet you when you arrived," the woman said to Caroline.

"It's OK, I'm just so glad to see you for at least a little while," Caroline responded as she pulled back to wipe her face with her sleeves.

"I was just about to talk about that, Caroline," the woman in the blue robes said, interrupting the reunion. "I noticed you weren't exactly glad to see us when we came in and I have a feeling I know why. You will not be expelled from Terradune for leaving to join the resistance. In fact, we are honored by your sacrifices and have decided you will always have a home here in Terradune. The Moon Born Council is unanimous on this."

Caroline, Gaspare, and several other Moon Borns in the group looked noticeably relieved and Juliet put her arm around Caroline's shoulders in support.

"Unfortunately, that isn't the only reason we came to speak with you all," Honore continued with a more somber tone. "Before she left, Rebecca entrusted something to me that I need to give to you."

Honore reached inside a leather satchel and pulled out an ornate book. Leo stared at it in surprise because it reminded him so much of the Book of Star Born. It was like a miniature version and he instantly wondered what the book could be.

"Is that… hers?" Caroline said, clearly holding back more tears.

"In a sense," Honore answered. "She created it for you. I believe she started working on it soon after she first met you."

Caroline walked around the table and took the book from Honore. She ran her fingers reverently over the intricate design, but she held back from opening it.

"Go ahead," Honore encouraged her and Caroline slowly opened the cover.

Words immediately started to appear in Rebecca's handwriting and Caroline read slowly as she wiped more tears away from her eyes.

Dear Caroline,

If you are reading this, my time has passed and it is now up to you and the rest of the Moon Born community to carry on our traditions. As if this is not already a lot to ask of you, the next great war is now unfolding. Yes, you read that correctly, I understood there would be war despite our best efforts to avoid it.

I have known Gabriel for a long time and first had suspicions of his true beliefs soon after he joined the

Council of tribal leaders. It has taken a great many years to understand his true intentions because he was so gifted at hiding them. He could have been a great leader, but instead he has become a sad, twisted person who has been corrupted by unchecked power. He will never be satisfied, even if he is successful in his quest to take over the world and pursue Advancement fully.

I knew all this and still sacrificed myself despite the fact that it would help him to release Warwick and absorb his core. Please know, I felt that we still had to try to avoid this outcome, even if it led to my demise, because it was vitally important for you and your friends to survive.

The tribes have been slowly shrinking for generations, with fewer and fewer members developing strong abilities. However, something has changed and we now have a group of young people who have reversed this trend and manifested skills we have only read about in far back records. To counter Gabriel's army, it will take all of your strength, but I have complete faith in you and have left you a path to follow.

This book will show you each step of the path when you and your friends are ready for it. I have found that most great things are achieved by a team rather than individuals.

I am sorry we did not have more time together, but please know I cherished every moment that we did have.

With much respect and admiration,

Rebecca

Caroline's tears kept falling, but she still flipped to the next pages to see several were covered with glyphs, but they were not the Moon Born variety. Feeling her grief beat out her curiosity, she closed the book and her shoulders slumped as Honore wrapped her in a warm embrace. Sobs wracked her, but Honore patiently waited and stroked her hair until Caroline was able to let most of it out. The others waited quietly in respect for the moment.

When Caroline finally pulled back, Honore placed her hands on Caroline's shoulders and gave her a warm smile.

"It's probably time for you all to get some rest, tomorrow will be the first of many busy days," she said and then looked around at the group who began to stir in their seats.

"I don't understand… What's in that book and what starts tomorrow?" Leo asked in a mix of curiosity and frustration from being in the dark.

"We prepare," Cecil said simply, peering over Honore's shoulder.

"Prepare for what?" Meimei pressed, not satisfied with the vague answer.

"For war," Caroline said soberly.

"That is something for tomorrow," Cecil interrupted firmly as the group erupted into anxious conversations. "Now is the time to get some rest. Juliet will show you to your rooms. We are sorry it will be such tight accommodations, but we are expecting many more arrivals over the next couple of weeks since Terradune is one of the few places that Gabriel can't reach right now. It has become the headquarters of the resistance."

Despite the fear of the fight ahead and the lingering sadness from Rebecca's message, Caroline felt a little jolt of excitement and pride that Moon Borns would be a part of it. Then Honore called out to the group as it made its way out of the hall.

"Be here bright and early tomorrow! Our combined faculty has prepared a new curriculum for you and I should warn you it is… very demanding," she said. Then turned to Caroline and said in a low voice, "Bring that book with you wherever you go. Don't let it out of your sight. It might be the key to our salvation."

Acknowledgements

Once again, the first thank you must go to Amy, my partner and editor extraordinaire. She has such an amazing mind that has helped make this book something of which I am very proud. I am also constantly in awe of her eagle eye that can spot a typo and grammatical error a mile away (if you find one, just remember everyone's human).

Thank you as well to all the readers who enjoyed "Star Born" and encouraged me to keep writing the full trilogy. Your words of encouragement have meant the world to me. What started out as a project just for my kids has gotten a lot bigger than I expected and it has been very rewarding.

Keep an eye out for the third and final book of the series!

ABOUT THE AUTHOR

Ben Barry lives in the Bay Area with his family. He discovered his love of storytelling while putting his kids to bed and making up fantastical tales on the fly. As they grew older, the stories became more complex and he began writing them down to feed their voracious reading appetites. Now Ben carves out some time every week to capture his imagination in words.